I0699668

THE KING'S DELIVERANCE

THE KING'S DELIVERANCE

Copyright © 2025 by Brittany Mack.

Contact info: writerbrittanymack@gmail.com

Cover Design by Maria Spada Designs

Map by Cartographybird Maps

Formatting Template by Derek Murphy

Chapter headers and dividers made with Canva Pro

ISBN : 979-8-9900737-5-3

First Edition : June 2025

10 9 8 7 6 5 4 3 2 1

THE KING'S DELIVERANCE

Fortitude Press LLC
Copyright 2025 by Brittany Mack

To all who dare to dream, who are bold enough to look outward and upward—we are better and stronger together.

CASTLE GROUNDS
THE HOLD
BARRACKS
CASTLE CIRCLE
POINTE
SALFORD
THE GROVES
THE ISLAND
OF
MIOTA
THE MONORAIL LINES
YORKINSON
KENDALL
CAPE
OUTER ROADWAY
THE FORT

DARK SEA
SECTOR E
JACKSON WILDS
SECTOR G
SPRING HILLS
WEST MONT
SECTOR F
SECTOR D
BLUE PRAIRIE
THE PACIFIC OCEAN

THE LEAGUE OF
INDEPENDENT SECTORS
SECTOR C
THE HEIGHTS
SECTOR A
THE OLD LAKES
NEW MILLS
RED FOX
NASH
CHARSTON
SECTOR B
VANNIS
OLD JAX
ATLANTIC OCEAN

PART ONE

"Blight to destroy crops, Anthrax to slay horses and cattle, Plague to poison not armies only but whole districts—such are the lines along which military science is re-morselessly advancing."

—*Winston Churchill, 1925*

CHAPTER 1

CORINN

I stared at the corpse in front of me. The living, breathing corpse.

Corinn, he'd said. *You made it.*

He was alive. The Prince of Miota was *here*, across the ocean, ripped from the very monarchy he was supposed to inherit within the year.

Cass was *alive and well,* despite having been deemed dead to his kingdom across the sea.

He was my friend. On the man-made island we hailed from, I'd belonged to society's bottom, while he'd sat at the pinnacle, the son of Miota's powerful queen and king.

Too many emotions—confusion, shock, joy—bled together, surging through my veins to fight for control. This wasn't real. *None of this* could be real.

Corinn. You made it. Those words echoed in my bones and inflamed my burned legs further, darkening my vision and pressing against my lungs.

I *made* it. As if this was my choice; as if I *wanted* to be here.

The thought curdled, poisoning the air around me, as I recalled how I got here, how I ended up in this cinderblock bedroom. I'd narrowly escaped death on Miota—only to be betrayed by Max Reno, who'd handed me off to strangers like I was nothing more than a commodity.

"What's happening?" I finally blurted, unable to sift through my thoughts to form a substantial question. My tongue tasted like the scalded flesh on my legs, where the Queen of Miota—Cass's own *mother*—had poured boiling water until they'd become unrecognizable.

How long ago was that?

Lorella Anzalone, the third and only other occupant of the sparse room, inhaled deeply as she ran a hand through her hair, revealing dyed layers of greens, pinks, and purples.

"Like I said," she started from her spot on the room's opposite wall, "there's a lot to catch you up on."

I ignored the woman. All I knew about her was that she worked with Max Reno—and any friend of his was an enemy of mine.

So I concentrated on Cass, fastening my gaze on the prince. He didn't look as I remembered. His dirty-blond hair was shaggy, tumbling over his ears and forehead, and shadows stayed fixed to his face, claiming him. The prince I remembered was carefree, and this man in front of me was anything but that, holding the weight of continents in his stiff posture.

"Cass." I tested the name on my tongue—I never planned on speaking to its owner again in this lifetime. "You're . . ." *Okay. Here. Alive. Not dead.*

Staring at me.

His eyes remained tethered to my legs, where jagged red scars peeked out from underneath bandages. A muscle ticked in his jaw, and when he spoke, I didn't recognize the depth in his voice. "What . . . what happened? Who did that to you?"

My throat turned thick. "Your mom poured boiling water on me." Uttering the words summoned heat, and I couldn't breathe. Couldn't think, couldn't see.

Salem is dead. Griff is gone. Cass is here. Max betrayed me.

Each beat, a sour reminder of what I knew to be true, sliced at me. I was going to suffocate in this bed, and *I couldn't move*, thanks to the loose snares around my ankles.

"Get me out," I panted. "*Get me out.*"

The world shrank to the size of my shackles, shielding me from the thoughts lingering in the corners of my mind. *Salem. Griff. Miota.*

"Get her out," Cass echoed, barking at Lorella. The bones of his knuckles pressed white against skin as he strode toward me. "Corinn, you're safe here. You're safe."

"I was kidnapped!" I gritted out, descending into panic. It was only a matter of time until I snapped. "Max gave me away—Max Reno— Lorella Anzalone . . . and now I'm *tied up.*" My face crumpled, and I tried blocking the entire world from view.

It was no use. I choked to death on this newfound reality.

Lorella unchained my ankles and waved one of the plastic bonds in the air. "Didn't mean to cause any harm," she insisted. "They were to keep you face-up in bed. To keep the topical on your legs—to heal your burns."

I moved my ankles, pointing my toes and rolling around the joint. The plastic bonds hadn't hurt me, but the idea of confinement sent me over the edge of my mind's fears.

"You weren't kidnapped," Cass said from where he hovered above me. Though his voice was silky, his sharp words bit into my skin. "You were saved. I promise."

Saved? Cass was wrong. This wasn't my salvation; it was my doom. And it could be Miota's destruction.

I'd been ripped from my family and friends—all still stuck on Miota, all still under the wicked hand of Julia Delldova, the island's jailor, shielding the country from the rest of the world. Miota was where I lived for eighteen years, my home despite its corrupt monarchy.

There'd been a plan to liberate Miota and its people from the evil queen. I was supposed to play a role in it, but now I was *here*, across the ocean and freshly unchained from a bed.

"What's happening?" I demanded again. "Why are . . . *we* here, Cass?" A pair of Miotans torn from the only world we knew. Why?

"Max said you already know about the supercontinent," Cass began. "Do you know anything about the trade deal between Red Fox and Miota?"

"Miotan people exchanged for Red Fox's supplies," I answered, keeping it simple. I knew pieces of laws and fragments of conditions that were so illegal on Miota, I'd never spoken them aloud before. I'd only ever fit facts together like a puzzle whose pieces weren't all present—but something told me the missing links were *here*.

It was so wrong, trading lives for goods. I'd first learned about the trade underneath my home city, Pointe. I'd been with Griff Howard, the man who'd gone from an irritating stranger to the holder of my heart in a few short months.

My chest pinched thinking of him now, knowing an ocean spanned the distance between us.

Cass nodded, gingerly sitting on my bed. Or, *his* bed, by the sound of it—Lorella said this was Cass's room. I glanced at each of the four walls, this place a perfect juxtaposition. It was scarce in furnishings yet potent in décor. Trinkets, unrecognizable to me, lined every bit of flat space available on the dresser and bedside table. Was this Cass's doing?

"We're going to stop that trade," Lorella cut in, marching to the bedroom door. She set her hands on her hips. "I've gathered a crew capable of doing it, but we need Miotans on our side. Now that we have you both here, you can help us gather information about your home. Let's go talk in the big group, okay?"

"Max," I said in a breath toward Cass, still refusing to acknowledge the woman from Red Fox. I could only handle one riddle at a time, and Lorella Anzalone was too big a problem to solve right now. "Max Reno sent me here."

Cass lidded his eyes, reaching out for my hand on some instinct that surpassed time, catapulting us back to our old meeting spot, an abandoned greenhouse in Pointe. For a fleeting moment, with his sloped shoulders and softened expression, I could almost pretend we were the same prince and Low-Tiered girl who used to meet in secret on Miota.

Almost.

But not quite. Because my heart was too empty. Salem, my best friend, was dead, and it was my fault. Griff was on another landmass. My family was still stuck in Queen Julia's grasp. Thinking of it all stretched me too thin, leaving me to gasp for air.

"Max is the reason I'm here, too," Cass whispered.

The words were an effective boulder dropped on my lungs, shattering my every thought.

"Why would he do that?" I couldn't draw a logical conclusion; there were still too many veiled truths.

Cass shrugged, hugging his arms across his chest. "I was hoping you knew."

Lorella huffed. "Let's go, you two."

"No," I snapped, finally looking at her. Lorella shifted her weight, fidgeting with a button on her black jumpsuit. "Why did Max send us here? Was it because of you?"

She tilted her head side-to-side a few times. "Kind of. I told him— look, this would be easier in a group setting. Long story short, my crew and I have been trying to find a way to save your country for the last ten-ish months. When we finally found a way to speak with your liaison between Red Fox and Miota—Max Reno—we told him to send a Miotan here to help us. We didn't . . . I wasn't expecting the country's only *heir.*"

I chewed on my cheek, meeting Cass's stare as my thoughts churned. The intensity in his hazel eyes threatened to melt me. Still, I held on as my mind spun frantically.

Some part of me still refused to believe this was real—that *Cass* was real. Miota's heir still lived, only it didn't seem to matter from this side of the ocean.

"Max knew the plan, right?" I asked, thinking aloud. "The plan for"—my cheeks flushed—"you and me to become Miota's next rulers and free the island."

Cass went still as he seemingly stole the room's gravity, weighing him down in his spot. "Yes."

I blinked, trying to sever the tension radiating off Miota's dead prince. "Then it doesn't make sense at all. There was a plan for us to free Miota. Why would Max ruin it?"

Maybe Max was rogue, working on an elusive agenda not even Lorella could sense. Or maybe there were yet again other forces at work. I couldn't sort it out here and now, though. Not from this bed.

Something inside me lurched. I needed out of this room, this apartment. I needed off this supercontinent.

"Let's get this over with." I sat up, bracing myself for the dizziness that would accompany it. Stars infiltrated my vision before slowly passing.

Cass stared at my legs and offered to help me up, but I refused. I didn't want to look at my legs; I didn't want to acknowledge them. They were my tie to reality, my indication that all of this was real.

What was worse than the pain in my legs was the wound on my heart. During Accolade, the competition to find Miota's new heirs, I'd tried sneaking out on my own. Salem had followed me, and . . . it had gone so *wrong*.

But while I paid for my mistakes with boiling water and scarred legs, Salem had paid with his life. I would never forgive myself for it.

Once I got my bearings, I used every muscle in my legs to stand. I didn't know the last time I stood, but my burns were still relatively fresh, only adding to the tenderness as I put weight on my feet.

Cass offered an arm for support, and though I wanted to walk alone, I ultimately caved, accepting his help. I steadied myself on his forearm. My right leg seemed to hurt more, although I knew Julia was equal in her torturous methods.

"I can't believe she did this to you," Cass muttered, his rough voice pelting me.

"Really?" I thought that, of anyone, Cass would expect this the most. He'd lived with his mother for twenty years; he knew her malice.

"How'd it happen?" he asked, pushing through my commentary.

I blinked, unable to walk and talk at once with much success. We'd barely made it to the bedroom door. "Do you know anything about Accolade?"

"Yeah, Max told Lorella about it on his last call with her. Said you were in it." His voice prompted an explanation, one I knew he'd want later. This wasn't the time.

Still, I nodded. "I was. I snuck out of Castle Circle, and this was my punishment. Salem was with me, and he . . ." My voice broke at the mention of him. "He didn't . . ."

Cass crushed me into a hug, and my cheek met his sternum. His heart battered in his chest, marching in tandem with my waves of grief.

"He's dead," I finally whispered. The words clawed the entire way up my throat, fighting to be spoken into existence. I didn't want them to ring true, but here we were.

Because of *me*.

How would I survive this feeling? The weight of Salem's death was already heavy enough, but paired with knowing it was my fault . . . it was too much. Bile rose in me each time that reality sank in with cold teeth.

"I'm so sorry," Cass murmured into my hair.

And as he held me, the world fell back into an old rhythm, a worn groove formed by years of habit, from before Cass's supposed death. From a time when it had been Cass and Bernard, Salem and me.

"I didn't exactly have friends as a prince," Cass said. "Everyone in the castle was only there because my mother would punish them if they didn't do their job correctly. But you and Salem . . . you were different."

Lorella shifted her weight behind me, widening this place back to its actuality. There were others here, ready to speak with us about saving Miota.

It was too late for me to save Salem. But there were so many others who could yet survive Julia. And I would be damned before I made the same mistake again. I would not let Salem Redding's death be in vain.

I gathered myself and let Cass lead me down the dark hallway, toward the gaping light at the end.

My legs radiated until we turned and the hall opened into the rest of Lorella's home. I tried keeping a neutral look, but my face betrayed me, and my mouth hung open.

The living room, a sleek space of reflective flooring and white walls, held plush sofas and a translucent column of *fire*, its flames crackling toward the ceiling. It sent a chill down me as the presence of excessive heat licked at my legs. A golden chandelier hung in intricate designs, alternating between blown glass and copper-colored metals.

But the room was nothing compared to the *window*.

The expanse of blue stretched upward and outward, a blanket covering the supercontinent. And though we were inside this building, we were also in the *sky*.

I could reach out the window and touch the clouds. The blue sky and buttery sun swallowed the window whole, and in the distance, *other* buildings stood tall, scraping against the heavens. This place made the Fort, the forty-foot wall encasing Miota, look like a mere stepping stone. Sun danced on steel, giving the structures an otherworldly appearance— more than any image a Miotan could conjure up.

Like a plant drawn to sunlight, my feet took me toward the window, one slow and supported step at a time. My eyes widened, unable to take in the scene laid out below me like the moving screen of a panel, our handheld devices on Miota.

Everything seemed to glitter—lustrous, floating pipes intersected with glittering horizontal tracks, and translucent tubes were filled with people the size of crawling bugs from this height.

"Makes me dizzy to look out," Cass said, shuddering.

I, however, felt drawn to this view and these heights; I'd always craved to see the world as the stars did. A quick tear slid down my cheek. Griff would've loved this, too.

Behind me, Lorella cleared her throat. "Corinn, I know you've already *technically* met, but these are the James brothers, Colton and Dalton."

I turned to see Lorella standing between two men: one blond, with cords of muscle bulking his arms and legs, and the other dark-haired, made of sharper angles and appearing very boyish.

My stomach dropped. *Not them.*

They were the two who'd intercepted me from Max Reno. The ones responsible for taking me from Miota.

CHAPTER 2

CORINN

The brothers stared at me. I stared back, hoping my defiance shone in my sharp gaze.

They were the reason I was apart from Griff and my family. *They* were the reason I couldn't save Miota anymore.

Well, with their help from Max Reno—a man whom Julia Delldova believed she controlled through the neural implant embedded in his brain. Except Max's implant was a fake, and it didn't work on him. He lived outside the queen's jurisdiction.

Making him the most powerful person on Miota. And he was working with Lorella Anzalone.

"Sorry about Miota," the dark-haired one finally said, snapping all tensions. His voice delivered in a higher intonation than I expected, much like the first time I met him on Miota's beach. He was chiseled, made of tight skin over lean muscle, but he sounded like what he was: a teenager.

I cocked my head after digesting his words, a cold pit growing in my stomach. "What happened to Miota? What do you *know*—"

"Nothing new," he said, waving his hands. "I just mean, sorry about taking you like that—forcing you unconscious and all. We were just following orders."

I froze. A weight settled on me. No one had yet to apologize for bringing me here against my will. Not Lorella, not even *Cass*. This boy, Dalton, was the first.

"Thank you," I said.

In that moment, I decided Dalton was my favorite—save Cass—in Lorella's crew. I only hoped I wasn't letting his brown hair and dark eyes cloud my judgment. The color had quickly become my favorite in the last two months.

"Can I get you anything to drink?" Lorella offered. "Tea, coffee, water . . ."

"Coffee?" I jumped at the offer.

Lorella grinned. "You and I will get along great." She went into a room I hadn't noticed before now, not against the competition of the sparkling window revealing the world outside.

It was a *kitchen*. Smaller than any kitchen I'd seen before—in Pointe, the city where I grew up, its two-thousand citizens ate at the Common, and it showed in the appliances' sizes. Everyone traveled to the Common to eat, but here, one could have a meal without stepping foot outside.

Lorella filled a mug from a carafe and jutted it toward me. "Creamer? Sugar?"

I inhaled to answer, but Cass answered first. "Creamer." He glanced at me with a knowing smile. "Trust me, you'll love it."

I snapped my mouth shut, trying to dull the sting of Cass's quick answer. I usually drank coffee black, but I stifled my indignation as Lorella doused the coffee with velvety liquid.

The smiling woman handed me the steaming mug, and I carefully held the handle. "Please, come take a seat," she prompted everyone, gesturing to her plush sofas, bathing in sunlight from the window. Dalton and Colton followed Lorella, plopping harshly on cushions.

I sipped the beverage. On Miota, coffee was earthy and bitter, a warm bite, sharp and familiar. This stuff, this creamer, shrouded the coffee flavor, and my throat bobbed as I tried not to fall apart completely.

The creamer didn't belong in the coffee, and *I* didn't belong on the supercontinent.

Images of Griff swirled in my mind's eye, and my throat seared. I turned away from Cass and made for a sofa. My legs throbbed after standing for so long, and my feet at least found reprieve as I walked from hardwood flooring to a thick rug.

I chose a spot facing the window, and Cass helped me sink onto the cushion. The coffee remained in my grasp, though I wasn't eager to drink the rest of it now.

"This is our crew," Lorella started the second I hit the couch. "Me, Colton, Dalton, Cass, and you. Also my aunt, but she doesn't escape the administrative district often. And Neave, a friend of mine from college, who doesn't get out much either."

I blinked at Lorella, who leaned on her knees and stared me down. She lived with such a glorious view, and she didn't even bother looking out the window. Didn't seem to care that she lived among the clouds.

"And you're all . . ." I trailed off. "Stopping the trade? People for supplies?"

"You know anything about Biourica?" the grumpier of the brothers asked. Colton. My eyes connected with his, moonlight atop green plants.

"Never heard of it," I answered plainly.

"Start big," Lorella said, cutting Colton a withering look. Colton's face darkened further, and I suddenly felt like I was intruding on an argument. "This place you call the supercontinent," Lorella went on, "is called the League of Independent Sectors—also called LIS, or even just 'the League.' It spans from the Atlantic to Pacifica oceans. We used to be united, but . . . after the war, we split into seven sectors. Just made things easier, being apart."

War. I'd heard the term for the first time not long ago, from my old tutor, Bernard Bartholomus. Cass's uncle. Bernard told Griff and me that war was a deadly game. I knew that this famed war took place in Miota's earliest days, and my home had been virtually unaffected by it.

"There are Sectors A through G. We live in Sector A, on the League's northeast coast. Red Fox is the capital city of Sector A, and that's where *we* are now." Lorella pressed her lips into a thin line, monitoring my reactions and comprehension.

"Got it," I confirmed. "Seven sectors. We're in Sector A's capital, Red Fox."

Lorella *hmm*ed, looking to Cass. "Chip in if it's needed," she told Miota's prince. "So . . . Red Fox, as the capital city, holds Sector A's government. The government dictates the laws here, same as the monarchy on Miota."

Cass nodded and laced his fingers together, a habit I also saw in his mother when she was anxious.

Lorella persisted. "But the government doesn't hold the true power. Only one thing in this sector decides power, and it isn't a government position."

I defiantly walked into her prompting. "What is it, then?"

On Miota, I thought the monarchy held power because of their name and heritage. A Delldova was one to fear and respect. But during Accolade, I learned the truth: Power came from secrets, and secrets sustained the Delldovas' power in turn.

"Money," Lorella answered. "Which is something Cass said you don't have on Miota. It's a way to measure something's worth. The value."

Cass interceded. "On Miota, there are trade deals: you get one commodity by giving another. But here, you get commodities by giving money. For example . . ." He motioned toward my drink, letting his hand brush mine for a second. I tried not to shiver. "This coffee would be worth something like seven dibs."

That hardly answered my questions—*What are dibs? How do you get them? Does everyone have them?*—but I pretended to understand. Miota had secrets, and the supercontinent had money. I wondered if this *money* was as evil as Miota's most valuable commodity.

"There's a company here in Red Fox called Biourica," Lorella cut back in, not wasting a second in silence. The James brothers shifted in their spots. Colton rubbed his shoulder, and Dalton quickly became very interested in a throw pillow's pattern. "They have a lot of money—*too much* money. Enough to buy Sector A's government. Which is precisely what they did a few decades ago. So, really, *Biourica* runs our sector, not the government."

"It's all an elaborate façade," I offered, echoing the same conclusion I'd come to about Miota during my time in the crown's underground prison.

"Exactly," said Lorella as Cass shot me an amused look in my periphery.

An elaborate façade. Another land, another country. Across the ocean, but not so different.

"Since Biourica runs the government . . ." Lorella studied the three men in the room, as if gaining permission from them to continue.

The act made my hair stand on end. What did Cass know that I didn't? He *was* a Delldova—did he have his own set of secrets?

"That company deals with the Miotan trade," Lorella continued. "Nobody in Red Fox knows about Miota, except a small handful of top government officials and Biourica executives."

Colton set his jaw, keeping a glazed stare.

I couldn't take this—couldn't take the secrets and cryptic information. I'd had enough of it on Miota, and I wouldn't maintain the cycle now. These people took me from my home; the least they could do was tell me what they knew.

I cleared my throat. "What's going on? What aren't you telling me?"
Cass loosed a breath.

I kept on. "Colton, you look like you're on the verge of shouting. And Lorella, you're acting like you're walking on a patch of ice! Just tell me what's going on."

Colton James laughed, though no warmth accompanied the sound.

"Careful, Januski. None of us *wanted* to risk our lives to bring you here, you know—"

"Well, I never asked you to—"

"Corinn," Cass interjected gently while shooting Colton a look of disbelief. "Look, this doesn't change anything, but it . . . complicates a few things. Biourica's leader is Arlo James."

James? My lips parted.

"Our father," Dalton answered.

I clenched my jaw to keep from displaying too much emotion. Dalton and Colton's father was in charge of Biourica, therefore in charge of the trade between Red Fox and Miota.

"Your father . . .?" I asked. "But you're both . . . *here*?"

"It's the right thing to do," Dalton answered simply.

A dizzying wave crashed over my head. We had inheritors of great empires gathered in this room—a prince of Miota, and two sons of Biourica's leader. This room held the power to change the world.

"So . . . what's the plan?" Surely a group with such authority would have some intricate scheme. Maybe this would be easier than I thought. Hope dared to swoop in, binding to my body for the first time since I woke here.

"Biourica is nothing but bad news," Lorella answered, clearly content with fielding all my questions. "They started as a retail company—"

"Consumer and capital goods," Cass whispered, putting Lorella's words into Miotan terms.

Every city on Miota specialized in providing a commodity. Consumer goods came from Yorkinson, and capital goods from Cape.

"—but over time, they got into weapons."

"Weapons?" I asked. "Like guns and knives?"

Colton leered, and his sharpness sliced through my stomach. "Try limb regeneration, genetic mutation, full neural compliance . . ."

"Biourica deals more with biological weapons," Lorella clarified. She leaned back in her seat and crossed her legs. "I hear Julia's guards on Miota are controlled by neural implants. That's not even a *whisper* of the tech Biourica has."

I swallowed the thick bile climbing up my throat. The company requiring Miotan people . . . dealt with *biological* weapons.

"Is that why . . ." I couldn't voice it. Couldn't walk down that dark path of logic on my own. But it was what I mulled over ever since learning about the trade. The supercontinent was massive, clearly with an abundance of resources and technology. What use could they have for Miotans? "The Miotans traded . . ."

All eyes turned toward the ground.

I couldn't swallow. Couldn't *breathe*. The leftover fire still stowed in my legs burned and burned and *burned*.

"Are they killed?" The words burned my throat as they spilled from me. I wanted the truth—the whole truth.

"No," Dalton said, his voice raw. He didn't meet my gaze as his expression broke. "Not usually, at least. It's . . . hard to say. No one but our dad can get into the segment of Biourica where he runs his experiments. All we know is there are different phases . . . different *uses*, per se, for the Miotans, and we don't know his system. He keeps it that way purposefully."

Lorella sniffed and blinked to keep tears from spilling over her lashes. Colton was a statue, broad and set in stone. Cass . . . was hollow, letting the conversation wash over him.

"You two can't walk in as Arlo James's sons?" I asked the brothers.

"We used to," Colton answered quickly, glancing at Lorella. She buried her face in her hands, shoulders shaking. "But no, not anymore. We had a pretty bad falling out last year, so we're banned from the place now."

I simultaneously felt like Cass—empty and numb—and Lorella—distraught and in mourning. I wasn't sure what to do with the different surges currently crashing into me, threatening to drown me.

I didn't know *anything* anymore. I hadn't since waking here.

I quivered, crossing my arms to conceal it. "So . . . this crew plans to take down Biourica? We could go destroy Julia, if that's easier, and end the trade from there—"

"Arlo would just capture Miota," Colton interrupted, shrugging. I curled my hands into fists. "There's no escaping Biourica."

"Not to mention you're talking about my mom," Cass mumbled.

I dared to look at the prince. Cass held so much of his mother in his face and posture, and in this moment, I *saw* it instead of ignoring it. He was her only heir, capable of destructive things.

During Accolade, Griff's and my plan was to inherit the crown and destroy Julia. To make her kingdom burn, as she'd done to me. To Griff's father. To every Miotan she sent off to Red Fox. Miota would never be free as long as Julia Delldova wore a crown, no matter what happened with Biourica.

Our tension was cut by Colton, who finished answering. "We'll take down Biourica first. Dealing with Miota's monarchy after that will be easy."

"Everyone in the crew has a role to help destroy Biourica," Lorella said, taking charge again after drying her eyes. She and Colton seemed to know how to play off each other's words—they knew where one of them stopped and the other started. "You have one, too, Corinn. That's why you're here."

I held my breath deep in my lungs, taking on a habit I knew Griff possessed.

"Neave is our technology wiz, and she's spent the past month getting you added to all our systems in Sector A. Because while we use Cass in my apartment as we have been, behind-the-scenes, we want *you* to be out there, in the city. Inside Biourica, even."

I ran my tongue over my teeth. Lorella huffed a hot breath, shoulders slumping, being as clear as possible. "Neave has essentially made you a legal citizen of Sector A."

CHAPTER 3

CORINN

A citizen of Sector A.

I couldn't decide if I should laugh or cry, feel joy or fear. Both paths seemed logical.

How was I supposed to blend in with a world I didn't know? And why was I needed for such a job? What purpose would I serve?

Lorella apparently read my mind. "You have something the rest of us don't: anonymity. I'm right-hand woman to the head judge of Red Fox's ultimate tribunal. Colton and Dalton, aside from being Arlo's sons, work in top government positions. My aunt works for the Health Prime, and even my college friend Neave has made a name for herself. You and Cass, though, would be invisible to people in power. And we *need* that right now."

I glared at Cass, wondering why *he* wasn't Lorella's spy. But Miota's heir only stared back. His royal training kept his features bent toward neutrality; he wouldn't give anything away right now.

"What will I do?" I finally asked, hardly able to find my voice. *Go to Biourica? Knock on their front door?*

"There are a few jobs you could find," Lorella replied. She shifted in her seat. "We thought you could apply for one and see how it goes, but I think we'll actually start smaller. Biourica has a treatment center on-location, and your burns are the perfect chance for you to get inside, get treatment, and then spy for us."

My throat turned to ash. *Spy.* For *them.*

Impossible. Why did these people think *I* could do that? They'd clearly never spoken to Abner, Cass's father and King of Miota. Because he would be the first to tell Lorella and her crew that I *crumbled* when people relied on me. I hurt everyone who put blind faith in me.

That was why Salem was dead. Why I'd been separated from Griff, and why I'd lost the king's support. And I was *done* hurting others.

"Spy," I mumbled. I wavered, and the room saw it. Colton probably *smelled* my fear and hesitation. "I . . . I don't know how to do that."

"We'll teach you," Lorella said quickly, waving a hand. "Don't worry, it won't be difficult. I'll start working with you tonight, and you'll have the behaviors down in no time."

I clenched my teeth so hard, my temples pulsed. I couldn't do this. "How long do we have? To take down Biourica?"

How long until I doom everyone here, too?

"Biourica controls Sector A entirely," Lorella said, "so we can't do anything rash. We just need to contain the company—stop them before they expand into other sectors."

"Which we expect Arlo to do once the new year rolls around," Dalton chimed in. His words were scarce but helpful, more potent than anyone else's. "Which gives us just over five months."

The floor tilted. *Five months.* It was too long . . . but also too short.

Five more months for Miotans to incur Arlo James—and no Miotan should endure something so *evil.* Simultaneously, only five months to infiltrate and demolish the company holding this entire sector in its grasp.

It seemed impossible.

I was completely helpless. Griff and I had a plan to free Miota, and now I was stranded from him. And I didn't know what to do without the Salfordian.

My brain barely made the connection—the thoughts whizzed by each other, interacting for only a moment. "Griff Howard," I gasped, looking to Cass. His face darkened at the name on my lips. "Griff is supposed to win Accolade. He and Abner want to get everyone off Miota, away from Julia. They could come here and help us take down Biourica."

"No can do," Colton spat, his voice overpowering every other noise in the airy apartment. It was hard to hide my scowl toward him. "They can't come here. Arlo would find them and *use* them all."

"But that was the original plan!" I exploded. I leaned forward, but my legs zinged and I pulled back. "Abner has always wanted to leave Miota—that means coming to the supercontinent."

"They can't come to *Red Fox*," Lorella said, partly agreeing with Colton. She gave a practiced grin, aiming to placate me with an artificial display of teeth. "It's not safe here. Southern Sector A could maybe hide them, but Sector B would be even better since they don't know about Miota, and Biourica doesn't hold any power there."

I was quiet for too long. This felt like I was back on Miota's beach, getting battered by wave after wave, unable to stand. Unable to *think*.

I looked to Cass for support, but he became too engrossed with picking his nails. Miota was *his* home, too—a kingdom he was meant to rule. Why did I seem to care about its outcome more than he did?

"You know Griff Howard?" Cass broke the silence, his voice a low roll. "Well enough to know his plans with my father?"

Had Cass just put it together? Accolade was a competition meant for two to win. Two to marry, to rule, to continue a royal bloodline.

In this moment, I could confess everything. I could spill that Griff and I were a team; we were intertwined. But some red-hot part of me wanted to keep Griff a secret, something I shared with no one else here. A hidden promise kept, linking us from across the sea.

"Griff and I met during Accolade," I said, leaving it at that.

I continued before Cass had the chance to reply—or ask a

question deserving a more concrete answer. I tilted my head toward Lorella. "What about the trade in the meantime? Five months means five more rounds of trade. More Miotans sent . . ."

What if it were my family, stuck in Miota's Low Tier? What if it were Griff's family? Then again, it didn't matter whether I knew the people or not—what was happening to Miotans was so wrong. I needed to stop it as soon as possible, whatever the cost.

"The trade can only stop once we take Biourica down," Lorella insisted. Her voice of iron left no room for argument. "Arlo is too smart a man. Too strong a leader. We can't chip away at what he's built—we need to blow it up, all at once. It's the only way we have a chance."

My face fell. For five more months, Miotans would be ripped from their homes and used for some unknown, evil purpose. They would be severed from their families, torn from their lives. Forced into whatever Arlo James required of them—which couldn't be anything good.

And after those five months were spent, the trade would only stop if we *won*. If I did my part and helped spy for Lorella's crew. If I did it successfully.

Fire churned not only in my legs now, but in my arms, my chest, my head. My vision dimmed as the walls of this apartment suffocated me. How could I be good enough for these people?

"I'm sorry it seems we aren't doing enough," Lorella said. Her apology sounded . . . personal. "I can promise you, though, we're doing *everything* we can while still practicing caution."

It wasn't supposed to be this way. *None of it* was. Yet here I was, with a lost prince, with enough knowledge to destroy Miota's monarchy but having no way to reach it. Meanwhile, Griff was across the ocean, stuck on that manmade rock with my family and my heart and soul and breath.

My body was on the supercontinent, but *I* was not.

"Right," I choked out. "Thanks for that." It didn't ring true, and the room's occupants shifted, seeming to notice. "So I'll learn how to spy and get information on Biourica. What's everyone else doing?"

Though I was nothing but curious, it delivered as an accusation. I stifled a flinch.

Lorella swallowed what was probably a retort, and she instead answered my question simply. "Cass has been helping by gathering information about Miota—the government, ways of life in cities, theories on how to get citizens to listen to us. We want you to help him fill in the blanks and give what information you can on the lower Tiers, actually."

Fill in the blanks?

What gaps were there in Cass's knowledge? He was the next Delldova fit for the crown; his mother had taught him everything there was to know about Miota, Low Tier, and all.

I peered toward Cass, and in turn, he sized me up as if I were a stranger. Maybe I was now—Accolade changed me in many ways. I wasn't the girl he knew the day his limo crashed. And something told me he'd changed as well.

We would need to talk alone after this. Roll over the implications: Cass's suspicion that I knew Griff better than I let on, and my worry that Cass lied about his knowledge to help get me into Lorella's crew.

All the glass lies and secrets needed to come crashing down, shattering anything delicate in the process.

"Colton, thanks to his job, *does* have a meeting with his father in three weeks, which'll be the first time any of us have spoken to Arlo James in . . . *months.* Dalton is preparing to join a logistical unit hosted by Biourica. Neave is busy creating *you* in all systems, so your identity and background are never questioned. My aunt and I are going through old information about this trade deal. I'm also relaying all our progress with Max, and I trust he's keeping our ultimate plan on course on Miota. Any other questions?"

Her last three words were clipped. I'd already overstayed my welcome, thanks to my accusations and doubts. I'd never been good at biting my tongue, and if I couldn't control it now, I'd let this group down, just as I'd already done to those counting on me on Miota. The tale would end no differently, and when people got hurt, it would once again be my fault.

"No." I stood, ignoring the blistering ache in my lower limbs. "Thank you for telling me. About the whole . . . our entire situation."

I wasn't sure if it would mend Lorella's spoiled mood, but it was all I had to give. I left my still-full cup of coffee behind and retreated toward Cass's bedroom.

As if he were a magnet drawn to me, Cass stayed in my shadow, ready to help me hobble away. And I easily let him, too tired to argue now. I clamped my mouth shut and kept my chin high until I made it back into the concealed hallway.

My shoulders drooped, and I leaned against Cass's torso for support.

There was too much to mull over. Too much to protest, yet also too much to *do*.

I didn't want to spy for Lorella's crew, but I would do it to help their cause. I would do it if it would save Miota. My family was still there, in the dark. And Griff . . .

My throat closed. He was set to win Accolade; he would need my help from this side of the ocean.

And I could give help—I would give Griff anything, *everything*. He was still mine, and our shared task was not finished yet.

I didn't have answers from within this apartment. I couldn't find useful information from within this beautiful *trap*.

Luckily, I was Lorella's chosen spy. And soon enough, I would unleash myself on the city outside. I would help Lorella, of course . . . but I'd be damned if I didn't fight to help Griff, too.

CHAPTER 4

GRIFF

I stared at the man in the pane of reflective glass. Or he stared at me—I wasn't sure which.

His eyes were so empty. His hair so tousled. His spirit so . . . dark.

I didn't recognize this man overcome by grief, nor did I *want* to know him. But here *I* was, and there my reflection was. And I feared we were one and the same.

I still remembered the all-encompassing sting of grief from the months after Dad died at Julia's hand. I'd been too shattered to pick up my pieces, and I'd fallen into despair, unsure of how to build myself back into anything meaningful.

It was the same now, after Corinn.

I hadn't thought anyone could take up so much space in my heart and mind before I'd met the Pointean girl. She'd held the moon in her eyes; the stars in the freckles across her face; the ocean's pull in her laughter. She'd been freedom. She'd been so . . . *lovely*.

And now she was dead.

Though she and I had schemed against Miota's evil queen, it hadn't mattered. Julia won in the end, just as she *always* did.

This was Julia Delldova's island, and we were all prisoners to her, to do with as she pleased. We were her well-oiled machine, much like Salford's contraptions used for timber refinement. We were nothing more than a fine piece of equipment to keep her island afloat.

And if a single cog rusted and fell out of place . . .

I blinked, forcing myself out of the trance and averting my gaze from the mirror. This was only wasting precious time, and I needed every spare second I could get. After all, these would likely be the last moments of privacy I ever received.

Hours ago, I'd been named Abner's heir. I would be the next King of Miota, with Addison Maybee as queen.

I was no longer a Top-Tiered Salfordian but an heir to a mighty bloodline. And I would use it to end Julia. To leave her choking on the power she'd given me.

My butler, Paul, barged into my room, and I jolted into motion, throwing more clothes into my navy bag. I kept my face downcast to hide my puffy eyes.

"Your Most Royal Highness," Paul addressed me. Something told me such a title would never cease to shock my every nerve and quicken my heartbeat. "Are you ready to leave?"

I tried to smile. I really *tried*. "Of course. This is all I've ever wanted."

Fate was funny. When I'd first heard of Accolade, I wanted nothing more than to enter the competition and win it, no matter the cost. I wanted to claim a throne and make Julia *pay* for what she did to my father. So I should've been happy, really. I won a crown, and I would soon hold the power that came with it.

But cost me, it did.

"We're going to my house first, correct?" I asked as I zipped my bag closed.

Paul's face wrinkled into a giddy smile. "Yours and Her Highness's both. You'll both enter both houses." And because Paul could evidently sense that I was still in love with a dead woman instead of my fiancée, he elaborated. "To keep the image of loving unity."

With my back turned to Paul, I rolled my eyes.

If I couldn't escape Addison, maybe it was a good thing I didn't possess the illegal papers anymore, the ones I'd collected with Corinn when we'd traveled to Pointe.

Maps of Miota's underground tunnels . . . proof of a trade between Miota and a supercontinental city called Red Fox . . . diary entries from the first Queen of Miota, wife of Aris Delldova.

Corinn had half those papers in her room, and as soon as she'd been imprisoned in the castle, I'd hidden the other half, the ones I held in *my* room. They were still buried deep in Castle Circle's greenhouse, scattered in random potted plants, where they would stay until I could safely retrieve them.

It was too bad, though. I wanted the map of Miota's tunnel network; it could come in handy during my time in the castle. But I couldn't risk retrieving the papers now, especially if my time alone was spent. If I was to live in a spotlight, it would be difficult to plot against Miota's queen.

"I'm glad to hear it," I gritted out. I cleared my throat and threw my bag over my shoulder. "When do we leave?"

"If you're ready," Paul replied, "immediately. We'll wait outside for Her Highness." His graying face scrunched as he looked to his panel.

Let's get this over with.

I followed my butler out of my room. This place had been mine for the past two months, and now I was leaving it for good, ready to take my place and carry Miota into a new era free from the Delldovas.

I hadn't realized what a paradox this would be, to have one of the best ranks in the whole country yet feeling helplessly, utterly *trapped*. While the other Salfordian finalists who hadn't won Accolade—Lorenzo, Selleca, and Hanna—rode home in their own limo, free of prying ears and eyes, Addison and I were forced to endure cameras shoved in our faces for the full ride to Salford.

Truthfully, the most difficult part was keeping a straight face through it all. This whole situation was amusing, with one of my arms losing circulation from Addison's merciless grip and my own visage within a breath of a camera lens. No doubt, Addison's and my faces were plastered to every screen in the country right now, and someone far away narrated what they thought must've been going through our heads.

But no one could know what I was thinking. Unless they speculated that I was thinking of treason against Julia.

Once the limo rolled into Salford, my stomach flitted with nerves. I was going *home*, to see my family, if only for a short time. One hour, tops.

I wouldn't have the privacy I needed, unless I schemed a way to speak with Mom outside of the vicinity of cameras. Nothing I wanted to speak with her about involved matters within Julia's laws.

I trained my eyes on my sturdy house as it came into view around the road's bend, and I grinned at the small figure jumping about the green yard. Jess never failed to put a smile on my face.

"Look, Griff, it's your sister." Addison pointed to Jess bounding around the yard.

Like I didn't notice, I wanted to bite. But with a camera shoved in my face, I had to play my part to perfection. I couldn't show any emotion outside of love and gratitude.

I focused on my younger sister. Her dark hair billowed behind her, falling nearly to her waist, as she jumped through the yard.

When the limo halted, I kept a sharp mind, getting out not to immediately crush my sister into a hug but to assist Addison with scooting out of the vehicle in her skin-tight dress.

"GRIIIIIFF!" Jessalyn's voice washed over me as I held a hand to Addison's back.

Addison let all her weight fall into me, and I staggered to catch her in my arms. When she leaned in to kiss me, I couldn't stop her.

It happened too fast.

I wanted to faint or sob all at once. My last kiss had been Corinn. And now it was Addison, and *now* I was breaking all over again, and *now* there was nothing left for me to do but fall apart.

I blamed the tears on Jess as she crashed into me. I sniffed, bending all energy toward missing my family instead of Corinn. Julia was watching this broadcast, and I needed to give her a spectacular show.

The better I did now, the grander I could blindside her later.

That thought alone kept me afloat.

"I missed you!" Jess squealed, delivering her part of our typical greeting.

"Missed you more," I said, tugging a tendril of her hair. She screamed and tried dodging me. "Let's head inside?" I started across our yard. It wasn't much, but at least we had *grass.* It was more than any Middle or Low could say. Had Corinn's house lacked greenspace? What sort of home had she lived in?

My hope of the cameras staying outside proved futile. I led the way to my room—Mom, Jess, Addison, Paul, and a cameraman all on my heels.

I gritted my teeth as I cracked a stale smile, trying to catch Mom's eye in a secretive second, but it was impossible with what seemed to be the entire *island* watching us. The whole time I packed my sparse belongings into a bag, I never got away from any of it.

There was so much to tell Mom. Mine and Corinn's adventure to Pointe, the trade with the supercontinent, where to find my illegal papers in Castle Circle in case I never got a private moment again . . .

My goodbyes to my family were as genuine as they could be in front of a camera. While keeping my hand in Addison's, and while Paul studied me with eyes like a field raven, ensuring I didn't mess anything up.

I dug my face into Mom's shoulder, using her hair to conceal my mouth. "We need to talk," I whispered, not sure it was even audible enough for her to hear. "About Corinn. And Dad."

Her fingers, once moving on my back, now stilled. She'd heard my words and the spaces between them, then.

Mom pressed her lips to my forehead, mumbling words beneath her breath. "Be happy, Griff. As best you can. And be safe." When she withdrew, she searched my eyes, my face.

She was looking for her son, and he was not here right now. Not really. I would have to work to find him again.

I was numb when we left. Julia had stolen everything from me, including the last moments with my family. This was all too practiced, too stiff. The camera efficiently dissuaded me from speaking privately with my only remaining family, and maybe that was Julia's goal. Maybe she still didn't truly trust the Howard family.

But if that were the case, I never would've ended up here, within an arm's length of the crown.

Whatever Julia's goal, she'd stolen my emotions nonetheless. I stood in front of my family, trying to memorize their soft smiles, trying to cherish these final moments with them. But I could only focus on everything else.

Smile for the camera. Don't brush Addison away. Smile wider, wider. Look at Paul for approval. Don't think about Corinn.

Don't think about Corinn . . .

But Corinn still led my every move. My heart pulsed toward her and the path we'd been on together. I wouldn't abandon our plan to save Miota.

The motions were too mechanical, and my heart was too heavy. As Addison and I walked away, six houses down the road toward the Maybee household, I forced my neck to be made of unmoving timber, large and sturdy, to keep from turning around to look at my mother and sister, likely still watching us from the front yard.

When we entered Addison's house, my throat bobbed once. Her parents and younger sister Mila flooded us with hugs and kisses, and I bent my mouth into a smile. It probably wasn't a convincing gesture, but it was the best I could do.

Because as time passed, more Top-Tiered Salfordians dared to leave their houses and venture into the Maybees' front yard, making me feel confined from within their home. And after Addison quickly packed her bag, we were being delivered to the castle. To Julia, the vicious queen, and Abner, the jaded king.

I hated the king nearly as much as I hated the queen. He was so spineless, so weak. So *willing* to let this deadly cycle continue. While Abner claimed he wanted to free Miota from the Delldovas' deadly reign, he'd worn a crown for over twenty years and was yet to do much of anything about it.

He was apparently *going to* pawn his son and Corinn off to that fate, and they were going to save Miota. But it hadn't mattered what Abner planned to do. Not when Kierran—*Cass*—and Corinn were reunited in death.

As we went through the motions, each one leading us closer to Julia and her lethal domain, I tried morphing my thoughts into wit instead of spite. I needed to remain sharp at all times—because I was going to live in the castle with the vile queen herself. I'd be at the disposal of her mind-controlled guards, behind walls of stone, where she wrote reality. Max Reno was not my ally anymore; he failed to save Corinn when it mattered most. And I didn't trust Abner either; he was only a necessary ally until Julia placed a crown directly on my head.

I would be alone in the castle.

If I wasn't smart moving forward, it would be the perfect storm for Julia to end me, as she did with my father.

But if I could maneuver my way around her court and learn how to scheme, it would be the perfect disaster for *me* to strike.

I channeled Corinn's beautiful determination now, holding fast to her ghost. I needed her strength if I were to survive this. Because I was scheming to uproot Miota.

I was charting to kill a queen in her own home.

CHAPTER 5

CORINN

Three days passed.

Three days of waking with the sun, drinking cup after cup of black coffee, and sitting with Cass in front of the sparkling window overlooking Red Fox as we wrote all we knew of our home.

Three days of tiptoeing around each other, too scared to fully come clean. I didn't dare mention Griff, nor did I ask Cass if he'd intervened with Lorella to get me—specifically *me*—here on the supercontinent.

Three evenings, which turned into three late nights, of lessons with Lorella on how to be an invisible, harmless member of society, one no one paid attention to.

It was funny. My whole life, I'd wanted nothing more than to be *worthy* of attention. But now that I'd escaped Miota, I was learning how to remain unseen and unimportant. Keep my eyes downcast; give a small, barely-there smile; slump my shoulders; walk with assurance.

"Fake it till you make it," Lorella said on the third night, tipping the neck of her beer bottle toward me. Alcohol wasn't something I knew much of on Miota, belonging to the Low Tier and all. I'd tasted wine during Accolade, but that was it—the commodity wasn't wasted on members of the Low Tier. But here, there were spirits and drinks of all tastes and colors, all with the ability to make one's head foggy after only a few sips. "That's how the saying goes. If you walk like you belong somewhere, like you know where you're going and what you're doing, no one will question you. Confidence is *everything*."

"It's more important than correctness," Colton chimed in, his voice bleeding in from the kitchen. He fished another drink for himself. Not beer, like Lorella, but a drink that fizzed on the tongue. "Which should make you feel a little better, Corinn."

I frowned into my coffee—my drink of choice, even at this hour—as I gathered his implication of my dimwittedness and gripped my mug harder. "Did you learn that much through experience?" I shot back, hoping he heard from across the apartment. The living room and kitchen were in the same space, each territory only separated by a marble slab Lorella called the island.

I couldn't help but picture Miota as the kitchen island: Julia ruled it, and everyone I loved was in the kitchen. Meanwhile, I was tethered to a couch across the apartment with Cass, and I needed *everyone* from back home to join me here.

When Colton plopped on the sofa adjacent to me, next to Lorella, he sneered at me before taking a swig of his drink and slamming it on the coffee table.

"Stop," Lorella scowled at Colton and waved her hands toward us both. "Seriously, you need to be confident. Not *cocky*—don't get arrogant. But always keep a sense of control and purpose, like you know what you're doing, even if you don't."

I nodded. This seemed an easy lesson, one Lorella could've given me on day one, with a few of the other basics: *Trust your gut. Don't speak unless spoken to. There's safety in numbers.*

"Right." I peered out the window at the bleeding sky now turning into a vibrant blue. The midsummer sky looked the same here as it did on Miota; the moon rose in the same arc, and the stars winked into view on the same ethereal clock. Maybe, somehow, I was more connected to Griff than I thought. Maybe we were both staring at the moon, thinking of each other.

For now, that was the most I could wish for.

Below the heavens, below *us*, the city sprang to life, as it did each night in an array of neon lights and glowing pillars. I knew citizens of Red Fox scurried about below, likely going to the bars Colton liked to mention being in close vicinity to the residential district we were in, or maybe going to visit friends in the other apartment buildings as tall as Lorella's.

Beyond the people, I glimpsed the void. Black as night itself, made of nothingness. Somewhere out there lay Miota; somewhere in the gaping blackness was my home.

And the only way I could save it right now was to spy.

"It's getting dark," Colton announced to the room, though his eyes targeted Lorella. "I should . . . get going."

"Okay." She gestured toward his drink. "Though you *did* just open that."

"I can drink fast, if you want me gone."

He spoke a question by uttering the word *if.* And I suddenly felt like Cass and I were intruding.

"Can you help me wrap my legs in cold cloths?" I asked the Miotan prince, ready to flee from the charged room.

Cass happily jumped at the opportunity, and he raced to Lorella's fridge for the compresses. I stood, retreating to the spare bedroom Cass had let me sleep in every night so far while he'd claimed a couch in the living room.

In the last three days, Lorella had given me painkillers and cold compresses, though no treatment outside of conservative measures— that would come from my first mission *outside* this apartment. I was going to become the crew's eyes and ears, receiving treatment for my legs in Biourica's main compound while also collecting any helpful information.

My appointment was set for two days from now. I was over

halfway through my confinement in this apartment, which was the only thought keeping me from going crazy. How was Cass still sane after being here for over two months?

I hobbled into the dark bedroom—how this room was constructed without windows when it had the potential for a beautiful view of the glittering city was beyond me. Creamy lamplight filled the space, throwing long shadows across the ceiling.

Cass trailed me. I lowered myself onto the bed and stretched my legs, still swollen and blistered beyond recognition. These wounds would scar and stay with me, following me all my days. They held the jagged memories of Salem Redding and my final moments with him.

Dead. Because of me.

Cass wrapped my shins in compresses with delicate hands, a tender touch capable only of a prince. Still, I winced, sucking cold air through my teeth.

"Sorry," he murmured and hesitantly pulled away.

"Don't stop," I said in a breath. "Get it over with."

Cass's hands now trembled as he placed each cloth on me and gently pressed them against my bare skin. I bit my cheeks through the initial sting and shock that always made me want to vomit. Then I slumped my shoulders and relaxed as best I could.

"Thanks."

Cass nodded and slowly sat on the bed near my feet. He hugged his knees to his chest as he watched me. "You'll get through this, you know."

I would. But the same was not true for Salem. And *that* was the part I found too difficult to live with.

So I changed the subject. "What's going on with Lorella and Colton? Are they . . ."

Cass sighed through his nose. "It's hard to say. Sometimes he stays here, sleeping in Lorella's room, for days at a time. Then he'll hardly come over. I think . . . well, I've figured out that they *had* a solid relationship, but there's bad blood between them now. And it has something to do with Colton and Dalton's falling out with their father."

I hummed. And then I asked the dumbest question possible. "Are you the reason I'm here on the supercontinent?"

Apparently, I could only hold my tongue for so long. *Three days.*

Cass's face fell, and he sat up as straight as a wall. "What? What makes you ask *that?*"

"Are you?" I didn't relent, though I averted my gaze, choosing to instead stare at my covered legs. "Lorella said I could help you *fill in the gaps* about Miota. But you shouldn't have any knowledge gaps—not as a prince."

Cass didn't speak for a few heartbeats. Then, "I did what I needed to protect you, you know."

The lump in my throat won, and I wiped a tear from my cheek.

"When I got here," Cass drawled, "and I learned what was going on between Miota and Biourica . . . I realized no one back home was safe. And you were in the Low Tier, and I *knew* you weren't safe there."

Though a thousand retorts grew on my tongue, I didn't speak any of them. I *couldn't.* If I opened my mouth, I'd fall apart, and there was no promise of putting myself back together.

"Corinn, I'm sorry. I had to do it."

"No you didn't," I choked out, my voice breaking in tandem with my spirits. Any tenuous hope I'd found here was now gone. I was only here because of *Cass,* because he felt like he had to save me.

"I *did.*" Cass reached out a hand across the bedspread. I did not take it. "Corinn, I wasn't lying when I said you and Salem were the only real friends I had. You were in Pointe's Low Tier, so I had to protect you first."

I finally snapped. "So you—what? Played dumb? Played weak until Lorella's crew agreed to accommodate you? You're more like your parents than I thought! Entitled like your mother, and a coward like your father."

As if the son of Julia and Abner could've been anything more than that.

Cass recoiled, standing from the bed. His eyes shattered into fragments I couldn't piece back together.

"I'm . . . I'm sorry," I got out, between the sobs spasming in my throat and the tears caking my cheekbones.

Cass crossed his arms. His jaw trembled. After a long moment, he spoke, his voice like a candle's flame sputtering out. "If I'd known that you'd hate me for convincing them to bring you here, I wouldn't have done it." He clenched his jaw, willing his teeth to stop shaking. "I thought—I thought I was saving you."

The genuine pain in his face told me he was still playing his father's game . . . still tying us together as Abner had forced him to do for the last four years back home. After being coerced to befriend me for that long, had some part of it become real to Miota's prince?

Fake it till you make it, Lorella had said.

"I knew Abner's plan," I whispered as I wrung my nervous energy out on the bottom hem of my shirt. "I know he sent you to Pointe, to *me*, on purpose. Because I was a Low, and Julia wouldn't suspect me to be a threat. And I'd win your Courtship, and we'd free Miota together."

Cass pressed two fingers at the middle of his brow. "I was obeying my dad's orders," he returned. Shadows and midnight claimed him. "At the start, anyway."

My eyes gravitated back to his, and he snagged on my gaze, refusing to let me go. As if I could read between his stare, his words.

"I'm tired of lies," I croaked. "So please . . . just say whatever you need to say."

Cass laced his hands as the tension in his shoulders melted. "I don't know what's true and what's *not* anymore. Ever since I got here, I feel like . . . like I'm learning more every day. And the more I learn . . ." He ran a harsh hand through his thick hair. "The more I realize how *useless* I am."

"You aren't useless, Cass—"

"I'm a prince without power," he shot. "And what does that *really* make me? Nobody." A snarl worked its way across his face. "I've always wondered how I could make both my parents happy when I knew they wanted different things for me. But now that they're back home, and I'm here . . . I keep wondering what *they* would do."

The cold from the compresses seeped up my legs and into my core. It was dangerous, someone following the molds made by a queen with no humanity and a king with no loyalty.

"Cass, you're better than your parents," I dared to say. He *needed* to hear that. He needed to know he wasn't doomed to follow their footsteps. "You're kind, and you're strong enough to walk a different path."

"I felt helpless," he admitted, turning his back to me. "I still do, truthfully. So I tried doing the *one thing* I thought I could: save my friend. I'm sorry it's not what you wanted."

My emotions hung, suspended in thick air, paralyzed by the prince's words. His actions weren't ones I would've chosen . . . but I knew what it felt like to be helpless. To do what you thought was smart, only to realize later how reckless it was.

I glimpsed the blisters beneath the cold compresses, recalling my own frenzied actions on Miota.

Yes, I understood Cass's desperate reasoning.

"We'll have to make do for now," I said. Whether or not I liked it, Cass's doing or someone else's, this was my life now.

I'd been cleaved from my home, and I was going to spy for Lorella's crew. It would be the quickest and easiest way to save those I loved still on Miota. I only hoped to the moon I was *good* at it.

"No more secrets between us, okay?" Cass promised, turning back toward me while wiping his cheeks with the heel of his hand.

"No more secrets," I agreed. I'd had enough secrets and betrayal from Delldovas to last me a lifetime; I didn't need them from Cass, too.

When Miota's prince offered a hesitant smile, much like the one he'd given when I first laid eyes on him here, I accepted it.

CHAPTER 6

CORINN

"Are you lost? What are you doing? Are you even from around here? I'm calling the cops—"

"I'm not lost. My name's Corinn Januski." I whipped out my grid—a device nearly identical to the handheld panels on Miota—and pulled up my photograph ID scan. "I'm from New Mills, just visiting for the week. The burn treatment in Red Fox is fantastic, you know." I lifted one leg of my loose pants, showing my uneven skin and pink-yellow blisters.

Lorella squinted, and I stared back, refusing to show emotion. This was the last test before I left this stifling apartment—I wouldn't fail now.

"I don't believe you," she ground out, playing her part of a stubborn Biourica security guard.

I sighed. "Look, I'm late for my appointment with Dr. Weston. I don't want to have to take my business elsewhere."

Lorella narrowed her eyes, bringing her face even closer to mine.

I didn't cave.

The woman grinned, straightening to her full height and giving a small squeal. "You're ready. Last thing: tell me of your route there and back."

Giddiness swelled behind my ribs. I was going to leave this apartment. *Finally.*

I explained my route in detail: the buttons I'd press in the contraption called an elevator, which was just outside Lorella's apartment, and the very corner I'd wait on for the correct maglev—a monstrous, metallic vehicle to take me deep into Red Fox's industrial district, to Biourica's compound.

"And what do you avoid more than anything else out there?" Lorella prompted.

I became queasy, remembering what Lorella had too casually mentioned yesterday.

"Rats," I replied. My mouth turned sticky as I thought of the disease Lorella called red bite. Transmitted by sickly vermin, the virus thickened blood until hardening it completely.

It ensured death to whomever it touched—a disease with a one-hundred-percent mortality rate, mercilessly killing every victim in twenty seconds or less.

I hadn't slept well last night with this disease now plaguing my fears.

Cass, who leaned his forearms on Lorella's kitchen island, frowned at me. "There isn't *any* way to avoid the rats? Guarantee safety?" he asked Lorella with an edge.

He stayed more composed now than he had last night, though, at Lorella's first mention of red bite. He'd shouted at her for not mentioning this before I'd agreed to spy for them. When Lorella had tried defending herself, ensuring us that infected rats were too rare to encounter or worry about, Cass refused to listen and locked himself in the spare bedroom.

"Immunity is something Arlo James is trying to work on," Lorella answered Cass from where she stood beside the pillar of fire in the corner of her living room. "Seriously, Cass, people still go outside every day of their entire life and never encounter rats *at all*, let alone infected ones. She'll be fine."

I tried shooting Cass a reassuring look, but it was difficult when my heart battered and lungs seemed to deflate.

Cass narrowed his eyes at Lorella. "You still should've told Corinn about red bite before last night."

Lorella didn't bother arguing with the Miotan after that. He did, after all, have a good point.

My first appointment was at noon, and at eleven, I slipped into a pair of shoes. Adrenaline claimed me completely.

I was caught up on painkillers, and with bandages wrapping my legs underneath loose pants, I could tolerate more walking than I'd been able to lately. The trick was convincing my brain that my legs could handle the force of walking normally.

Also armed with a grid from the mysterious member of this crew, Neave, I was ready.

I'm ready to go.

For Griff, for my family, and for Miota, I would do my best to find information to help my home—and, of course, Lorella.

Eleven fifteen rolled around, and Lorella and I had to leave despite my queasiness. According to Lorella, there weren't cameras in the halls or the elevator, so we just had to leave at the same time for her own coming and going to add up.

Cass embraced me, holding me for a small eternity. "Be safe," he whispered against my hair.

When he'd hugged me before, after my Commencement in Pointe, his fingertips had sent little shocks to my skin. But now . . . all I felt was an ache, wishing his arms were someone else's.

Lorella and I left her front door—which only *she* could lock and unlock with her fingerprint, hence the reason why I hadn't tried sneaking out already. Her door, and then the elevator, which I still had yet to see.

I sucked in a breath, bottling air deep in my lungs, to keep from letting out a squeal just from witnessing this small chunk of hallway. I drank in the tiled corridor—from the light fixtures of red metal adhered between each doorway, to the golden double-doors at the end of the hall.

This place looked like Castle Circle, in all its glitz and glory. Not a speck of dirt littered the cold, reflective floor; not a tile lay out of place on the ceiling, where they created a gradient of hues from colored slabs of stone: gold to white to sea-green.

The gilded doors at the end of the hall slid open, revealing a box adorned in ruby carpeting and reflective walls. I walked like I was made of molasses.

"This is the elevator," Lorella muttered, her breath hitting my temple. "Now get in, and stop gawking. You'll see a hundred things crazier than *this*."

I gave my best impassive expression and kept my chin parallel to the floor. *I belong here. I live in Red Fox. Everything is mundane.*

But it was the most new and exciting thing I'd ever done.

If only Griff were here to see it all, too. He and I were supposed to do this together. It was meant to be us.

Before Griff Howard completely overtook my thoughts, the elevator lurched *downward*. Though the pace seemed steady, I still didn't trust it to know when to stop. I squeezed every muscle in my legs, ignoring the irritated burns, and I gripped the railing until my knuckles turned white.

The elevator slowed to a gradual stop. I braced myself to look outside, to *step* outside, but Lorella set a restrictive hand on my wrist. "Not our floor."

What did that mean? As I opened my mouth to ask, the elevator doors opened and more people flooded into the box, filling it to the brim. Lorella exchanged pleasantries with a few of them.

By the moon. These were citizens of the supercontinent! Maybe I'd underestimated how calm I'd be able to stay. I'd seen citizens from Lorella's window, though they appeared to be no larger than specks.

Now, they were breathing the same air as me; I could reach out and touch them.

Once we reached the lobby, I had to dissociate to keep from whirling at a hundred miles an hour. It was the most beautiful thing I'd ever seen, on any continent or island.

Citizens bustled about the room made of slabs of black marble with gold veins. Instead of chandeliers, which were all the intricate light fixtures on Miota, this lobby had tens, if not hundreds, of glowing crystal tubes hanging from the ceiling. Windows fell flush against the ground, letting in the watery sunlight. The floor was opposite the walls: white marble with black veining, with gold etched in intricate rectangular patterns.

"No gawking," Lorella repeated before separating from me.

"Okay."

Lorella couldn't have heard me, though; she was already walking toward a counter with a dozen built-in screens, veering from my path through exterior doors.

I was *outside*.

I couldn't keep up with Red Fox. No matter how slowly I crept onward, I didn't have time to take it all in. Especially against the racing clock of my appointment.

The first thing I noticed was the heat. Muggy air stuck to my body, fueled by the random gases that seeped through the air, making my skin sweat and my nose twitch.

The streets were packed with so many people, there wasn't a way for me to comprehend them all. They wore clothes of every style and color imaginable, a medley like that of the rare rainbow. The swarms of people were tightly packed, and even more so as I navigated to the correct spot to wait for my maglev.

It was so easy to get turned around down here, among the chaos. I tilted my head upward for only a moment. Could Cass see me from up in Lorella's apartment?

And then I remembered the rat situation, and I looked back down at my feet, sweeping the area ahead of me with both eyes. Even in the sweltering heat, a seemingly slight majority of people wore either pants or high-topped shoes—I assumed for warding off potential rat bites.

When Lorella first told me of red bite, I'd exchanged a crazed look with Cass. Miota had fieldmice, vermin, rats . . . all words used interchangeably. And in all circumstances, they were harmless creatures. But Lorella said the war on the supercontinent *changed* the rats to make them lethal. People had first discovered red bite right here, which apparently played a role in changing this city's name from *York* to *Red Fox*.

So as I made my way to the correct corner, I scanned for rodents scurrying across paths.

It was one of the advantages of being rich, like Lorella. While she'd gone downstairs to escort me out, she wouldn't step foot outside; she'd instead go back up to a higher floor, where she could walk out onto the Platform to travel across the city.

Again, briefly, I glanced upward, now eyeing the clear tubing dozens and dozens of stories above us: *the Platform*. It was how those rich in money chose to travel, having access to the roads *above* the city— Lorella said for less crowds, safer travel, and no rats, thanks to some electrifying technology I didn't understand.

I tried tucking away my resentment as I waited in the appropriate spot for the maglev due to arrive in three minutes. With the wealthy, the fortunate, living literally *above* everyone else, they were Red Fox's Top Tier. And there was no differentiating between the other two Tiers—we were all the same down here.

From what I could tell, the main street I stood on existed solely to funnel people along, either by maglev or by foot. Smaller buildings lay in the side alleyways, where throngs of people sat on bricks, leaned against mossy walls, or ran along the path. No matter where I stood, I seemed to be tightly packed in Red Fox's vessels, the swarms moving mechanically against time.

From up above, where Lorella had to be by now, she couldn't smell the stink of sweat and unwashed bodies. And she likely couldn't taste the sticky chemicals on her tongue, given off by the vehicles that whirred by, nor hear the chatter of every conversation running together in a jumbled conglomeration of noise.

I couldn't believe people lived like this, so separated from each other. The wealthy above and everyone else below, all because of an intangible commodity called money. Was money easy to accumulate, or were people practically stuck in the position they were born into? Maybe this truly wasn't so different from Tiers after all. Only, while Julia kept her country in order overtly, placing social status on a silver platter to be displayed for all to see, the supercontinent tried hiding it more by shoving the less fortunate into alleys and side streets. To keep the rich from being bothered to care.

Maybe Miota and the supercontinent, and all their associated people, weren't as different as I'd imagined. Maybe humanity was strung together across countries and oceans, all burdened with the same problems.

And maybe that meant we were also all hoping for the same unreachable things, all dreaming impossibilities.

The maglev appeared exactly on time, and I hadn't expected it to be so . . . *big*. From up at Lorella's window, these things hadn't looked so bulky and intimidating. Keeping my face as straight as possible and pulling my lips tight, I stepped up and into the metallic beast that hovered slightly above the street by magnets. The entire thing was taller than my shack in Pointe and longer than a dozen limos combined.

After entering the maglev through a side door, I looked for an empty seat in the rows of chairs lining the compartment. I ended up next to an old woman with knobby joints and a bow in her spine, just like my grandma back home.

Lorella said not to engage with others unless they spoke to me first. But in this moment, it took all my strength not to acknowledge the woman. It would never be enough to replace Grandma Yvette, but any sense of familiarity right now would be nice.

Odd, how even though all I'd ever wanted was to be out here exploring, I now thought of home.

I looked out the window, staying occupied with the view, to keep from speaking to the stranger. Small sidewalks chiseled their way into ribbons off the main road, though they became less frequent as we moved from the residential to industrial district.

Massive signs hanging higher than the Fort littered buildings' exteriors, promoting products like medicines, lotions, and technology. I noted a Biourica symbol in the corner of one sign, and its bold *B* stayed branded in my mind's eye.

After about ten minutes whizzing across the city and stopping to both unload and receive new people every few blocks, the maglev rattled to a stop in front of a sky-high building of sleek whites and metallic materials. It dangled like a prize in front of my eyes, and I wondered where in this building Miotans resided. They were kept *somewhere* within.

I dismounted the maglev, took a final deep breath, and made for the entrance. I was a Low-Tiered Miotan now entering the heart of my enemy.

CHAPTER 7

CORINN

"Heart rate is high," the mechanical thing mumbled.

I cleared my throat and stared at the machine clad in plastic. Though it looked semi-human, enough like a woman with a face, torso, and arms . . . it was *fake*. Nothing more than a machine.

Ultimately, I responded to . . . *it*. "I've been running around this morning," I said.

"Biourica recommends taking deep breaths to calm your nervous system."

"Sure." Was I supposed to acknowledge the machine-lady?

Now that I was here, within Biourica, my nerves stayed bound tightly together, trying to contain themselves. I channeled all thoughts toward a common purpose of collecting information without getting caught.

I'd kept myself calm on the walk in here. While my hands had become slick with sweat and my eyes had wanted to wander around the fluorescent-lit halls and nooks, I'd played my part.

I'd scanned my panel—my *grid*. And I'd waited for my name to be called. And I'd followed a motorized box—yes, a *box*, about three feet tall and complete with four sets of wheels—down the hall on its heels, not letting my head whip around in apparent search.

My eyes had scanned the hall, counting how many doors lay on each side. I'd mentally tracked how many steps and how many turns we'd taken—hopefully, the numbers wouldn't blur.

This place, the halls, were pristine and crisp, made of clear-cut angles and smooth white tile shiny enough for me to catch my reflection in.

The robot finished assessing my vitals and medical history, which Neave must have put together somehow. I still hadn't met the technological whiz, but when I did, I would owe her a lot. The humanoid med robot finished and went to sleep, turning off and tucking into a portion of the wall.

I waited for a human to enter: Georgia Weston, a doctor who Colton said had mentored him when he'd gotten his first certification. Here on the supercontinent, if I'd gathered correctly, students *chose* careers. It was so different from Miota, where you were assigned a job based on many different factors, some modifiable and others not.

While I waited, I scoured the room from my spot, but it was devoid of anything useful. This treatment bed, lined with some sort of paper, took up the small room's main floor space. A sink and blank countertop stared back at me, and other than that, only the med robot slept in its corner.

I considered rifling quickly through the cabinets, but a woman around my mother's age entered the room. She wore a friendly smile, and her tight updo pulled at her forehead and eyes.

"Hi, Corinn." She sanitized her hands and donned blue gloves. "I'm Dr. Weston."

"Nice to meet you." I kept my back straight and my eyes set on the woman. *Be confident. Be covert.*

"I heard you spilled a kettle of hot water on yourself?" The story Lorella and I had agreed on telling others. "How is the pain now compared to when it happened?"

The pain. Her question clawed at my brain, taunting me. It had been so much more than Julia's torture. It had been Salem's death, and my recklessness, and Abner's justified betrayal.

"A little better," I answered.

"Good." Dr. Weston pressed a button on her panel—*grid*—and within the minute, one of the cabinets flew open, producing a tray of shining and sharp objects that looked like they could accompany someone in a surgery. "How long are you in town? We may need to do a few rounds of this treatment method."

I sighed. "There isn't a definitive date. As long as it takes, I guess, for me to heal properly." I hoped these answers sounded believable to *any* extent.

Because if I were caught in *here* . . .

A chill shuddered through me. There were Miotans somewhere around here. *Miotans.* They needed my help—anyone's help.

I'd discover what I could today, and I'd return with vengeance next time. I knew better now than to run into danger without a solid plan, no matter how worthy the cause. Because even though this cause was enough . . . *I* was not.

I am not enough. The sentiment carried over in my body, in my cells, as Dr. Weston instructed me to take off my bandages. I followed her direction, letting the wounds breathe. With a quick, muttered warning, she injected a bright blue serum into my legs, jabbing me with a needle in each lateral shin.

The world blurred and I was robbed of breath. I wanted to scream, but I couldn't speak. Couldn't move or do *anything* but stare at the ceiling, mouth agape, as my throat seared in a silent scream.

The world burned, *burned, burned*—

And cleared.

"Finished," Dr. Weston stated, discarding the needles in a red bucket.

I blinked, staring at my legs. Blisters were less welted, staying flatter against my skin. The bright red spots were now a less pigmented pink, and more tissue took on a yellow color, signaling healing and regrowth. My lips parted, and victory swelled in my lungs. That was . . . so *simple*.

"You're good to go now," the doctor finished.

Wait. That was it? I hadn't discovered anything remotely helpful yet. "Wh-what about next treatment? When will that be?"

Dr. Weston observed me as she stood. "You can come back any time after forty-eight hours. Our web-bots can answer any questions and schedule your next appointment. Nice to meet you, Corinn."

I recognized the dismissal cloaked with courtesy, and I inhaled to speak. But before I said anything, Georgia Weston told me she had other patients to see. She left, and another motor-operated plain metal box appeared to escort me out of the compound.

We retraced our steps to the waiting room, and I looked for something. *Anything*. But before I knew it, I left the back hallways, having seen nothing but white-washed walls and reflective floors. Other citizens waited in the secured lobby area, and I noted some of them, but nothing stuck.

And then I was back outside. Rejected from Biourica. Cast out, and with nothing to show for it.

During the maglev ride back to Lorella's, I racked my brain for anything useful for either Lorella or Griff, secretly fighting for *both* sides.

But I came up with nothing. I tried to contain my tears and rein in my trepidation. But a whispering voice whittled away at my mind, telling me I was on an impossible mission, one I was predestined to fail.

And who was I to fight fate written in the stars?

I paced Lorella's living room on my new legs. Though they would need more healing sessions, I was able to keep weight on them for much longer now, able to walk untethered to furniture or Cass's forearm for support.

"You mean to say you can't think of *anything*," Colton confirmed, breaking the room's silence. The James brothers lounged on Lorella's sofa, while Lorella stood by the crystal column of fire with crossed arms. Cass stood in the kitchen, leaning back against the island.

"I can tell you how many rooms there were," I mumbled, hating this feeling of defeat. It was something I was used to, after eighteen years of being stifled in Miota's Low Tier. But it still didn't make it any easier, admitting my shortcomings to Lorella's team. "And how many steps I took. How many turns I made."

"And what the hell does *that* tell us?" Colton snarled, leaning forward so his elbows rested on his thighs. "You're supposed to be useful—"

"I know!" I raked my hands through my hair. "Look, there was always something watching me. I didn't know where else to *go*."

"Did you not realize what spying meant?" Colton asked. "The whole point is to blend in, find ways *around* the people watching."

I couldn't breathe. Not with Colton James barking at me, humiliating me in front of the others.

"I know what spying is," I gritted back. Cass's eyes stayed pinned on me, following my every move from across the apartment. I knew he would step in if needed. Our latest mutual promise—*no more secrets*—boiled within me. I still hadn't mentioned Griff to him, and at this rate, I wasn't sure when I would.

"But I never asked for any of this to happen! I didn't want to come to the supercontinent in the first place, and I didn't want to be put to work, to do the job no one else wants to!" Anger bubbled over, heating up my freshly healed burns. "Why can't Cass do this instead? I'm not good at this, and I never pretended I *would* be."

The occupants of Lorella's apartment didn't move. Everyone looked off in the distance, anywhere but at me. Their bodies were still and silent, each likely pondering their options.

Of what to do with me, now that I was here but useless.

Why *couldn't* Cass do this? He'd already been here. And though anyone on Miota would know his face, no one here did.

Right?

I looked to Cass, the question in my eye. *Why not you?*

He understood. The prince cleared his throat and straightened his posture. "Back home, I used to go to meetings with my mom and Sillian Reeves, the president of Red Fox. He's directly controlled by Arlo James, and both have seen me, thanks to the cameras we use during the meetings. So the odds are slim, but if Arlo or Sillian saw me in Biourica, I'd be a goner."

I stared off, defeated. So this job *had* to be mine. There was no alternative.

"You're not alone in this, Corinn," Lorella offered. She played with the purple rock on the end of her long silver necklace. "You need to spy, and if you're caught, you'd end up in my court. I hold power, and I'd do whatever I could to keep you safe. But, for the record, I don't think you'd be caught. You're a young woman; men like Arlo James will naturally want to count you out. But little does Biourica's leader know that you could wreck them all. You could destroy them when you show them what you're made of."

I could do that. I *had* to, if I wanted to see those I loved again.

This was the plan, and I had to stick with it, because when I didn't . . . people got hurt.

I didn't like the plan, and I didn't want to spy. But I *had* to go along with it. I *had* to once again enter Biourica.

And if I didn't emerge with useful information, I wasn't sure what Lorella's crew would do with me.

CHAPTER 8

GRIFF

I bumbled in my seat next to Julia. Even with a full day between moving into the castle and now, I wasn't prepared.

Nothing could have prepared me for this. Julia announced this event last night, but even then, Addison and I hadn't received our speeches until an hour ago.

The words from the speeches Julia wrote for us now clattered through me in a taunting cacophony. I could hardly keep from fidgeting in my seat wedged between Julia and Addison. On the other side of Julia sat Abner, and the four of us claimed one side of a long, rectangular table overlooking the rest of the dining room.

We watched the revelries unfold like clockwork as butlers rushed in lavish foods and drinks. As maids opted to light candles instead of using the room's electric bulbs embedded in the chandelier. As a small slew of Queen's Guard members, blank as ever, arrived with instruments: a metal pipe, a fiddle, and a drum to add to the lone piano that had been lugged in here earlier today. This was the only piano on the whole island, Julia had bragged. As though Addison or I really cared.

This room was etched in gold, from the table itself, to the veins in the black-marbled fireplace, to the stems of the wine glasses. The dining room was decorated too jovially for the occasion, and though we all knew it, no one seemed to care but me.

This dinner was cruel. As fragrances of meats and breads and stews hit me, I wanted nothing more than to run away. I didn't know where . . . my room had last belonged to Ivan Delldova, Julia's father, and his cruelty seemed to still reek in there. Ideally, I'd run back to Salford, grab my family, and leave this entire island. I wanted to feel the ocean and inhale the stars, and even that would only be worth it if it could somehow bring me back to Corinn.

Addison's hand found mine beneath the table, and I stilled, tightening every muscle to keep from leaping out of my skin, away from her. I let her hold my hand, though, and Julia noted the gesture with a quick downward flick of her head. She was watching—always watching. Nothing escaped her eye.

And this dinner was a test. If I failed, Julia wouldn't hand me a crown anytime soon. But I needed to get my revenge as quickly as possible. I needed Julia to taste the pain of losing pieces of her heart, just as she'd done to me.

But I couldn't do that without a crown.

So I acted out my role as a perfect prince. I kept an upright posture, with shoulders sloped downward, a warm half-grin, and a slight lean toward Addison.

Gwynn, Julia's lady-in-waiting, curtsied as she sliced her way through the bustling castle staff. "Your Most Royal Majesties. Your Highnesses. Guests have just entered the castle grounds and will arrive in a few minutes."

"Thank you, Gwynn," Julia hummed, all too calmly. "When they arrive, please escort them inside. We will be waiting here. Begin rolling the cameras once they are in the castle."

Gwynn dipped her head and left.

I quit breathing, hoping neither woman at my side noticed. They were almost here.

This dinner was supposed to celebrate Accolade's victors. Julia and Abner would accept us as their heirs on camera, for the island to see, and Addison and I would deliver speeches ensuring our prosperity and fidelity to Miota.

And while that would still happen, Julia planned something else.

She'd invited three families to this dinner, spanning all three Tiers. The Top-Tiered Redding family. The Middle-Tiered Stanzifer family. And the Low-Tiered Januski family.

The families of the fallen, Julia told us an hour ago. She invited the families of the candidates who'd died in Accolade, families who now had holes in them, missing members like vital organs in a body.

And she invited them to our damned celebration dinner. As though food and party could mend their broken hearts. As though this would replace the people they'd lost.

"Smiling faces, everyone," Julia gritted through her own bared teeth.

"What isn't to smile about, Your Majesty?" Addison replied in a sickly-sweet tone. "There won't be a day that passes where I forget your generosity for allowing Griff and me to become Miota's next king and queen."

Julia made a small noise, amused.

"Yes," I agreed, saying *something* to keep Julia from burning her sights into me directly. If she looked my way, she'd likely find poorly concealed misery and contempt. "Thank you for your kindness. It's an honor to be seated at your side, tonight and every night."

I *hated* myself for speaking the words.

"I am glad you think so." The queen's hand dove into her dress, and my heart battered in my chest as I remembered hearing that she kept weapons and poisons concealed in her pockets. She instead produced folded papers. While paper was a limited resource in Salford, it appeared to be used much more in the castle. "I wrote additional speeches about the fallen candidates for you two to give. These will come after the main course."

A command, not a request.

Addison's hand tightened on mine, and I kept my fingers leaden. I had to direct my unease elsewhere: in my chest, and in my toes. Places Julia wouldn't see, and Addison wouldn't feel.

My future vengeance would only be as invisible as my current suffering.

"Of course," Addison and I droned in sync.

"Your Majesty?" Addison continued, leaning over me to speak with the queen. "When should we speak about a date to become coronated? On *our* twenty-first birthdays, as your son's coronation would have been?"

My tongue turned thick. Customarily, the heir of Miota took over on their twenty-first birthday so they would rule with, hopefully, the guidance of their parents. It helped solidify their cruelty and power. Addison and I were the same age as Cass . . . my birthday was coming up near the peak of Salford's harvest, and Addison's was later, just after the new year.

Either way, we'd both be twenty-one within a matter of months.

"I had not given it much thought yet," Julia replied, her tone dismissive. If I'd asked the question, Julia likely would've grown suspicious, wondering why I was hurrying. But everyone in this room knew Addison was only eager to grasp at any authority offered to her.

She would do whatever it took to gain—and keep—power. It was why Julia so easily aligned with her, and why she'd ultimately won Accolade. Besides, as daughter of Salford's mayor, she believed she was entitled to most anything.

"It would help maintain tradition, Your Majesty," Addison persisted. "Though you must do whatever you see fit. I was only curious."

Julia glanced sideways, looking toward *me*, and I stuffed all my nervous energy deep into my chest, my belly. My heart froze.

"If I find you two to be worthy," Julia replied levelly, "then you will be crowned around the new year. You will both be of age, and a coronation at the start of a year would be symbolic."

"Worthy, Your Majesty?" Uncertainty laced Addison's voice, undermining her innocence.

Julia spoke to Addison while looking at me. "Yes. *Worthy.*"

I couldn't swallow my fear. Was she worried about my loyalty? Had she already suspected my ulterior motives? I thought I'd masked my pain well.

I was saved by a butler prying open both doors to the dining room. Five cameramen, one from each city, entered behind him. Their lenses burned into my skin. We were now on display to Miota.

It meant the families were coming next. My heart drummed.

I recognized the first two to enter from the sporadic weekends Pointe and Salford had overlapped in Castle Circle. Genevieve Redding, who was on Pointe's executive council, and her husband, Esteban. Genevieve patted her fiery red hair into place before taking her husband's hand and leading him to their seats. The black-haired, mustached man rubbed Genevieve's shoulder. The couple clung to each other, mourning the loss of their only child. In turn, my lip quivered for Salem, the boy who could have lived, if not for Julia's violence.

The next to enter the dining room was a woman with dark hair and pallid skin. She looked worn, like she'd lived more years than her body was worth, and she kept her sunken eyes on the floor.

"Bernet Stanzifer," the leading butler announced. "Mother of Holland Stanzifer."

I waited for more to trail her, but no one did. Was Holland's mother the only family the Accolade candidate had? I ached for Bernet, now doomed to live in exile without her daughter.

The next family threatened to destroy me. *I can't do this.*

A blonde woman I'd met before entered, and grief twisted in my chest, marring my heart and lungs. Mrs. Januski wore the face Corinn would have, if only she'd lived into life's later decades. Beside her walked an ashen-haired man whose eyes, the color of glowing moonlight, were identical to Corinn's. Last came Corinn's brother, Theo, who possessed too much of Corinn in his features for me not to succumb to the lump in my throat. I recalled Corinn saying she lived with her grandmother and cousin, but they evidently hadn't been invited.

The Queen of Miota stood, dressed entirely in the country's navy-blue color, stuffing it down these people's throats. "Welcome," she started, her voice ringing across the polished floors, bouncing off the glassware. "Thank you to everyone watching from home as we celebrate the naming of our newest heirs of the Miotan crown and dynasty, hand-picked by myself, with the counsel of my husband. Both Addison Maybee and Griffith Howard stem from mighty bloodlines, rich in justice and overflowing with charity . . ."

Julia's voice drowned out, only for a moment, as my eyes drew toward Corinn's family. As much as I needed to see her features just *one more time*, this was also torturous, seeing her eyes, her face, her hair, but not *her*. She was veiled from me, behind a wall, somewhere I could not follow.

" . . .And thank you to these three families for coming into my home," Julia said. "It is an honor, truly, to host you tonight. And I want to give my deepest and sincerest condolences to you, who are here to celebrate with us three lives lost."

This wasn't fair. Julia was here, telling these people about candidates *she* killed. The families were here, alive and well. Addison and I were here; Julia and Abner were here.

But Corinn and Salem and Holland were not. A tear tracked down my cheek.

My stomach dropped as I prayed to the moon Julia wouldn't notice.

Max Reno and I had a falling out the day of Corinn's trial that ultimately killed her, and we hadn't spoken since. But that day, he'd told me something that still rang true.

Until Julia gives her power to you and Addison, we're still walking on glass. She can do whatever she wants.

It seemed to sate my anger and redirect my focus, though only until I recalled my response to Max's statement.

She'll always do whatever she wants.

Julia was a master of manipulation and deceit. Whether or not Addison and I held a crown, she would be our mentor. And she would wield her power to make us do her will.

I *had* to end her.

I scratched my head with my free hand and discreetly wiped my cheeks of tears. Julia didn't seem to notice, though everyone on Miota might have if a camera was on me. When I glanced back at Corinn's family, I found their gazes trained on me.

They saw. They knew my tears were for Corinn—my moonlight, who'd waxed brighter and brighter, until Julia forced her to wane.

To *die*.

I held my breath deep in my lungs, filling them until the pressure squeezed in my throat, my stomach. I couldn't stand the thought of Corinn's demise, of Julia's triumph. This island needed to be flipped upside-down.

Once Julia finished speaking, Addison and I gave our initial speeches about our eagerness to rule Miota. My tailored suit squeezed too tightly on my chest. This banquet, these words we droned written at Julia's hand, were all so *stupid*. Everyone already knew we won Accolade. And having these three families in front of us now didn't help them.

It hit me once I sat back down, after delivering my frivolous words and pointless promises. This wasn't a mourning meal for these families; it was Julia's victory feast.

Over a spread of Miota's finest meats, cheeses, vegetables, and wines, Julia grinned, keeping her eyes trained on the castle's visitors. She'd killed vital members of these families, and all she offered them was a buffet.

I was glad to have dinner dragged out, since I now knew that afterward would come these new speeches Julia just sprang upon us: words about our relationships with the fallen Accolade candidates.

I never spoke to Holland Stanzifer, though she'd been Corinn's head-to-head partner the week she died. Salem Redding was more of an ally than I ever expressed to him. His friendship with Corinn kept her afloat long before I crossed paths with her. And Corinn . . .

I shoveled roast beef into my mouth, using the smoked taste to distract me. How was I going to deliver a speech in front of Corinn's family, in front of the whole nation? I burst at the seams just thinking of Corinn; I couldn't *speak* of her in the past-tense for all to see.

I couldn't do this. I didn't *want* to do this. These people in front of us, and the candidates they represented, deserved so much *better.*

My legs shook, turning restless, though I quickly stiffened my muscles. But even my hands quivered, and my jaw rattled, making my teeth ache.

Find the light, a whispering voice caressed me. But I couldn't. My moonlight was dead, and I could not find the stars without her. I was going to succumb to the darkness, to this grief.

As I glanced at the latest speeches Julia sent to our panels, my eyes glazed over, unable to read the words. The sentiment was of *our* sorrow, of *our* sincerest condolences, from the crown.

No. I couldn't associate myself with Julia like this, the true murderer—

"Griff." Abner leaned in front of Julia, over his plate of food, to see me. Julia, seated between us, picked at her food, clearly listening to whatever the king was going to tell me. "Drink this, and get a grip. I know you get stage fright, but it's not a very kingly quality."

Abner slid a chalice of dark liquid across the table, in front of Julia's plate, toward me. I intercepted it. If Abner saw what a mess I was, Julia certainly would, too. As would every Miotan watching at home.

I know you get stage fright. Abner's excuse for me in front of his wife. Even though I didn't trust the king, I remembered we were essential allies until I wore a crown. Abner's lead eyes, hardened like steel and rock and the unrelenting Fort, spoke of our mission to dethrone Julia. I needed to stay composed, even now.

I needed to deliver this speech.

Begrudgingly, I sipped from the goblet, tasting soured wine that gave more of a bite than I'd thought.

"Thank you, Your Majesty," I mumbled, feigning a smile. "Just what I needed." Hopefully, it kept Julia subdued, chalking up my state to nerves and nothing more.

Nausea clenched at my stomach, though, as each second whirled by, as the moment to give our next speeches hurtled toward us. The wine, unfortunately, seemed to undo all attempts to steel myself, condemning me to fall apart entirely. I tried eating a wheat roll to calm my belly, though it did just the opposite.

Pull yourself together, Griff.

I tried channeling Corinn's determination into my bones, knowing I *had* to do this. I *would* give this speech. Even as my mouth turned to dust and my skin grew cold and slick with sweat. But I couldn't muster her spirit.

Maybe because she was dead.

A deep chill seeped into me, first of dread, and then annoyance. I was going to be sick. Why couldn't I just grit my teeth and read the words from my panel? Why was my body fighting this so hard? I *had* to give this speech; I *had* to go through with it.

My vision dimmed, transforming the dining room into a place of vile shadows and icy doom. Only then did it dawn on me that this might not be completely mental. As the world turned blacker, I grew enlightened. I turned my head in time to see Abner's expectant visage.

He'd laced that drink with something. This was purposeful.

I stood to excuse myself and escape to the nearest bathroom, but the world spun. I fell to my knees, behind our table of four royals, and the vomiting started.

CHAPTER 9

GRIFF

The nausea remained for a full day, along with an unruly fever, successfully mimicking the typical flu that swelled every autumn and winter. I was deemed an early receiver of the sickness, but the castle's doctor, Jameson Klemmins, told me I had nothing to worry about and the symptoms would disappear in a few days.

It wasn't the sickness that worried me, though. It was the *king*. Why had he laced my drink? What game was Abner playing? We might both act against Julia, but that clearly didn't mean we were on the same side. Trusting him at all had been a mistake.

I stayed in my suite, glued to the bathroom floor, happy to lock everyone out. It was my first moment of solitude since Accolade ended. Only Paul, unrelenting in his butler duties, entered my room with plain foods every few hours. I chewed on hunks of fresh bread and sheets of salted crackers, relishing the seasonings present in the food here. Spices were one of Miota's more regulated commodities, so the light punch of flavor made even the simplest of foods more enjoyable.

"Your Majesty?" Paul's voice reached me as he set a fresh bowl of broth on my desk. The butler then peered into the bathroom, to where I lounged against my tub. "I brought dinner . . . and His Most Royal Majesty."

My stomach roiled, as though still feeling the sickly wine. "I don't want to see him."

"Respectfully, Your Highness, he outranks us both."

"Griff." Abner's voice, gravelly like steel against rock, intruded. I gave an instinctive eye roll.

The king dismissed Paul, and once we were alone, surrounded by silence, Abner stepped over the bathroom threshold, studying me with unsympathetic eyes. Everything about him was stone-like, cold, and unfeeling.

I turned away from him. "Why'd you do it?" There was no sense in masking my sour tone; it was written on my bunched face, in my bent spine.

I was *so tired* of Abner—tired of his lack of support for Corinn when it mattered most. Tired of the secrets he still kept from me. Tired of his supposed *desire* to save Miota, and tired of his apparent cowardice to actually do so.

"I did you a favor." Abner stepped closer. "You were risking *everything* by letting your emotions get the best of you! It looked like you were about to have the meltdown of the decade. Julia will take as long as she feels she needs before handing over her power. What were you *thinking*?"

"I was thinking of Corinn!" I exploded, irritated by the words that rubbed me raw at this point. I *knew* I had to stay calm; I *knew* Julia would take her time. I grabbed the glass of water sitting on the lip of my tub, and I drank the cool liquid, letting it soothe my acidic throat. "Corinn's family was right there. I did my best—"

"And it wasn't anywhere near good enough." He studied his nailbeds. "You need to do better. Everything is a test to her, and right now, you're failing."

I glared sharper daggers at the king. "Did Julia know what you did? With the wine?"

If she did, it could give us away as allies. Not allies, maybe, but . . . people with a mutual enemy.

"Not at all, and let's try to keep it that way."

My expression curdled. "You mean you were able to lace a drink then and there, and then you used it on *me* instead of *her*?" Electricity zipped through my body. "What are you doing to help these days? Or are you still just sitting around, waiting for me and Addison to do your dirty work?"

Abner's face rippled in waves of shock, then anger. "Trying to sound as reckless and accusatory as Corinn won't bring her back."

I recoiled. Corinn had only acted that way because Abner *left her*. He let her fend for herself in a game she couldn't win without help. My blood boiled, singeing as it churned through me.

"Julia needs to burn," I muttered. The sentiment extended to the king in this moment, though I kept that to myself. He couldn't be trusted; no one on this island could be. I lived alone in this royal court, with only the knives in my back to keep me company.

"And she will," Abner responded with a dismissive flick of his hand. He shifted his weight onto his heels, leaning back against the doorframe. "But only if you get a grip. Don't let anything get under your skin. Then you'll get your crown, and we can move on with the plan. Julia said it herself last night: your coronation will fall around the new year, to coincide more with Addison's birthday. To drag out the festivities and distract the people."

A tear slid down my face. "What do I do until then?"

How can I save Miota when no one in the castle will lift a finger to help?

"Act the part. Be in love with Addison, and bend to Julia's every command. Maybe you can convince her to move the coronation closer to *your* birthday instead."

My birthday. In just over three months.

I felt trapped. I wanted to avenge my father and Corinn as quickly as possible . . . but victory was tied with a marriage to Addison. I couldn't get one without the other, and it paralyzed me.

I finally nodded numbly, unable to give a coherent response. How could I speak when I wasn't even sure what to think? I couldn't open up to anyone in this castle of ominous kings, secretive guards, venomous queens, and bothersome fiancées.

Maybe I didn't *need* to open up. Maybe I only needed to remain agreeable. Do nothing, say nothing against Julia. Even though she was the island's warden, the one orchestrating Miota's secrets, the one hiding an entire supercontinent from us, the one who conducted some elusive trade with them. Despite it all, I'd remain pliable to her.

For a fleeting moment, I glimpsed why Abner was so passive and vacant. He hardly had an alternative from within the castle walls.

"I'll do better," I said, appeasing Abner to get rid of him quicker. "Thank you for the advice."

And thank you for poisoning me, I nearly added out of cruel spite. I wasn't grateful toward Abner at all. Not when this entire situation was mostly his fault. He could've freed Miota long ago.

As I hoped, Abner left after that. I ate the broth Paul had brought, though it lost its warmth and I couldn't finish it.

Addison slipped into my room before retiring to hers next door. "Feeling any better yet?" she asked in her practiced, silky voice.

Its effect didn't work on me anymore. "Not really," I said quickly, hoping sickness would drive her away. "Thanks for checking, though," I added upon remembering my words with Abner.

Her eyes only glittered, pinning me to my desk where I lounged. "I can stay in here with you. Take care of you tonight."

"*No,* Ads." I gave the statement like a bullet, sharp and precise.

Her brow folded, along with her lips. "That's not my name."

"To me it is." I didn't care *what* was on the line; I would never utter Addison's name to her face again. In her family, where names correlated with power, calling her a stupid nickname was like a swift blow to her stomach.

She ran a hand through her hair, smoothing out the thick black locks, setting them in place. My intestines writhed into knots as she sauntered toward me. "Griff Howard, I'm going to be your queen before long. And you'll be my king. And we'll have to be able to—"

My bedroom door opened. Usually, the guest would send me into a panic, but in this moment, Julia's presence was a relief.

The queen's gaze volleyed between Addison and me. "Am I interrupting something?"

"Nothing we can't finish later, Your Majesty." Addison smirked at me before heading for the door. "I'll see you in the morning, my heart."

Julia's face slackened, her emotions betraying her façade of stone for a breath of time. "'My heart?'" she echoed after Addison left. "Do you call her that, too?"

Why did she care?

Julia shook her head, swallowing once, before stepping closer to me. Her skirts swayed at her feet, and I wondered what weapons she kept folded in her pockets. "Actually, it does not matter. Do not tell me." She paused. "I have questions, Griff Howard, and if I were you, I would answer them quickly and truthfully. Otherwise, your life will become rather difficult."

Though my limbs went cold, I dipped my head, agreeing. "Of course, Your Majesty. What can I do?"

"How are you feeling?" she asked, studying my posture, my face, my hands. "You look . . . unwell still."

I offered a ghost of a smile toward the queen, whose hands were laced together, whose eyes were surprisingly soft. Well, maybe not *soft*, but . . . calculating. Not *bent* on destruction, and instead only *considering* it.

"I'm starting to feel a little better," I answered plainly. "Food is going down easier now and coming up less."

"Good." She pressed her lips into a thin line before sitting on my bed, just out of my reach. "What do you know of Corinn's trial?"

My ears rang. She just asked about . . . Corinn? Why?

I swallowed my heavy fear. There was nothing in the castle to incriminate me, luckily. The evidence was all still stuffed away in Castle Circle's greenhouse, and it would stay there until I could ensure my safety.

But Julia wouldn't ask about Corinn if she didn't have reasons.

"Her trial?" I echoed, bunching my lips and recalling what news the island received about her trial in the Queen's Court. "There were reports that she attacked you, and you ended her life in self-defense."

Saying the words, materializing them, was torturous. We'd had a plan for Corinn's trial—one that relied on Max Reno to get Corinn out of the courtroom alive. But he'd failed her that day, losing all my trust in the process.

"It begs the question," Julia mused, "what could Corinn possibly have attacked me with? Why would she try such a thing at all?"

I knew the answer: she'd been armed to the teeth with deadly supplies from the hospital wing. *I'd* been the one to retrieve the materials for Corinn, while she'd been strapped to her bed.

Was Julia toying with me? Did she already have evidence to incriminate me? My insides tightened with hesitant terror.

"She couldn't have had any weapons from the Hold," I answered. As far as the public knew, Corinn had been stuffed away in the Hold, an underground prison, until her trial. I only knew she'd been put back in the hospital wing because I'd been there. "So I assume she just ran at you and tried to beat you in a physical fight."

Julia fiddled with her dress, grabbing her panel from her pocket. "And how would she have ever beaten *me* in a fight? You remember the state she was in, correct?"

This was a test. I wasn't supposed to know about Corinn's burned legs, scalded beyond recognition by Julia's hand. Corinn had died marred, and that made me want to rip the queen to pieces now, here in my room, here in solitude.

"I don't know, Your Majesty," I answered, my voice meek. Corinn had been a fighter, with strength in every way that mattered. Her spirit, though invisible, had been unbreakable.

"But at that point," I continued, "she wouldn't have had anything else to lose. She was stubborn and headstrong, and I wouldn't have expected her to go down easily during her trial. She would've put up whatever fight she could."

Julia made a small noise, an amused huff. My bedroom door burst open, and five members of the Queen's Guard entered. Two stalked toward me with vicious speed, and they pinned my arms and legs into stillness. The other three ransacked my room, throwing everything out of my drawers, shredding my pillows, and throwing all my clothes on the ground.

I tried not to panic, but the mind-controlled guards chilled my very bones. They had cranial implants that deleted their conscious thoughts entirely. *Julia* controlled their wants and needs.

"Please understand, Griff," Julia said, floating across the room as her guards unleashed chaos within. "I want to believe you, but you worked closely with Corinn for too long, and I will never forget the face of your father. I just need to ensure I am not handing over power to someone I cannot trust."

"Your Majesty, you can trust me," I hissed. I didn't struggle against the guards; it wouldn't help my case. But I could vow my allegiance to Julia. I could weave words of unyielding promise. "Whatever I can give, it is yours. *All of my service* belongs to you."

I didn't choke on the words now. Each lie I spun, each flattering word I chanted, was a future lash to Julia, an upcoming wound of betrayal.

Julia's face remained flat. She turned toward the biggest guard once they'd successfully obliterated my room. "Did you find anything?"

"No, Your Majesty."

Julia focused on me once more, fidgeting with her pocket's contents again in apparent habit. "Then we will leave you, Griff Howard. You may not know what I am looking for, but let me make a blanket statement." She inched closer, swathed in a predatorial air. "Should I find any evidence of any wrongdoing, or of your betrayal to the crown, you will suffer."

She couldn't kill me so easily, though. That would require finding someone to replace me as Abner's heir.

She must have sensed my thoughts. "If I find you guilty, I will not kill you, but your mother and sister. I will torture them and leave you to watch, unable to do anything about it. So for their sake, I hope you are as innocent as you claim." She spun on her heels. "Good night, Griff."

And in that moment, nothing combated the terror coursing through me.

Sleep didn't find me after that.

Why did Julia believe I was guilty? Had she found something suggesting my crimes against her? Would she search my home in Salford, if it came to it? All our illegal artifacts were stored in our backyard, underneath our chicken coop. The Queen's Guard hadn't found our stash when they'd searched our home following Dad's death . . . but maybe Julia had grown smarter in the last few years.

Something must have set her suspicions loose. This had to be a very new development, or else she never would've let me win Accolade.

Each time sleep tried tugging me under consciousness, I jolted at the thought of Mom and Jess dying at Julia's hand. She'd then successfully have ended my whole family—all but me, anyway.

They were all I had left on this cursed island. I couldn't lose them, the only two remaining stars, my sole sources of light. Without Mom and Jess . . . I would be nothing.

The lack of sleep didn't help my nausea and fever. At some inhuman hour, I padded into the bathroom—still strewn with stray clothes and items displaced by the Queen's Guard—to take a few fever-reducing pills, but the bottle was empty.

Had I not noticed finishing the vessel of pills earlier? Or maybe the guards had even poured out my medication.

I couldn't call Paul; I'd feel guilty for waking him at such an hour, and for something so trivial. Technically, this was my home now. We were allowed to leave our rooms and walk the halls unescorted.

Right?

I'd only done so twice before, and it had been in broad daylight.

Even then, with sunlight protruding through the windows, I'd felt Julia's eyes somehow boring into my back, like she could still see every moment from within her realm.

I grabbed my panel for its flashlight and slinked out of my room. The hallway was empty and eerily quiet. Maybe I'd feel better if someone found me, to witness my harmless behavior. I trekked down the hallway of bedrooms to the back stone staircase, tucked into its own concealed corner of the castle. I emerged on the ground floor, stepping across the blood-red carpet toward the hospital wing on the opposite side of the castle.

My lip wavered as I approached. This wing was the last place I'd seen Corinn. This was where I'd heard her final words, kissed her for the last time, and seen her eyes of glowing moonlight, a beacon not even death could take from me.

But my thoughts reflected back to the present as voices bled from under the door. They were hushed, and the hall's carpeting only made matters worse.

Still, I leaned close, tilting my ear downward.

"Remind me of what is missing." The cold, vile voice unmistakably belonged to Julia.

What is missing. From the hospital wing?

"Three syringes," an answering voice chimed, "two scalpels, and a vial of antiserum." This voice was laced with the same icy intonation as Julia's, and I assumed it belonged to the royal doctor, Jameson Klemmins.

"She could not have gotten across the room on her own," Julia said. "She undoubtedly had help."

"Agreed, Your Majesty."

The pieces clicked, sucking the air from my lungs. *She—she— couldn't have crossed the room on her own.*

Three syringes, two scalpels, and a vial of antiserum . . .

The supplies I'd gathered for Corinn the night before her trial.

Julia knew Corinn couldn't have retrieved them herself.

So the queen knew there was an accomplice. And she likely suspected me . . . which explained her earlier appearance in my room. The search, the questions, the threats . . .

If Julia outed the truth, she would never hand me a crown. Even now, I couldn't expect to push Julia's timeline forward. I'd need to work harder than ever to stay on the precipice of power.

Crown aside, if Julia discovered the truth, she'd kill my family for it. The final two on this island I cared for—my non-negotiables. All my happiness and humanity hinged on the heartbeats of my mother and sister. I couldn't fail, couldn't let Julia claim them as she had Dad and Corinn.

I hurtled back toward my room and decided medicine could wait. I was ready to let my fever claim me for a few more days.

Until I figured out if the deadly queen was going to come for me again. Until I knew if I was her prime suspect.

And until I figured out what I would do if she caught me.

CHAPTER 10

CORINN

My second appointment came and went, no different than the first. And in the same manner, Lorella's crew doubted my spying skillset after I returned with nothing worthwhile to report.

I couldn't blame them. I wasn't made to be a spy, after all. I hated doing this more than anything. I'd snuck around powerful leaders before, and it was the reason Salem was no longer alive. I was only doing this because I didn't have another *choice*.

The disappointment, the hesitancy, in Lorella's and Colton's eyes had been enough to confirm that it wasn't just *me* who thought I was failing these people—therefore failing Miota, too.

This third appointment *had* to be better. Even without Lorella's team growing impatient, Dr. Weston would soon stop approving me for visits since my legs were healing well. But these appointments granted me the easiest route into Biourica, and I didn't want to find a new way to sneak around the place.

I rubbed my palms along my shins, a new habit I'd developed upon feeling their new skin growth and smoothed-over wounds. Fleshy pink skin now glossed over where marred burn tissue had been only days ago. While the supercontinental technology was incredible, leaving me with the newfound ability to walk and function as normal, it was also bone-chilling.

The tech and medicine were revolutionary in this city, this company, and in my gut, I knew the innocent Miotans traded here had something to do with that.

Which was also why I *had* to do something worthwhile today. For Miota. For my friends and family who didn't deserve any of this. Spying was the only way to find relevant information against Biourica, take them down, and save my home.

"Corinn Januski." The same motorized box from my last two appointments called me and took me from Biourica's open tile and metal lobby to the smaller white hallway of treatment rooms.

I'd already counted the number of doors and steps in these halls.

I'd asked Dalton and Colton if they knew of any secret passageways—in Miota, there were plenty of underground tunnels that hid people and their secrets. They told me there was nothing, though Colton had stuttered, hesitating to give a straight answer at first.

The metallic box veered into the typical treatment room. I let the machine-lady take my vitals before it fell asleep in the room's corner. I waited for Dr. Weston to appear, and once she did, we went through the same routine as before.

Sanitization of my legs. Then the serum, burning and searing me alive. Then *nothing*. The absence of all feeling, all thoughts.

Then the admiration, laced with disgust, at how much *better* my legs looked. After this third treatment, there were even spots that were *pearly* again, appearing like fresh skin.

Erasing my mistakes. Erasing my past, erasing the last marks I'd borne when Salem was still with me.

For that, I hated myself. For eliminating the evidence of my shortcomings, and for deleting something so tightly connected and interwoven with my last memories of Salem.

"Your legs are healing tremendously," Dr. Weston said, offering me a forced grin, pulling too tightly across her teeth. "You can treat the rest with conventional creams and bandaging. And time. So this will be our last visit here today—congratulations!"

Her words fell on me like a hammer to my chest. I was done with these visits; this was the end of my easy way into Biourica.

Not that it really mattered if I couldn't prove useful as a spy. It didn't matter *where* I was if I couldn't execute a plan.

Dr. Weston cocked her head toward me, blinking. Waiting for an answer.

I lifted my chin. *Fake it till you make it.*

"Right," I said. "Thank you. I just . . . these appointments are helping a lot. What if I came less frequently?"

Dr. Weston's brow knitted together, pulling her face inward. "By spreading out your visits, you'll have even more time between—even more time to heal. I don't think it'll work out. Sorry. But I'm prescribing a gel for you to pick up at your pharmacy. It's on the pricey side, but it's worth it, for how much better you'll feel."

She went on about gels and creams and prices, but I filtered out her voice, left to wonder *how* I would find anything useful about Biourica from now on. If I found no upper hand on this company, I'd be useless. Worse, I'd be a liability.

The phantom burns on my legs stung in rhythm to the chant. *You are not enough on your own.*

"Okay," I finally blurted. "Thanks, Dr. Weston. For all your help."

She grinned and hurried away to her next appointment.

My first two appointments had been in the afternoon, and Georgia Weston had been rushed. I'd scheduled this appointment for the morning, hoping she wouldn't be in such a scramble, but the time of day clearly hadn't mattered.

Time nearly seemed as valuable a commodity as money or secrets sometimes. It was the one thing I wanted more of—and the one thing I couldn't get. More time to save Miota . . . more time to spy in here.

The metallic box came to escort me out of the building, and on some instinct of self-preservation, my legs moved of their own accord, spinning me around, taking me deeper into Biourica's halls.

I had to spy—had to save Miota.

The bot whirred after me, and I pretended not to see it. Pretended not to care or know what it was doing. Pretended I was invisible and set in my own ways.

After turning down a new hall, one of inset metal doors and blinding fluorescent ceiling lights, the bot sent something after me, *shocking* my spine, making my teeth buzz and scalp burn.

I turned on the thing, scowling, ready to put up a fight with my new legs.

"Wandering is not permitted," it said in a grainy, monotone voice.

"I'm not wandering," I insisted, fighting with this stupid little box. I put my hands on my hips and looked down at it. "I need a bathroom."

"Wandering is not permitted," it repeated. "Turn around now."

I stood my ground. I needed to find *something* useful here.

"Upgrading shock level," the thing said, buzzing at me.

"Fine!" I turned around and walked toward the front door leading into Biourica's lobby. In this labyrinth of halls, and with a robot on my heels, I'd never learn anything worthwhile. "I'll just go somewhere else. Thanks for the hospitality." Poison seeped into my voice, and I let it take over, honing my anger and frustration toward Biourica and their evil schemes, and toward Lorella's team for making me spy.

I counted the eight rooms on either side of the hall and the thirty-eight steps to the lobby door. Since I wasn't approved for more burn treatment, I didn't stop at the appointment screen as I had the last two times, and instead marched out of the building.

I'd failed yet again. I *couldn't* return to Lorella's apartment empty-handed, but I didn't know what else to do.

My maglev ride back to Lorella's wouldn't come for another twelve minutes, which left me some time to devise a new plan. Clearly, getting medical treatment inside Biourica wasn't enough—it was too structured and closely inspected. I needed something with more flexibility.

Strange, how I was on the supercontinent, with the freedom to move around the city as I pleased, yet I'd never felt more *stuck*. My heart wanted one thing, but my brain said another, and I didn't know which to follow.

"On your left!" someone shouted from behind me. As I wondered if she was addressing *me*, a girl with a birdlike frame flew past me in a sprint. Handfuls of others followed her. Where were they going in such a hurry?

I'd hardly realized I'd stopped in the yawning green field outside Biourica's front doors, a picture of freedom and verdant land amid the metallic world surrounding it.

The group of runners slowed to a stop in front of me, nowhere apparently significant.

"Nice cool down!" the lead girl offered her group, smiling brightly and resting both hands atop her head. Dozens of long, dark braids tumbled from her head, splaying out around her shoulders.

Everyone heaved, breathing in labored and loud synchrony.

"Our pace is still on track for hopefully making the logistics team."

Logistics team. That sounded similar to the program Dalton was hoping to make, which was hosted by Biourica. Though I couldn't help but wonder how Dalton would be allowed to make a selective team when it was run by a place he was banned from.

Curiosity led me near the running group.

"Same time for training tomorrow?" one of the girls asked as she bent over to prop her palms just above her knees.

The leading girl nodded and threw her many braids into a knot at the top of her head. "I'll be here."

"Thanks, Anya." Two of the runners peeled from the group, leaving at a creeping pace. Within a few minutes, the others left, leaving the young girl—Anya—to walk off, too.

"Anya?" I clapped a hand over my mouth. What was I *doing*, talking to strangers like this?

But it was too late. The girl looked at me and grinned.

Reciprocate what others give you, Lorella had told me during our lessons.

They smile, you smile. They ignore you, you ignore them. Only time you don't follow this rule is when someone is picking a fight—you'll lose, Corinn.

So I smiled back. "I'm Corinn," I said. "I've . . . heard about you and your training."

The girl cocked a dark brow, and the gesture summoned Salem's ghost. I swallowed the knot forming in my throat. "Really?" It didn't deliver as a challenge, but more of a surprise.

"Uh, yeah . . . aren't you training for the logistic thing Biourica is hosting?"

"Yeah, the logistics team? Do you want in? There's room for everyone—"

"No," I interrupted, waving my hands to claim innocence. My cheeks burned. "Oh, no. I'm not . . . I can't *train*. I was just wondering what happens if you make the . . . team. Squad. Whatever it is."

Anya gave a shrug and cracked her knuckles. "Kinda unclear, but Biourica's offering tons of money for it, so—well, not tons of money, but a lot to *me*—anyway, no one knows much. It kind of sounds like Biourica's moving into a second location, outside Red Fox, and this team will help make sure the transition goes smoothly."

"And to make the team, you need to . . . run fast?" I wasn't sure why I pried, but something about Anya's demeanor put me at ease. The way she'd encouraged her running group felt genuine, and if I had someone like that on the supercontinent, someone to trust and believe in . . .

I killed the thought.

"Run fast," Anya confirmed. "And lift heavy weights, and take commands, and possess the skills to fight . . ." Her eyes flicked toward Biourica's building looming over us, and she shivered. "Something's not right about it all. Luckily, we're all starting on the same playing field, since no competition like this has ever happened before. None of us know what we're doing or what's going on. And right now, making this team is all the hope I have."

Hope for what? I nearly asked, but kept my mouth shut. It didn't matter.

"How many make the team?" I wondered aloud.

"Seventy-five, so it's pretty selective. Plus, rumor has it Arlo James's own son is going out for the team, and he's pretty much a shoo-in, so make it seventy-four spots."

Shoo-in? I wrinkled my nose at the expression. Still, my mind worked. Dalton would make the mysterious team comprised of people to enact Biourica's ploys. The team needed to be fast, furious, and sharp . . . they needed skills for war. The word that plagued my mind constantly these days.

Biourica already bloodied their hands in biological warfare, but could they use their technology to create *more* war? Could they use an elite fighting force for their own malicious purposes?

And if they did, would Arlo truly let Dalton in on it, if their relationship was as spoiled as Lorella's crew made it out to be?

That was when the idea blossomed, with this smiling girl in front of me. The sun seemed to shine brighter on her brown skin, as if making her a beacon of hope.

Let in the light, Griff's spirit told me now, echoing across oceans.

"Could I train with you?" I asked the girl. "If you'll let me."

Maybe this logistics team would be my new way of infiltrating Biourica. Despite the tasks at hand, doing something with a crowd of people seemed much safer than wandering the halls of Biourica alone.

"So . . . you *are* training?" Anya drawled.

"Yes." I stood straighter, smiled wider. *Accept me, please.* "Yes, I am."

Anya's visage of hesitancy slowly melted, and her smile slowly returned as decision settled into the lines of her face. "Fine. Corinn, welcome to the training team."

CHAPTER 11

CORINN

Welcome to the training team.

Anya's sentiment followed me all the way back to Lorella's, all the way through the afternoon lull. Only Cass occupied Lorella's apartment when I got back, and though I told him I found something out, I wanted to reveal it only once the whole group was together.

"At dinner tonight?" Cass gawked. He scratched his neck, which pulled at the hem of his shirt and bared a thin strip of pale skin. "You won't tell *me*? I'm your best friend, Corinn."

Salem was my best friend. But since he was gone, and it was all my fault, I supposed Cass was somewhere among the top options now. That thought did nothing but sour my mood.

I rolled my eyes and collapsed onto the couch nearest the window in Lorella's living room, letting myself take up the whole piece of furniture.

The sky was bright blue today. Back home in my city of Pointe, the upcoming months would bring increased farming production and preparation for the harvest season, always accompanied by cold air and brisk wind. Did the supercontinent have a harvest season, too? Would the air grow stale and chilled?

I stared out the window at the vibrant, cloudless blue, as if the heavens could answer my question.

Finally, Cass drew me from my trance. "How are your legs? Can I see them?"

I looked at the prince, whose question was so gentle, I couldn't help but melt to his command in this moment. I rolled my loose black pants, revealing the smoothed and glossy wounds.

Cass knelt at my side. He reached out a hand of splayed fingers and brushed my shin, and I did my best to conceal a rough inhale.

His hazel eyes, deep blue dipped in shadowed brown, snapped to my face. "Am I hurting you?"

"No." His touch was a caress, incapable of *hurting* me.

Still, he withdrew, and the cold apartment air sank its teeth into my legs.

"I'm training for Biourica's logistics team," I confessed, ultimately deciding to tell the prince of my plan as I remembered our vow to each other. Keeping Griff a secret from Cass was bad enough; besides, Cass would discover my training plan tonight anyway. "The same one Dalton is prepping for. I think . . . well, they require fighting skills, and you need to be fast and strong." I sighed through my nose. "I think they're planning something big, something . . . dangerous."

Cass settled into his spot on the ground, his gaze locking on mine. "Do you think . . . do you think Arlo James wants to raise an army? To fight for him?"

I shrugged and broke eye contact, staring at the soaring ceiling. "It seems like I'm jumping to conclusions, but . . . we know more of the whole picture than most. Sector A, these people wouldn't know his motive for wanting an army. But *we* know about Miota. The trade." My throat turned to ash. "It makes me *sick.*"

Cass knelt and reached for my hand. "Corinn, look at me." The prince's gaze and touch smothered me into stillness. "Lorella's crew will figure this out. They're a good team. Don't worry, okay?"

While I wanted to find comfort in the promise, I snagged on his phrasing. *They* will figure this out. *They're* a good team.

He was pawning this off on them—not including himself in the move to end Biourica. It was a line of thought echoing that of Abner Delldova, Cass's father, a coward and a deceiver.

Upon making that connection, I shifted on the couch then stood up. "Don't talk to anyone else about this, okay? I'll announce it at dinner tonight."

Tonight was the first crew dinner since I'd arrived. I was still yet to meet the whole team—including Neave, the hacker who'd jammed me into every system and made me a legal citizen of Sector A, and including Saoirse, Lorella's aunt, who'd apparently started this whole movement after finding forbidden texts referencing Miota and its trade with Biourica.

Lorella arrived first, home early from work, in a whirlwind of rushing to clean and cook. Cass and I offered our help where we could, though she mostly turned us down. When I told Lorella I'd share my update from today's appointment at dinner, she'd stubbornly accepted it.

Closer to dinner, Dalton and Colton showed up—the latter with yellow flowers, which stung more than I cared to admit. Salem's favorite color, in an object so *Pointean* . . .

Colton handed the stems off to Lorella at the door, which also triggered the memory of Griff Howard handing me flowers during Accolade.

Tears blurred my vision as I excused myself to the bathroom tucked into the spare bedroom. I now longed not for a place, but for the past. A time when Salem was alive and Griff was mine.

When I emerged after a few minutes, Neave had shown up: a girl around my age with russet curls, a rumbling laugh, and husky voice. She wore a puffy hat made of yarn and had her panel—grid—glued to one palm wherever she went.

As the sun retreated for the day and the moon rose, Lorella's kitchen filled with warm chatter and aromas of baked chicken. Neave went around and lit soy sticks—or what we on Miota called candles.

While on Miota, candles were on the rarer side because of their prestigious status, apparently here, candles were simply archaic, a thing of the past. When Neave said such a thing, Cass had clucked his tongue and pursed his lips, keeping silent.

Lorella's aunt arrived, a box of dessert in hand, only minutes before dinner, which was already scheduled for late in the evening—evident by the glowing moon and midnight blue sky outside the gaping windows. She was an older woman, with deep smile lines and silver hairs, and the brass cackles turned to warm, honeyed chuckles in her presence.

"This is Saoirse, my aunt," Lorella introduced Cass and me. "But everyone just calls her Aunt Sea."

Saoirse gave a close-lipped grin, wider than a moonbeam, and hugged us. "Miraculous," she said in a breath between mine and Cass's faces. Behind Saoirse—Aunt Sea—Cass and I had no choice but to interlock our own arms. "Two Miotans, *here*. Alive and well. Bless you."

Cass and I exchanged entertained glances.

Once we all sat down at Lorella's long wooden table, surrounded by plates of baked chicken and buttery vegetables and fresh fruit, Lorella insisted I share my news from today's appointment.

I blinked from my disbelief at how elegant Lorella's table looked. Back on Miota, I was granted one ration of food per meal as a member of the Low Tier. *This* candlelit table, adorned with ceramic dishes of well-seasoned foods and sleek metal silverware, held a meal fit for Miota's royalty. We ate like this in Castle Circle, during Accolade only; not even Miota's Top Tier regularly ate in such luxury. And no one from Sector A seemed to notice the grandiosity of this meal.

I swallowed my first bite of chicken, cherishing the accompanying zing of lemon that stuck in the back of my throat. With all eyes fixed on me, my thoughts tangled, and I suddenly wondered if this was a good idea.

I looked to Cass from where he sat diagonal from me, and he gave a curt nod, imperceptible to everyone else.

"The appointment went as usual," I started. My voice trembled.

"My legs are essentially healed; Dr. Weston won't approve me for any more treatment."

Lorella leaned forward over her plate, waiting for me to deliver my news. Dalton stared into his lap, and Colton chewed away, maybe not even listening.

I swallowed and folded my hands. "But I found a group actively training for the logistics team Biourica's putting together. The one Dalton is hoping to join." I glanced at the dark-haired boy, who now watched me with churning brown eyes. "I want to join, too. I think . . . I think Biourica's doing something big—"

"You can't," Lorella decided. She set down her silverware and slumped in her seat. "You'd never make it. Only seventy-five spots, and you aren't someone like Dalton James, and you aren't exactly . . . don't take this the wrong way . . . but are you physically fit enough for it?"

My blood sang beneath my skin as the room steadily rose in temperature. "Probably not right now, but maybe there's a chance I can train and *become* good enough."

"The logistics team becomes finalized September first," Lorella countered. "That's over a month away."

"It gives me some time to hopefully train and become good enough." My skin seemed too tight. This was now a private conversation on display for the table, laid out like the platters of lavish foods around us.

Lorella folded her napkin and draped it in her lap. "*No*, Corinn. I'm sorry." Her brow wrinkled, and she continued. "What if you train for a month and don't make the team? And what are you going to do in the meantime? You could do a lot of spying in the next month. We're working against a timeline we don't exactly know for sure, so we can't waste time on this. Dalton is already training for the team."

"Arlo James is doing something *big* with the people who make it," I ground out. From the corner of my vision, Cass heeded me with caution, and I tried stifling my temper. "I don't know if he intends to invade Miota or expand into another sector with the team, but he plans to do *far* more than logistical work. Do you think Arlo would really let on that much to a son he's disowned?" I glared at Dalton. "No offense."

"None taken."

"Besides," I said, pointing a look at Lorella laced with challenge, "can you really say that I've made a good *spy* so far? I will never be good at it, and my appointment days are over. I need a new way into Biourica, and what better way than joining this group? I'd be hand-fed Arlo's plans."

"So will Dalton," Lorella threw back, pointing her fork in turn with her tone, "once he makes the team. We don't need two people going for the same position—we're already spread thin as it is. Neave has risked a lot so you can spy for us."

With each new word, the table simmered into stillness, holding their collective breath as Lorella and I hashed this out. I glanced at Cass, who wore an expression as calculating as the Queen of Miota's. While it spliced me, sending a chill deep through me, it also churned hope. He was scheming for *me*, not Lorella.

Help me, I silently urged, letting my eyes speak to the prince.

He shifted in his seat. "You know . . ." He diverted his gaze downward as he fidgeted with his silverware. "She'll still *use* all the information Neave gave to her. And wouldn't someone else trying out only help our odds of either Dalton or Corinn actually making the team?"

Cass's royal blood thrummed strong right now. His argument seemed to melt some tension around the table. Dalton nodded at the theory.

Lorella's brown eyes burned holes into Cass, though. "*Do* the odds increase if they both try out? Or do they decrease because they're now competing against each other?" She glanced at Colton, whose jaw remained clamped shut. "This is stupid. Dalton is a James; why wouldn't he make it? If Corinn put you up to this—"

"No," the Miotan insisted. "If she'd already pitched this idea to me, you'd already know about it because I would've told you." The lie flew so effortlessly off his tongue, I nearly believed it myself. "Miota is my home—*our* home." Cass's gaze skittered over me. "And if Corinn joining the logistics team endangered them or this team here in any way, I would say something. Because we're all here for the same reasons, right? To help Miota?"

The invisible question hung tautly: *Isn't that why you're doing all this?*

Lorella slumped in her seat, hopefully accepting her defeat. "If you shift your time and energy into training instead of spying," she grumbled toward me, "and you *don't* make the team . . . you'll have wasted *everyone's* time, and you won't find much sympathy or forgiveness from me. In fact, at that point, you'll be a liability more than anything."

Each word pierced me, though it was nothing I hadn't already internalized. Lorella wasn't wrong; I *was* a liability. But the sentiment rang true whether I spied or trained—whether I did what *Lorella* wanted or what *I* wanted—so what difference did it make?

Unless Lorella cared about control more than she let on, like most others in power. This only built my defenses higher.

I lifted my chin. "What would you do?" I wondered. "If I stopped spying and instead trained for this group?" I shoved a bite of chicken into my mouth as I waited for Lorella's answer. The meat seemed to get tougher and harder to swallow with each passing moment.

Lorella glanced around the table. "Everyone here has a role to play, Corinn. And we've all risked *too much* already to get you to be our spy— Neave and me to make you a citizen of Sector A, and Colton and Dalton to get you off Miota in the first place! Don't you see how selfish you're being right now?"

"I make a terrible spy," I shot back, my mouth still full. "The safer thing for everyone here is for me to train for this group instead."

Lorella ran a hand through her colored hair. "Why not throw all your efforts into being a better spy, then? Why do you think you need to change my plans entirely—"

"Because I *will* get caught!" I burst at the abrasive sound of Lorella confirming my suspicions. She didn't want to lose her grip on my role in her schemes; her ego placed *her plans* above everything else. My voice dropped to a whisper, dancing across the floor. "You want me to spy, but I *will* get caught. I'm not . . . *good enough.* I can't do what you want me to."

My confession cracked my spirits, and from the shards, Salem's ghost rose.

After a contemplative silence yawning across minutes, Lorella inhaled and stiffened her posture. "I can't stop you, I guess, if you want to try out for the logistics team. But with only seventy-five slots open, I don't expect you to make it, and you shouldn't, either. So I need you to promise you won't stop spying entirely. You need to keep *trying*, Corinn, because your home depends on it."

I nodded numbly. I could keep trying. For Miota, and for my family, and for Griff. "I will," I vowed. "I still want to learn Biourica's secrets and help destroy the company."

"Fine." Lorella stacked her silverware on her empty plate. "If you train for this group, you'll be on a completely different schedule than me. I can't let you stay here any longer—you'd have to live on your own for a while."

The gravity of the words weighed on my shoulders. To live on my own in Red Fox, in the heart of Miota's greatest enemy . . . could I do that and survive it?

This decision had to be my own. I could continue solely spying for Lorella and stay tucked into the safety she offered, or I could train for the logistics team and risk not only my success in making the team, but my entire future and wellbeing through surviving on my own accord.

I would fight against the odds, but this was the only way to get what I wanted—what Miota *needed.* What if the logistics group *was* going to target my home? I needed to be there to stop it and undermine Arlo's power.

Resolve settled into the marrow of my bones. I was *going* to fight for this. I was done spying, an act that always revived Salem's spirit in the worst way possible. If I made this elite team, I could help end

Biourica from the inside out, from the safety of a group—it would be the quickest and safest way to ensure freedom for the people of Miota. And once we destroyed Biourica, taking down Julia would be easy.

Lorella must have seen the determination obscuring my face, shadowing all doubts. I was going to train, and I would risk whatever conditions she conjured up, even if it meant leaving the haven of her radiant home. Though Lorella grinned, appearing to accept these terms, I noted the undermining bite to her show of teeth.

Sometimes I forgot these people were like their own breed of supercontinental royalty; they held power, and they used it to get what they wanted. Up until this moment, we'd desired the same things, but now . . . we'd spliced.

It was a story spanning oceans and weeks, unchanged since Accolade. I would fight for my country. But whereas recklessness had once ruled me, it was now replaced with steeled determination and light.

I would try to make the logistics team with all I was.

The crew split up after the main course, each of us claiming separate spots now, strung thinly across Lorella's apartment. After arguing in front of everyone earlier, this seclusion offered peace.

"Where should I stay tonight, then?" I asked Lorella over dessert. My voice carried to Lorella's spot on a sofa from my location in the kitchen. "Since I start training with Anya in the morning."

I'd just told the crew about Anya—to which Lorella had stormed into her room for a while before reemerging—and how I would train with the girl. In Lorella's absence, Dalton had quietly offered to help, too, since we both eyed the same goal now.

I glanced at Cass from across the kitchen island, each of us leaned over one end of it. And so the slab of marble persisted to be my stupid symbolic home: the island of Miota, where the prince stood at one end and I, the Low, at the other.

Cass picked at his chocolate cake, Saoirse's dessert contribution. He eyed me lightly, offering an expression I'd seen before, and I didn't need to hear his words to feel their weight: *Be careful.*

I *was* being careful, though. *Spying,* sneaking around Biourica's halls, was what hadn't been careful. This plan was a much better one—a plan in which I actually could help Miota without endangering anyone I cared for.

Lorella's lips bunched as her face heated. Couch cushions nearly swallowed her whole as she lounged. "A hotel. That's a building full of temporary people visiting—people who were, say, here for burn treatment." She flicked her gaze to Miota's prince. "And you have to take Cass with you, too. I have some maintenance things that need to be addressed, and I haven't been able to do it while storing fugitives in my spare bedroom."

"Seriously?" Cass went pale as the moon. His fork clanked to his plate of cake crumbs. "You want me to *leave* the apartment—"

"*Yes*, Cass," Lorella snipped. "That is, only if Corinn leaves. Which'll only happen if she decides she still wants to train for the logistics team."

My temper rose, and though it happened steadily, I would soon burst, rolling like a pot of boiling water. "It's already decided," I seethed through gritted teeth. "I *told* you. I'm not going back on it. If Dalton and I both make it, how is that anything but a win for us?"

"Because it's over a month away!" Lorella sat up on her couch. "And the odds are stacked against you. It'll do nothing but waste time when we already don't have much of it."

"I already said I'll keep spying as I train," I reminded her. "I'll figure out what I can from other training members. I'll even try to soften them and turn them against Arlo's commands. Wouldn't it be helpful for me to plant those ideas in these people's heads?"

To that, Lorella didn't conjure up a response.

Within the next hour, with the reluctant help of Neave, I'd secured a hotel room. My welcome in Lorella's home had come to its end.

Cass didn't speak the entire way to the hotel.

Not on our short trek down Lorella's hallway. Not in the elevator. Not on the streets, which possessed an ethereal vibrance they didn't during the day. Citizens strutted around in metallic clothes, and the maglevs glowed as they whirred by. Cass and I were two Miotans, two rogue stars among moons and constellations, and still, he said nothing.

Nothing as we mounted the maglev, sat across from a man baring a toothless smile, and eventually got off in front of a gilded hotel the color of rich honey.

The hotel stretched into the sky, thrusting upward in a grand column of gold and glitter. Cass didn't react, didn't care. Granted, *I* didn't have words, either. Speech wouldn't do justice to the structure we were about to enter.

The inside, equally magnificent, was swathed in rich golds, deep reds, and lush purples. The ceilings stretched upward, creating large caverns of cool air, letting the sea of voices melt together in a brassy dissonance. I marched up to the welcome pad and checked into my room, like Lorella and Neave had taught me to do only thirty minutes ago.

After the room key dispensed, I held it tightly as Cass and I entered an elevator. Since Neave hadn't made me a member of Red Fox itself, but a different city just north of it, I didn't have access to the Platform—nor would I likely have the status to access it anyway. So, regardless, Cass and I were stuck on a lower level of the hotel.

Maybe Cass was scared of the rats. While I understood, because I'd been too conscientious of them initially, Lorella appeared to be right so far: they were rare, something not worth wasting worries on.

Especially when we had enough to fear as it was.

Cass still said nothing as we approached the room and as I opened the door.

The room, painted in gold lights and lavish furniture, held a kitchen smaller than Lorella's, a round table fit for two, a closet for our clothes, and a single bed.

My eyes flitted to Cass, and in that breath of time, his cheeks bloomed with color. When I closed the door behind us, locking us in this room, I finally snapped at the prince.

"Okay, when are you going to talk? Say anything?" I set a hand on my jutted hip.

He blinked, keeping a practiced, calm façade. "Look, the bed is only going to be weird if you make it—"

"I'm not talking about the *bed.*" I threw my hands in the air and marched toward the window. Outside, the moon rose, keeping the distant ocean company. "I mean me dragging you into this. I know you didn't want to leave Lorella's, and I'm sorry about that. But I *had* to do this."

Cass stuffed his hands in his pockets. "It's fine."

"That's all?" I charged.

"Well . . ." said Cass with a sigh. "I guess I'm just glad we didn't die of rat bites on our way here."

I rolled my eyes.

We unpacked our sparse bags of borrowed clothes—mine from Lorella, and Cass's from Colton—in silence. We then ransacked the room, fawning over its small appliances and fancy gadgets. I only froze once I readied for bed and realized how this night would end.

I couldn't sleep in the same bed as the *Prince of Miota.*

"Only weird if you make it weird, right?" Cass repeated and peeled back the covers. I bit my cheek and lay on my side. Cass made a barrier of pillows down the middle of the bed, which made me feel a little better.

"Sleep tight," Cass said as he turned off the lights, plunging the room into darkness.

I snorted. "Sleep tight? What does that mean?"

Cass shifted, and the mattress dipped beneath his weight. "You don't say that in Pointe? Mom said it all the time growing up."

I huffed, finding nothing more jarring than Julia Delldova putting a young Kierran Cassius to bed. Kissing his forehead, tucking him in . . . telling him to *sleep tight.* Maybe even the cruelest, most evil person I knew still harnessed a natural goodness—the kind to make her love and protect her child. Maybe, then, *anyone* held the power to be both good and evil.

My throat thickened. "Sleep tight, I guess," I echoed the sentiment.

I closed my eyes and didn't wake until the clock beeped, signifying training with Anya.

Hazy light bled through the cracked curtain. The sun hadn't emerged from above Red Fox's skyscrapers yet, but the sky broke from black to blue, foreshadowing the radiance to come. Fog drifted low to the ground in thick plumes, not yet baked off by dawn.

I shimmied out of bed, and Cass, still on his side of the pillow fort, rolled in his sleep. Padding to the window, I shivered, then slit the pane open. While it didn't move much, it was enough to let in the dewy morning air still laced with stars.

I inhaled deeply, wondering if any particles had swept in from the ocean, from *Miota*. Maybe I was more connected to my home than I thought.

I changed into appropriate workout clothes, careful not to wake Cass. With healed legs, everything was so much easier now. So much quicker. With a bite of granola still in my mouth, I slipped out of the hotel room for my first day of training.

PART TWO

"An annual review will take place within the first week of each new year, between MIOTA's reigning blood monarch and Red Fox's president, in order to adequately raise or lower the ratios and/or frequencies of this fundamental trade. Terms must be agreed upon by both parties, willingly."

—The Royal Codex, Section 1, Para. 2: Trade Rules

CHAPTER 12

GRIFF

I braced myself before asking Julia the question, thinking of every logical answer and each potential rebuttal she could throw at me. I needed the Queen to let me go to Castle Circle this weekend, Salford's first assigned weekend since Accolade finished.

But Julia had agreed immediately, stating it would be good for us to become familiar faces for each city's Top Tier. Cape's Top Tier would be present, too—Julia had decided it was best to maintain the Castle Circle schedule as it would have played out if Accolade hadn't taken place. And it was Salford's turn to share the luxurious lane with Cape, Miota's southernmost city.

Julia approved Addison and me to go under supervision of the Queen's Guard, but it was still the most freedom I'd been allowed since moving into the castle. This was my first true breath of fresh air.

I reflected on my agenda as the limo rolled on the castle's dirt roads, slicing through the land toward the rich lane of buildings and people alike, where Miota's wealthy stayed.

My family would be in Castle Circle's gates; I needed to see them for no reason other than pure selfishness. All of this—Accolade, fighting Julia, going along with Addison's painful presence—was for them, and I needed to keep them fresh in my mind to stay sharp. Julia's threats about them last week still haunted me, often leaving me paralyzed in sleepless trances.

I also needed to find Lorenzo, my accomplice in everything. I'd at least been productive in my long nights stretched out by sleeplessness, and I'd thought up a scheme requiring Lorenzo's help.

Lastly, and only if I could deem it safe, I would retrieve my diary pages from Castle Circle's greenhouse if I could. Now that I knew Julia was actively searching for Corinn's accomplice from her time trapped in the castle, I wasn't safe. I'd seen Corinn the night before her trial, and I'd given her the tools to try to survive it. If Julia linked me to such a crime now, she'd kill my family, slowly, for me to watch.

It seemed too big a threat at first, but I began wondering if maybe it was because Corinn survived her trial as planned.

I tried not to fly free with the thought, with the blinding hope, but . . . it made sense. Julia was bent on finding the culprit who'd helped Corinn the night before her trial. Julia cared about the medical weapons stolen . . . which included that vial of antiserum.

Corinn had told me antiserum was for preemptively counteracting poison, making a person immune to anything they ingest. And I didn't think Julia would be quite so enthralled with the antiserum if the queen had simply shot Corinn with a killing blow, like she said she'd done.

Thinking about it ignited some fighting ember behind my ribs. I couldn't fully trust the feeling and risk being wrong, only to plunge into a deeper grief . . . but it was a possibility. And for now, that was enough. For now, it kept me going with mine and Corinn's original plan. Because if Corinn *was* alive, living in the tunnels underneath Pointe, she couldn't survive off a small ration of stolen greenhouse food forever. If Corinn was somehow still here, she would be waiting, poised and ready for me to secure the crown as quickly as possible.

The mere possibility that Corinn was actually alive was enough to snap me from my lethargy. I couldn't *wait* for Julia to hand me a crown, submitting to her every command, living comfortably in her court while

Corinn barely survived beyond the castle walls. I had to chip away at her empire, piece by piece, until nothing but crumbs remained, and a killing blow would come easily.

The limo hurtled over a divot in the dirt road between the castle grounds and Castle Circle. Though the ride was short, being alone with Addison and two Queen's Guard members prolonged the seconds. The uneven ground jostled me, and I braced my arms on the empty seat next to me.

Addison's eyes flicked toward me. "Careful—"

"I know." I didn't know why I snapped; everything in life seemed to weigh heavier on my shoulders, my chest, these days. Where life had once been a vengeful, colorful thing, it was now dull and defeated. When Addison rolled her eyes and slumped in her seat, I apologized only due to the guards present, listening in. They were Julia's brainwashed eyes and ears, after all.

"For what?" she asked, more jagged than I'd anticipated. While the Addison I'd always known was like a rose—made to entice, yet sharp and unwelcoming—she'd recently become like a soured wine, steeped too long, dull and bitter. She was the collateral piece who'd cluelessly spun herself into my mess of a tapestry the day she chose me as her new partner, leaving Corinn to fend for herself.

I'd never forgive Addison for it. The moment Addison had taken Corinn from me, everything had gone drastically awry. It was childish, maybe, but I didn't hold much room for forgiveness these days. It was an emotion too light for an island so dark.

I blinked, searching for my answer in the gilded gates quickly approaching. "I don't know," I admitted. I'd only apologized to appease, not to absolve.

"Of all the things you've done to me," Addison ground out, "you can't think of one thing to be sorry for."

It was a statement, not a question. She knew, then, that I wasn't sorry for any of it. For placing Corinn above Addison's well-being; for speaking poorly about Addison on national news; for ignoring her now behind closed doors.

"Funny," I retorted, my temper rising unchecked, "how I could say the same about you."

Addison scoffed. "What did I ever do to *you?*" Her emerald eyes bored into mine.

I let my mouth gape. "Are you serious? Your whole life, you've forced me to be tied to you! You've never given me the room to breathe on my own!"

Her churning glare festered. "At least I never spoke negatively about you in front of the entire country. I never pretended a *Low* was worth more than you—"

"Don't bring her into this!" I shuddered, allowing only the temporal second for my grief to run its course. "You knew what she meant to me, and you took her from me, and now . . ."

"I am *not* the reason Corinn is dead," Addison snarled. Her words now flew with a vicious timbre, spoiling like most of our longer exchanges tended to do. "She ruined herself."

Though her sentiment stung, it reminded me of the mask I was supposed to be wearing—one placing blame on no one but Corinn. Julia couldn't know I blamed anyone else for her death. And not just *anyone* . . . I blamed Addison for starting it and Julia for finishing it.

"You're right," I choked out, *hating* myself for the lie. "I'm just . . . taking my anger out on you. I guess that's why I'm sorry. You weren't supposed to get caught up in all this."

Addison studied me. "Say my name," she blurted.

The only true test of forgiveness. One I would not pass now, or maybe ever.

"Don't ask me that—"

"*Say it.*" For a heartbeat, her guard dropped, and the plea shone bright.

I clicked my jaw, refusing to bend to her. It was the vow I'd made the day after Dad died: I would never let Addison Maybee control me again.

"Ads, I know you're not the reason Corinn is gone." It was the best I could offer her.

She rolled her eyes, spinning her legs away from me, looking out the window. Retreating from the conversation. "Whatever."

Good riddance.

We crossed into Castle Circle through its sleek gate, and the lane summoned too many memories. There were old ones, trickling in like the passing years: Lorenzo and me drinking our limit of wine on his last birthday and sleeping on the sidewalk, much to the disdain of his parents . . . Dad and me scheming how he could evade the mandatory Executive Council meetings with Their Majesties . . . younger versions of Addison and me sprawling on my family's balcony, seeing who could get more skin pigment from the sun.

Those were from *before* Corinn, but the memories from *during* Corinn came just as potently. The first head-to-head competition, when she'd been annoyed by my very presence. The group competition where the only word that escaped her lips was my name. Our secret planning on balconies and in the greenhouse. Our first kiss in her apartment.

I sniffed. There wasn't supposed to be an *after* Corinn. But maybe, somehow, she was still alive beneath Pointe . . .

We soon parked, slicing through a growing crowd of Salfordians and Capeans, and I exited the limo first to offer Addison my elbow. The guards came next, quick to shoo the crowds back.

Citizens from both cities pressed in, bottling tightly, warded off only by two guards. I recognized the Salfordians, along with a few Capeans from Accolade. But even those I didn't recognize *certainly* knew me now.

How was I going to speak with Lorenzo alone?

Jess materialized in the crowd. The larger guard tried detaining her, but my sister sidestepped him and latched onto my waist. The guard's failed efforts, though comical with Jess, didn't ease my fears about his ability to take on this crowd if necessary.

"Missed you," she whispered against me.

"Missed you more."

"What are you doing here?" She withdrew from her embrace to study my face.

"Am I not allowed to visit my favorite sister and mother?" I patted her arm.

Jess stuck her tongue out and tossed her long tendrils of hair over her shoulder. "Favorite sister? Thanks, Griff, I'm *flattered*."

I laughed at my sister, who'd always held the family's dramatic flair—well, her and *Dad*, really, but now it was only Jess.

"Who finally taught *you* sarcasm?" I mused.

She shrugged. "Noah, this girl at school."

Mom made it past the two guards and wrapped her arms around my neck. "Thank the moon for this," she said against my forehead. "Started to wonder if I'd ever get to see you again."

Keeping our family apart was a cruelty neither Mom nor I would put past Julia.

"Is Lorenzo here?" I asked as carelessly as I could muster. He was going to help accelerate my plan to destroy Julia.

Mom nodded. "Somewhere. Maybe at Club Castle, drinking away the sorrows of your absence—"

"Come on, Mom. It was Lorenzo's birthday!"

"And you two slept on the *sidewalk*, Griff." She peeled her arms from me and set her hands on her hips.

"It was comfortable," I defended myself with an exhaled laugh. "At the time. Anyway, I've worked up an appetite. Snacks are still in The Gathering Hall, I assume?" I knew wherever food and drinks were, Lorenzo often followed.

"Nothing's changed," Mom confirmed with a nod.

I glanced at Addison, whose family found her, too. She stood stiffly with her parents and sister, younger than her by only one year. Addison and Mila, with the same heart-shaped faces, shining black hair, and lanky bodies, were copies, yet they couldn't despise each other more.

Addison used to ask how I got along so well with Jess, and I told her it was because Jess and I worked together, not against each other. To that, Addison had only said it must be different between siblings with an age gap—because between herself and Mila, *everything* was a competition.

I decided to peel from Addison, and one guard followed me and my family down the lane of dazzling buildings, toward The Gathering Hall at the end, a massive, foreboding structure fit for royalty. Its cavernous insides had always felt larger-than-life. Though I'd enjoyed this place before Accolade, it was now riddled with memories of Corinn, and I tried not to squirm in its shadows.

The hall of soaring ceilings, exposed wooden beams, and delicate windows bled with chatter, laughter, and silverware clanking. After a minute of scrutinizing the crowd, I pinpointed Lorenzo standing with his father, the pair chatting over small plates of bite-sized foods.

When Lorenzo spotted me, he bowed deeply, a sarcastic gesture; I shouldn't have expected anything less from him.

"Yeah, yeah," I swatted a hand, feigning boredom. "What's next? Calling me 'Your Highness'?"

"Maybe," Lorenzo sang, straightening his spine. "If you aren't a royal pain in the—"

"*Enzo.*" Mr. So shot daggered eyes at his son. "You are speaking to the *future king.*"

"I just see the same old Griff Howard." Lorenzo grinned at me after glancing at his plate. "I need more food. Come with me, King Griff."

My face bunched as we left Lorenzo's father. "Never call me that again."

Lorenzo let out a chuckle and ran a hand through his hair, which now grew past his shoulders. Its length likely drove his family toward madness. *You're Lorenzo So!* I'd heard his father chide him too many times to count. *You must keep your hair cut, your clothes pressed, and your mind sharp.*

But Lorenzo had never cared much for the opinions of his father.

After amassing my own plate of soft cheese and sweet fruit, I led Lorenzo to the hollow room's perimeter, where we walked with our heads together and voices low.

"I need to ask you for a favor," I mumbled, keeping my words nearly indiscernible to even myself. But Lorenzo and I had spoken in this manner for so long, it was like a code.

"Anything," my friend replied, stiffening. Likely weighing the possibilities of what I could ask of him.

Time to unleash the plan I'd been brewing and mulling over for the past week. "The night before Trials started, during Accolade, there were prisoners who escaped the Hold."

I knew this to be true because I'd *been there* when it happened. I'd helped Abner and Max hatch the scheme so I could see Corinn from the castle's hospital wing. The prisoners had all been wrangled up, none gone permanently, but it was still information Julia hadn't shared with the public. It could still spur the doubt I needed to undermine her authority.

"And I need you to make sure Salford knows it," I continued. "Don't tell people outright, but . . . start rumors. Theorize with people who work at *Salford Summit*. Something—*anything*."

Lorenzo nodded, knitting his brow. "Easy. I'll tell Mila." Addison's younger sister *was* known for starting rumors, letting words spread quicker than fire through a pile of our city's timber. "What's it get you?"

"People to doubt J." *J*—the queen. If Lorenzo sparked suspicions, it could create cracks and divots in Julia's iron-strong power. And it would be easier to take her out with a single blow.

"I can have Selleca help, too," Lorenzo offered. "Get the Middle Tier involved—"

"Maybe." While I appreciated the commitment, it seemed too big a risk. "But I think the Middles and Lows will be more willing to betray J. I need the *Tops* to turn against her."

The Queen of Miota was nothing without her Top-Tiered minions, who ate out of the hand she fed them with. They were spoiled; they were content. The Middles and Lows would be more open to the idea of change. But Tops . . . it only took one look around at those feasting on snacks, laughing with old friends, skipping weekends in their home city to be here. Why would they ever want *change?*

It was a spoiled routine I'd taken for granted for too long, before I realized the lengths of Julia's malice. Before she'd killed my father, and long before I'd met Corinn. How many other Tops would modify their ways if they knew how askew their sense of reality really was?

Lorenzo shrugged. "Then I'll get Wendy and Mal on it, too."

"Thank you." Wendy and Mal were Lorenzo's teenaged cousins, twins, known for their gossip. Still, even with their tales blown out of proportion, Lorenzo risked all of this coming back to haunt him, and I wouldn't discount his courage. "I mean it. I know this takes guts, and I want—"

"Easy, Griff Howard. Don't get sentimental on me now."

I shook my head, smiling and looking to my feet. He could never take a moment *too* seriously—

A frail woman fell into my arms.

I caught her, noting her knobby joints, wrinkled skin, and disheveled gray hair.

"By the moon," she hissed. I didn't recognize this woman, which meant she was from Cape. I'd nearly forgotten, for only a moment, that Salford was sharing Castle Circle this weekend.

"Are you all right?" I asked, steadying the woman old enough to be my grandmother.

"You're Griff Howard," she answered. Her voice was rickety, sounding like rotting, creaking wood. She lost her balance yet again, this time collapsing directly onto my sternum. Her face fell in my shoulder, and though her words delivered garbled, there was no mistaking them when she spoke so only I could hear.

"Be careful, Griff Howard. I know you plan to take Julia down."

CHAPTER 13

GRIFF

I bit my cheeks to keep a neutral expression.

Who was this lady? How did she *know*?

My fears must not have stayed buried, because the woman offered a grim smirk. "Don't worry, no one else is listening. And even if they could hear you, these people wouldn't really be *listening*. Me, however . . ." She smoothed her hair as she looked over my shoulder at Lorenzo. "I know what you two are doing. There's a group of us in Cape trying to do the same."

I stepped backward, letting my confusion saturate every line in my face. "I don't know *what* you're talking about—"

"The name's Jyn Hepper. And yes, I think you do." She forced me to share her gaze, and I noted her cobalt blue eyes, ringed with a thin hazel band.

Hepper. I recognized the surname . . . Was she on Cape's executive council?

"It's nice to meet you, Jyn," I started, remembering my manners, "but I don't know what you're talking about."

"Why would Griff do anything stupid when he's about to inherit the crown?" Lorenzo sided with me, despite not completely knowing the topic at hand. Gratitude flooded my veins.

Jyn's eyes stayed pinned on me. "You know Miota's dark secrets, Howard. Thanks to your father."

Someone might as well have thrown a bucket of ice water over my head as chills skittered up my spine and around my skull.

By the moon.

Who was this woman? I crossed my arms to keep my skin from crawling.

"His father?" Lorenzo whispered. He whipped his head toward me. "*Your father—*"

"You plan to dig at Julia's perfect monarchy from the inside out," Jyn interrupted. "You want to turn the Top Tier against her."

"No," I insisted, dropping the word with the weight of the Fort surrounding Miota. "I would *never* do that. You should be arrested for treason."

"It's a good plan, Griff," she continued, cracking another leer. "And you're in the right position to do so. I'm *glad.*"

Every inch of my body shook. Was Jyn . . . on my side? Or was she only baiting me? I couldn't trust anyone outside Lorenzo and my family; I'd been burned too many times, lost too many people, to put faith in others again.

Lorenzo and I exchanged shocked glances, to which Jyn Hepper cackled, a sound making my skin pinch too tight around my bones. "You should see the looks on your faces!" She reeled herself back in, hunching her shoulders. "Look. Holland Stanzifer? From Accolade? She knew a lot more than she let on—until Julia found her and ended her." A knot worked at Jyn's throat. "My family works to rid Miota of the monarchy's oppression. Know this much, Griff Howard: You may feel alone in the *castle*, but you are *not* alone on Miota."

Her message, dipped in hope, nearly undid me.

The guard loosely following me tightened the distance between us, picking up on Jyn's continued presence. The old lady's eyes widened, nearly protruding from her face.

"Come to Cape. I work in Factory Alpha—talk with me there. It's more private. I'll share the plan with you."

"What plan?" I demanded, putting strength in my voice. "And who's your family?"

Jyn bowed her head, shielding her gaze. "It'll come to you. Think of the company you keep." When her chin became once again parallel to the floor, she spoke through bared teeth. "Find me in Cape, Howard. We'll talk then."

Before I could say another word, she walked away.

I didn't sleep well that night, or the next. Too many thoughts danced in my head, making me dizzy as I pondered their implications.

The odd Capean woman and who she was. The fact Corinn could've been alive—and if she now hid beneath Pointe, I needed to move a lot faster. I'd won Accolade over two weeks ago, and I had virtually nothing to show for it. I needed Julia's trust *now*.

I nearly fell asleep Tuesday morning at breakfast, over an array of poached eggs and shredded potatoes fried to a crisp. My eyelids drooped, and Addison cleared her throat. When I startled awake, I found her prying eyes stippled with suspicion. At least it kept Julia from barking at me in front of the table—which only consisted of Julia, Abner, Addison, and me, but it was still a tasking thing to sit through.

I kept my consciousness by brewing more tea, pouring the water over the leaves slowly, drawing out the task. It also helped still my limbs, grounding myself in such a mundane task when *nothing* in my life seemed normal anymore.

After racking my brain for why I knew the old woman's name, Jyn Hepper, it had finally come to me in the young, dead hours of night. *Mind the company you keep*, she'd told me.

Julia Delldova. Her father had been Ivan Delldova, born royalty, and her mother . . .

Born a Top in Cape. Elizabeth Hepper.

I didn't know how Jyn exactly fit into Julia's family—as an aunt or something else—but she was related to our queen, and she held knowledge of my father. She was also bent on bringing Julia down.

Jyn suspected I planned on destroying the queen's reign. I wasn't sure if I should've let her leave my sight so easily in Castle Circle, considering how destructive her suspicion was. Rumors on Miota spread like fire, quickly and mercilessly.

I'd denied Jyn's claims, though she hadn't been wrong. I *was* trying to end Julia, and I was now walking a double-edged knife, hoping to the moon the deed didn't bite me. If a stranger from Cape had figured me out, who was to say others wouldn't follow her thought process?

I shivered. It warranted a glance from Julia, and I pounced. I needed to offer my proposition, and this was as good a time as any.

"Your Majesty," I started, giving a small smile. "I have a question, and I hope you'll entertain it. It's an idea for how to bring peace to each city."

Julia's daggered gaze pinned me; her scrutiny always felt like I was a breath away from being poisoned, a quick movement from death. "And what do you propose?" asked the queen.

I sipped my tea and summoned my most recent lessons, undertaking the commanding tone I'd found within me last week. Julia's lady-in-waiting had been charged with teaching Addison and me all the ways of castle life, though so far, it had been nothing more than superfluous information on manners and posture.

"It appears that each city has something needing to be mended," I replied. "It would make sense, I believe, for Addison and me to visit each city and help remedy their apprehensions ourselves. It would help people see us as future rulers, as people in charge. And by appearing in each city, we would also show Miota that we care about *them*."

Julia frowned and set down her fork. "Royals do not visit the cities, save the annual Commencement journeys. Placing our citizens in their rightful jobs—*that* is what the royal family does. We do not just . . . parade around the country for show."

My gaze crossed Abner's for only a moment; the king picked at the fruit on his plate. I never failed to notice how he seemed afraid of the food grown in Pointe. When he tasted the labors of Pointe's Low Tier, did he taste his own betrayal against Corinn?

"Respectfully, Your Majesty," I started, "what was Accolade, if not that?"

My head inflated three times as every eye in the room centered on me, stifled into stillness.

Stupid. How stupid could I be, speaking against Julia herself? Abner's warning flitted through my scrambled thoughts: I needed to stay on her good side.

"It was an ingenious plan," I tried recovering. "A necessity that kept the people entertained instead of focused on fleeting uncertainty. And now . . . the people are uncertain again. Three hundred young adults experienced living a life outside of working, outside of their cities. If we don't pacify them quickly, I'm concerned for the implications." Time to clinch the true prize. "If there isn't a seamless transition of power, to make matters more certain and permanent . . ."

I trailed off, letting Julia work her way through that one. Hoping she saw what I did: I needed power, and fast.

The queen sipped on her tea and watched me with vigor, as though she could pry open my head and read my mind with her eyes. *Quit eyeing me like a field raven*, they'd say in Salford's Low Tier, referencing the ominous birds that resided in the thick forests outside our city.

"You say each city has something that needs mending," Julia finally spoke. "Tell me, what specifically do you speak of?" She leaned against her chair's back and stuffed her hands in her pockets.

I should've known she wouldn't agree to vague terms so easily. I took my time answering, selecting each word carefully. This was, after all, nothing more than a critique of Julia's reign. But if I were to get a crown anytime soon, to theoretically help a maybe-alive Corinn, this was my one shot.

"To start, Your Majesty, it's been made clear that certain citizens in Yorkinson wish to see those from other cities, like they did in Accolade. And in Castle Circle, I heard Tops from Cape speak about increased turmoil since the death of Holland. The same goes for Pointe, with Salem and Corinn."

My throat constricted. I'd deliberately said Salem's name first, hoping to make myself less threatening to Julia by placing Corinn as an afterthought. I *hated* myself for it.

"In Salford, citizens are questioning what happened during Accolade—some think the whole truth wasn't told, and they're questioning information exchange between the castle and cities. Meanwhile, Kendall seems to think Salford is attempting a government takeover."

When I laid everything on the table like the breakfast before us, it seemed futile. How could I ever help Miota become a better place when there was so little to have faith in?

Julia cocked her head. "And you believe *diplomacy* is the answer over brute force." Though it was a statement, I knew her true intent. The queen was quizzing me.

"I do, Your Majesty." I sat straighter. "If Addison and I can gain the citizens' trust, I believe they'll be more inclined to listen to the laws once we're ruling."

Julia set her teacup down, clinking porcelain on wood. She was truly pondering the scenario. Using compromise instead of coercion wasn't something she was familiar with, but her island was a changing world. She could no longer fight the inevitable alterations that had been sealed upon Prince Kierran's death.

"There are merits to your idea," Julia admitted before glancing at her husband, still picking at his plate. "What do you think?"

Abner startled slightly, sitting up and hitting his knee on wood underneath the table. "It makes sense," he answered. "The people will have to listen to them eventually, right? Why not start now while you and I can guide them?"

"Would you have us go on this parade, too?" Julia persisted. "Or do you mean guidance from afar?"

Abner popped a grape into his mouth to keep from responding immediately. Finally, "If you believe we should go with them, to keep a close watch on how cities react, that would be appropriate. Or, if you think we should let them step into their role on their own, that would be practical."

Appropriate or practical. I smothered a facetious huff. Did Julia notice how little her husband offered to conversations? He never gave approval until Julia had given hers. It was one way to survive with her, yes, but it was the coward's way. It didn't encourage me to trust him again anytime soon.

Julia studied her nails. "I will trust you two in Salford alone," she decided. "If that goes well, we will speak about visiting the rest of the cities."

"What if it doesn't go well, Your Majesty?" Addison chimed in. *Finally* deciding she was interested in the topic, now that negotiations were about finished.

I didn't think Addison realized winning Accolade would be more than waving for crowds, dressing in gowns, and accepting praises and good graces. Lasting in this castle required grit—and if my plan went as it should, things would turn messy, with the downfall of the monarchy. I didn't know how Addison would react to it all.

It was my looming question for another day.

"If you two fail in your home city," Julia started, "then Accolade was the grandest waste of time, because you two will have proven yourselves completely inept to rule."

Addison's jaw slackened. "Will we still be crowned queen and king?"

"No," Julia snapped. "No, I am not sure I could do that."

That sobered the table. Addison and I were supposed to be the next link in a dynasty that transcended both generations and humanity. If we couldn't complete the tasks Julia put us up to *now*, she wouldn't risk us overtaking her throne.

"But if we *do* pacify the people . . ." Addison spoke slowly, "we'll be crowned?"

"By the new year," Julia promised.

By the moon. This was my way to climb past Julia's restrictions. This was the beacon toward freedom.

Fix the turmoil in each city and gain a crown, or fail and surrender our spots as heirs to the throne.

I chanced looking at Abner, now wearing a cold shadow across the bridge of his nose. He knew what I did: this would either be a needed step toward Miota's freedom or the thing to doom us all.

I cleared my throat, simmering the nerves growing in my stomach. "When should we start, Your Majesty?"

She grinned. "Tomorrow."

CHAPTER 14

JULIA

Once Griff and Addison left for Salford, I slipped into my office, the place where Father's spirit roamed most freely.

This had been his residence before mine. His essence stamped the furniture and filtered into the dust in the air.

Jules. Father's incessant voice pounced onto me the second I closed the office door, rendering us alone. *You can't cross Sillian Reeves. You're going to ruin my empire.*

I will not doom Miota, I assured Father. I was going to play my hand as best I could, and with any stroke of luck, I might hold my own against a powerful man from Red Fox, our cryptic trade partner connected to Miota only through the networking of my forefather, Aris Delldova.

I would not doom Miota because, while Sillian might hold power in a faraway land, *I* was a shining *queen.* Sillian Reeves was plucked from a normal life, whereas I descended from a long line of monarchs. I was a jewel in a crown of diamonds, a tempered link in a powerful chain.

Even though it was not meant to be *me* ruling Miota, but Josiah. If Father had not butchered my brother, Josiah would be King, ruling with splendor. But Father had thought it easier to train *me*, the one naturally inclined toward destruction, than to guide Josiah away from his gentleness and kindness.

Any child of Elizabeth Hepper left to their own devices would possess an instinctive goodness, and Father had realized that the second time around, with me. He had intervened and ensured he killed my kindness early on.

I was death, I knew no real love, yet I was *powerful*. A proper Delldova.

Stop dwelling on the past, Father snapped, making me blink hard. I knew spirits were real, and some were cursed not to prowl the ocean, as most Miotans believed, but to stay within the Fort and feast on the living. Father's voice was too real at times; surely, some shadow of him still existed.

I rapped my fingers on my desk in passing as I approached the steel door tucked behind a curtain. It was one of the lone doors in this castle operated by a physical key instead of a panel's touch.

These monthly check-ins with Sillian Reeves were nothing more than a reason for him to be redundant and condescending. I usually sent Max Reno to them instead, letting him pass through the metal door while I sat in my office and tended to *relevant* Miotan matters. Max Reno was my oldest friend, gracing me with his presence for as long as I could remember, and he had become liaison between Miota and Red Fox almost two decades ago without resistance from Mother, Father, or myself.

But now that my friend was nothing more than a mind-controlled body, under the effects of a cranial implant I ordered my doctor to instill, he did not have free will. Max's critical thinking had greatly decreased, and I did not want Sillian catching on and taking advantage of the man. While Sillian sent us the implants, he did not question who I used them on; it was better if he never knew of Max Reno's involvement.

Mostly because it would be information Sillian could use against me. But partially because the guilt of ruining Max Reno, my dearest and closest friend, ate away at my insides.

Maybe Sillian would catch on regardless when Max stopped showing up entirely. Yet Sillian still had not seemed to realize Cass was not busy with his Courtship, but that my only son was *dead*.

The familiar knife of grief twisted in my chest, and I pried my thoughts elsewhere.

I heaved open the metal door, leaving the office and Father behind and trading it for a chilly chamber filled with clunky equipment of another lifetime.

Under the dim lighting that always flickered sat archaic screens and bulky keyboards. The equipment took ages to power up, to which I held my breath until everything pulled up smoothly. Every so often, I became rank with the fear a machine would not work and Miota would be on her own, abandoned in the ocean.

But the monitor turned on as expected, at its crawling speed. I wrung my hands together, wondering why I did not feel as unstoppable today as I typically did in my dress of Miotan blue. I could not be *nervous* about bargaining with someone who possessed no real leading expertise. Even though the supercontinent was large, they were not governed by a *dynasty*. I had an island to safekeep; I would not bring it to ruin now, after ten generations of Delldova rulers. I had already grazed the fate, and despite Cass's death, this would not be our end.

The monitor screen glowed, projecting my face, shadowed in the dank room. After a moment, Sillian's own face appeared, thin and gray.

"Julia, my dear, it's you," Sillian Reeves started, grinning too wide to be real. "However *have* you been?"

I wore my own practiced smile, soft enough to keep my features slack. "Good morning. I am well, and I hope you are, too." It seemed such a waste of time, exchanging pleasantries like we were not holding each other's throats.

"No Max today?" Amusement adorned Sillian's tone. "Where's he off to?"

"He has more pressing matters," I replied, hoping it chipped away at Sillian to insinuate these meetings with him were merely trivial tasks.

To that, Sillian's smirk only widened. I bit back a snarl. "If I didn't know better," he started, "I would think you're here in his stead because of your near-colossal failure last month."

I clamped my teeth until my temples pulsed. "We made our quota, did we not?"

"And not a second too soon!" Sillian snapped.

"I tried warning you about this back in January," I replied, attempting to keep my spirits sharp. *I am Julia Delldova, Queen of Miota.* "I told you the quota could not increase; it is unsustainable. We are now only reaping the consequences I told you about."

"Unnecessary consequences," Sillian rattled. His face contorted. He did not seem angry, but rather . . . annoyed. "Anyone with a grid—panel, excuse me—can quote-on-quote *die* at your beck and call. Hell, anyone *near* a panel at any point in their life has the potential of dying from your silly little disease. So what's the hold up with the quota, my dear?"

There it was again, the *stupid* nickname that burrowed beneath my skin. In Sillian's mouth, it was always laced with such hubris and arrogance.

"The *problem*, Sillian, is not in the technology."

Faking deaths was easy when panels held such explosive radiation capabilities, enough to shock the life from someone for more than a full day. Their heart and lungs . . . It was technology unlike anything on Miota. And it was why doctors believed it to be death itself.

In reality, the bodies were taken to the beach not to float off into the afterlife, but to do whatever Sillian Reeves did with them on the supercontinent . . . except for the few unlucky ones, chosen at random, who truly died each month. They were sent off to their city's labs in the heart of the hospital where healthy individuals, killed by electric shock, were cut open and analyzed in the name of finding a cure.

It was vile, and I knew it. But it was necessary.

"The problem is you increasing our quota by force every year," I concluded. "We are not able to fill jobs as needed; we cannot recover so quickly from such a loss every month."

"I would love to help you, Julia, but the codex outlines everything, clear as day. We decided on a number back in January, and the codex says—"

"The Royal Codex was nullified the minute *you* increased our quota by force," I surged. Sillian was officially causing my blood to boil. My pulse thrummed through my ears. "The trade agreement was supposed to be mutually beneficial, but it has recently become something of torture. Miota will collapse if you suck our people at your current rate. So you will either decrease our monthly quota willingly, or I will cease relations with you entirely."

Sillian drew his lips into a thin line for only a moment. Then, he did not do what I thought he would.

He howled with laughter. It was so magnanimous, there almost seemed to be a second, deeper voice.

"Julia, my dear!" Sillian wiped the ghost of a tear from his eye. "You cannot do that. For *many* reasons. Think of your people—you wouldn't have our tech to surveil them or control them. You wouldn't have the means to medical tech that saves lives. Would you so easily give all that up?"

"Yes." It was a lie, but I would not let up.

"If you cease to send your people and comply with the trade," Sillian stated, "I'll have no problem paying you a *visit*."

A visit. Sillian *coming to* Miota . . .

"We'll soon have the people to march onto your island, Julia, and claim it. Don't forget that you're nothing more than the warden of Miota. I could expose what you've been hiding, and your people wouldn't side with you. You'd be ruined."

I scoffed, seeing red. Sillian was threatening *me*. He insinuated *he* owned Miota and I was nothing more than a pawn. But he was twisted greatly; *my* forefathers built this place from nothing. This spot had been nothing but desolate ocean, and a Delldova built a prosperous nation here. *Not* Sillian, and not anyone else from that hunk of land, however big and mighty they may have thought themselves.

While I seethed, I inwardly counted each breath. "Decrease the quota, then, and neither one of us will have to take such drastic measures."

"I miss your little friend, Max Reno," Sillian said with a low chuckle.

A surprising lump bobbed in my throat because *I missed him, too.* It was pathetic, how Max's neural implant pained me, but between my son's death and a fragile transition of power to two Salfordians, losing my childhood friend and trusted liaison was simply too much.

It had been a necessary step, though, after the man had let Corinn Januski and Salem Redding survive upon finding them on Miota's beach. Sometimes I wondered if the thing that truly hurt was not what I did to Max, but what his illusion of contrived loyalty did to *me.* He and I were both paying a debt now.

"I am just a queen who loves her country," I replied, my voice cracking. "And I am willing to defend it from people like you. I will not ask again, Sillian: you need to decrease our quota."

Sillian's eyes floated behind his screen, then focused back on the camera. "Julia, let me repeat myself. I will soon have the forces available to come to your island and take over, knocking you down in a heartbeat. There will be no *drastic measures* taken from our side; it'll be as easy as anything else I do in a day. I'll *assure* you, for your own good, that I'm not bluffing. But if you'd like to try and play a game you can't win, be my guest."

Listen to him, Jules, Father said, his prowling voice finding its way through the metal door and back into my head. *Don't jeopardize this monarchy now.*

Sillian thinks he can control me, I gritted back to Father's ghost. *This is our island, not his. And we cannot continue sending citizens at this rate.*

We can for the time being. You're only one person against thousands; your people would destroy you if they learned the truth. Don't be insolent, Jules—

I slammed a veil between Father and me. He could not be here right now; I did not want him.

"You cannot decrease your quota by even one person?" I challenged Sillian. He would not best me when speaking of my citizens on *my* island.

Again, Sillian's eyes roamed behind his camera, pausing before answering. Finally, "No. If you don't have next month's quota ready, we'll take over your island and simply cut the Delldova rule out of the picture."

Julia, Father resurged, never failing to creep back into me when my hatred went unrestrained. *I beg you, listen to the man. Meet his quota.*

If we continue sending people at this rate, I reasoned with my dead father, *it will doom us just as easily as his threats.*

It'll be a slower death. Meet the quota, and give yourself the time to find a better solution.

Why are you on his side? I accused Father.

I'm your fear, was all he said.

I was not in the mood for riddles, so I instead chewed on my fibrous pride, not ready to spit it out and succumb to Sillian Reeves.

But it was either let the pathetic man control me this once or give him permission to take over Miota and turn my people against me. I would have to find another way to protect my dynasty.

"Very well." I hardly mustered it. "I will meet your silly quota."

"Wonderful," he purred. "And to think, you were about to throw your life's work away for something so trivial."

I stifled an eye roll. "I have a favor to ask of you, though. Is there anything on the supercontinent that . . . scans fingerprints, perhaps? Something to identify who has touched certain objects?"

Sillian's brow lifted. "Perhaps. What do you need it for?"

"Someone stole something of mine." It was not a whole lie. "And I would like to know who has been in the room where it happened."

Had Corinn been so insistent on drinking my poison during her trial because she knew she would be safe from it? With a vial of antiserum missing, she could still be alive, festering and growing like a disease.

It was all theoretical, but it was plausible, and that was enough to cause concern. Whoever helped her deserved to die for their crimes.

"I can do that," Sillian promised. "Give me two months of meeting the quota, and I'll send the means your way."

I nearly gawked. "*Two* months—"

"Yes, so we can talk about it at our next meeting here. Anything else I can do for you, my dear?"

I had miscalculated. It had not mattered my title against his; it was about our people and power. And Miota, a stranded rock, would not win against a supercontinent.

I would have much to think about now.

"Nothing," I answered, ready to return to my office to plot.

"Good." Sillian rested his chin on his hand. "And Julia? Next meeting, send Max. I like him better."

"I will send whoever I wish."

Sillian bleated in response.

CHAPTER 15

CORINN

Anya's morning training was somehow *not* considered torture in the eyes of society, but I couldn't see it as anything else.

The group consisted of about a dozen people, and when I recalled that only seventy-five would make it onto the logistics team, I quickly realized how futile this all could be. Maybe Lorella had a point; what were the odds *I* would make this team?

I didn't immediately recognize Anya, despite knowing the time and place to meet. She'd been eclipsed by my blind hope yesterday, and today, while staring down the daunting eyes of this task, recalling her face became difficult. There were multiple different groups training in the greenspace beneath Biourica's looming structure, but I eventually found Anya flagging me over.

"Guys, this is Corinn," Anya said as she threw her braids into a loose bun. "She's training with us now, too."

The group eyed me, slow to trust, yet quick to accept. It was the most I could ask for right now. Why wouldn't they be wary of a new member joining their training group? It was one more person to compete against.

I smiled, as Lorella taught me to do when first meeting people. A few sets of shoulders sloped, and some smiled in return, though while the group stayed civil, I was nothing more than an outsider to them.

I *was*, after all, an outsider trying to infiltrate and destroy the company they were all competing to work for. Maybe they were right not to trust me.

Those thoughts chewed away at me as we started training.

First came lifting weights, which we entered a muggy building for. The place made me sweat immediately, and it smelled of grime and soured bodily secretions. The twinge of metal coated the air, sharp on my tongue, and I tried to ward off decaying thoughts of abandoning this plan now and going back to spying within Biourica's cooler and fresher building.

Lifting weights wasn't something I'd done before or even heard of people doing—back home, most people I knew stayed physically strong from their work on Miota's farmlands. The rest of us just tried staying sturdy by sucking every nutrient out of our limited food supply. On Miota, we were functional cogs in the labor wheel Julia directed; everything on that island of finite resources served a purpose, and meaningless strength had none. Those with physically demanding jobs gained strength through job experience, and that was that.

Anya was kind enough to walk me through their typical exercises. While most people gravitated toward massive round weights, I started small and *still* struggled.

We worked through set after set of tasks; even with my eight-pound weights, my arms nearly gave out. I sat out one of the three sets of rows because I'd fallen too far behind—my arms became jelly, unable to respond to my commands. Being on the medical track back in Miota, knowing the names and locations of muscles, didn't help me now. *Nothing* could will my muscles into becoming stronger.

Once we'd finished, I prepared for the running. But we instead moved onto push-ups and pull-ups. I'd hung limply on the pull-up bar as Anya and her friend Charlie cheered me on. But the girls' support didn't matter; my body never budged. I eventually jumped off the bar, teeming with humiliation.

Running didn't come after *that* either. We stayed in the shed, stuffed with slick bodies and reverberations of metallic weights hitting the ground, and moved onto leg exercises.

Sweat pooled in my palms and at my ankles, but I forced my body onward. We worked through weighted bridges, step-ups, lunges, jump squats, and single-leg activities I never caught the names of. My legs cramped, and my arms still sang. Summoning images of my family and Griff, and all the innocent Miotans stuck under Julia Delldova's rule, helped soften the burning of my muscles, though it didn't summon my usual spiteful fire. My spirits were being exhausted on this training.

And this was only day one.

After legs came abdominal work, which I fell behind on and had to give up and collapse flat on the floor. I lay helplessly, a sweaty mesh of grated muscle. After the core work finally came the running. Two miles, Anya said. To keep it easy.

I couldn't even finish one.

"I'll meet you guys back here," I told Anya and Charlie after nearly a full mile. My legs seethed, still feeling like I shouldn't bear weight on them. And after the lifting we just did, it didn't matter that my burns were healed; I'd taken on new strains to my muscles.

My lungs went ragged with each gulp of air I swallowed, and an incessant pain formed at my side, which stretching hardly helped. I lay in the field in front of Biourica and tried prying open the structure with my mind. What hid within its shiny walls? On Miota, pretty things were oftentimes a diversion, guarding dark secrets. What did Biourica do with the people traded to them, and were they all dangled in front of me now, unknowingly?

Maybe spying *would* be more useful. If only I was any good at it. It didn't seem difficult, but in the moment, each step felt stiff and heavy, like someone breathed down my neck, ready to clamp my shoulders. I'd gotten Salem killed by sneaking around; it wasn't fair to him to make that same mistake now and endanger others.

Salem Redding was marred on my heart. I'd heard life's challenges usually made one stronger, but this wasn't the case with Salem. Though his fate would never make me stronger, I needed it to make me wiser, to prevent it from happening again.

When Anya's group returned, I'd started catching my breath, and the stitch in my side subsided with stretching. The group dissipated without much interaction, and no one spoke to me before peeling away from the training field.

Anya squatted near me, eyeing me. "You ever worked out a day in your life, Corinn?"

"No," I answered honestly. "Is it obvious?"

"Painfully." Her eyes gravitated from me to a man's figure, and her visage darkened. "Dalton James?"

"Yes?"

To that, I lifted my head off the ground—irritating my abdominals—and gawked at Dalton, here now, clad in all black.

"What are you doing here?" I got out, my cheeks burning at how pathetic I must look, a limp and sweaty heap.

"Training for my father's team," he said, a cold tone slicing his words. *Right*—I couldn't reveal I knew him. "Same as you, I think. Except my odds are looking a lot better than *yours*."

I huffed. Did Lorella force him to say that?

"Corinn just had a long day," Anya jumped in, constricting her gaze on Dalton. "Leave her alone. She's training with *me*."

"And if I offer to train her instead?"

Anya threw her arms in the air. "Then I guess you could, because you're a pretty, rich boy with a famous father who's used to getting what he wants!" Pent-up anger whittled its way into her voice and posture. Even from my spot on the ground, frustration ensnared itself around her, circling Anya's limbs like jewelry.

"My father disowned me," Dalton grumbled, a dark sound, "so I'm certainly not rich, and I have *never* gotten what I want." This was a Dalton I'd never seen before; someone of the new moon, donning shadows instead of light.

Anya's throat quivered. "Then why change things now? Corinn's in *my* training group. It's her decision if she wants to change that—not yours." She turned, walking away. "See you tomorrow, Corinn." She threw a look at Dalton. "Well, maybe."

I stared at the girl, dumbfounded, admiring her bravery to speak to Dalton in such a manner.

"She's charming," Dalton spat, scowling after her. "I'm glad you're training with someone so caring."

I cringed—I'd called Anya caring and compassionate last night, when I'd broken the news to everyone about getting trained by the girl.

"Doesn't matter," I grumbled. "I'm *never* making the team. That couldn't have gone worse."

Dalton shoved his hands in his pockets and stood stiffly a few feet away from me. "If you didn't puke, that's a win."

I sighed, craning my neck at the glittering building of Biourica. "So . . . you don't know anything about what's in there? Passageways, tunnels, anything like that?"

Dalton blinked furiously, his face crumpling. He finally choked. "No, nothing."

I froze, not placing my trust in such a delicate answer. "Right . . . well, I guess I'll head back into the building. It's honestly about the only hope I have at still helping around here."

Lorella had been right; I couldn't train to become good enough in the next five weeks. I couldn't spy, and I couldn't train. I didn't even know for certain what the logistics team was going to do under the reign of Arlo James, so this was all guesswork anyway.

I was so stuck, so blinded and unsure, and *nothing* would fix that until I clawed my way back to Miota. Until I ensured their safety and once again held my loved ones close.

I didn't know who I was here, but it was not a spy, and it was not a soldier. I was not enough to save Miota or fight Biourica. I was scattered, sprinkled across sea and sky, shorn between two countries, pried between my own heart and mind. I was no one.

"Now?" Dalton asked. "No appointment first?"

"I don't get appointments anymore, remember?" Slowly, I pushed off the ground and stood. "Not for burns, anyway."

"Be careful."

I stared levelly at the boy in front of me. "I know." And without a plan, without anything guiding me, I returned to Biourica's front doors. I had nowhere to go but through them, hoping to find a beacon, any bit of information to help me find the right path. Because I was a shooting star, throttled toward oblivion, needing to be found. Needing to find my way home.

I was again trapped in the cogs of a medical machine, pumping patients in and out of the building in a strategic and rigid manner. No person was ever left unattended; robotic cameras escorted everyone past the waiting room.

I could either find a way past the waiting room or return to a doomed mission of training. These were my only ways to get back to Miota. As much as I wanted to simply *flee* the supercontinent, I didn't have the means to do so. I needed to succeed in spying or training, and for the next month, I would swing between the two to make at least one of them happen.

I braced my aching muscles and stood, ready to try slipping beyond the door to the waiting room. I didn't feel people's eyes on me as much as the artificial weight of cameras and microphones, surely watching my every move.

I opened the door to the hallway of treatment rooms—it remained *unlocked*.

Victory unfurled within me, followed by frustration at my past self. Why hadn't I tried this sooner?

Then the alarm went off. I flinched, stupidly hoping my arrival in the hallway hadn't caused the blaring sound, and I darted into the nearest treatment room.

Aside from the echoing alarm, my pulse drummed in my ears, a quick and thundering beat. What would happen if someone found me here? I'd have to plead guilty.

I really need more burn treatment, I practiced internally. *I made an appointment! Check your schedule again—*

A frail, blonde woman entered, fury filling her features, and I forgot how to breathe.

"Hallan?" I blurted. The name escaped me, short-circuiting every inch of my brain, and I struggled to catch up with what I'd said, rifling through my memories.

Hallan. Hallan Janson, a Low-Tiered packer from Pointe who'd worked alongside my father. She and her husband were assigned the same dining table in the Common as mine back home; we ate every meal together when I was young.

Until the Jansons were taken by asympton.

It happened eight, nine, maybe even ten years ago, but time couldn't break all bonds. This wasn't a trick of the eye, no. This woman was Miotan, and she was within Biourica's walls.

"Hallan, it's me—"

"Who the hell is Hallan?" the woman said, whipping behind her to ensure I wasn't talking to someone else.

"M-maybe I'm getting names mixed up," I said. I shouldn't have expected her to recognize me. Last she'd seen me, I'd been a child. Now I was eighteen, and life had managed to fill each possible second, especially these days. "What's your name? Where are you from?" It gave her a gateway, an easy way to bring up Miota. Maybe she was trapped here, needing help from someone like me.

"Questions I should be asking you," she spat, extending her fingers so her hands took on the shape of claws.

"I'm Corinn Januski," I said, emphasizing the last name, waiting for hesitation or realization to flash in her eyes of sharp glass. None came. Her face bore more wrinkles than when last I saw her, and she wasn't wearing her usual bubbly smile. "You know me and my family, remember?"

Please remember.

"Never met a Januski in my life," she said with a scowl. "You also from Bantry, up north?"

Her words registered like molasses. She didn't know me . . . she didn't remember . . . she claimed northern Sector A as her home . . .

This was Hallan in looks, though she stopped there. It was her body, but the woman and person inside was someone else entirely.

My mind slipped out of focus, reflecting on what this meant.

On Miota, the Queen's Guard was brainwashed, living blank lives, though it was clear. They were empty, devoid of emotion in their voice and sparks behind their eyes.

But Hallan . . . she'd been sentient in every visible way. Had she been screaming for help behind an unescapable mask, or was she gone, erased for good?

"I thought I had an appointment," I bumbled to Hallan. As I looked at her one final time, I knew this was real. This was Hallan, a living relic from Pointe, alive yet something I didn't recognize. "I'm sorry. I'll leave."

Hallan scoured me, eyeing my every move until I'd returned to the waiting room. She locked the door behind her with a *click*. That small noise, trivial as it sounded, was my demise. It locked away the Miotans I could help; it kept Arlo's secrets out of my reach. The lock was the final strike of a hammer on my heart, and it bent me out of shape.

I didn't know who I was here, on this gigantic rock. I was stolen from my home, just as others were, and I wanted to *save them.*

My muscles screamed at me, begging for reprieve; still I ran to the maglev stop, relishing in the pain.

CHAPTER 16

CORINN

For the next week, I tried to be both spy and soldier. Listener and warrior. Cunning and brutish.

I failed at both. But Anya helped me with my lifting form so I became more efficient simply with small tweaks to my posture and spine. And Dalton helped by delivering frothy drinks filled with proteins to soothe my muscles and force them to adapt quicker.

The running didn't become easier, but I knew how it would shred my lungs and sting my legs and rob me of air—and expecting that much *did* make a difference.

I couldn't run at Anya's pace, but I forced my body to carry me the whole distance, no matter how long it took. The first time I spanned the correct distance, I vomited. The second time, too. But not the third time, or the fourth.

I lived in a constant state of sore muscles, and my limbs would sometimes buckle on me when I first stood up. Though this pain was not of someone else's doing—it was a necessity of my own making.

Seeing Hallan was the push I needed to *try* with everything I was to get better. To either make groundbreaking discoveries as a spy or to force my body past its limits to make the logistics team.

When I wasn't training with Anya or Dalton, I studied up on Biourica's history and I watched their building for covert entrances and weaknesses.

Cass and I stayed together in my hotel room.

"I can go back to Lorella's whenever, I think," he told me over the weekend, on my one rest day per week from Anya's morning training sessions.

"It's fine," I replied. Refusing to meet the intensity of his eyes. "Probably easier to just stay here at this point."

"Yeah." The prince's voice was too thin. "Probably easier."

He and I *had* fallen into a comfortable rhythm. I spent my day training and studying while Cass wrote pages of notes to hand off to Lorella. He cooked dinner with the ingredients we'd selected on my grid to be delivered to the door. I iced my shoulders and legs nightly, sprawled out on the couch, while Cass told me about his day. Our conversations usually twisted onto Miota. We were bent on returning home, our words reflecting our hearts.

At some point each night, the conversation would die down, simmering into silence, and we'd build our pillow barricade down the bed's middle. Cass would tell me to sleep tight a number of times, and I would eventually tell him to shut up.

It was mundane, but it was easier, wearing smoother with each passing day. Cass was as constant as the sun, even when Anya increased the number of miles we ran in a day. Even when Dalton piled *more* training onto me after my spying continued to fail.

A full week passed since starting my training with Anya, and I felt no closer to freeing Miota than I did seven days ago. By the moon, *how* was I supposed to be any good at this?

I leaned back against the couch cushion, letting the ice further burn my shoulders and neck from where I'd tweaked it this morning, trying to lift more weight than I could.

"Here." Cass smirked, approaching me and setting fresh ice packs on my knees, which were also swollen from usage.

I closed my eyes and released a sigh. "Thanks."

Cass retreated to the kitchen, where a pot of water boiled on the stovetop. "Seriously, if there's anything I can do to help more, tell me."

Defeat infiltrated my skin. "Unless you can figure out why Hallan didn't recognize me . . . or magically make me run faster and lift more weight . . ." I sank into the ice pack and winced. "I just don't *get* it, with Hallan. Makes me wonder how many more Miotans there are like that." I opened my eyes and frowned toward Cass, who stirred the pasta as he salted the water.

"That reminds me . . ." He set the salt down and peered toward my couch. "Lorella gave me news this morning. My parents were talking, and Max overheard, and he told Lorella, who told me."

I worked to follow the chain of communication. Sometimes I forgot Cass and Lorella still interacted through meetings of their own accord, planned by phone calls of scrambled signals, thanks to some invention of Neave's. It meant Cass could talk to Lorella from our hotel room's phone and no one could trace Lorella's speaker to the hotel. It guaranteed anonymity.

With Neave's skillset, I often wondered why *she* wasn't the set spy, prying information from unsuspecting people in power. But she was bent on making a name for herself here in Red Fox, and it meant *I* was the only one left to do the work of a spy.

"What's that?" I wondered, my mind walking onto a ledge, unsure of what I was about to hear.

"My mom apparently tried negotiating with Sillian Reeves to decrease Miota's monthly quota. She wants to send less people every month."

I raised my brow. Julia hadn't grown a set of morals in the last few weeks—not even a full month ago, she covered me in boiling water. The mere memory made my legs throb. She must've had some selfish reason for wanting the number of innocent Miotans to decrease.

"Why would she do that?" Maybe her son knew her mind better than I pretended to.

Cass shrugged and shook his head, staring into the pot. "I don't know. I'm almost positive Mom doesn't even *realize* what happens to the

Miotans she sends here—to her, they're just a means to an end. So to decrease the number . . ." The pace of his stirring slowed into a stop. "It would be for herself. Maybe Sillian's asking for too many people now? And she can't keep up, even with asympton?"

The cold from the ice burrowed into me. "I still can't believe you *knew* asympton was fake. That you've known about the trade for years."

"Corinn." Cass faced me, abandoning dinner, showing me his eyes and heart. Forcing me to remember our agreement not to keep secrets from each other. "We didn't *know* what happened to the Miotans here. All the Delldovas know about the supercontinent is it's a land of opportunity. If I'd realized . . . if I knew what was really happening to them . . ." His voice wavered, and he grounded himself in me. "I never would've let something so *evil* continue if I'd known about it. You have to trust me."

"The Miotans were ripped from their families. Either way—"

"My mother told me they were getting a chance at a better life, and I believed her, because she's my *mother*. Because she believed in *herself* so damn much."

Our stalemate was nothing new, and it wouldn't change now, with both of us firmly rooted in our dissenting views of the trade. Maybe that was due to nothing more than our backgrounds, our parents—the way we were raised. If I'd viewed asympton not as a deadly plague that separated families but a chance to give people a better life elsewhere, would I have hated it so much?

I advanced the conversation. At least Cass and I shared an opinion on the trade *now*, both aware of the facts.

"So Julia wants to decrease Miota's quota. What did Sillian say?"

Cass ran his tongue over his teeth behind closed lips. My stomach dropped in the short second. "He said if she tries sending him less people than usual, he'll attack Miota, and he'll have the means to send a small army soon enough."

Panic lanced down my spine as gravity shifted toward Cass. "The logistics team."

"Yeah." He bit his lip. "If Arlo attacks Miota . . ."

"They're doomed." But I knew Julia would likely agree to Sillian's terms. She wouldn't submit her people to an army—wouldn't submit *herself* to someone else's rule.

Even if Arlo's threat only intended to scare her into maintaining her quota, it showed his hand. It gave away *his* charted stars, his plans with time.

"The logistics team is going to Miota," I stated. "So I need to make the team. It's the way home."

Cass returned to his cooking. "Go home, and then what?"

"First off, make sure everyone I love is okay. My family . . . my friends." I couldn't bring myself to say Griff's name, which only churned guilt through me. But Griff was still my measured secret, the one I tucked into my heart, living there like he was a part of me.

It wasn't fair to Cass or Griff. Griff wasn't mine anymore—he was Addison Maybee's. Maybe *that* was why I endured this secret. It immortalized a flicker of Griff from when it was just him and me. Protecting him here extended the small slice of time when he first kissed me in Castle Circle, when it had thundered outside instead of within me, when he'd called me *lovely*.

I recentered myself on the ice packs. This was doing nothing beneficial, wasting away in the gilded memories of Griff Howard.

"Then we raise our *own* army of Miotans willing to fight Biourica."

"And what of my parents?" Cass asked, barely audible.

When his eyes met mine, I looked away. "Cass, I . . . the things your mom has done . . ."

"That's what I thought." He reeled in his emotions, masking them from me. "I don't blame you. What she did to your legs . . ." He clenched a fist as every muscle in his body went taut. "I *hate* her for it. But I also know there's good in her. And I hope you can give her the chance to prove it."

I wasn't sure how I could. But I kept that part to myself.

Cass fished out the limp noodles from their pot and doused them in a cream sauce. "I just wish everything could go back to the way it was before. When we were both on Miota, and we saw each other in the greenhouse, and . . . and you were going to join my Courtship."

"I never officially said I would join," I shot.

The prince smirked at me. "So it was nothing more than my wishful thinking?"

I shrugged, tossing the playful tone back at him. "I guess we'll never know."

Cass hummed. "Careful, Corinn, I have your dinner. If there's one rule I know, it's that you should always butter up your cook."

He carried two plates toward the couch, each complete with a heap of noodles and seasoned chicken breasts. This was a finer meal than anything I ever ate back on Miota, yet here, it was made of simple ingredients, something easy and quick. How different life was.

And Cass wanted to go back to the way things were before.

He *had* been a prince, though, part of the family that created reality and dictated society. The Delldovas were royalty, living in a too-big castle with too many people to wait on them. And now he lived in a hotel room, subject to these four walls, speaking on the phone through hidden channels.

Cass and I had lived lives completely opposed from one another, two repelling ends of a spiraling cord, but we held strong to each other here on the supercontinent.

I shared a smile with Cass as he handed my plate over, and we ate in comfortable silence. When thinking of Miota, I often thought of the Low Tier. But I'd recently started thinking of how *Cass* saw everything more than I cared to admit. I wanted to know his thoughts, learn his mind. Scheme like a true royal.

"So Arlo plans on sending the logistics team to Miota," I finally prompted after finishing my chicken. "I guess I really *should* make the cut, then."

"How would you get the army to go against Arlo's will?" Cass challenged. "You'd have to infiltrate the ranks and rally people against him."

I chewed on my cheek. "No, I could always . . . the army wouldn't have to . . ."

"They would." Cass's words dropped with my heart at the realization he was *right*. It wouldn't be enough for *me* to make the logistics team and get to Miota. I'd have to raise *this* supercontinental army against Arlo, or else they would overrun Miota, and I might be part of the group leading the slaughter against my home nation.

I would have to make the team. And then summon spirits against Arlo. I would still have to scheme, sneak around Red Fox's major powers in the heart of their territory, and continue playing a game bigger than myself.

This was more dangerous than anything I'd done yet.

CHAPTER 17

CORINN

I had no alternative after learning this information. I *had* to make the logistics team to help save Miota. And I'd have to turn the team against their own leader, so once we made it to Miota, the team wouldn't destroy my home.

Cass told me Lorella stopped complaining about my efforts to join the logistics team. Even though I didn't see Lorella daily anymore, knowing that much still settled my spirits. Her disapproval had managed to breathe down my neck, even from a distance.

My running times became better—by only a matter of seconds, but it was still something. I began lifting more weight, and I pushed myself until my arms and legs gave out. Anya's group would soon begin splitting what days we exercised arms and legs, doing them separately to spend more time with each muscle group. I braced myself for it.

Anya introduced us to an old fighting style popular on another supercontinent, one that dealt in kicking, striking, and punching. While I wasn't precise with my movements yet, the activity helped me get out my pent-up energy.

A whispering breeze cooled the sweat at the nape of my neck during my second fighting lesson with Anya. It distracted me from my current series of movements: stepping, then extending each arm in alternating punches.

"Your step wasn't precise," Anya said, kicking my left leg instead of simply motioning to it. "Again."

Since we'd already gone through over two hours of strength training and running this morning, my muscles bumbled, moving against my will. It proved difficult during lessons of this fighting style, when I was supposed to stay planted like a tree, tall and forceful.

"What happened to the supercontinent where this fighting style came from?" I asked, once again stepping while baring my fist in an upward hooking motion.

Anya swatted my arm this time, her honeyed eyes of amber ablaze. "Eurasia? You know as much as me, I'm sure. We haven't had real contact with them since the war. Now stop throwing your arm up like that, and be meaningful with your footwork!"

I hooked again, stepping stronger this time. Again, Anya hit my arm. I flinched. "What?"

"It's not a punch," she said, "it's a *block*. And you aren't blocking anyone with limp arms and half steps."

"I'm tired, Anya. My muscles—"

"Won't get stronger if you let them rule you! You dictate your body, not the other way around. Your blocks need to be more like this"—she threw a fist with seething accuracy—"and your punches like *this*."

Anya turned and channeled her most precise form of rage into throwing a middle punch—unfortunately, at the same second, Dalton drew near, hands shoved in his pockets. He swerved, swiftly moving his torso to dodge, but Anya's punch still cut him, and he doubled over for a brief moment.

Anya watched with wide eyes as Arlo James's son succumbed to her techniques, crumbling within, yet straightening himself out enough to pinpoint Anya with his brown eyes, glowing with the same lethal spark emitted from fire.

"Sorry—"

"It's fine." But Dalton's tone didn't sell his words. His eyes danced toward me. "Why is Anya Steele yelling at you, and why can I hear it across the field?"

It was *my* turn for my cheeks to scald crimson. "Don't take this the wrong way, but why do you care?"

"You both want to make the logistics team, same as me," Dalton continued. In Lorella's apartment, he'd been a softer version of himself, one of lulling ocean waves curling against the shore. But each time I saw him in public, with an audience, he was like stone on steel, the churning currents of deeper seas threatening to drown anyone who crossed them. "So if there's a chance we'll all be on the same team soon, it's my job to care. Why not work together?"

Anya and I shared a look, each of us assessing the other. Would Anya figure out Dalton and I knew each other outside of this training group? Would she wonder why he was invested?

"You're the leader here," I told Anya softly, putting the decision on her.

Anya's eyes clashed with Dalton's.

Finally, Anya clenched her jaw. "What, did you realize Corinn wasn't going to train with you, so now you're trying to join her team? And why do you care so much?" Anya whipped toward me. "You two know each other or something?"

I should've known Anya would connect the pieces.

Dalton answered for me. "Have you seen her in training? She's awful. And she's not even from Red Fox, so consider me *curious* on why she's putting herself through all of this."

Not from Red Fox. My heart pummeled for a brief moment before I realized Dalton referred to New Mills, my fabricated home just north of Red Fox, and not Miota.

Anya furrowed her brow and jutted a hip before glancing at me. "Up to you, Corinn. *I'm* not the one he's weirdly obsessed with. Wanna deal with a James?"

I swallowed hard and pretended to size up Dalton James. The boy narrowed his eyes at me, and that was when I finally realized this was his great façade. While Lorella had taught me to smile and mirror others, feigning harmlessness and anonymity to blend in, Dalton was fighting against his nature to *stand out* and command others. He was a star trying to play the part of a menacing moon, clearly hoping to gain something from it.

"Sure," I finally said. "Why not? It could help to have a James on our side."

"Fine," Anya spat and glared daggers at Dalton. "Like I told Corinn, *all* are welcome. But don't think I won't have my eye on you. If you're spying or something for your dad, or trying to sabotage my training group—"

"I have much better things to do with my time," Dalton promised. "We'll all be a team soon enough, hopefully." He glanced at me.

"A team." Anya shrugged. "Together. See you tomorrow, then. We start at six, and not a second later."

A team.

Together.

The words landed in my rib cage, sticking the rest of the day and haunting me into the night.

A team. Together. After over a week of training, I'd grown friendly with many of the members. Charlie, a stout woman who could lift four times my bodyweight, taught me how to stand to be able to lift more— she was training to prove to herself she could do anything she put her mind to. Gunnar, a lanky man with braided hair, hoped to make the logistics team and use the money to support his newly pregnant wife. Another man, Rollins, wanted to help his sick father with the money.

And Anya . . . I didn't know, really. She kept quiet about her past, but she was the stitching between us all, the foundation keeping us from crumbling apart.

These people were patchworks of their own, all of us a fabric of different paths and backgrounds, and we each had our own warranted reasons to be here, fighting for a spot on the logistics team. And according to Cass's latest news, we would all march into Miota together.

I needed to create dissent somewhere, and I needed to chop the team members from Arlo James at the head. It would require making friends of these people—real friends—and then hoping they'd listen to me about *saving* Miota instead of attacking it as Arlo would have it.

I would have to convince these people to go against the most powerful man in Sector A. How was I to do it and live to see it through? How would I not get caught? It would only take one person to stop me . . .

To keep these thoughts at bay, I ran harder around Biourica's complex that morning, until I fell from my legs collapsing. I skidded on my palms, cutting them up, and Charlie fell back to ensure I wasn't hurt.

"What happened?" she demanded, offering a sweaty hand then freezing when she saw the blood on me.

"Nothing," I insisted. My lungs burned as I spoke. "I'm okay. Keep going, Charlie."

She did.

Slowly, I collected myself, assessing the chafed skin. Scarlet bit me, though the wounds were superficial, and I'd only need to worry about washing my hands.

After sterilizing and wrapping my hands with supplies from our training group's medical aid kit, provided by Charlie, I finished the run with clenched fists because *I had to*. Only after I made this stupid team would I once again sneak around powers greater than myself, waging a losing war. Who was I to raise forces against Arlo James? I couldn't do it on my own.

But what other choice did I have?

After finishing my run, fatigue struck me, bringing me to my knees again. And after I'd already pushed myself with weight training, I didn't have the strength to rise. I stayed on the ground.

Until Dalton approached, sweat beading along his brow. He'd been in the front of the pack with Anya, untroubled the whole time.

"You're shutting down," he said, glancing around the open field. Other training members of a multitude of groups littered the field, running or stretching or fighting, spanning the large greenspace in violence and determination. I didn't belong out here among it. These people thought themselves enough; I was only here out of necessity.

"I'm not going to make the team," I grumbled, staring at blades of grass. "Besides . . . that's only the half of it. You . . . you heard about the call, right? Max figured out what the team will be used for?"

When I craned my neck up at Dalton, he grimaced. "Yeah, Colton told me. So . . . what's your plan? Make the team, then turn everyone against him?" *Him.* Arlo James.

I huffed a laugh. "It's that obvious, hm?" I flicked the grass nearest to me. "I thought about it, but that requires . . . the secrets. Working around powerful people."

"Like spying?" Dalton suggested, flicking a brow up in perfect Salem fashion.

My chest twisted.

"Get up," Dalton said.

I stayed planted in my spot. This was all too insurmountable. How could I scheme to save Miota when it was never the plan to come here at all?

"Why are you quitting?" he said. "You'll run yourself to the bone, and you'll lift until weights fall out of your hand, and you're practicing fighting styles pretty well. But the second anyone mentions the spying, you close yourself off and *give up*."

I stood, just to spite him, getting as close to his eye level as I could, even as my muscles withered. Dalton still held critical inches on me. Only when I was this close could I see the boy in him—his smooth skin and wide eyes. I never once felt older than him, no matter what the numbers said, calling me one year his senior.

"There's a reason for that," I gritted out. "I've learned that lesson before."

Dalton dipped his chin and lidded his eyes toward me. "And what was that lesson, Corinn?"

"I'm not doing this." I spun on my heel, but Dalton grabbed my wrist, yanking me back. I batted him with my free forearm, pulling one of the initial martial movements I learned from Anya. "Let go of me."

Dalton didn't relent. "If you can't do this now—can't even *face* it—what makes you think you'll be able to do it if you make the team?" He offered a swift punch, and I threw another block. My forearm buzzed upon the contact.

"Because"—I grunted in sync with his kick—"I'll *have to*." I spun and gulped for air.

Dalton stepped back, letting me escape. I choked on his mercy. "Who hurt you? What happened?"

"No." I fled and ignored Dalton's footfalls behind my heels. "Not talking about it."

"Keeping it locked inside only makes it worse—"

"I said I'm not talking about it!" I whirled and shoved him hard in the chest. Dalton hardly swayed, while my sore muscles and bandaged hands screamed at me.

I was pathetic—this situation was pathetic. Griff once told me I was like a waxing moon, made of growing light, if only I learned to let it in. But here and now, I felt like a dying star winking out in the night.

I wouldn't share Salem with anyone else. He was *my* burden, *my* best friend. His weight heavied my shoulders, but I stuffed him further in my soul, keeping him safe from the supercontinent.

I didn't need to talk about it with anyone, let alone Arlo James's son.

Still, when Dalton let me walk away, it didn't feel like a victory at all.

CHAPTER 18

GRIFF

Addison stepped out of the limo first, eager to bask in Salford's adoration. I let her steal all attention as I collected myself before emerging from the vehicle.

My eyes grazed the thin, chattering crowd taking up space on the asphalt road. While I hoped to see my family, I knew Jess would be at school and Mom would be at work, overseeing the allocations of Salford's weekly trade offerings.

I just needed to know how they were holding up. Had Julia sent guards to search the house? Were they being watched? Did Julia have concrete evidence *I* was Corinn's accomplice?

No, the queen couldn't know yet, because I was still here, on a clear-cut path to coronation.

Salford's mayor, Tulane Maybee, emerged from the thin Top-Tiered crowd and bowed in reverence. Addison smiled at the sight of her father bending to her instead of the other way around. Their family had always been about power moves and stiff respect; I knew better than most that love wasn't potent in the Maybee family.

Tulane's keen eyes reminded me of the task at hand: successfully appease each city and mend the chaos, or give up the crown.

"Thank you for meeting with us," Addison greeted her father.

Tulane's spine straightened, and his lips split beneath his thick mustache. "Anything for my two winners—heirs to the throne." He studied the few Queen's Guard members now piling out of the limo before flitting his eyes toward me. "I hope you two are trying for children? There's nothing like securing our families' spots on the throne."

I choked and looked away from the stocky mayor. Nothing made my stomach churn more than the thought of having children with Addison Maybee. My goal was to free Miota before it came to that.

"Good." Tulane sidestepped us, waving toward Council Hall, the metallic o-shaped building in Salford's exact center. The place had always made my skin crawl. Dad once told me stories of odd voices from within the walls, which always put me on edge.

Addison grabbed my arm, igniting a red flare in me as we trailed her father. Three guards walked behind us, keeping a healthy distance.

"Her Most Royal Majesty hardly mentioned why you've come," Tulane said, not bothering to look over his shoulder at us. "But something tells me you're all aware of the situation in Salford, rumors against the crown and all."

I didn't acknowledge the victorious plume in my chest. Lorenzo had done his part of our plan, then. Of course, my power *now* relied on sating the people, which went against what Lorenzo and I were hoping to accomplish. This was going to be trickier than anticipated.

"So we've heard," I mused. "What are the rumors saying specifically?"

"That prisoners from the Hold escaped and are now running through Miota's fields, free as ravens." He swatted a hand in front of him. "It's a heap of manure, of course, but people are believing it. And if it continues, well . . ."

He yanked open Council Hall's door, and I squeezed through with Addison.

"Her Majesty's control may continue slipping, and therefore yours will, too."

Addison's father made a point. While I wanted Julia to crumble, I was integrally connected to her, and I would also doom myself if I wasn't careful. Julia's rule was like an unraveling thread, and it had reached the end of its spool. However, I still needed something to inherit aside from a world of turmoil. I couldn't doom the entire country. If the chaos wasn't organized, and if I didn't lead it, there would be no escaping Miota—we'd sooner destroy ourselves.

Council Hall was exactly as I remembered. Shadows saturated the chilly corners, and every sound ricocheted off the harsh walls. Our shoes clacked in unison as we went down the hallway toward Tulane's office. Goosebumps erupted underneath my shirt.

I wished I could trust Abner and Max; we could burn Julia's island together. But they'd abandoned Corinn, and in turn, me. Abner poisoned me mere weeks ago to keep me in check, so I knew there were certain moves he wanted me to make before he told me his true plans. And I would rather devise my own strategy than conspire with someone who'd only speak to me when I wore a golden crown.

"I can't believe you two will be newlyweds soon," Tulane continued. "If only Charles could see this, hm?"

His casual mention of my father stung my throat, sharp and hot against the drafty hall. Dad *had* supported my relationship with Addison, requiring me to amuse her. And I'd never learned the reason. After all, Dad was also on Salford's Executive Council; the Howard name held sway and power on its own, without help from the Maybees.

"Who do you think started the rumors?" I diverted the subject back toward where I needed it. "I mean . . . prisoners escaping the *Hold?* How could anyone believe that?"

Tulane opened his office door, and the three of us shuffled in, leaving the guards behind. Tulane shut the door and collapsed in the chair behind his desk, heaving a sigh. His dark eyes jumped between Addison and me as we sat in silver chairs across from him.

"Everyone's starting to theorize," Tulane answered, "and it makes the most sense those in Accolade would've started the rumors. If that's the case . . . the list of suspects is small. It's a list including *you* both."

"What?" Addison shrieked. As she threw her hands up, her jewelry clanged together. "How could people think *we* started rumors in Salford? We don't even live here anymore!"

"Don't worry, my darling, I know it wasn't you." Tulane reclined in his chair as his eyes slid to mine, and my stomach dropped. But his next words shook the bones in my body. "It was Selleca Wooveson."

Selleca. This was my fault—I'd told Lorenzo to start the rumor, and he'd offered recruiting Selleca's help.

"Are you sure of that?" I asked. "Besides, they're just rumors, right?"

Tulane stuffed his hands in his pant pockets. "Well, the rumors surely came from someone in Accolade. While the rumor itself is unsettling—I mean, prisoners roaming free?—that's not what has Salford spun up in dramatics. It's the scouring of trying to figure out who started the rumors, to see if they're of substance. Once we know how this all started, Tops can shut the information down at the drop of an axe."

The pieces settled into place. "So you're blaming Selleca . . . because she's an easy target?"

"She's the *logical* target," Tulane corrected me. He sat up. "The only Salfordians left then were you two, Lorenzo, Hanna, Killian . . . and Selleca. Once I report her intent to rile up Salford to Her Majesty, Selleca will be put in the Hold. So you can tell Queen Julia I have the situation under control."

"The Hold?" I demanded, my tongue becoming rubber. Beside me, Addison slumped low. "On what grounds? Potentially starting a *rumor?* If that were a crime, Mayor Maybee, the Hold's cells would be overflowing."

"I think it's the perfect punishment," Addison chimed innocently while studying her nails.

Tulane ignored his daughter and pursed his lips, which wrinkled his mustache, as his sights burrowed into me. "If I say it was Selleca, then it was her—"

"It wasn't, though," I interrupted. Both heads of dark hair

whipped my direction. "And even if it was, you can't declare her to the Hold for starting a rumor."

"Are you offering an alternate suspect?" Tulane questioned, narrowing his gaze. "Was it *you?*"

"Of course not," I dismissed. I straightened my shirt, finally seeing through the mayor's plan. "I don't know who started all this, but you can't truly think it was Selleca with how quickly you just tried blaming me instead. But you need to hold *someone* responsible, and I think you want it to be the only Accolade finalist who isn't Top-Tiered."

Addison let out something like a whimper. "Griff, *please.* Don't be difficult. If this Tier stuff is because of Corinn—"

"Can you guarantee," I started again, smoldering Tulane with my scrutiny, "that it was *one-hundred percent* Selleca who started these rumors?"

"Griff Howard," Tulane droned, equal parts amusement and annoyance leeching off him. "*What* has gotten into you?"

I cracked at the resolution written in the cracks of his face. He was ready to blame everything on Selleca without providing evidence, and the worst part was knowing Salford's Top Tier would believe their mayor, taking his words as written fact.

It was something I likely wouldn't have considered or even *realized* if I hadn't grown to love Corinn first, to see life from a perspective completely opposite of all I'd ever known. Life in the Top Tier was comfortable, but Corinn had been prey, living in an upside-down Miota. She'd fought daily for the chances others were granted without question, solely because they were born into a better Tier. Corinn hadn't deserved it then, and Selleca certainly didn't deserve this now.

The system was so broken, flawed. Yet it was exactly how the Delldovas had successfully managed their monarchy and imprisonment for generations. It kept the same people in power, and they became blinded to all other life.

The Top Tier was the problem—*we* were the problem. And I couldn't let Selleca fall because of that, because of me.

So Addison could call me difficult all she wanted. I would always be *difficult*, if that was what standing up to injustice meant. If fairness was difficulty, if equality was troublesome, *so be it*.

Tulane's nearly-black eyes glowed like embers in a fire. I was challenging his authority, proving him wrong, and he wouldn't let me live it down anytime soon.

I didn't care.

"Mayor Maybee, it would be prudent for you to remember I'll be King of Miota before long. And if you falsely imprison Selleca based on her Tier, I'll remember. I won't take your word seriously on the executive council, and I'll have to wonder if everything you say is pushing some personal agenda."

"Griff, *stop*," Addison pleaded, grabbing my hand and holding it in a restraining grip that blanched my fingers. "Stop."

"Don't worry, Addison," the mayor said. While he spoke to his daughter, his eyes never left me. "He wouldn't *dare*."

"I assure you, Mayor Maybee, I would." I wore Corinn's light in my eyes, the same determination I'd seen steeled in her time and time again. She wouldn't have given up this fight.

Neither will I, lovely.

Tulane shifted in his seat, ready to bend to me. I'd wagered correctly, then: he'd rather maintain his own power than rely on his daughter's future hold on the country. "That Low did a number on you, didn't she?"

My voice cracked. "I'm a better person because of her."

Tulane sighed and stood. "You just made life a lot harder on yourself, Griff Howard. But fine, Selleca won't see the Hold. Happy? But we still need to gain control of these rumors before they spread even more and create chaos. We can't have Salfordians questioning the monarchy."

"No." I cast a sideways glance at Addison, who looked to the floor with wet eyes. My jaw worked before I focused back on the mayor. "Luckily, that's why we're here."

CHAPTER 19

GRIFF

After a week of working with Tulane and other council members to placate Salford and sedate the rumors about the monarchy lying, Salford became more pliable to mine and Addison's words.

We promised they were safe. We swore the Hold had never been broken out of. Addison even promised Salford she would speak to Julia about communication changes.

"How will you ask Julia about those reforms?" I asked on our limo ride to Pointe, the next city, whose obedience was in question. I tried ignoring that this was Corinn's home, but the fact dangled in front of me alongside Corinn's ghost. "If you propose communication reforms, Julia may take offense, or worse—"

"I'm not *actually* going to ask," she brushed me off with the flick of a hand. She opted to stare out the window at Pointe's fertile lands, bustling with Low-Tiered farmers preparing for the upcoming harvest season. "This is all about pacification, remember?"

I creased my brow. "I thought it was supposed to be about diplomacy."

"And *I* thought I'd already have a crown on my head and ring on my finger."

I heard her next breath of silence: *I'll do whatever it takes to get what I want*. It was such a Julia way of thinking, and I let Addison wear the implications like tough armor. She was what Julia wanted in a queen: someone to pacify the people, someone to promise change yet deliver nothing. Addison and Julia were both sickly sweet on the outside and hollow on the inside, filled with nothing but empty promises.

We entered Pointe's gates, and Corinn's blonde hair and moonlit eyes infiltrated the streets, nearly leaving me gasping for breath. This was her home. I'd *been here* with her—and she could be hiding in the same spot even now, for all I knew, beneath an abandoned greenhouse. All my hope for Miota hinged on Corinn's life.

We made it into Pointe's innermost ring and stepped out into a world riddled with unrest boiling in the very air. Their poles of society were in mourning: the Tops for Salem Redding, and the Lows for Corinn. This city had paid too steep a price for Miota's preservation and continuation.

The thought nearly made me sick. To these people, *Corinn* was the price paid for *my* victory. Corinn and Salem's blood belonged to Addison and me.

Before I could keel over on the stone street, a flimsy man floated toward us, seemingly no heavier than the winds. This was Tanith Peabody, Pointe's mayor who'd lived long past his prime years. But until the monarchy declared him incompetent, he would remain Pointe's leader.

"Welcome to Pointe," Tanith rasped out, his voice as rickety as the bones beneath his sagging skin. "It's our honor to host Miota's next heirs."

"Thank you, Mayor Peabody," Addison cooed, grinning.

I cleared my throat, ready to hurry through our conversations. I had better things to do in this city than negotiate peace with the mayor. I needed to know if Corinn was *alive*.

"Our deepest condolences go to you and your city," I said. "Who can we pass along the message to?"

Tanith smiled with his eyes only. "Follow me." He slowly shuffled into Pointe's Council Hall, the round building seemingly marking Pointe's epicenter, identically mirroring Salford's layout.

Pointe's Council Hall wasn't as eerie as Salford's, as it was made less of steel and more of wood. Still, the dark corners and high ceilings created the hissing of spirits, of Corinn and Salem alike.

Addison and I spoke with multiple members of Pointe's executive council—which included Tanith and Salem's parents. In Salford, we'd worked against a fixable problem. Rumors could be dismissed, truths and lies blended, and accusations discredited. But in Pointe, lives were lost, and there was nothing to do about that. It brought us to a quick stalemate and ended with Addison and me leaving with unfinished promises. We'd reconvene tomorrow.

On the way back to our limo, I caught glimpse of a face that made my heart thunder and palms slicken. Bernard Bartholomus, Abner's Top-Tiered, Pointean brother. The keeper of Pointe's underground tunnel, and the only person who knew of the location Corinn was supposed to hide, assuming she survived her trial.

His stormy eyes the color of rainclouds collided with me as he approached, headed the opposite way of Addison and me, and I poured every ounce into silently questioning him.

Is she alive? Is she here?

Bernard's face fell at the sight of my blind hope. And it *killed* me.

That only meant one thing. She was gone.

The quick shake of his head confirmed my fear.

In the limo, I nearly broke all over again. *This* was why I didn't want to hold hope; this was why faith was poisonous.

Constellations were made of Corinn's eyes and laugh and smile. The moon was her beacon into the unknown, into a place I could no longer follow.

How was I supposed to care about appeasing cities when I could no longer soothe myself? Besides, didn't I *want* cities to riot against the crown?

The weight of Corinn's death held me hostage, haunting me entirely. Everything I'd ever done had led me to *right here and now*, and I hated it.

This was unbearable. I couldn't keep outliving those I loved simply because they didn't fit within Julia's boxes, her checkerboard stage of black and white.

If Corinn was dead, so was my belief for a better Miota.

I cleaved in two.

We spent another week in Pointe, until Mayor Peabody opted for us to stop visiting, as it wasn't particularly helping matters. I hated being the undoing of Corinn's city, but Tanith insisted this wasn't a problem anyone could fix. Pointe was in mourning, and they just needed the proper time to mend.

It was time I didn't have before, partly believing a hidden Corinn was waiting for me to usurp Julia. But now I knew the ugly truth, there was no real rush. I just needed to stay facing a crown, and I needed my family to stay safe. The rest of my plan had crumbled away, simply leaving my survival up to me, transforming life into a long, moonless night.

While Pointe had been somewhat of a failure, Julia still sent us to Kendall next, so I figured our crowns were safe.

For now, at least.

But Addison and I found Kendall to be tricky. The city's Low Tier played a crucial part in servicing power plants and parts distribution centers, so this posed a problem for Miota and its power grid. Kendallian sentinels had increased brute force on the Low Tier, and as I could've guessed, it only made the Low Tier *less* productive and motivated, now run by fear and contempt. To make matters worse, the lower Tiers were already exhausted from taking on extra work hours during Accolade.

Kendall's problem, I realized after a few days, wasn't any particular

Tier or sector of work, but the whole city. They balanced delicately on the edge of a razor. The Low Tier handled basic machinery they didn't know anything about, as their duties consisted of transporting parts and completing the mind-numbing tasks deemed too lowly for the Middle and Top-Tiered managers. The upper two Tiers intercepted the Low's foundational work—which was becoming increasingly faulty and scarce these days.

Kendall's monarchy-assigned task of supplying Miota with power was one requiring cooperation between all Tiers, and without that happening, it would send Miota into a dark spiral. I'd never quite realized how much power Kendall held before now. They could practically govern Miota and dictate ways of life more than any crown or executive council could. We could learn to survive without the monarchy if needed, surely, by altering our ways as a society. But it would be damn near impossible to outlive Kendall's power grid, monorail lines, and water desalination system.

Addison and I spent the week in Kendall's factories and gated power plants, speaking with citizens of every Tier to learn how we could help better their conditions. Addison was quick to promise people anything they wanted, though I knew it was only a ploy to make quicker progress. Her words were fruitless. She and I held no jurisdiction; we only needed to succeed in appeasing the masses to gain power. Once Julia had our trusted allegiance, she could hand off her crown.

After Kendall came Cape, the city I wanted to simultaneously plunge into and avoid at all costs. That was where I'd run into Jyn Hepper, somehow related to Julia, and somehow knowing of my plan to usurp the Delldovas.

Find me in Cape, Howard. We'll talk then. The old woman's promise to me rang in my bones. I didn't want to do anything to incriminate myself, and I was no longer frantically jumping toward every solution. Now that I wasn't rushing for Corinn, I had time. I could afford caution.

At breakfast before our first day in Cape, over a selection of grains and meats, Julia briefed us on how to address the city. Apparently,

Holland's death had affected every Tier, causing the three stratifications to unite against the crown.

I would've considered using their solidarity to my advantage if I wasn't already bearing the weight of Jyn Hepper. I didn't need to add another layer of secrets to this trip—my family would pay the price if I overestimated my skills.

"Speak to the Lows first," Julia instructed us. "Get them out of the way and over with. Then you know inside their minds, and you can use it against them later on when speaking to the Tops of Cape."

By this point in her life, Julia had mastered the art of oppression, and it bled into every facet of her mind.

Had Corinn ever held a fighting chance as a Low? Miota wasn't made for her people, despite this rock being her home. While she'd had just as much claim to Miota and its land as anyone else, she'd been denied for simply being born into a lowly Tier.

Within the hour, Addison and I traveled to Cape in silence, watching the world around us as we sliced through it. As we headed south, our right window displayed Salford's thick timber forest, and the left window showed the daunting base of the Fort surrounding the island.

I saw Cape's factories before we entered the city. I knew the two buildings, Factories Alpha and Beta, claimed almost one-quarter of Cape's entire city space, and they extended into the sky far beyond the height of Cape's perimeter wall. The dark, looming buildings possessed a different air, a unique and foreboding atmosphere that was audible, palpable, even from outside the city. Upon entering Cape, it was clear life revolved around these two buildings.

The limo stopped outside Factory Alpha first. Addison gripped my elbow as guards escorted us inside the building. Sounds of slicing metal and whizzing machines engulfed us, making speech nearly impossible as a constant ringing filled my ears. Occasional sharp shouts bounced off equipment as we mazed through the building's levels, encountering people busy at multiple different equipment pieces of dull iron and black leather.

We attempted interviewing Low-Tiered citizens in their brief breaks. Some held us in high regard, bowing between each sentence, and others gave us detested glances, refusing to speak to anyone associated with the monarchy. Some warily eyed the Queen's Guard members present, and some . . . eyed *me* with intent.

Did any of these people know Jyn? Was she here somewhere, watching in the shadows? Had she shared her suspicions with anyone else? I *never* should have let her leave me so easily in Castle Circle those weeks ago.

During one interaction with a Low-Tiered man, I accidentally touched an oil spot—for some reason, I'd thought the stuff to be black as night, though it was apparently clear.

"Where can I wash off?" I asked, revealing my slick palms.

The freckled man motioned toward an outlet beneath a set of metal stairs. I smiled and excused myself to the nook, where I found three toilet stalls and two sinks tucked away.

As I washed my hands, two burly men entered, spines bent toward each other, paying me no attention.

So I didn't see it coming when they tackled me to the ground and threw me into one of the toilet stalls. My ears rang as I fought to reorient myself.

I heard her speak my name before I saw her.

Jyn Hepper had found me.

CHAPTER 20

GRIFF

The woman's crackling voice was hardly audible over the whining machinery beyond this nook.

"Griff Howard?"

The stall door swung open, and Jyn Hepper entered, immediately cupping a grimy hand over my mouth. I wrinkled my nose and fought to keep the world from spinning.

"*Listen*, Howard," she said and released her grip on me. I spat into the toilet. "Finally, you made it. Look, I'm going to talk, and you're going to follow my instructions. Got it?" The shaky woman spoke in hisses I could hardly decipher above the factory noise. Her gaze bobbed between my eyes, left and right, faster and faster. "You figured out who I am? Who I'm related to?"

"Julia," I answered, my mind whirling at this storm of a woman. "What are you doing—"

"I'm Julia's aunt. Queen Elizabeth, Julia's mother, was my sister." She took a backward step and darted her eyes in the murky lighting. "I'm also Holland's grandmother. And the leader of Maintenance—our group here in Cape against the crown."

My lips parted. "Maintenance?" A forbidden group?

"Yes. *Shh.* I've discovered something that endangers the whole island—" Footsteps approached, and Jyn's eyes widened. "What do you know of the Royal Codex?"

I shook my head. "Never heard of it."

"Gah!" Jyn placed her thumb and index finger between her eyebrows. "Okay, promise me something, Griff Howard. *Promise me.*" She hung the weight of her gaze on my face. "My sister, Julia's mother, discovered many things while she was in the castle, and she was able to communicate them with me once her husband, the late King Ivan, died. I was revisiting old notes she gave me, secret information and trade deals, and . . . I've figured something out. But I'll have to test its legitimacy first, which is where you come in. Are you listening?"

"Yes—"

"Listen *closer.*" Each word blended into the next as Jyn became more frantic with every passing second, hurtling toward insanity, descending into a frenzy. "Something dark is happening—something all the Delldovas are in on. Elizabeth theorized it, but I believe I've found evidence. It's a reach, but . . . it's a solid conclusion."

"What are—"

"I said *shh!*" Jyn clamped a greasy palm over my mouth again, and I cringed, wriggling out of her grasp. I needed to get away from this panicked woman. "Griff, I'm going to commit a very specific type of treason, one Julia won't want getting out to the general public. But I won't know if my theory's right or not, which is why I need you."

My stomach dropped.

"If the asympton reports roll out," she continued, "and my name is on the list, I need you to leave the island immediately. There are boats on the southern beaches. *Large* ones; I've seen them. They'll carry as many people as you can convince to go with you."

"Jyn—"

"*If my name,*" she gritted out again, eyes bulging from her skull, "is on the asympton reports, so help me, Griff Howard. *Get off* this damn island, and take everyone you can with you."

"What are you going to do?" I uttered.

"Doesn't matter." She waved her hands. "I can't risk telling you anything. Not yet. You need to stay uninvolved until necessity calls— you're Miota's hope, you know. Maintenance is counting on you." She lifted her brow at me. "Understand? Maintenance is large here, and we're working to undermine Julia. The group is at *your* disposal. Abner's on your side, as is Max Reno. The guard was just patrolling down here a few nights ago, and he says you don't trust him. You should, though."

No. I already barely understood what she wanted—for me to get everyone off the island as quickly as possible, but only if she died of asympton. Why asympton?

But now she urged me to trust the king and the elusive Max Reno, who played both sides, whose true allegiance I still wasn't sure of. How could I ever trust them again? Why would I *want* to?

"Don't commit treason, Jyn."

"I have to. *I have to.* If my theory is wrong, I'll go into the Hold and die for my crimes. I'm okay with that—I'm ready to see Elizabeth again." Her throat bobbed once. "But I don't see that happening . . . I think I'll be taken by asympton, and *you* will have to lead these people off Miota."

A banging on the door made me jump, and Jyn bit the back of her hand. "Your Highness?"

It was a Queen's Guard member, given away by the vacant tone and thudding steps. My pulse drummed, racing through my body too quickly.

"I'm in here!" I called, keeping my eyes locked on the graying woman in front of me. "I'll be out in a minute!"

Jyn nodded and slowly, silently, pushed a stack of papers toward me. *Paper*, a highly controlled commodity. "Take these," she hissed, jutting her hands toward my stomach.

"Jyn, *no.*"

She shoved the papers into my suit jacket. "We don't have time, and these papers explain everything—"

"Stop. *Jyn, stop.* Julia searches my room whenever she wants."

"Then find a good hiding spot."

"She'll kill my family."

"She won't."

"Tell me what's happening."

She clamped her mouth shut, pursing her lips. "I can't. But I won't actually be dead, Griff. If my theory is correct, and it's asympton, *I won't be dead.*"

My thoughts died, cutting off sharply. *What?* She wouldn't be dead?

Before the pieces settled into place, a knock rapped on the stall door. "Griff?" It was Addison this time.

"I need a second, Ads," I called out.

She didn't relent. "The guards are pushing for us to leave."

By the moon. Julia controlled the guards—did the queen know Jyn was with me? Would she search me the second we got back, or skip straight to killing my family?

I reached for the lock, and Jyn struck, grabbing my hand and pinching my wrist. "Promise me, Griff. Promise me *right now* you'll hide these pages, and you'll get everyone off this cursed island in the next month."

I blinked, my temper rising. "No."

"Promise me!" Her blue-brown eyes grew, holding me too tightly. "Do it, Griff."

"No!" I blinked as my temper steadily bubbled. Jyn was coercing me into a rash plan I knew nothing about; this wasn't logical.

"Griff, I'll open this door right now if you don't agree. Do this for the good of Miota. Please. *Save us.*"

Save Miota. That *was* my goal, right? And Jyn's papers held the instructions on how to do it. I wanted to leave Miota, to free everyone.

It should've been an easy yes. But the implications . . . I'd have to work with Abner and Max again. I'd have to trust their plans, their conditions and terms. It would mean being content with becoming a fraction of a plan instead of devising the ploy.

It would also endanger my family. My agreeance could bring their demise.

"No."

Jyn swatted at my hand, placing her free palm atop the stall door's lock over mine. I wrenched her grip away, locking our arms in a tussle. I would win, and she knew that, but she could easily raise her voice and give away her location with me.

"If I agree," I said in a breath, knowing one more decline would bring her to shout for the guards. "Can you keep us from getting caught right now? Julia will kill my family if we're both found in here."

"Yes." Her face glittered with hope. It was the expression I'd seen in myself, up until the day I discovered Corinn was dead. "Yes, I can get out of here alone. Just promise me you'll get everyone off Miota in the next month."

"I swear." The oath delivered my fate, altering it as necessary.

The old woman rubbed my shoulder. "Thank you, dear. Thank you." She grinned and memorized my face. "Stay here for another minute. I'm leaving now." She ducked underneath the wooden plank and into the adjacent stall with a nimble grace I hadn't expected.

I stayed frozen in my stall, unmoving, drinking in what Jyn just forced me into. What I'd promised her through coercion.

Had I truly meant it? Would I stay true to my oath? I wanted to believe I would. But a kernel inside me wondered if I'd only said what I needed to in order to secure my current safety; after all, she hadn't given me much of an option.

But if I didn't keep my word, I would be no better than Julia and Abner. Addison was already learning the art of false promises, and maybe I was, too.

Maybe I was no better than Julia Delldova herself. The thought ripped into me.

As I listened to Jyn retreat from the adjoining stall, I wondered with a thousand questions still burning on my lips if this would be the last time I ever encountered her.

CHAPTER 21

GRIFF

The room blurred as Gwynn's voice droned on about the infamous Treaty of Miota, the document Julia liked to mention but not follow. With my feet propped and trunk reclined, my heavy eyelids dragged me toward sleep, and I could hardly put up a fight.

Until Addison would make a sudden movement to break my trance, and I'd startle and blink the fatigue away as best I could. It left Gwynn, Julia's lady-in-waiting, to shake her head at me while still chattering away.

This cycle continued for hours.

When Addison and I weren't fixing each city's problems like our titles hinged on our success, Julia forced Gwynn to give us long and tedious lessons in one of the first-floor sitting rooms. My eyes had already roved over every square inch of baby-blue wallpaper, every intricacy in the gold-plated furniture. The windowless room provided no external distraction, no hope of freedom. I wondered if Julia ordered Gwynn to lengthen these lessons simply to keep Addison and me under supervision for longer.

Sometimes the lessons caught my attention because of their blatant inaccuracies, muddying the truth. Had this been how Cass was raised? Gwynn told us the Fort was built to protect us from sea monsters—with no mention of shielding us from an entire outside world. She said the Queen's Guard was a prestigious program breeding stone-cold law enforcement—nothing about the mind-controlled shells they truly were.

" . . .The treaty is a living, breathing document." Gwynn slid a thick, textured piece of paper toward us, the stuff unlike anything I'd ever seen before. Ink-ridden words poured into the paper's cracks and lines. "For example, we made an amendment decades ago about giving a certain number of diseased bodies to each city per month to look for an asympton cure. Her Majesty is changing this amendment currently, so only *one* body per month is sent to each city. Can you think of why she would do this?"

Addison lifted a hand, sending her metal bracelets clanging down her arm. "I'm sure most Miotans would rather be floated off the island, left to the elements of nature, than experimented on in their city's hospital."

"Precisely, Addison." Gwynn grinned at her, followed closely by a frown toward me. "The more that can be floated out to sea by the Guard, the better. Even though we all see the experimentation as a necessary step for our future . . . until there's *any* progress toward finding a cure, it just seems a slight waste of resources."

The subject of asympton made me squirm. Jyn had been so caught up on asympton, on fearing the disease. It seemed like the Capean had given me all the pieces but kept them scrambled, and I now had to sort them out on my own.

"This is the list of all who've fallen to asympton this past month," Gwynn said, motioning to the thick paper.

A deep chill settled in me. If Jyn's name was on this list . . .

She wanted me to get everyone off Miota. Work with Abner and Max again. Endanger myself, and therefore, my family. Her name *couldn't* be on this list.

I hadn't looked at the papers she'd forced into my jacket that day in her factory; I'd instead marched to the small royal book collection and shoved them in a tome covered in a thick blanket of dust. Hopefully, that would keep them unrelated to *me*.

The less I associated with Jyn, the better. She'd forced me into a deal, one I still wasn't sure would be wise to act upon.

The weight bore on my chest, hanging heavily on my shoulders. My light was waning, and I would soon be a new moon, invisible and hidden in darkness. I'd held so much light with Dad, with Corinn. I *wanted* to unearth Julia's secrets, and I would give anything to do it. But now . . . Aside from my mother and sister, my fragmented family, I wasn't protecting anyone. I didn't *trust* anyone.

The forces of this island had turned their backs on me, and I would not be so insolent as to do anything but the same. I would not risk Mom and Jess, my only lifeline left.

Besides, I was already working with my own veiled knowledge— the stuff Corinn and I had discovered together, underneath Pointe. I didn't need Jyn's help then, and I certainly didn't now. I'd already uncovered the depths of Julia's evil in the trade document I'd briefly scanned with Corinn.

I strained to remember it now, and I wished I'd somehow found a way to repossess my own set of papers still hidden in Castle Circle's greenhouse. They'd outlined a trade deal between Miota and the supercontinent: supplies for people.

People. That always turned my stomach. People were *not* commodities to be traded; they were free, autonomous beings. It made Julia Delldova a worse monster than any story someone could conjure up about field ghosts or the spirits beyond the Fort. Julia was giving people to another country, another *world*, without permission. It didn't matter if the supercontinent was a freer place—people deserved the choice. People had livelihoods here, family and friends.

I wasn't sure how Jyn could uncover anything darker than the trade. Julia gained supplies at the cost of viable Miotans. And now, whatever theory Jyn hoped to prove to herself would be lost if she died.

Well. I grasped at the memory of speaking to Jyn, reaching to recall every detail. I'd nearly forgotten, in the frenzy of it all, she'd said something about not truly being dead. Right?

If it's asympton . . . I won't be dead.

My stomach dropped. The floor tilted beneath me, and my propped legs came crashing to the floor.

"Are you all right, Your Highness?" Gwynn pointed at me.

I blinked and righted myself in my seat. As quickly as the scene came together, it tore apart at the seams, unable to fit together wholly. I lost the thought before fully grasping it.

Or maybe I just refused to believe something so *impossible* . . .

"Yes." I feigned a smile that didn't feel at all believable. "Sorry. Just got . . . lightheaded."

For a transient second, the loose ends had tied together. I'd received an instant of clarity, only to be shrouded by doubts and . . . *helplessness.*

Because if the people dying of asympton weren't actually dead, as Jyn made it seem . . . if they were the people Julia traded to the supercontinent . . . and they were still alive . . .

By the moon.

I couldn't jump to such a conclusion. Was I forcing the pieces together? Making this up?

It made too much sense, though. Who else would Julia be sending? The only Miotans leaving the island in mass numbers were the ones dying from asympton.

Asympton, the disease Jyn spoke of with fear in her eyes. She'd said we were in danger, that if she was claimed by asympton, she wasn't truly *dead.*

And if this was the case, I really *did* need to get everyone off the island in the next month. Before Julia did her next monthly trade. Before anyone else could be abducted from their home by force, instead of given the option to leave by choice.

If this were all true, I'd just uprooted Miota's darkest secret of all. And I was completely powerless against it. How could I compete against not just Julia, but the supercontinent?

This affected the entire island—my family included. No one was safe from asympton, from being abducted to the supercontinent. Yes, certainly *this* was the secret Jyn wanted me to discover. I needed to find a way to work with Abner and Max again for the sake of every person on this island. I'd have to plunge into treasonous territory again for the good of Miota.

The sense of doom didn't fully strike until I scanned the list of asympton names. Sure enough, in letters that stamped Miota's demise into my eyelids, sat the name I didn't want to see.

Jyn Hepper.

Asympton wasn't real.

Ghosts didn't stop haunting me after that.

Every person I knew who'd ever been taken by asympton, every Miotan I thought was gone . . . were they? What was real? I didn't know.

Later that week, I slipped into Abner's office on a routine visit. The king seemed too foreign, always out of reach, since I'd moved into the castle. But I would collide with him today.

I'd made a promise to Jyn. A forced one, yes, but a vow nonetheless. Whether she was truly dead or off to the supercontinent didn't matter. Jyn said there were cataclysmic consequences of not getting off Miota in the next month.

It even made me wonder if those taken to the supercontinent didn't walk into good graces. Maybe there was another side to this puzzle we were blind to on Miota, and we'd only see the full image by going to the supercontinent ourselves.

"Ah, Griff." Abner didn't look up from his seat at his wooden desk, tucked against the room's back wall. Against the large window of blown glass, he was nothing more than a dark figure, playing tricks on my eyes. Maybe he'd set up his office like this purposefully.

But I needed to see the king's face, his eyes, during this conversation. Or else I'd never be able to trust him.

"Take a seat," he said, gesturing to the chair opposite his own.

I lowered myself and let my eyes adjust to the colored sunlight bleeding in, outlining Abner in a halo. Once I could make out his features, I spoke. "Your Majesty. I've . . . heard news."

For the first time today, his gray eyes snapped toward me. I finally held his attention. "News?"

"Of Jyn Hepper."

"Oh, yes." The king returned to jabbing at his panel, typing out a message to someone. "She's died."

"Of *asympton*," I added, now shaking. Jyn gave me Abner's assurance, but I still didn't like the risk. He'd dropped Corinn without batting an eye; he'd let her die. Fire fueled my belly.

"Yes," Abner drawled. He seeped into stillness before leaning back in his chair to study me. His eyes shone with a slippery challenge. "And?"

Right. Abner didn't trust *me*, either. I couldn't forget how he'd poisoned me only weeks ago, not trusting my current decisions to be of a sound mind.

This exchange, if successful, would take a leap of faith—one I'd put in Jyn Hepper, a stranger. A woman who'd coerced me into her plan. What made Jyn's tactics better than Abner's, than Julia's?

Jyn had risked herself for Miota. She'd sacrificed her life and freedom with the assumption *I* would free our island. Wasn't that my ultimate goal? I *wanted* to save Miota. So why couldn't I just go along with this?

I swallowed hard before taking the plummet. "We both know asympton isn't real."

Abner's features stretched. "Who told you?"

I went cold. I'd guessed correctly, then. Asympton was a royal scheme, an evil deception. "Jyn Hepper gave me clues," I answered honestly. "I met with her when Addison and I went to Cape, and . . . she told me to work with you and Max. That you two are good, and I should trust you."

"She was right," he said with a flick of his nose.

"She also said we need to get as many people off the island as possible in the next month."

"No," Abner barked with a sneer. He stroked his gray beard. "Max and I have a plan, and *that's* the one you'll follow, not the wishes of a dead woman."

"She's not dead, though." I rose to my feet, looking down at Abner. "Is she?"

His stare sliced me. "Not yet, but she *will* be. Do you think my wife would allow her to live after she tried to expose Miota's biggest secrets?"

"How'd she do it?" I asked, ignoring his fear tactics. "Jyn, I mean. How'd she give herself away?"

Abner sighed and stood, matching my height. "She was found outside Cape, in Miota's central fields. And she spoke of the supercontinent and the Royal Codex to the guards—they're programmed so those words will get you detained every time."

Something taut snapped in my chest. Once again, Julia killed innocent people for having knowledge against her rule. Dad, Corinn, Holland Stanzifer, Jyn Hepper . . .

"I promised Jyn I'd get as many people off the island as I could within the month." My heart battered, lungs contracted. "She told me there are boats on Miota's southern shore—Jyn's seen them herself. She gave me papers, too. I haven't looked at them, but—"

"Griff, you're *mad.*" Abner's ever-present storm, usually latent, finally bubbled over. "Have some common sense. There isn't a way to get everyone off the island in the next few weeks."

"Not with the way you live!" I hissed and leaned over the desk. "You only care about yourself. And it's costing people their *lives.* Do you realize that?"

"I do." The king smoothed out his shirt—as though this subject was something trivial.

"And you're okay with that."

"My plan to free Miota depends on my survival. So yes."

I returned to my seat, at a loss, wondering how I could ever afford to trust this man. He was so stone-hearted, he'd neglect the lives of everyone around him if it meant maintaining his peace.

Abner was no better than his wife. She was the murderer, the easy target. But he was compliant, and therefore just as evil. The royals were on the same side after all. Jyn had been wrong; there was no trusting Abner. There would *never* be a world in which I trusted him.

"What if I have a good plan?" I hypothesized. "A plan so strong, so *sudden*, Julia would never see it coming?"

"You have one?" Abner threw.

I blinked. "Not yet. But I *will*."

Abner's shoulders rose, then fell. "It would need to be so unshakable; Julia's loss would have to be *guaranteed*. There couldn't be a single hole, and she couldn't have reason to suspect anything. It would need to happen like *that*." He snapped his fingers.

Defeat tried slamming into me. I pushed back. "That's the only way you'll agree to this? If you aren't put in any danger?"

"I'm damn tired of endangering myself. I do it for my brother, and I did it for my son. For Corinn. I'm *done*."

This wasn't getting anywhere. I understood his line of thinking. I really *did*. It was a path I'd become too familiar with myself these days, without a guiding light. Jess and Mom were my only beacon left, and protecting them meant playing this royal game safely.

But Jyn dared me to play for *more*.

She'd also given me two names—Abner was only my first option. He didn't seem eager to mend our alliance.

I stood to make my exit. "These people that are being stolen from their homes every month?" I bit out. "That's on you for knowing about it yet doing nothing to stop it. That's on *you*."

Abner growled. "If you don't have an exact plan, you'd be

rounding up people to leave Miota—rounding up the rebels and doubters—making it easier for Julia to kill them. Don't peg this as cowardice. It's just being logical. Talk to me once you have a *real* plan."

I huffed a dry laugh. "Whatever you say, Your Majesty."

Abner was too willing to sit comfortably in his iron box, tucked away as he watched our island burn to the ground. No matter—I wouldn't become reckless quite yet. I still had one other option, courtesy of Jyn, to help me. To give me hope.

I had to trust the old woman again. It was time to visit Max Reno.

CHAPTER 22

GRIFF

I invited Addison to the barracks too, so Julia wouldn't grow suspicious. Not that she couldn't simply spy on us the whole time if she wanted to, using the guards' implants. Not that she wouldn't have them keep a close eye on us, something I was expecting.

But I had to try working around them. I had to get everyone off Miota in a matter of weeks, and Max was my only hope left on this entire island.

Rain splattered on the windshield as our limo sliced through the weather. Back home, on days like these, I wanted to sip tea in the Common and listen to the thundering of raindrops on the roof. Since moving into the castle, I could even do such a thing from my bedroom, with the balcony doors thrown open to amplify the sounds. But there was no time to waste today; besides, it felt wrong to bask in such a luxury.

"You have the checklist?" Addison asked as she mindlessly brushed the ends of her damp hair.

"Of course." *Obviously.* This entire trip would be null without the checklist; Julia thought we were completing training on how to conduct a routine barracks visit.

As the limo zipped through the barracks' surrounding electrical fence, Addison scooted closer to me. She weighed on me now more than ever these days. If I were to get as many people off Miota as I could, she would have to be near the top of that list. Even though our engagement didn't feel real in any substantial way, I still bore the responsibility of her well-being. If leaving Miota meant freedom, I wouldn't be able to live with myself if I didn't extend the offer to her first.

But doing that much would require telling her about the supercontinent, and I couldn't risk that. She was Julia's ally now, as she'd been during Accolade's entirety. It didn't leave me the room to tell Addison anything conspiratory until the plan was happening.

The vehicle stopped, and Addison and I leapt from it, running into the barracks as quickly as we could. Addison hitched up her skirt, keeping the purple fabric out of the muddy grass. I only cringed as my running cadence had my feet hitting the ground with so much impact it forced squelching mud onto my pants.

Two burly guards I didn't recognize welcomed us, and I only hoped word had traveled about our presence so Max would know I was here.

"Your Majesties," the middle-aged guard addressed us. She gave a thin smile, which further wrinkled her skin of leather and showed off a white laceration scar slashing her jaw. "I'm Harrie, and my partner is Jolon." She motioned to the man whose bulky muscles writhed beneath his dark skin. "We will be assisting you with your checklist. Follow us, please." Like all guards, Harrie's voice was devoid of all emotion, signifying she was a subdued version of herself Julia created and controlled.

As the four of us started down the carpeted hallway, I took up as much space as possible and created as much noise as I could muster. I hadn't been to the barracks since we'd toured them during Accolade. It still smelled of mold—especially in the wet weather—and gave me a headache. Wooden slats lined the walls, and I knew any of them could reveal a secret compartment or passageway, as most things of royal manufacturing did.

It also revived Corinn. Harrie and Jolon led us to the supply closet, which was a cold shock to the lungs, leaving me hiccupping for air. I let Addison lead these tasks as I tried not to look at anything too closely. I'd hidden with Corinn in this stupidly small supply closet, nothing more than a musty outcropping. I'd almost kissed her senseless here, but there had been too many problems at the time. I'd ultimately let worries dictate my actions.

What I wouldn't give to go back and kiss her despite the circumstances, savoring every moment with her. I would've kissed her in that closet as she deserved, kissed her until we used all the oxygen in the room. From the beginning, Corinn had lit my nerves, and I wanted nothing more than to burn beneath her touch, to be undone by her.

I blinked away visions of her as my heart warred with itself, set on its own cycle of waxing and waning. While I needed to move on from the past, I didn't *want* to. I needed to remember Corinn in her full splendor, as I'd tried so hard to do with Dad years ago, too.

If remembering Corinn's freckles and smile and spirit came with pain, then I would suffer a hundred times over.

While Addison and Harrie swept the closet, I stood back with Jolon—and noticed when Max Reno walked by. I snagged his gaze, and his brow twitched slightly.

I cleared my throat. "I'm going to the restroom," I told Jolon, commanding it instead of asking. "I drank way too much tea this morning. Stay here and help Addison."

"Of course, Your Highness."

Before Jolon could say more, I peeled from the group, stalking to the end of the hallway. I slinked into the men's restroom and wrinkled my nose at the mildewy scent. Beneath flickering lights, two small stalls occupied the back wall. A rusting water fountain, much like the communal fountains sporadically placed around Salford, sat in one corner, and two shower areas still wet with pools of water sat in another. To complete the space, one sink basin squatted beneath a grimy mirror.

Max Reno entered a moment later.

"Thank the moon," I whispered. "I need to talk to you. Abner won't listen, and . . ."

"Spit it out," Max prompted levelly and ran a hand through his pale, curling hair. When he first received his sham cranial implant, his hair had been cropped short, but it had since started growing back. "Tell me what you know, Griff. And I'll do the same."

There was something too calculating, too cunning, in his voice. It bristled against me, leading me to keep a keen eye on the bathroom's door: my exit, if needed. I retreated from his reach.

This was the problem with Max: I couldn't *trust* him, as he'd grown up in the castle as one of Julia's closest friends. Max was meant to save Corinn from her trial, yet he'd failed her, even after guaranteeing her safety. I wasn't sure whose side he gravitated toward; maybe his allegiance changed, shifting like the oncoming autumn season.

So I chose my words carefully. If Max knew what I did, the message would ring clear about Jyn and Julia's monthly trade. "I know she's alive." *For now.* I hoped Julia didn't truly kill her own aunt. "And I know that every month . . . Julia and the supercontinent . . ."

Max's eyes widened. "How long have you known? How'd you figure it out?" He rounded his shoulders and nearly covered my mouth with his hands, now scanning the bathroom for eavesdroppers.

"She told me," I answered.

"This whole time?" the guard hissed, flashing teeth. "By the moon, Griff. Still, you get why I had to lie to you, right? I needed you to play the part of a mourning lover so Julia believed she was gone."

I opened my mouth. Then stopped breathing. "Mourning *lover?*"

"Look, I don't need to know the details of your relationship with Corinn." He waved his hands in a way that would be comical in another situation. "I just mean you played the part well. Aside from the medical supplies' disappearances, Julia really thinks she's dead."

The world tilted on its axis, hurtling toward a grand pause. The room faded to gray. I didn't want to speak, to move, and shatter this moment, this newfound feeling of *what if.* My tongue went limp, and my legs hardly kept me upright.

"What?" I finally uttered.

"What do you mean, *what?*" Max shoved me hard, sending me to the ground. My palms smacked against the chipped tile floor. I didn't care. "You were just talking about it!"

I spat, ignoring the vibrations in my arms. "Tell me word for word what you're talking about."

"Corinn is alive. She's on the supercontinent . . . like you *just said.*"

By the moon.

I reached for the nearby wall, trying to stand, but my knees buckled. The last few weeks of my life flew out from under me, dissipating into nothing. I thought I was finally getting a sense of what was real, what my plan was supposed to be. But now . . .

I let out an ugly laugh. "She's alive?" Tears intruded my vision, blocking out everything but this moment. "Are you serious? You better *damn well* be serious, because I can't think right now, and I can't keep doing this—"

"Get a hold of yourself." Max offered a hand, pulling me to my feet. His colorless eyes scoured mine. "Who were *you* talking about? Who's still alive?"

I sharpened my mind, trying to focus on the conversation at hand instead of Corinn. I couldn't lose myself now, in the home of Julia's spies. "Jyn Hepper." I swallowed. Time to take another leap. "She told me that if she was announced dead because of asympton, it meant she was alive. I pieced together the truth, that asympton isn't real, and those are the people traded—"

"*Shh.*" Max's face went frantic. "Damn, Griff, took you long enough to figure it out. Well now you know just about everything."

Despite it all, I grinned. Corinn was *alive*. My moonlight still shone; she would not be so easily ruined. I silently worshiped every star, every constellation, every sun and moon.

I *knew* she wasn't gone.

Yet before my next breath, my stomach turned to ice. According to our plan, she was supposed to end up in the tunnels beneath Pointe, not across the damn ocean.

"Max." My jaw clenched. "Why is Corinn on the supercontinent?"

Max took a step backward. "She's safe, trust me. There's a group on the supercontinent I'm working with, and they have her. We'll meet her there soon."

"In the next month," I said, repeating Jyn's command. Corinn went from being a lifetime away from me to someone I could see in mere *weeks*.

"Jyn's timeline wasn't ours." *Ours.* His and Abner's. The taunt roared in my mind, and I lashed out.

"It is *the timeline!"* I accentuated each syllable, making myself clear as day. "That's what Jyn said, and that's what I'm saying now."

I'd thought Mom and Jess were the only ones I had to look out for, though now I knew the truth. I couldn't sit aside as Abner and Max did, letting random citizens leave the island into the unknown every month. As much as I wanted to believe these people were tasting the rumored freedom of the supercontinent, I couldn't blindly accept it—because nobody decent traded *people* like a commodity.

The gameboard and its pieces just expanded by an ocean.

Max paced the tile floor. "You aren't in charge, Griff."

"I don't care." I crossed my arms over my chest. "I can't just sit back and *watch*, now that I know what's happening! Now that I know Jyn was right . . . and that Corinn's alive . . ."

"Careful, now," Max hummed, a facetious smile overtaking him. "I can't tell if you're trying to be self-righteous, or if you're just impatient now that you know your girlfriend's out there—"

I whirled on Max, ready to hit him square in the chest. Ready to chop him down. He stared at me too smugly, thinking he was *right*. Believing my emotions were getting the best of me.

My upper lip twitched, but I otherwise channeled my rage into my fists, clenching them, nails biting into my own flesh. Maybe Corinn *was* within me again; I could still fight here, as I knew she would.

"I won't sit back and do nothing," I grumbled, hoping to simmer the energy between us. This was hardly going better than my interaction with Abner. "I *can't*."

Max narrowed his eyes. "You're sounding a lot like Corinn."

"It's time someone did." I knew my dark eyes lived—*breathed*—fire, showcasing her spirit melded with mine. By the moon, living with this much determination lying in my bones was exhilarating. But I'd once told Corinn she was strong enough to do anything she put her mind to; I believed it for her, and I'd now believe it for myself.

She was alive. And I was going to get her back—while freeing this entire island.

"Not when her recklessness got her put in the Hold," Max said. He adjusted his uniform and resumed his pacing. "Abner and I aren't evil for not wanting to ram our way to victory. We're all doing what we think is best. I can promise you, if you act out and end up in the Hold, no one will be there to save you."

"Why'd you say you got a fake implant?" I challenged, slowly falling into despair with each relaxed muscle in Max's shoulders, with each line of satisfaction etched into his face's wrinkles. "Because there are people there counting on you to help? I'm assuming it's the same people who have Corinn, right? So she's counting on you, too."

Max blinked, fighting himself. "Stop."

I would not. In fact, I was just getting *started*. Max was cracking, and I would make him crumble. "The Max I met months ago was willing to risk himself. You would do what you had to for the good of Miota. But I see now what a coward Abner turned you into."

"It's not that simple." Max raked a hand through his hair, pulling near-white strands out of his scalp.

"Who told you that?" I pushed. "Abner? Don't forget, Max, you're dealing with Miotan people being stolen from their homes. How can you know the truth about asympton, do nothing about it, and live with that choice?"

I mimicked Jyn's fervor now that all the pieces were laid out in order. The more I dwelled on it, the more I knew she was right: I *had* to save this country before Julia's next trade. It was time for a stand against Julia for good.

Max's next words, delayed after a heartbeat of thought, were quick. Sharp, hushed. "I speak with my contact, Anzalone, Friday night. I'll see if I can find anything out about getting us off this island quicker."

I blew out a sigh. "Thank you, Max. Thank you."

"Get out of here before I change my mind." His gaze fell to the floor. "Now."

I didn't risk disobeying him as I clamped my lips shut and left the bathroom with newfound hope, a light feeling I hadn't known in months.

CHAPTER 23

JULIA

Nothing claimed the beach but brine and sand. Wind and sun. The elements whipped about in chaos; there was no control out here. No sense of stability. I detested it.

I scraped my tongue along the upper row of my teeth, attempting to rid myself of the salty taste, but it was no use. Ignoring the ocean's sting as best I could, I focused on the woman bound in shackles, kneeling in the wake. Water crawled toward her in uneven waves, occasionally hitting her ankles and knees.

Most Miotans would possess the sense to bow in my presence. But this was Jyn Hepper. Her nose tilted upward, and her eyes squinted against the sun. She watched me, which gave way to the hazel ring in her blue eyes.

Her eyes held all of my ghosts, matching those of my greatest heartbreaks: my mother, my brother, and my son.

"Your Majesty." Jyn's sarcastic twinge made me want to douse her in the multiple poisons I possessed. "How are you, dear?"

"Jyn Hepper." I addressed my aunt with necessary disdain. "There is no need for pleasantries. We both know why you are here."

"Yes, I guess so." My aunt tipped her nose toward the sky. "Since I'm on the beach, I'm assuming I was right? Asympton isn't real?"

"It is none of your concern," I snapped. "Speculation on the matter is treason enough and calls for your death. Did my mother theorize anything like this when she was alive?"

Jyn's face rippled at the mention of her sister. "Elizabeth is dead. Don't bring her into this."

I clenched my jaw. "Each unanswered question will be one finger separated from your body. So I suggest you *answer* me."

Jyn scoffed and gave a wretched grin. "Listen to you. You'll never be half the ruler Josiah would've been—"

"My brother is dead." I threw her own words back in her face. "Do not bring *him* into this, either." I jutted my concealed blade forward. Its iron tip pressed against Jyn's throat, the ruby hilt and metal adorning her like a piece of jewelry. "He is gone."

Even though I am looking into his eyes now.

"He's gone," Jyn said, "and whose fault is that?" Jyn refused to break eye contact, as though knowing their hue was my destruction. Each blink chanted their names: *Mother, Josiah, Cass.*

My knife did not waver against her throat; in turn, she did not crumble against my blade.

"It was Father's fault," I finally answered, humoring the woman for reasons only the heavens knew. "*Father* turned my brother inside-out."

The image would forever sear my mind.

"Your father failed you." Jyn swallowed against my knife. "And your mother never wanted you to turn into him. She wanted to *help* you."

I recalled lying on my bed as a young girl, staring at my cream-colored ceiling. Mother would come in after Father's lessons, and she would rub my head and brush my hair to comfort me.

You are good, she would say, lulling me with gentle nails along my scalp. *You are Julia Delldova, and you are good.*

But she said such things after Father had called me a weapon. A deadly disease. Were parents not supposed to tell the truth? One of my parents had been lying through their teeth, and I had not known which one.

I learned later on that Father was right and Mother was wrong, when Josiah was bloodied and dead, and a fleeting thought ran through me as I looked on in horror.

I was *glad* to become Queen of Miota. Josiah, always kind and compassionate, would have risked Miota's destruction.

The thought had been infinitesimal. And it had triggered such a potent reaction from me—I had vomited to expel the thought from my body, and sobs racked me. I would have given *anything* to have my brother back.

Still, I had the thought, no matter how quick. And what sort of monster felt anything outside sorrow and grief for the death of an only sibling? It proved I was as deadly as Father wanted.

A rare tear fled my eye. I blamed it on the sharp winds carrying sea salt.

"Mother did not help me enough," I said. "She lied to me. She told me—"

"That you're Julia Delldova, and you're good?" Jyn guessed. The woman leaned into the blade at her neck, and I received her message. She would not cower here and now. "She loved you, and she never wanted you to turn out like Ivan."

"Then you admit she hated who I became." I was Father's spitting image, his daughter through and through. His ghost still lived in my head, tucked into my every thought. *My* bones and blood were my father's; *Josiah* had always been Mother's child.

"You are not Ivan," Jyn insisted. Her eyes stretched wide. "You are Julia. Sister of Josiah, and daughter of Elizabeth. And you are good."

Slit her throat, Father barked. *Now. Don't you see what she's doing? She wants your mercy. She knows she's as good as dead.*

Killing her now would only take a quick slip of force. Such a small movement could have such destructive implications.

But I could not do it yet. She held information I needed. I hated how similar this felt to the moment I questioned Corinn after she and Salem appeared on the beach without my knowledge. I had not discovered her secrets in time, and the thought still preoccupied me. If I could do no better with Jyn now, what sort of queen would I be? A spineless one. One incapable of protecting her country from insurgents, risking its demise.

"Stop trying to distract me," I commanded with a tone of cold steel. "You committed very clear crimes: running about outside of your city and speaking the *utmost* treasonous words to my guards patrolling the southern island. This was your goal, was it not? To be detained and killed?"

There was no fear in Jyn's eyes. When I had caught Corinn in her crimes, the girl had denied them. She had been a wreck, not planning to be caught. But Jyn stayed collected. A picture of resilience; a state of composed rebellion.

She wanted this to happen.

Chills exploded on my arms. Even Father retreated slightly, unsure of what to do with her. He and I wanted to be the attackers instead of the ones piecing everything together, solving the riddles.

"Was I wrong about asympton?" Jyn challenged. "I'm asking because I believe you killed Holland Stanzifer, conveniently claiming asympton. And that breaks my heart because you were related to the girl."

I withdrew, dagger and arm and feet, taking large steps away from the shackled woman.

"Related to Holland Stanzifer?" I mocked her with a chortle. "I am not—was not. She was a Middle."

"She was," Jyn explained. While Father screamed at me to end this life in front of me, my limbs clenched tight, rendering me paralyzed. "I never had children, but little did I know until your mother's last year of life, Elizabeth and I had a half-brother. Our father, you see, had an affair with a Middle he oversaw in Factory Alpha. Since they were both in their own marriages, and different Tiers, they didn't tell anyone for a long time. But they had a child, Leith Stanzifer, who my father's lover claimed as her and her husband's."

For once I was truly shocked. My mother . . . had a half-*brother*. The fact must have stayed concealed for decades, for if my father or grandparents in the castle knew about this, they never would have allowed Elizabeth to win Father's Courtship.

Leith Stanzifer. The name curdled my blood.

"Leith died about a decade ago," Jyn continued all too casually. "He and his wife both. Asympton." She threw me a pointed look. "They had one daughter—she's your cousin."

Cousin. I hardly remembered what that word meant—some sort of distant relation. Something Cass would have been to Josiah's children. Not that it mattered much when my brother and son were both dead.

Jyn did not grant me the mercy of time to process. She instead hurtled forward. "Your cousin, Leith's daughter, had her own family. Husband and daughter. Her husband went first, four years ago. And her daughter, well . . . you remember what you did to Holland."

I paled.

I realized, with a start, I had met this cousin of mine not long ago, at Griff and Addison's victory meal in the castle, when I had jointly invited the families of Accolade's fallen. I recalled Holland's only guest—her mother.

My cousin.

The woman and I had shared straight brunette hair. She had possessed my mother's angular nose. I had destroyed her family. The same as Jyn's family. The same as *my* family.

It made me dizzy.

"Who else knows of your theories?" I asked. "About asympton? About treason?"

"No one."

I tilted my chin. "Not even Holland's mother?"

"No. I swear to you, Bernet knows nothing. It was . . . the only sure way to protect her." Her eyes, irises I knew too well, told no lie.

"Is there *anyone* in Cape you've talked to about this?"

Her mouth opened, though no sound came out.

"Remember what I said?" I tsked in her silence. And then I expertly cut a digit off. Pinky first, being easier to slice through, with more independent muscles and tendons.

Jyn's screams filled the lull between the ocean's waves. I tried to ignore the dark blood on the sand. Still, Jyn did not waver.

"*Who else knows?*" I demanded again. "This will not end well for you if you do not answer me, Jyn."

"I know . . . my fate," she panted between whimpers. "But *you* can be better, Julia . . . *you* can be . . . *more.*"

I shook my head violently. "You are wrong."

Mother used to tell stories of how the best souls went to live among the stars in the afterlife, shining down on those they left behind. Meanwhile, the cruel souls stayed stuck here, feasting and prowling on those still living.

I knew the stories were true; why else would Father follow me around now? He was not good enough to reside in the heavens above. It was the same fate I would one day meet.

"There is *good* in you." Tears caked Jyn's cheeks. Blood coated her hand. "There's good in . . . in everyone related to Elizabeth! To Josiah."

I snapped and brought my blade flush against her neck. Jyn raised her chin, pressing against the blade. Giving me the chance to end her.

Putting her life in my hands would be her last mistake.

You are deadly. Father cackled. *Your fate is already decided. Finish off your family, Jules.*

Fate despised me. Jyn held the last light of my mother, my brother, and my son. And now I had to kill her.

When Father was a thing of the material world, he taught me where the life-ending vessels in the neck were. I eyed them now, watching Jyn's pulse jump in her throat.

Kill her, Father commanded.

I cannot do this, I told Father. *I am not strong enough.*

You must be.

If Jyn were younger, I could preserve her and send her off to the supercontinent. But my trade partner longed for younger people, for whatever ominous reason, I did not know. The last time I sent someone as old as Jyn, with stiff joints and a gravelly voice, Sillian Reeves did not let me live it down for quite some time.

It only left one fate for Jyn. I looked at my aunt one final time. The light in her eyes did not go out, even now.

"I will find your secrets in Cape after I kill you." I did not recognize my detached voice. "It will be fun. But you, Jyn, have worn out your welcome."

Jyn did not back down. She did not cower. She only looked at me with an expression that said *You deserve what's coming to you.*

Were my secrets in Cape? I supposed I would have to find out. But for now, there was only one thing I could do to ensure Jyn's knowledge did not leave her.

You've killed family before, Father said. *Do it once more.*

I found my target and turned myself over to Father. The rubies on my dagger's hilt glittered in the sun, foreshadowing spilled blood.

I averted my gaze. I could not take the weight of my family's eyes staring me down in this moment.

With Father's help, I slashed my blade.

CHAPTER 24

CORINN

Life moved quickly on the supercontinent. One week of training led to two weeks, then three weeks. Running two miles turned to three, to four. My dumbbells doubled in weight. I practiced my fighting skills with Anya and Dalton, the steps becoming easier, slightly more natural.

Then things became more complicated. Anya commanded her training group to work on one specific body region while weightlifting, which caused more soreness than I'd ever felt before. It made the subsequent running nearly impossible, and once I was back at Cass's and my hotel, I'd fall onto the couch and spend hours recovering.

I also learned more about the qualifications to be accepted into Arlo James's logistics group. Turned out, there was a *small prerequisite*, in the words of Anya: a logics exam. Only those who passed this test could try out for the logistics team.

So I had to start putting in hours of work toward bettering myself mentally, too. Dalton gave me books to read—some written by leaders and legends of Sector A, and others by humans long before this land was divided into sectors.

I always thought bound books of paper could be nothing more than journal entries and reciting life, recording it for memory or for future generations. Books were virtually nonexistent on Miota, but the few I'd seen had used the rare commodity of paper to document important events and details of life.

But the books Dalton gave me were different. Some were about Red Fox specifically and how it became Sector A's capital following war, and others were about the entire League—LIS, as I had to remind myself.

But some books contained stories of completely fictional lands. At first, I didn't understand the concept—in Pointe, we had field tales, truths simply stretched too far and wide, which were common among the farmers in the Low Tier. They were the closest thing to these supercontinental fiction books.

Even after grasping the concept, I still wondered *why* books like this existed. But upon finishing one, I realized: they, too, contained vital information to the preservation of humanity. They contained potent lessons learned not through experience, but entertainment. They highlighted courage and believing in oneself; kindness and gratitude; of being a force of good in the world, no matter how dark your surroundings. And I couldn't help but wonder if Miota might be a better place if it housed books filled with fiction.

These books, Dalton claimed, would help me pass the logics exam. Still, I asked Anya if I could study with her.

"We're teammates," she answered like it was a vow, some promise we had to keep to each other.

I chewed on my cheek. "So . . . that's a yes?"

She shot me an incredulous look. "Teammates work together, Corinn. No matter what."

I hated how her words tied around my intestines, constricting my insides.

Work together . . . no matter what . . .

I was part of something greater than myself. I was dependent on others, and in turn, they counted on me. But I didn't need anyone tying themselves to me—especially not Anya, a complete stranger, someone unaware of Miota. She didn't know the baggage I heaved around. The hidden nation I carried with me.

My days stretched, now starting even earlier. I met with Anya before training, long preceding dawn's first light, when the night sky still ruled.

Which part of a maglev provides shock absorption? What type of current runs through the Platform's support beams to keep potentially infected rats from climbing them? How do you use the word "abrogate" in a sentence? If someone ran 14% of a 5-kilometer race, how many centimeters did they run?

There were too many random facts, numbers, words, and formulas bobbing around in my head by the time the whole group met for physical training.

Dalton taught me how to use different forms for lifting heavier weights. Anya coached me in my running form, showing me how to keep my core tight and open my stride to go farther faster. After training, I'd brush up on my fighting techniques—sometimes with Anya, sometimes alone, and sometimes with Charlie, the bulky woman who could easily knock me unconscious if she wanted. Charlie seemed old enough to nearly be a mother to me, and she'd adopted such a role in our training group. She looked out for everyone, ensuring our success and celebrating victories with us.

After simultaneously too much time and not nearly enough, it was the night before the logics exam. Tucked away in my hotel for the night, I pored over notes I'd scribbled with Anya and digital memory cards with equations, definitions, and other bits of information.

Cass turned on a lamp, and the amount of light shocked me. I hadn't realized it was nearly dark outside, and I'd been squinting to read the words on my papers.

"Thanks." I grinned at him.

The prince sat next to me at the table, pursing his lips as he glanced at my ink ridden pages. "You're nervous about this test."

"Well, yeah." Too much rode on this exam. If I didn't pass, it would wrinkle every plan I'd made since being brought here.

"Because of what Lorella might do if you don't make the team?" Cass wrung his hands together, showcasing his nerves. "She's said some things that scare me, Corinn. She . . . you might . . . we could be completely on our own if this team doesn't work out for you."

I chewed on the thought. While this added another layer to my determination, it wasn't the foundation.

"I just want to do something *good* for Miota," I replied. "I want to help our country, and I want to see everyone I love again. And I think this team is the way there."

Cass hummed. "I get that. I miss my stupid family more than anything."

I grinned toward him at the mention of his *stupid* family. That much, they were.

"Have you and Lorella made any big breakthroughs lately?" He and Lorella worked when they could to piece together information from both sides of the ocean, trying to connect threads of history and sum them into a tale of time.

"It's starting to look a little bleak," Cass admitted, sighing and shifting in his seat. His hair, grown out to the base of his neck, became a blond veil across his forehead. He pushed the locks out of the way, causing them to stick up. The image would surely make his mother cringe, and that thought summoned a smile from me.

"We're learning a lot, sure, but none of it seems to help right now," Cass elaborated. "There's nothing about Biourica's secrets, how to exploit them, anything like that. Lorella would never admit it, but she wants you to make this team *with* Dalton. I think she's starting to realize the more eyes and ears we have on that team, the better."

It narrowed my consciousness back to making the team. "If I make the cut, I'll have to turn the people against Arlo. If I can't do that much, we'll invade Miota, and I don't know what kind of a chance our home will have."

Cass's hand twitched, freezing, before he ultimately reached for my hand, holding it softly. My heart battered, and I felt the sudden need to swallow. But I remained still, letting Cass's hand roam over mine, providing silent comfort.

"You can do it," Cass said, his now too-rough voice slowly dragging across my skin. "You'll pass this test tomorrow. You'll make the team. And you'll save Miota."

I quivered. "And where does the Prince of Miota fit into all that?"

His blue eyes, ringed with brown, swallowed me whole. "Wherever I can. Wherever you'd like."

I didn't know what to say—what to *do*. I glanced out the window at the low-hanging moon. It rose each night despite its phase of waxing or waning. I bottled the courage Griff gave me on Miota and capped it with Cass's faith.

"You're a prince," I said. "You have the power to *shake* Miota, if you go back with us."

"Go back," he repeated, withdrawing his touch. The hotel's cold air hit my skin. "Go back to Miota, and . . . fight."

"I'm Low-Tiered," I continued. "I'd have to fight with force. But *you* could fight with your words. You could command anything of anyone on that island." I leaned back and crossed my arms. "Cass, you could rewrite reality within the Fort."

A slick layer of fear seemed to cover Miota's heir as he waged internal war with himself.

"That's getting ahead of ourselves, I know." I returned to my pages. "But it's the future I hope we have."

"Well, one step at a time." Cass retreated to the bathroom, and seconds later, the shower water ran.

I continued studying for the logics exam.

The morning came in full force. Cass offered me oatmeal before I left, though my stomach felt like a solid rock, unable to digest food.

"You need to eat something," Cass urged. He picked at his own bowl of oatmeal, dressed with entirely too much brown sugar and milk. "I know you're nervous, but you don't need to be. This is logic—and you're not stupid."

I shot him a vexed glare, though it was doused with too much amusement. "*Thanks*, Cass."

He snorted. "I'm just saying. You'll be back tonight, and we'll be celebrating your victory."

"I hope so."

After forcing down a few bites of oatmeal, I got dressed and digitally mapped out my maglev route using my panel. *Grid*. The exam was taking place at a local university, High Citadel, which I'd gathered was an optional school some attended after finishing primary school.

I left early, giving myself extra time in case I got lost on the maglev or got off at a wrong spot. Luckily, Anya ended up getting on my maglev with a few stops still to go.

"Hey!" She smiled and plopped into the seat next to mine. "This is exciting! I've been saving for this maglev ride. Figured it would be a good morning to ride instead of walk."

My lips parted. "You don't normally use the maglev?"

Red tinted her dark cheeks. "I could probably count my maglev rides on one hand. Which helps keep me in good shape, at least."

"What about rats, though?"

"Eh, the odds of an infected one finding me are slim." She frowned. "Well, not *slim* slim, because I've seen people die of red bite before, but it's not something I just worry about all the time . . ."

"I'll pay for your rides," I blurted. "At least to and from Biourica when we have training."

"No, Corinn—"

"It's the least I could do. You've done so much to help me, and I wouldn't have gotten this far without you." The rest of my sentiment clogged in my throat as the heaviness of the words hit me.

Anya's eyes watered. "You're a good friend, Corinn. Thank you."

Friend. Was Anya my friend? Some fraction of my heart wanted to open up, but the title came with too much weight, too much responsibility. It only summoned the memory of Salem's lifeless body. His pale skin, blue lips, closed eyes . . . Dr. Klemmins smiling over me, and Julia Delldova's kettle of boiling water.

My vision went black, and my head felt too light, made of air and haunted memories.

I didn't respond to Anya, and the ruffling of people around us filled our silence until we reached High Citadel, an environment looking like something of another world. Red Fox was metallic, made of soaring buildings and blinding lights. But this university was built of green lawns and blank space, of bronze and shrubs. It looked like a place Griff and I had dreamed up, made of freedom.

"If I had money," Anya muttered to me, "I'd go to school here."

We unloaded the maglev, and I nearly collapsed at the sea of people waiting to take the logics exam. Swarms of citizens gathered, lining up in messy columns to enter a glass structure.

I hadn't felt like this since the thick of Accolade. Times and people and places had changed, but I hadn't. I was the unlikely contender.

I'd made a mess of Accolade, but I could remedy it now. My second chance—my *last* chance.

I didn't see Dalton, Charlie, or anyone else from our training group before employees ushered us inside to a room consisting of neat rows of monitor screens. I found my assigned seat at a sleek screen and waited for the test to start.

All attempts of reeling in my worries proved futile. The odds stacked against me only pushed heavier on my chest as time ticked on. As we opened the exam to begin. As I answered each question, poring over the words and contemplating every answer. As people finished the test when half my test still remained.

It's logic—and you're not stupid. I hoped to the moon Cass was right. But I was from Miota, and certain aspects of life worked *very* differently on that island.

Every thought threatened to melt my brain by the time I reached the end of the test. I didn't know how to feel after answering the last question—I'd developed such an apathy toward everything while in this room, and I submitted the exam.

I *passed.*

My breaths became fuller; my spirits rose higher.

But as I recalled all I still had to do—make one of the seventy-five team spots and turn the recruits against Arlo's commands—I realized this fire may still burn me yet. I'd avoided the ashes for now, but this mission was far from over.

CHAPTER 25

CORINN

Competition threaded Miota and Sector A together.

Accolade had made beasts of people, morphing silver into steel. Similarly, training teams bashed heads and teeth the following week, during tryouts for the logistics team.

Everyone from Anya's training team had passed the logics exam, which meant we all contended for one of the seventy-five spots available in Arlo's discreet army.

Five days called for five contests.

It helped me scale the world down, to take it one day at a time instead of thinking in terms of fighting off the entire supercontinent. Each day would bring me one step closer to Miota.

Five days to give it my all. Five days to prove I hadn't been wasting the last month of my life. To prove I was stronger than doubts and fears.

The first day came with heavy rain, which would hopefully help my case. All recruits would be running today, given a rank among the masses upon reaching the finish line.

Just over three miles. I'd run that distance over a dozen times now . . . but I didn't know how fast my pace would be. Anya told me to pace with her in the first mile, then pace with Charlie, a little slower, so I didn't wear too quickly.

"We can do this," Charlie heaved when we connected in the second mile.

"Dig deep," I said, spouting water as rain fell into my mouth. "And find strength."

Charlie huffed. "I like that."

It was the saying I'd learned from Bernard, my tutor back home. Cass's uncle. My secret-keeper for four years. Though he and his brother, the king, had used me, the advice would always stick, lodged so deeply in my heart, it couldn't be shaken.

Not even now, in the pouring rain, an ocean between us.

I gasped by the end, sucking in rain and muggy air alike, flopping and bounding toward the finish line with legs and arms of rubber. Still, I finished with my best time yet, and I held my rank close.

167th place.

Yes, this was like Biourica's abridged version of Accolade. And I was not off to a strong start. Dalton placed in the top fifty, and Anya barely crossed her way into the top one hundred.

By the next morning, sunshine had driven the rainclouds away and replaced them with hot moisture. I sweated before we even began today's event of weight-lifting. If there was a method to the rounds and small groups, I didn't know it. But some sort of electrical equipment tracked us, and when I glanced at the leaderboard outside Biourica at the end of the day, I found my place.

153rd. I was stagnant.

It remained that way until day four, when I discovered I could climb debris well, summoning the strength I had to pull my body up and over structures.

It was as Griff taught me when we'd broken into Pointe. I'd seen him navigate my city's brick wall with ease, and I mustered Griff's movements into my own now, letting his grace filter through my muscle and bones.

It also helped that the higher I climbed, the freer I felt. Life in Red

Fox, for as big a place as it was, sometimes felt pinched too tight, forced in all the wrong spots. I didn't belong here. This wasn't the plan. And sometimes it seemed the only way out was *up*.

After finishing the climbing activities with cramping fingers and tender toes, I found myself in eighty-eighth place.

Thirteen slots. The number clanged through my brain all night. Maybe that was why there was a night in between each event: more time to let nerves win. It was another test in itself, one requiring not physical fortitude but mental grit.

The fifth and final test day required holding a plank position for as long as possible. Thirteen to beat; thirteen people to overpower.

For Miota. For my family—Mom, Dad, Theo, Tellie, Grandma. For my friends. For Griff, who surely remained within an arm's length of Julia these days. For Hallan, who'd been alive but hadn't known who she truly was. For justice. For a kinder world.

My arms buckled. But I did not fall completely. I forced my shoulders and hips to hold. I relented. I endured.

I ended in seventy-fourth place.

Lorella's apartment basked in candlelight and laughter. The space welcomed me, feeling like a familiar groove. Though I hadn't particularly enjoyed my few weeks in this apartment, they'd been my introduction to Sector A. This was the place I'd first discovered Cass was still alive.

"Welcome!" Lorella squealed, embracing me in one arm and Cass in the other as we walked through her entryway, into the bright kitchen I'd missed. Cass's and my hotel had been nice temporarily, but each day in it felt like wearing worn shoes growing too small.

"And congratulations," Lorella told me, smiling as bright as the candles littering her home. "I know I had my doubts, but I always *wanted* you to make the team."

"Thank you." I returned her grin, pushing from my mind the fight we'd had last time I was here.

I would remember that side of her, though, and I would remain wary. I knew she could bite with that same smile.

Cass and I sat at Lorella's table, laden with hamburgers alongside an assortment of snacks: crunchy chips, crumbling brown sugar cookies, and chewy candies.

Cass offered to make me a burger, and I let him. When Dalton and Colton entered next, I hugged Dalton, eager to thank him for all his help with my training.

"I couldn't have done any of it without you," I told him.

"I'm glad we're both in this," Dalton responded.

Colton's predatory green eyes danced, feasting on me from behind his younger brother. He didn't speak, but he didn't need to. I understood his message.

He didn't think I was worth anything. Colton believed I was only what his brother made me.

After Neave and Saoirse, Lorella's aunt, showed up, the celebration fell into vibrant motion. Colton handed out glasses of champagne to everyone; Dalton and Neave made a game of throwing popped corn into each other's mouths; Lorella and her aunt spoke in the living room, the pair hovered near the glowing glass column filled with fire.

Now that September was here, the nights would soon begin getting colder. This was the first month I thought of as autumn back home. The season called for cooler weather and gray skies—for the last great harvest of Pointe's Low-Tiered farmers before the cold subjected grounds to infertility. Before any chance of snow came, keeping us indoors and rubbing our hands together underneath thin, matted blankets for warmth. My family's shack never had temperature-regulated air like the buildings in Castle Circle had, nor like the buildings here in Red Fox. In the winter, we were left to pack together like canned vegetables, relying on our bodies for warmth.

Meanwhile, Lorella had a glass column of fire in her living room.

"I can't believe this is all for you," Cass murmured, leaning his head playfully onto my shoulder for a moment. We sat together at Lorella's kitchen table, basking in the scene around us.

"It's not," I brushed him off. I took another sip of my bitter champagne, steadily warming my chest. "Dalton made the team, too."

"He has much-needed backup now." Cass slid an arm across the back of my chair. "If you're going to Miota, there needs to be someone on the team who's been there before. Someone who knows how life works there."

Cass's sentiment grated against me. He spoke like his father's son too often these days, speaking of *my* involvement with saving Miota and never his own.

I'd asked Cass where he fit into the plan. *Wherever you want me.*

I swigged my champagne, liquifying my bravery, and I spoke outright. "When we go to Miota, I want you with us. We'll need a royal—we'll need *you.*"

Cass angled his face toward mine so his lips hovered at my ear. "Corinn . . ."

"*That's* where I want you," I ordered, turning my head to better face him. Miota's prince stilled, dampening even his breath. "That's where I *need* you. With me. On Miota."

"Do you want me there for your sake, or for Miota's?" he whispered, barely able to draw out the question. His eyes turned tumultuous as the sea, rocking steadily between peace and destruction. As if my answer would be the thing to either steady him—or undo him.

My mouth went dry.

Cass blinked in a frenzy, turning pale. "If you don't want to answer . . . oh, *by the moon.* Sorry I asked." He withdrew his arm.

It expanded my awareness back to the entire apartment, and I realized just how folded into each other Cass and I had been.

Both. It was for both. But I couldn't force my mouth open to say that much, terrified of the retribution it would bring. "It's fine." I cleared my throat. "I'm . . . I'll be back."

I stood from the table and retreated, fleeing, longing for the freedom I'd experienced when climbing the other day. Wanting to feel anything but stuck. The only problem was I didn't know where to run or what to feel. I was a mess of a person, still collecting the mismatched pieces of being brought here against all my plans.

" . . .talking to Reno tonight, and he'll probably know the answer." Lorella's voice bled into my ear, and I perked, my steps acquiring a new target.

I approached Lorella and Saoirse, whose heads were tucked together in a conspiratory manner, the same way I'd often seen Griff and his friend Lorenzo during Accolade.

"Max Reno?" I questioned, looking at Lorella for any tips of information. "You're talking to him tonight?"

Her face hardened, slamming me out of her thoughts. "None of your concern, Corinn."

"It *is*," I argued as I planted my feet, unwilling to move from this spot until I gained more information. "I'm about to go live in Biourica for who knows how long. If there's any sort of plan between you and Max, I need to learn it *today*."

Speaking the words into existence slammed my future into my posture in a way I hadn't expected. The seventy-five of us were going to live in a designated, secure place while we learned to work and train together into a functioning, well-operating team. I wouldn't come home to Cass every night, and I wouldn't hear about Miota through distant paths of Lorella and Max.

Dalton and I would be on our own. We needed to learn everything *now*, before Arlo James tucked us away into his realm.

"She's right," Saoirse muttered to her niece. The woman's eyes crinkled. "No one here can afford to keep secrets right now."

Lorella scanned the room before taking a shuffling step toward me. "If you come by tomorrow, I'll tell you everything Max and I discuss."

"I won't have time," I said, straightening my spine to grow an inch. "Neither will Dalton. We have Elementary all day tomorrow."

Elementary: the basics required to officially become an inducted member of Biourica's logistics team. From what I could tell, I'd get a haircut, injections of vaccines and preventative medicines, and a chemical shower. I'd give blood, start a new diet, and more I couldn't remember. It sounded like I was signing my life away, becoming nothing more than a sentient piece of equipment.

As if that wasn't exactly what I'd been my whole life on Miota. This place and my home weren't so different after all.

"Hmm." Lorella tapped her foot and thrummed a finger on her chin. After glancing at her aunt yet again, she finally broke. "*Fine.* You can join the call. But it isn't open to other people—only you and Dalton because of Elementary. The call won't even happen until later tonight, though."

My shoulders sagged. "I'm okay with that."

"And you can only join if Dalton agrees to join, too."

I decided not to ask if she trusted Dalton more than me, warranting her reason for wanting him present.

Besides, it didn't matter much. Something deep in my soul knew Dalton would side with me on this. This boy and I were now deeper allies than anyone else in our small rebellion.

We would be present for Lorella's call. Tonight, I would speak with Max Reno for the first time since his betrayal on Miota's beach.

CHAPTER 26

GRIFF

I tapped my foot, the dull sound filling Abner's otherwise silent office. My occasional sigh also filled the room as I waited for the king.

In the meantime, I flattened a hand against my stomach, feeling the papers tucked beneath my shirt. The papers Jyn had given me—I'd retrieved them from their hiding spot, and I'd read them thoroughly. They were plans to leave the castle, made by Elizabeth Hepper, Julia's mother. They were also the instructions on how to maneuver and control the boats placed on Miota's southern shore. I kept them close now, ready to show them to Abner and Max as the end-goal of my concrete plan. These boats were our saving grace from tyranny.

I used the room's shadows to my advantage, painting myself among them in case someone other than Abner entered. But the room remained still until the king arrived. Moonlight peeled through the window's thick layers of painted glass, dressing him in creamy light. When he saw me, his face tightened as he tucked himself behind a mask.

"Your Highness," he ground out.

I gave a closed-lip smile. "Your Majesty."

"How did you get in here?"

"I'm going with you," I started, ignoring his question and getting straight to the point. "Into the tunnels." When Abner didn't speak, I tilted my head. "Unless you're in here to do some late-night work?"

Abner snarled, accepting I'd figured him out. He was escaping to Pointe tonight to meet with Bernard. "My brother doesn't want to see you."

"I won't be going to Pointe," I assured the king. "I need Max. He's talking to whoever Anzalone is tonight."

Abner dug a small carving knife from his vest pocket, and my breath lurched. "If you don't even know who Anzalone is—"

"*I know* Anzalone is Max's contact from the supercontinent," I interrupted, leaning onto my toes, ready to spring into action if Abner decided his best move was to attack me. Without a weapon of my own, I wasn't sure how I would beat him, but I believed in my ability to outrun the man. "And the person keeping Corinn right now."

Abner halted, features slackened and knife midair. His knuckles were paler than moonlight as he gripped the hilt. "*What?*"

My insides crawled, ready to eat themselves alive. Didn't Abner know Corinn was alive? Didn't Max and Abner share all information?

Or were there secrets even among teammates?

My tongue turned to dirt. "Corinn is alive. She's with Anzalone."

Abner knitted his brow and adjusted the multiple straps on his dark vest. "Why do you think that?" Curiosity undermined his neutral tone.

"I *know* it because Max Reno told me." I didn't mind revealing my source. The three of us couldn't afford to have secrets. Besides, maybe Abner trusting Max Reno a little less could work to my advantage.

Abner grunted. He spun the small knife in his hand, and I tensed, ready to run. But the king instead stuck the hilt at me, offering it over.

I met his gray eyes. Sometimes they embodied steel and other times storm clouds. But right now, they were unlit charcoals, the material made of Salfordian wood—tamed for now, but ready to burn if necessary.

"There's just one rule in the tunnels," Abner said as I intercepted the weapon. "Every man for himself down there. You never quite know who you'll see or what you'll find. But if you end up at the tip of someone else's knife, there's no saying I'll be able to save you."

"Got it." I tucked the knife into my pants, keeping it available to unsheathe. "I've been thinking of a plan. To get us all off this island within the month. I'm going to tell Max about it tonight so he can figure out the details with Anzalone, if you want to hear it, too."

Abner shook his head. "No time now. If Max approves of it, I'll hear about it then." He stalked toward his office's bookshelf, which housed trinkets and ink and half-used candles. "And he'll only approve if it's completely, undeniably feasible. Without getting caught. And even then, I'll still be able to shut it all down if I don't think it'll work."

"Understood." I watched Abner produce a metal key and slide his sofa away. He jabbed the key into the ground, and a trap door opened, not unlike the door Corinn and I had found in Pointe's abandoned greenhouse.

The king's eyes leveled against mine. "Time to go. Follow me, and I'll point to where you branch off. Follow the tunnel to its very end— that's usually where Max speaks to Anzalone with the comm device she sent him."

She. My cheeks reddened; I'd assumed Anzalone was a man.

The bottom half of Abner's body disappeared into the door. "You don't have your panel, right?"

"I'm not an idiot." I produced my flashlight, one of the last relics of Dad. "Just got this and my pocket watch."

"Good. Remember what I said. If something goes wrong, I'm not saving you."

"Yes." I got to the ground, ready to slink into the darkness of Miota's intricate tunnel network. "Every man for himself."

After half an hour of creeping along behind Abner, we parted ways. He ventured into a narrower artery of dirt and caked earth while I followed the main path, constructed of a metal skeleton.

I didn't like admitting my bravery faltered, crumbling at the edges, without Abner's company. Though I didn't trust him, he'd at least navigated these underground channels before. I was now blindly following this carved trail to its end, where I only hoped on the moon I'd find Max Reno.

Automatic lights flickered on every couple dozen feet, meaning I didn't need my flashlight. I wished they could turn off, though—it left a trail of my whereabouts, which was the last thing I wanted down here.

I kept my eyes and ears peeled, walking on my toes to prevent my shoes from clacking and leaving even more proof of my treason, until I reached the end.

The same second the lights turned on, revealing Max Reno from around the tunnel's bend, he fired a gun.

The ricocheting bullet pinged the floor to my side, hardly missing me.

Max didn't fire again. "And that's why I purposefully miss the first time," he started. "In case it's an ally."

My heart battered in my ears, and my hand gripped the knife Abner gave me. *Ally*. Max was my ally. Even though he just shot a weapon at me—near me, rather.

"What the hell does that mean?" a voice filled with static asked from within Max's communication device, a sleek black piece.

Max motioned me over with a flick of his head. He spoke to the woman, Anzalone, while looking at me. "Lorella, put her back on. Before we go further here, there's someone she needs to talk to."

When Max held the device out to me, I shook. I was . . . supposed to speak?

I swallowed, blinking fast as nerves almost knocked me to the ground. What had I walked in on? "Hello?"

After a light pause, a voice I would never forget in a thousand lifetimes hit me. "Griff?"

I made a small noise as relief almost knocked me to the ground, threatening to drown me. And I would *gladly* go, gladly meet my doom at her hand. "*Lovely.*"

PART THREE

"He [Sillian Reeves] did not give me a choice. I had to agree to raise the quota. If we cannot find a way to stop this from happening in future years, Cass's rule is going to end very bitterly."

—*Diary of Julia Delldova, entry from 05 January, 26 JD*

CHAPTER 27

CORINN

As Lorella waited for Max Reno to answer his own comm device, my pulse bounded against my skin, each beat of silence sentencing me to holding my breath.

Lorella, Dalton, and I formed a standing circle in Lorella's living room. Saoirse had left first, claiming she needed a full night's sleep to survive. Colton and Cass went next—the former walking with the latter back to our hotel because of how many times Cass mentioned he didn't want to be bitten by a rat. Neave was slow to leave; she eventually departed, though not before stuffing a few extra beer bottles into her bag. Lorella had told her friend she was acting like she did in their university days together, though she'd said it with a laugh, and I doubted Neave took the reprimand to heart.

It left only the three of us to witness this call with Max.

The guard finally picked up, and when he spoke, I heard the Miotan loud of clear. "Four-five-seven."

"Five-seven," Lorella answered.

Dalton and I exchanged a glance, wondering what significance the numbers held.

"I . . . have two accompanying me," Lorella continued.

"Let me guess," Max chimed. "Corinn and one of the James brothers?"

I lifted a brow.

"Yeah," Lorella answered. "Corinn and Dalton. They're joining Arlo's logistics team, and they leave tomorrow to basically live under Biourica's jurisdiction."

Max remained silent for too long. "So they made the team? Both of them?"

"Yes."

Max cursed. "Corinn? Can she hear me?"

"Loud and clear," I answered.

"By the moon." Silence. A sniff. "You're okay, kid."

I swallowed the lump in my throat. I was okay, despite all that had happened. Tears overtook my vision. "I'm okay." I needed to hear it just as much as Max did.

"You need to be careful with Biourica," Max started, shifting into a tone of reprimand. "Ideally, you'd be staying as far away from the company as possible. Lorella's already told me about your plan to join this team—I was pissed when I found out. I sided with Lorella, for the record. You shouldn't have risked that."

Heat flared in me as Lorella gazed elsewhere, likely basking in Max's scolding.

Before I could defend myself, Max moved on. "But since you made the team, all you can do is be careful. Don't do anything stupid. Stay in line, and do exactly as you're told—nothing more, nothing less. Got it?"

Lorella spoke for me. "She's still going to spy for us while she's part of this team." The woman looked at me. "That was part of her bargain."

"Spy?" Max laughed drily. "No. She's going to stay *safe*. I can't be worrying about Corinn, too, when I already have Griff trying to make a break for it with the entire island under Julia's nose . . ."

His voice faded out. My vision darkened. "What's Griff doing?" I interrupted.

Max cut himself off. "Griff? He wants everyone off the island in the next month. I can't find a reasonable way to make it happen, though."

By the moon. Griff must have figured it out, about asympton. At our last meeting, in the castle's hospital wing, I'd forgotten to tell him about the disease's falsehood. I thought I'd single-handedly doomed Miota for letting the secret disappear alongside me.

But Griff had figured it out, as I should have known he would.

Laughter bubbled within me. Of *course* he knew. He was Griffith Howard. He could do anything. He was going to save Miota.

"He knows about asympton, then," I whispered.

"Sure does," Max confirmed. "He wants to get everyone off Miota before Julia sends next month's people."

Griff knew everything. This was as close to him as I'd felt since arriving here, yet he couldn't have been farther away. I needed him *with me.*

"Which is why you need to stay put," Max finished. "Corinn, I can't deal with you *and* Griff trying to take on the biggest names in the world. You two were a match made in the stars for that, you know."

"Are you helping him get people off the island?" I asked. "You can't bring people to Red Fox—"

"As I've told Max time and again," Lorella butted in. She and I hovered over the comm device while Dalton leaned back, opting out of this liaison business. "It's why Max is under my orders to not let Griff try anything funny. Plus, they don't have a good way off the island. Biourica only has a few boats—enough for maybe a couple hundred people if you crammed."

Max's silence met Lorella.

My own brain spun this time. If there wasn't a good way off Miota, no matter how noble the cause, attempts to leave would only endanger people instead of liberate them.

Before I could say anything, a throttling *bang* drowned out Max's side of the call. "And that's why I purposefully miss the first time. In case it's an ally."

Lorella, Dalton, and I exchanged puzzled glances.

"What the hell does that mean?" Lorella spat, unamused.

"Lorella, put her back on," Max ordered, commandment filling his tone. "Before we go further here, there's someone she needs to talk to."

She. Me. I tried piecing it all together, too slowly. Because before I knew it, that rough voice sounded from Max's side of the line, and time and distance collapsed into each other, slamming me out of my body.

"Hello?"

I knew Griff Howard's low voice from anywhere. Hearing it made my face go numb. My limbs lost all connection to my brain, and I was now operating on gravity alone, the kind that made me believe the moon was equally as drawn to the tides as they were to the moon.

"Griff?" I uttered.

He let out a shaky exhale. "*Lovely.*"

The world outside of Griff's voice simmered away. Lorella, Dalton, the apartment . . . I fell to my knees, taking grip of the comm device like my life depended on it. "Griff. By the moon, it's you! *Griff!*" I laughed.

He let out a noise sounding like a sob. "*You're alive.* Are you okay? Are you all right?"

"Yes." I sniffed. "I'm alive. I'm okay."

"You're sure."

"Yes," I said on a shaky laugh. "Ugh, I *miss* you."

"I *promise* not as much as I miss you." I envisioned his tentative smile too clearly.

I knew the tears on my cheeks mirrored his own, both of us apart yet still connected. My heart simultaneously melted and sheared, pressing itself together at the sound of Griff's voice, only to rip apart at the realization he wasn't *here.*

"I *knew* you were alive," he choked out. "*I knew it.*"

"You had faith in us," I said, feeling like a half-moon, grinning for Griff while churning with darkness beneath. By the sound of Max's earlier words and Griff's current reaction, the guard likely *hadn't* told Griff I'd survived my trial.

Griff had thought I was dead. I wanted to ruin Max for having Griff believe such a thing.

"And you figured out asympton," I finished.

"I had help. From Julia's aunt, actually. Capean. Nice lady." Even from across the ocean, he couldn't mask the restriction of his throat. Something told me Julia's aunt had met a fate she hadn't deserved, simply for her knowledge. "She wanted everyone off Miota in the next month."

My heart ripped at the hope Griff embodied.

"Griff . . ." I didn't know how to say this. "You can't bring Miota to where we are—where I am—now. It's a huge city, populated and regulated, and hiding *two* Miotans has been hard enough. Forget thousands."

"But there's a way—wait, *two* Miotans?"

I ran my tongue across my teeth. I hadn't wanted these two to collide yet, but I couldn't keep the truth from Griff. "Cass is here, too."

Griff swore, then he and Max spoke in hisses, too grainy to make out. While they sorted out matters on their end, I stood back up, adjusting my clothes and handing the device back to Lorella to hold.

"Sorry about that," I whispered so the other side of the line couldn't hear.

Dalton elbowed me, his brow knotted and eyes wide. "I thought you and Cass were . . . together?" he said, hushed.

I *burned*. "No." When Dalton opened his mouth to respond, I shushed him. "It's a long story."

To that, Dalton twitched his brow and clamped his mouth shut.

"Say there was a place to bring everyone," Griff mused, his voice rough, a brewing storm.

"We'd still need the means to do it," I countered. "There aren't enough boats here to bring everyone in that short amount of time."

"Corinn, *I* have the boats." Griff dropped the information, knowing how vital it was. Lorella froze, and Dalton leaned closer to the device.

"You?" I clarified.

"Jyn. Julia's aunt. There are boats bigger than cities on Miota's southern shore, hidden from the supercontinent. I think that's for a reason. I think . . ." A heartbeat of silence. "I think Miota's founders put them there on purpose, to give us a secret escape plan if needed."

I met Lorella's gaze, where she hung the weight of the world. She . . . *knew* something.

What? I mouthed.

Her throat bobbed. "Do you *know* the boats could get you here?" she asked Griff.

"Yes. I have instructions on everything. How to find them, start them, steer them, where the resources are kept on them . . . there are two boats, and they each fit over five thousand people. We could sail all of Miota to the supercontinent at once."

Both sides of the call were too quiet, trapped in thought. This changed everything. If Miotans could safely come here, no one left behind . . . our home could be saved in one shot.

Lorella shattered the silence. "I might know a place."

I reached for her forearm, holding hope hostage to her. She held the lives of everyone back home right now.

"In Sector B," she continued. "I've heard talk from people higher up in the government that there's a huge plot of land Biourica just bought"—she looked to me and Dalton—"to invest in Arlo's expansion plans. Anyway, I hear it's big enough to be a metropolis, and it's on the coast . . ." Fear ladened her eyes. "Obviously, Miotans couldn't stay *on* the land entirely, but maybe in a nearby town, they could pass as approved foreigners." She blinked furiously. "Griff, are there rations on the boats? Food, water, things like that?"

"Yes." He huffed. "Yeah, it sounds like these things are built for survival if needed. Nonperishable rations for five-thousand people on each, for up to three months, if you ration well."

"Hopefully by that point, you'd have another sustainable food source," Lorella thought aloud. "Has Max told you anything about Arlo James's plan with his logistics team?"

Not a chance, I thought, internally answering the question.

"I don't even know who Arlo James is," Griff said.

I rolled my eyes. What *had* Max told Griff about the plan here? Was the pair even working together these days? How had Griff come to hijack this call? What I wouldn't give to see the pair's interactions right now.

Lorella briefly explained Arlo James, Biourica, and his logistics team.

"Based on recent communications with Julia, we have reason to believe Arlo will use this logistics team to invade Miota, should she not produce enough people for her side of the trade," Lorella finished.

Griff hummed. "And you aren't . . . worried about that."

"I'm on the team, Griff," I interrupted. Nerves swarmed me at the thought of speaking this next part aloud for both parties to hear. "Dalton and I are going to turn the team to Miota's side. That way, when we come in, we'll fight *with* you. *For* you." My mouth went dry, and my voice turned low. "I'm always fighting for you, Griff."

"By the moon," he murmured, expertly turning the curse into a promise, a celestial vow only he possessed the power to fulfill. "Lovely, *nothing* can stop me from getting to you."

In this moment, I saw the fruits of what I'd somehow always known: we were unstoppable together, explosive and unwavering, with enough grit and strength between us to do the unthinkable. In my short time with princes and lost heirs and rich sons alike, no one had radiated the energy of an earth-shaker, a bone-breaker, like Griff.

The five of us schemed, balancing our unknowns with our concrete steps.

Max, the escort of asympton's victims, would ensure not everyone was sent at the next trade in three weeks, triggering Arlo to send his team to Miota. Dalton and I would work to turn the tide against Biourica, using every free second to crumble the trust between recruits and Arlo. Griff would scope out a path to Cape, pinning the easiest access to the southern boats. Lorella would serve as a bridge between worlds since Dalton and I would be cut off from these communication opportunities starting tomorrow. She would also seek out word on the status of the empty land in Sector B, judging how safe it would be to temporarily house Miotans there. But when our team was ready to mobilize, Lorella would send word to Max, who would relay the message to Griff and Abner.

Then it would be a matter of waiting for our arrival, shaking Miota to its core. And escaping with the island's population, freeing them from Julia and her wicked ensnares.

"Any questions for this call?" Lorella asked.

"Not from me," Max responded. "We'll have things to work out on this end, but with the logistics team's help, I think we'll be okay. Without you guys . . . I'm just not sure how we'd go about ushering the entire island toward something that would get them killed any other day of the year."

"I want Cass to come back with us, too," I said. "When Miotans see him, alive and unharmed, that should help."

Yes, with all of us working together, we should succeed. We should liberate Miota, once and for all, in the matter of a single day. The empire Julia's family had built in centuries would crash and burn in a matter of hours.

Max and Lorella exchanged parting words, leaving me and Griff to separate for now.

Except, now that I'd heard his voice and witnessed his energy, I didn't want this call to end. I just wanted to run home, to Griff.

"I'll see you in a few weeks," I said meekly. "Be careful, Griff."

"I'm *always* careful." But his smiling tone was cocky enough to say otherwise, and when I rolled my eyes, some part of me knew he sensed the motion.

We were two stars colliding now, spanning the great unknown to reunite. But until he was with me, until his dark gaze bathed me and lips glided on my skin, he would be *too far*.

"Just come back to me," I whispered. "Please."

"All my stars point to you."

It was the most Griff thing he could've said. Though I knew he'd won Accolade and was living in the castle with Addison, likely training to become king and reap Julia's work, he hadn't changed.

He was still *my* Griff.

Lorella disconnected the device, and I was too distracted to stop her—too enthralled in thoughts of Griffith Howard.

Once I realized what she'd done, my mouth gaped.

"I had to do that," she said, stuffing the comm device into her shirt and smoothing her clothing. "You never would've hung up on your own."

She wasn't wrong. I crossed my arms, and Lorella shared a cloudy look with Dalton before smirking back at me. "You know, I'd heard the rumors from Max about you and Griff nearly being able to become Miota's next king and queen. And if that was any proof . . ."

I used my shirt to wipe below my eyes. "Clearly, a lot's changed."

"I'm not so sure about that." Lorella eyed me with a small grin.

I huffed and ran a hand through my hair, brushing it out of my face. Tomorrow entailed a haircut, and I hoped they didn't cut it too short. On Miota, hair length didn't matter—if someone felt they needed a trim, they'd have a family member or friend use a spare pair of shears.

"Thank you," I said. "For letting us join the call. I . . . I really needed that." *I needed to hear his voice.* "And don't tell Cass about Griff, please. He needs to hear it from me."

Dalton and I were staying the night at Lorella's since it was the earliest hours of morning—hours that usually invited nothing but turmoil on the streets outside. I readied myself to sleep in Lorella's spare bed, the place I'd slept for a few weeks when first arriving here.

Dalton skirted into the room, raising his hands. "I come in peace. I just didn't know if you . . . well, if you wanted to talk about any of that."

From the bed, I hugged my knees to my chest. "No."

"Corinn." Dalton was softer in private, choosing to show more of his soul. If we'd been on display in Biourica's front lawn, as was our typical meeting place these last few weeks, he'd undoubtedly start sparring with me, using his words *and* movements to provoke me. But in here, he was smoothed out. "You lost someone close to you. Was it Griff?"

My eyes clamped shut. "No," I shot. "It *wasn't.* It was my best friend. And I'm *not* going to talk about that, so let me go to bed if that's all you want." I plopped onto my side, turning my back to Dalton.

No movement ensued. "Then I won't ask," the boy replied *too* softly. "But if you want to . . . tell me about your home."

I swallowed the painful lump rising in my throat. I would not cry, even as tears welled in me. "I can't."

"You can't, or you won't?"

"Both." I tugged the blanket up to my chin.

Dalton heaved a sigh and drew nearer. I braced myself. "I know survivor's guilt when I see it, Corinn—I've been there, too." His voice stretched thin. "And I'm just saying, from experience, it may help to talk about Miota. I *am* trying to help."

I rolled over, daring to meet the boy's eyes. They glowed, showing no signs of trickery. He was genuine.

He was being brave, inviting me to do the same. And since we were teammates, about to be closed off within Biourica together, I caved.

I first told him of my family: Mom and Dad, my brother Theo, my cousin Tellie, and my grandmother. I decided not to mention Tellie's parents, my aunt and uncle, who'd died of asympton. Were they here somewhere?

I didn't speak of Salem. But I briefly spoke of Griff, tasting his name as if it would draw his presence nearer. I told Dalton of how we met, how he'd known me, and how we planned to win Accolade.

"But like I said," I finished, raising my eyebrows, "a lot's changed."

Dalton shrugged. "In circumstance, maybe. But I notice how you cave inward so easily, and I just wonder . . . if maybe *you're* still . . ."

"Trapped?" Tethered and chained to the day it all went wrong, when Addison stole Griff from me—the day I'd sealed Salem's death, sealed my ruin on Miota.

"Yes."

I averted my gaze, pinning it to the cotton bedspread. And I nodded. "Always."

CHAPTER 28

CORINN

Within twenty-four hours, I was no longer of my own flesh and blood. I was a weapon made for Biourica, one part of a seventy-five-person whole.

I entered Biourica as Corinn Januski, Low-Tiered Miotan passing as a citizen of Sector A, and I emerged Corinn Januski of Arlo James's logistics team.

Biourica employees in all-white prodded me, studying my skin and noting my potential identification markers: freckles, birthmarks, and scars. They then stuck me with needles, some of which injected serums into my veins and others which drew blood to be collected in small vials. After that came the haircut. My blonde strands, which had always brushed near the bottom of my rib cage, now fell just past my shoulders. I didn't recognize myself in a mirror, and it almost felt like I was missing a limb, some part of me I'd always known.

There wasn't much packing to do, since Biourica would provide us uniforms and essentials. I didn't make it back to the hotel room I shared with Cass until after the sun had set. At least I'd get to tell him goodbye this time around, receiving a chance I wasn't given when he'd been abducted from Miota.

The moment I entered our room, Cass jumped up from bed and crushed me in a hug.

"So . . . tomorrow," he said in a breath against my hairline.

I shivered at the brush of his lips on my skin. "Tomorrow. Five o'clock report time."

"I'm proud of you," Cass murmured. "I know you have to turn the crew against Arlo, but please be careful with how you do it. I can't . . . I can't lose you, Corinn."

"I'll be careful," I promised. I couldn't guarantee anything else, like my success or my safety.

Dalton had been right last night: I was trapped. Trapped, not only in the past, but in the present, stuck between achieving two opposing goals. How would I remain stealthy while planting the seeds for Arlo's destruction? And if I couldn't turn the team against Arlo, what good would going to Miota bring?

I let Cass hold me for far too long as I wrapped my thoughts around the insurmountable tasks at hand. I would hold the power to either save Miota or destroy it.

The sun hadn't yet risen when we congregated in front of Biourica, ready to be welcomed inside. I'd ridden the maglev with Anya, sticking to my promise of paying for her rides. This would be the last one for a while, given that we were now going to *live* in Biourica.

I wondered if I'd run into any other Miotans, those subject to Red Fox's trade with Julia.

The group of seventy-five bounded with a nervous energy, winding tighter together by the second as everyone clashed, speaking and baring teeth.

"What was your final rank?" some asked, ready to brag about their numbers. Though we were all a team, this felt like when I'd gathered with all of Accolade's competitors.

Three clad in black—two women flanking a burly man in the

middle—came out of Biourica and raised their hands, standing in front of the main entrance.

Those in the front of the group squatted or sat. "Quiet down!" a small handful shouted to the rest of the group. They shushed everyone, smirking with cocky grimaces, embracing the sense of control. I rolled my eyes, crossing my arms and standing in the back with Anya, Dalton, and Charlie.

The three leaders from Biourica introduced themselves before the man in the middle, Zephyr, shouted orders at us.

We'd be moving into one of three pre-assigned barracks on the outskirts of Red Fox, outside the bustle of city life. In these combines, we'd learn to work together in small units, building comradery. We wouldn't live within Biourica at all, but outside Red Fox. Cut off from the city.

While this would make it easier to sway my team against Arlo, it would also mean I'd only live with one-third of the recruits—I'd never get to speak with the majority. And what if I was assigned to a different barracks than Dalton?

Already, the plan we'd hatched mere days ago was foiled. And now it was too late to change—Max was going to force Arlo's attentions onto Miota by not providing enough people next month. Arlo was *going* to send his team.

And at best, only twenty-five of us would know the truth. Fifty people would add fuel to the fire, fanning the flames and bringing Miota to its death even faster.

I met Dalton's gaze, and even in the murky lighting, I knew his thoughts mirrored mine. We'd tried outsmarting an enemy whose moves we didn't completely know, and we would now pay the price.

"Don't spiral just yet," Dalton muttered. Anya perked, though she said nothing. Had she heard?

Zephyr called out names, giving assigned barracks to each of us, telling us our futures.

I was assigned to Scarlet Barracks. When Dalton and Anya were too, I hoped it was by some stroke of luck.

Only later did I realize what this meant. If Dalton and I had been assigned to different barracks, we could spread the word of mutiny farther. We'd each reach two full groups—a majority of recruits. But now . . . we'd only have influence over twenty-five recruits.

It wouldn't be enough.

Scarlet Barracks was a small building dotting the northern perimeter of Red Fox. Our barracks tucked nicely into folds of countryside, witnessing the land's transition away from the artificial. The building outlooked rolling hills of green and yellow, with only one maglev track splicing the earth. It was otherwise untouched by man, flitting solely with wild winds and critters. To the left, farther north, fields met a patch of thick trees, much like the woods I imagined outside Salford, before the land sloped upward into giant masses of hills. Even the earth out here reached for the skies.

This was a view Griff would delight in too, his star-dipped soul wanting the same things as mine. I wanted to run through the grass, climb the trees, and shout until my lungs went raw.

Zephyr, the burly man who'd emerged from Biourica initially, was apparently Scarlet Barracks' leader. Even from afar, his brown skin rippled with muscle, and his dark eyes fixated on objects like little lasers.

I wasn't sure how dividing us would help us cooperate and learn to function as a full unit—unless *these* small groups were made to act as one, and Arlo had sufficiently created three armies.

How were Dalton and I supposed to operate against Arlo when we didn't know his full plans? We didn't have a full view of what was happening, and maybe that was purposeful. We were just cogs, cells of different parts.

I learned that much quickly, and it was only proven as the week lurched forward. With each passing day, each hour, I heard the invisible clock ticking faster, hurtling toward killing the people I loved if I wasn't careful—if Dalton and I and the rest of Lorella's crew couldn't seamlessly mesh our plans with Griff's and Max's back on Miota.

Step one of this plan working was for me to turn people against Arlo, and that required first gaining their trust. The task weighed on me, growing stronger, spreading like a disease through my body with each passing day.

Not that I had much time to befriend the recruits. Our barracks—nothing more than a quaint building of small bedrooms lining a top hallway, communal bathrooms and kitchens downstairs, and a large auditorium in the basement—ran on our own accord. We recruits were the beating heart, keeping the barracks operating.

The daily schedule remained the same, at least, and it gave me something to ground myself in. First came waking up to the shouts and clanging of Zephyr and two other nameless personnel, whom Anya called Brood and Broody because of their enduring scowls. Then came a quick breakfast—a scoop of powdered nutrients mixed in a glass of water. The breakfast here reminded me of the slop Low-Tiered citizens in Pointe would eat if they qualified. Dalton's face curdled at the first sip of breakfast each morning, while Anya and I simply took the stuff for what it was.

After breakfast came two hours of fitness training—running and perfecting our fighting styles, mostly, which saved weight-lifting for later in the day.

After morning basics came a quick break for showering in one of the limited number of stalls, if you were quick enough to snag one, and then four hours of lectures. The whole barracks was in the same classes, and Zephyr, Brood, and Broody took turns cycling through material, each lecture taking one hour. Subjects ranged between military organization, company logistics, battle tactics, and team conduct.

Then came lunch, afternoon weightlifting, dinner shifts, homework hours, and cafeteria cleanup crew. Each of us was assigned a chore, and as the week waned, we all grew stronger at our assigned tasks, falling into a necessary rhythm.

We signed documents of secrecy, swearing our oaths to Biourica. Sending Arlo James our full allegiance. I bonded with recruits over things like disdain toward homework and the struggle of sleeping on stiff mattresses. It was never anything about Biourica, though. That part would prove difficult.

On the fourth morning, during breakfast, Zephyr marched to the front of the cafeteria and rolled up his sleeves, showing off the dark ink wrapping both his arms.

"QUIET!" he snapped. Anya and I, sitting next to each other across from Dalton, turned to face the Scarlet leader. "I have a message from Arlo James himself." Dalton's shoulders caved inward at the mention of his father. "It says recruits will soon be tested on their teamwork skills by undergoing a series of trials, to deem where your group will fit best among the logistics spots available. The winningest group will have their pick of a job: expansion, enforcement, or allocation."

Buzzing started, voices chattering and swelling into a steady roar.

"SHUT IT!" Zephyr boomed. "A hundred burpees after breakfast for everyone." That suffocated all sounds. "You heard your boss. Arlo James will reward the best team, and I expect it to be Scarlet Barracks."

Dalton and I shared a look. Arlo had some ulterior motive; I was sure of it. What need would he have for us to compete against each other? Was he going to split us up, using us in different ways? Would only *some* of us go to Miota?

Was there a point in wearing Scarlet Barracks' spirits against Arlo if we didn't even leave the supercontinent?

My doubts infiltrated everything, once again clouding my judgment and rendering me motionless. I didn't know what to do. For one of the first times since arriving in Red Fox, I truly believed I was in over my head.

CHAPTER 29

CORINN

"We have to win these trials," I muttered. My voice went raw as I heaved for air. Our run this morning wound through the trees beyond the field outside Scarlet Barracks, and the watercolor leaves fell in arrays of reds and yellows. I tried basking in this scene, but I was instead distracted by my itchy knee-high boots—given the higher chance of rats residing out here—and side cramping. "It's the only way to pick our assignment." *And we need to go to Miota.*

Dalton huffed in agreement, which sent a cloud of breath in the air. "We can. We have some of the top recruits—three from the top ten."

Our first trial against Emerald Barracks was set for two days from now, first thing Sunday morning, after a full week of living in Scarlet Barracks. Almost a full week in, and I'd made no improvements toward shifting the tides against Arlo.

"I can't do this," I whispered, confessing my shortcomings and fears to the falling leaves. To Dalton. "Our plan . . . I can't do it."

Dalton staggered, almost losing his footing on a stray tree root. "We aren't alone," he said in a breath after huffing out a curse. He regained his running form, staying upright, even against the wind's teeth. "Remember that."

It was hard to remember, though, when we couldn't contact any of them. I missed Cass and Lorella, and even Colton. I knew my desperation thickened when the Queen of Miota's words found me: *Keep your eyes and ears sharp; you do not know what you are getting yourself into.*

Cass's mother had delivered the advice as a threat, but it still served a purpose, here and now.

I decided I'd begin making enemies of Arlo after our first trial against Emerald Barracks—winning seemed more important right now, or at least more immediate. These competitions meant something, or else Arlo wouldn't have bothered with splitting us up and dividing his resources.

That was it. After we faced Emerald Barracks, I'd start asking questions about what *exactly* we were doing here. If I could stir up doubts and raise suspicions, maybe I could undermine Arlo without completely attacking him.

In the meantime, the twenty-five of us trained, slowly becoming closer in ways I'd never thought possible. I ate meals with Anya and Dalton, but my connections didn't stop there. I had dinner clean-up duty with Garrison, a lanky man who helped people manage their money for a living—a job he hadn't wanted, but one he knew he'd excel in. I shared bunks with Stella Hong, a woman who had an athletic knack only because she used to run away from bullies. Everyone here had a story, and they were fascinating. Things of another world brought to life, illuminated by reality, and softening them around the edges.

The day came to face Emerald Barracks. We ate dinner before leaving for our match time set at sundown. While most ate unbothered, I found it difficult to swallow food when my throat stayed clogged with worry of what was to come. What sort of implications would a loss have on us? What about a *win*?

I hated not having answers.

"Eat up," Anya coaxed, tapping my plastic tray with her fork. "You can't fight on an empty stomach."

"I'm just scared," I admitted. "Who knows what this competition is for, what it'll bring . . . what it means."

Anya shrugged. "Who knows, and who cares?" She threw a grape into her mouth. "If it was important, they would've told us."

I shared a fleeting look with Dalton. His measured eyes warned me to stay quiet. But I couldn't. "No, Anya, I think they're not telling us *because* it's important. We aren't Biourica's brains . . . just the brawn."

Dalton rolled his eyes and took the slab of ham off my tray. "Have some faith, Corinn." He ate my food, seemingly unbothered by the implications of tonight's competition. "We'll be fine."

His sentiment echoed one of Griff's: *I just have faith in us.* Griff's hope and light always seemed to be enough; maybe I could carry it here and now, too.

"I hope so," I threw back. "And stop taking my food!"

"He wouldn't take it," Anya defended Dalton with a grin, "if you were eating it!" She then snatched a handful of my fruit.

I covered my face in my hands. *Why* was no one else concerned about this? Dalton, at least, should've carried some worries; he knew what the choice in assignment meant, should we win these trials.

After Garrison and I finished sanitizing dishes and tabletops, we joined the rest of our team at the foyer, awaiting our ride to the meeting point.

All twenty-five of us, plus Zephyr, piled into a yellow vehicle, which Dalton called a bus, a tall thing fitting rows upon rows of plastic seats inside. We sat two to a seat—Anya with me, and Dalton across the aisle with someone whom I believed was named Finn.

"I miss Charlie," Anya said. "And the rest of our training group."

I nodded. "Wonder if any of them are in Emerald Barracks." Most everyone from Anya's training group had made the logistics team, though we'd been fracked apart. Only Dalton, Anya, and I remained in Scarlet Barracks.

The bus started into the wilderness, driving not on a paved path, as vehicles did in Miota, but straight through the countryside on its own accord. The setting sun dyed the sky orange, and the sporadic open bus window let chilled twilight air into the vehicle. Just as on Miota, September brought longer and cooler nights.

After a ride lasting far too long for anyone's patience, we arrived at a campsite nestled at the bottom of what everyone called the mountains: sleeping giants made of earth and rock, pine and dirt. I vaguely recalled Bernard Bartholomus telling Griff and me he hoped we'd one day learn what mountains were, but words couldn't do these masses justice. If it hadn't been approaching night, I'd get a better look at the rising earth against the sky, but for now, I settled for admiring the view and mentally noting to take Griff here one day, after freeing our home.

When we piled off the bus, a thin man with gray hair, wearing a puffed jacket and fuzzy earmuffs, waited for us in front of a black limo. He grinned, cheeks painted pink as we gathered around him.

He eyed Dalton warily, and my stomach dropped. Was this Arlo James? Biourica's leader—

"Sillian," Dalton whispered, as if reading my mind.

Oh. This wasn't Arlo James, though he might as well have been. Sillian Reeves was Sector A's president, if I remembered correctly, the one who'd been bought out by Arlo James, working alongside him at the pinnacle of the sector.

"Hello, Scarlet Barracks," Sillian welcomed us. "Congratulations on making Biourica's logistics team. I know I speak for Arlo James when I say you *all*'—he tightened his gaze on Dalton—"deserve to be here. Your task tonight is simple. Climb the mountain with this map and solve the riddle at the peak." He produced a folded parchment map from his coat and handed it to Zephyr. "Emerald Barracks is at the opposite mountain base, fighting for the same thing. Each barracks has a separate riddle, and whoever gets to theirs at the top and solves it first, with *all* barracks members present, will win."

I thought of the lingering rats out here, who would certainly be attracted to warm bodies. I also thought of the sharp winds and perils hiding under night's veil. But they all simmered away at Sillian's next words.

"See you at the top in a few days."

Days.

Sillian had said *days*.

My head inflated as Zephyr folded his brow, brooding over the map as he unfurled it. After getting his bearings, he studied us. "I'm not allowed to go with you. Stick together and remember what I always say: the mind will break a hundred times before the body."

Though Zephyr had never said that before, I appreciated his sentiment. It gave me an inkling of hope; maybe I was stronger than I believed, limited by my thoughts and mind, not my physical strength.

"You can't give advice, either," Sillian said with a beam toward Zephyr before looking at the recruits. His gaze snagged on me, as if trying to split me open. As if he could read my secrets like ink scrawled on a page. I averted my gaze, hoping the flush on my neck and cheeks passed as an effect of the cold instead of secrecy. "Now hand them the map, and leave your recruits to their fate."

Zephyr's jaw ticked before he gave his final good-bye.

He and Sillian left, leaving the twenty-five of us in the dark, beneath the rising moon, amid shadowed forests crawling upward to the mountain's peak.

I shivered. Prickling goosebumps rose on my skin, rubbing painfully against my tight-fitting fleece jacket. It was too cold out here to last a few days; we'd surely turn to frozen hunks of meat before we made it to the top.

Recruits slowly scanned the rest of the group, and most gazes settled on Dalton, rendering him leader due to his lineage. Once the boy noticed, he straightened his spine, adding an inch to his height and dampening all emotion from his expression.

"Anyone volunteer to be our navigator?" Dalton asked. When no one spoke, he crouched down to retrieve the map from where Zephyr had dropped it. Arlo's son brushed off the map and squinted, wordlessly accepting navigation duties. "We need firelight," he stated to the group. "Not a lot—no attracting rats. But some, to figure out where the hell we're going. And keep your eyes peeled for a water source, too."

A small group collected branches from the forest's underbrush, and Garrison rubbed the wood together until it smoked, then sparked, producing flames. The scent of burning wood flooded my nostrils.

Dalton calculated our whereabouts, then snuffed the small fire and led our ascent. Anya and I trailed immediately behind him, trying to emulate his footfalls and steps to avoid loose earth. Pale moonlight guided us, our beckon toward victory.

As the full hold of night sank in, it darkened every aspect of the trees, melting the world into blackness. The winds also swelled with the temperature drop, creating harsher hiking conditions. While my skin was laden with sweat, pooling at my feet and in my armpits, my face and head remained too cold.

Time passed as slippery as mud. The moon and stars served hazy timekeeping duties, though no one cared too much when we weren't racing against the night but against another team somewhere in this same wilderness. Were we on track to win? Were we too far behind?

Beat Emerald Barracks, I reminded myself, replaying the course of thought with each new step. *Then beat the other barracks to choose our logistics task. Go to Miota. Reunite with Griff.*

Free my people.

Save my home.

It seemed to light a small ember of warmth inside me. There was a purpose to all of this, even if it seemed elusive right now. I wasn't on the road I'd originally planned to take, but I was still on the path toward saving Miota nonetheless.

When sunrise welcomed the new day, every muscle in my body cramped from shivering all night. We must've been at this about twelve hours, and from our small spot, dropped like pins, I couldn't tell how much more we had to go.

We needed to stop for a break, but the thought of giving Emerald

Barracks an advantage was enough to keep us numbly continuing. While my body regained some feeling from the now rising temperature, I remained sore, unable to do anything more than simply *walk*. The tree line thinned as we hiked upward, granting us small patches of sunlight on the forest floor, and we took turns basking in the golden rays.

"How much farther?" I asked Dalton, who studied the map.

He smirked, eyes still glued to the parchment. "You sound like me when I was about five years old, Corinn." His gaze brushed over mine. "At our current pace, another night. But we need food, and we'll need to rest. So . . ."

The hike progressively turned vertical. We climbed rocks almost my size, and we tried not to trip over sporadic tree roots jutting out of the ground. I fell to the back of the group. Judging by the sun, it was midmorning, and our pace had slowed to a near-stop. My muscles sang for reprieve, and my eyelids weighed heavy with sleep.

"That's it," Dalton sighed from the front of the pack. "Take rest. Emerald'll have to do it, too. We'll nap in shifts, and we'll send people to find food and running water." He eyed me in the group's back and turned away.

I thought these trials were about communication and teamwork; but this one was more focused on the individual, each person needing to cross the finish line on their own for the whole team to win.

Stupid trials.

I meant to volunteer to hunt. But I collapsed to the forest floor and fell asleep where my face met pine needles.

I woke to a light boot to the shoulder. I winced and looked upward to find Dalton towering over me.

He set his hands on his hips. Gusts of wind brushed dark hair across his head. "Get up."

I threw my arms over my head. If only this was all over. There was no *reason* to beat Emerald Barracks—except for the implications of winning these trials. So for now, I had to play Arlo's game.

I hated how this felt like Accolade—like a lost cause. My control slipped, even now, and I wasn't sure how I was supposed to keep everyone around me safe.

Slowly, I sat up and eventually stood, rising to Dalton's level. A pounding headache met my upright posture.

Dalton's gaze roved over my face. "You look awful."

I curled my lip. "I could say the same about everyone else here."

"Can you take guard while others sleep?"

I nodded, folding my arms as a wind gust ripped through my jacket. The higher we climbed, the more exposed we became to the elements.

Those who'd been awake, on guard, were now curling up against tree trunks to take rest. A few others gathered around a mass of berries and leaves, all deemed edible by Veronika, who recently graduated from High Citadel and recalled her lessons from a plant differentiation class.

The sparse pile lay thin when I reached it. A large handful of us still needed to eat, and two berries each wouldn't be enough to sustain us. My head already spun, and hunger gripped at my stomach, holding me hostage.

"Can we hunt?" I asked. "We need meat."

A muscle twitched in Dalton's cheek. "It's not safe. These woods are crawling with animals that are only staying away because of how many of us there are. If we separated . . ."

"I'll go with her." I recognized Anya's bright voice from behind me. I spun, and she shrugged as she toed the rocky dirt. "I've had to survive off my hunting skills before."

Dalton scratched his neck. "Fine. Steele, keep Januski safe. And vice versa." He whipped a knife from his pocket as an offering to the girl, and in response, Anya unsheathed the twin blades at her waistband—one for each hand. Dalton's mouth twitched into a quick smile, and he gave the blade to me instead.

I hadn't realized we were supposed to come to this event armed. My cheeks warmed, as I knew color surely stained my face.

"Boots are laced?" Dalton asked, surveying our shoes.

"Highest rut," Anya replied. She surveyed my boots, a protective motion that did nothing but rub me the wrong way, before we peeled from the group. We stuck to what appeared to be a path through the orange and red trees, though I hoped we weren't merely losing ourselves to the woods, carrying nothing but wits and knives.

We didn't speak for the first hundred feet. When a twig snapped across the small leaf-littered clearing, Anya put an arm in front of me.

"Look out—" She cut off at the sight of a squirrel prancing to the nearest tree.

My annoyance festered in the merciless wind. "Why are you trying to protect me?" *I'm not a child.*

She threw me a sideways glance, undoubtedly noting the bite to my tone. "Because you're my friend. And I want you to be safe."

She used the word again. *Friend.* The one thing I never asked for upon coming to Sector A. "Well, I can take care of myself."

We turned onto a rockier section of earth. "I'm sure you can," she responded levelly. "But that doesn't mean you *have* to. Teammates take care of each other."

I *knew* that was how Anya felt about all of this. And if it continued, she'd soon rely on me, as she expected me to rely on her. And I couldn't have that.

So I said what I knew would sting.

"I didn't choose any of this, Anya." *None of this.* Coming to Red Fox, joining the logistics team as my only way home . . . this path was nothing more than the unfortunate sum of my actions. If I could change any of it, I would. "I'm not here to make friends; I'm here by force. We're all just *recruits.*"

Anya stayed quiet a beat longer than expected. Finally, "That was low, Corinn."

"I know." Guilt clawed behind my ribs. In a matter of short and sharp words, I'd ruined this team for her. "Sorry." But the sentiment didn't bleed through.

We trudged on in silence. Why *had* I snapped at Anya so fiercely? She didn't deserve that. This anger . . . it wasn't toward her. She was only the ill-placed collateral. This uneasiness, this contempt, overshadowed all other emotions these days. Everything was shrouded in uncertainty, and I *hated* how torn I felt because of it.

On this land mass, I didn't know who I was supposed to be. A spy, a soldier, a friend, a teammate, a rebel . . . My bones vibrated with each step onward. Did I want to run *away*, or did I want to run *toward* something? I wasn't sure.

I was running from who I'd been, from what had led me to doom Salem. I was also running from this life here and now, where nothing was assured except uncertainty.

And I was running toward anything to point the way, anything to guide me home. I was running toward an answer I wasn't sure I'd ever find.

It slashed me in two.

We remained silent for a long while, creeping through the bushes and trees, finding no luck with tracking down meat. Our team needed it, if we were to sustain a steady pace up the mountain. I wondered how far Emerald Barracks had made it by this point. Were they just as desperate as we were?

"When should we turn around?" Anya grumbled, her voice tight. She looked at me with tears welled in her eyes, nothing but sadness pent up within her.

So she couldn't have seen it coming.

The furry, rabid creature that dove out from a pile of dead leaves. The red eyes. The foaming mouth.

My body went cold.

In any past moment, I would've stayed frozen in fear. But I was so bent on *running*, on moving, not a moment passed before I screamed Anya's name and dove for the creature about to bound up her leg.

I grabbed the rat. My jaw rattled as the ground rose to meet me.

The damn creature bit my wrist.

And the world spun.

30

CORINN

"Corinn!"

I couldn't pinpoint Anya's voice. Not as the world teetered. Not as my head inflated.

"No!" Anya screamed. Her hands were on me, above my wrists. "Why does this *keep happening?*" Sobs laced her voice, each one stabbing at my heart. *"Don't take her, too."*

This rat disease . . . red bite . . .

It killed people—*everyone* it touched. And I was its latest victim.

No. I could *not* die. I couldn't have my last words be something so cruel to someone so light . . .

I centered my gaze on Anya. I couldn't form thoughts. Couldn't think. Couldn't do anything but stare at the girl above me, tears streaming down her cheeks, heartbreak contorting her face.

Somewhere in my brain, the number twenty rattled around. *Twenty seconds*, Lorella had taught Cass and me. *Twenty seconds before you're dead.*

My brain refused to count. But my sights hitched on Anya's lips.

Seventeen, she mouthed. *Eighteen.*

"Griff," I uttered.

Nineteen.

I closed my eyes. Waited.

Kept waiting. Had death found me? Was this the end? It didn't feel any different.

I cracked one eye open, too terrified to acknowledge the fact I didn't think I'd succumbed to the bite. I . . . I was living on borrowed time. Slowly, I stretched my limbs as the dizziness subsided. I blinked both eyes open.

"Thirty," Anya whispered, still counting, staring at me with parted lips and wide eyes. "*Corinn* . . ."

"Um . . ." I choked, gagging on the shock. "I think . . . I'm okay."

"You're . . ." Anya wiped her eyes with a trembling hand. "B-but . . . but the *rat* . . . Corinn . . . it was *infected* . . ." She made a noise akin to both a laugh and a cry. "No one survives red bite. *No one.*"

I knew that, too, from the research I'd done in Lorella's apartment, in my early days in Red Fox. Red bite coagulated blood quicker than one could sing a Pointean field song chorus. The infection curdled blood into a thickened, solid mass, making survival impossible.

Yet I was alive. And I knew by the blood pounding through my temples, it was very much still a liquid, still coursing through me.

"Is . . . are people lying about red bite?" I dared to ask. I sat up, ready to flee from this area of the forest. I didn't want to test my luck again. My wrist radiated, pink and swollen at the site of the bite, but I was *fine*, otherwise unaffected. "How else would I be alive?"

Anya shook her head wildly and tugged at her bottom lip with her teeth. "They're not lying. I've seen it too many times to count. Red bite kills every time, usually within seven seconds—they're the lucky ones." Her eyes raked me up and down, still expecting me to drop dead at any given second. "In some, the blood thickening takes longer, but . . . I've never seen anyone make it past sixteen seconds."

Until now; until you. Her unspoken words were written into the surrounding wind.

I shivered, moving back toward the way we came. I didn't want to go any deeper into the forest. "Well . . . I guess I'm lucky."

"That wasn't luck." Anya shook her head and knitted her brow.

"You shouldn't be alive right now, Corinn. Don't you get it? No one in the entire *League* has ever survived this!"

My blood went cold—fear's doing, not the rat's. Something deep inside me told me I *should've* died from the bite. For some unknown reason, I was still alive . . . but if someone like Arlo James discovered I survived red bite, I didn't think I'd outlive *him.*

"Keep quiet about this," I blurted. "Anya, *please.* Don't tell anyone. Especially Dalton."

Arlo's son. Maybe he would know what to do with this information. But *I* needed to tell him myself.

"Why not?" Anya crossed her arms, her gaze still wild. "This isn't the type of thing you don't tell people!"

"I'll tell people myself," I insisted. Anya's steps grew swifter, and I fought to keep up. "Anya! Let *me* break the news."

She pursed her lips and slowed, stopping in a patch of sunlight. Golden light brushed her dark skin, making her glow. "You're a walking medical anomaly, you know. You should be on the front screen of every grid. On the front page of every news story."

My trust snapped, and my face paled. "*Anya.*"

"I'm just saying."

"I'll tell the right people. Make this promise to me, please. I'll never make you promise me anything else, but make *this one.* You can't tell anyone."

She sheathed her knives and set her hands on her hips. "What are you hiding? What do you know about red bite?"

"Nothing!" My mouth gaped. "Please just trust me. This isn't your news to tell."

She huffed, dropping her arms so they hung limply at her sides. "Fine. Not telling anyone." She scanned the forest for food, as if we'd be lucky enough to catch anything during this backtrack to the rest of the group. "Even though it's stupid."

I rolled my eyes and changed the subject, desperately wanting to escape this. "Why did you want to join the logistics team?" I asked harmlessly.

Anya stiffened and retrieved her knives, mindlessly turning to sharpening them against each other, as if it was a nervous tell. "What makes you ask?"

I shrugged. "Curiosity, I guess."

She stalked forward, silent for about a dozen steps. "To belong somewhere," she answered as she sharpened her knives again. "And I heard we'd get housing if we made the team—I was tired of living in alleyways."

Alleyways? I almost chanced a look toward the girl, but I kept my eyes plastered to the ground ahead of us, scanning for more rats as Anya surveyed the woods for food sources.

"You lived in . . . alleyways?" I recalled Anya telling me she never took maglevs around town; she couldn't afford the rides.

"Not always." She quickened her pace once again as her ears perked at something. "My dad left first. Then my older sister. It left me and my mom, and . . . she told me to just go. Made it easier for us to choose to leave instead of having some huge falling out." She blew out a loud breath. "But don't worry about it. That was five years ago now."

My mouth dried as I did the math. Anya was my age, meaning five years ago, she'd only been thirteen. So young to be cast away by her mother, to live in alleys among red bite, in the city infamous for the deadly disease.

My mind wandered to what I'd said to Anya before my bite. This team was all Anya had—this was her family now. It was the first sense of belonging she'd had in five years, and I'd tried to crush it all.

"I'm sorry, Anya." I couldn't swallow the guilt consuming me. "For what happened. And for what I said back there . . . You *are* my friend." Adrenaline punched me. My spirits begged to retreat inward, to close myself off and run away. But Anya challenged me to open up, and it was the least I could do right now. "I just can't have anyone else getting hurt because they care about me."

I realized my mistake too late. Anya turned toward me. "Anyone *else?*" she asked, catching on. "Who's Griff?"

"What?" All blood seemed to drain to my feet, and they became too heavy. "Where'd you hear that name?" If Dalton told her—

"You said it. When I was counting your twenty seconds. I thought . . . maybe he was someone you lost."

Ah. I swallowed and caved to the girl. "I did lose him." He was across the ocean from me, and though I was fighting to get back to him, I didn't know if I was doing *enough*. The feeling before crying gave way in my lungs, and I struggled to gulp air in.

"Corinn." Panic riddled Anya's voice. "No, no, *no*—"

"It's not the bite," I heaved. "I'm fine. I just . . . don't like talking about it. *Him*—Griff." *Or anyone else from Miota, for that matter.*

"You can trust me—" Anya stopped, sucking her lips shut and crouching into the nearest bush. *"Shh."*

I hoped the question simmered into my alarmed expression as I followed Anya, ducking into the prickling greenery.

She cocked her head, and I listened. My ears picked up the distant gobbling, and I grinned.

Anya flicked her brow upward and readied her knives. "I hear breakfast, lunch, and dinner."

Our meal of roasted turkey came only because of Anya—her knives had proven useful, as we'd used them to carve sharp points into stones and secure them to sticks. Three makeshift spears had produced two skillful throws from Anya and one lucky shot from me.

Three turkeys for twenty-five of us. A host of recruits helped cut and trim the meat, and others roasted it over a brightly burning fire, moving with such haste that the turkey ended up charred.

The food revived our spirits; everyone woke for food and for conjuring up a plan. Dalton passed around the map, letting others calculate the quickest way to the summit.

Dalton shared a victorious grin with Anya and me, though fear splintered my happiness. Anya wanted me to tell Dalton of my bite, but

I couldn't bring myself to voice it to him. I trusted Dalton with my life, yes, but for some reason, I couldn't articulate *this* vital piece of information to him. He was Arlo James's son, after all, and if this ended up in his hands . . .

I buried the secret. I *would* tell Dalton.

Eventually.

We took our time recovering: packing what food we could, and collecting fresh water from a nearby stream. Our team then began again, ready to continue until we reached the summit.

We traveled as a group—slightly spreading out at times but otherwise staying together, refusing to separate. Through the watery sun's descent, and through the moon's rise. Griff's fierceness filtered into me at the sight, and I forced my burning legs onward, trudging relentlessly.

The sooner we finished this, the sooner we could go back to Scarlet Barracks.

"Almost there!" Dalton shouted. Some cheered, though no vitality found them. Even the strongest among us were walking corpses by now.

When we reached the glowing shack at the top, tears blurred my vision. We *made it*. From what I could tell, Emerald Barracks wasn't here yet.

We were going to win.

Dalton approached the shack, and a hazy figure handed him a scroll. He scanned it before walking slowly back to the group, all of us now sprawled on the ground in need of reprieve from using our legs.

"Here's the riddle," Dalton started, not breaking his gaze from the words. "'I will grow deeper the longer I am, so long as you nurture me. One mile or a hundred miles makes no difference, for I am already with you, should you beckon me. What am I?'"

No one spoke.

Then, "A tree?" from Garrison. "But I don't think it could grow a hundred miles . . ."

"Courage!" Veronika squealed.

But Dalton submitted the answer to the figure in the shack, and the man shook his head, visible from the illuminated building against the dark night.

Others threw out guesses, and on our fifth try, distant stomping rumbled closer. Then they appeared through the hedge, entering the clearing in their own state of disheveled misery from the last day and a half in the woods.

Emerald Barracks. They received their own riddle, and their chattering derailed my every thought. They were *here*. They could win, with a single correct guess.

What grew longer, then deeper . . . *no*, what grew deeper, then longer? What was a hundred miles long? Or *one* mile?

At least tonight wasn't as cold as last night had been, so the temperature wasn't also distracting me. But Emerald Barracks . . . each time they approached the shack with an answer, it undid me, and I lost all ideas.

Our group thought more frantically. We descended into madness, into desperation. Dalton and Anya paced in tandem, and the sight put a wrench in my chest. If we didn't win this, it could potentially destroy my friends and family across the sea.

I shot up, spurring into motion. *Miota* gave me an idea. My home would help win this for Scarlet Barracks.

"I know it!" I hissed to Dalton, grasping his arm.

Dalton hurried over to the shack. When he gave *friendship* as an answer, the figure within the shack nodded.

"Congratulations, Scarlet Barracks. You are the winners."

CHAPTER 31

GRIFF

Three weeks until seeing Corinn quickly turned into two.

The racing clock kept me moving, kept me bending to Julia's will and playing Addison's games. It forced me to place unsteady trust in Max and Abner alike—I could put delicate faith into something for fourteen days, after all.

Two weeks, and Corinn would be back on Miota, with this team she was part of. I didn't fully understand this group she belonged to, but she'd soon be able to just tell me outright.

Hearing her voice had been a glimpse of the moon on a dark night; her laugh amounted to every constellation.

I'll see you soon, lovely.

The sentiment drove me onward. As Max helped scope out the safest underground tunnel path to Cape from each city, I planned with Abner how the night would go.

Abner wasn't easy to convince, though with Max and me both assuring him Lorella and her crew had figured this out and would carry the brunt of the burden, he'd slowly eased into it.

The recent trouble was convincing Abner on how to handle Julia.

"I won't kill her, so don't even think about suggesting it," Abner said before biting into his sandwich. He propped his feet atop his desk, leaving me to hold my plate of food in my lap. The king still refused to meet with me unless we sat in his office; he didn't trust another inch of the castle for privacy.

Considering the subject matter, I didn't blame him.

I only took slight offense to his remark; the thought had admittedly crossed my mind, though it was something of impulse. I didn't truly want Abner to kill his wife.

"I wasn't going to," I responded and folded my hands. "But . . . you could give her something to knock her out for a while. Something strong, giving us plenty of time to get off the island without her waking."

It wasn't what I wanted. If I had it my way, Julia would *watch* us thieve her island from under her nose. She would feel the same pain she'd put me through, more than once.

But Abner's cooperation relied on certainty. If we could successfully take Julia out of the picture, we'd only have to worry about her loyalists, and at that point, they'd be outnumbered.

Abner, however, shook his head curtly. "Not possible."

"Why not?" I charged. I ripped a bite of my own sandwich, an effort to simmer down.

"Because she's always looking out for that sort of thing. She's paranoid about her food, her drinks . . . everything has to go through a meticulous process before she'll even touch it." I inhaled to respond, but Abner continued. "She's a trained killer, Griff. Her father taught her from . . . an age much younger than you're probably imagining. I can't force anything onto her without inviting her to hurt me first." The king blinked. A lump wavered in his throat. "If . . . if she were easy to poison, Griff, I would've already done it."

Poison. It unlocked a memory, one from not so long ago.

"You poisoned me," I uttered. Hope found me once more. "You poisoned me in front of Julia at our first dinner in the castle. On a live camera feed, of all places, for the whole island to see! But Julia didn't know I was poisoned—and she definitely didn't know it was *your* doing."

Abner adjusted his shirt's collar. "Yes, well, that was different. Her guards were low; she didn't think I'd poison her for all Miota to see."

"But you poisoned *me!*" I refuted. Did he truly not see my point, or was he scared of where this conversation was directed? "And nobody noticed. *Nobody.*"

The king coiled his lips beneath his bushy beard and closed his eyes. "Griff . . ."

"You can do it," I willed him. "Don't you *want* to fight to see your son again?"

Abner lost his delicate balance and fell from his seat. He jumped back onto his feet, quickly for an older man, and stared at me with wild, storm cloud eyes. "What did you say about my son?"

Surely Abner *knew* Cass was alive. It was a fact *I* tried to forget, because thinking of Cass being Corinn's only sense of familiarity on the supercontinent . . .

My vision went red.

I blinked it away and acknowledged Abner. "Cass? He's—on the supercontinent, with Corinn! And I thought you'd want—"

"My son is dead," Abner growled. He went from stillness to chaos in the matter of a heartbeat. He swiped at the trinkets littering his desk, letting them fly to the floor. I braced myself, ready to fight if needed. Abner clawed at his hair and paced the room. "*My son is dead,* Griff Howard."

I held my ground. "He's alive, and Max knows it."

Max, it seemed, *was* keeping his own set of secrets. He was caught in a delicate web, some confidences placed in others' hands, and some hidden entirely. Max needed to be careful, though, before he became prey to his own trap.

Abner pinned me to my spot on the floor. My feet turned to molten liquid. "If you are *lying* to me . . ."

"Ask him yourself." I paused. "Will you help get rid of Julia for one night if you find out I'm telling the truth? That Cass is still alive?"

Abner's eyes turned to black fire. "If my son is still alive," he ground out, each word deliberate, "I'll do *anything* to get him back. I'll help you burn this entire island to the ground."

The rest of the plan weaved together in small pockets of time, in secretive bits of scheming.

Max routed the way to Cape using Miota's underground tunnel network—he would aid Corinn's logistics team to usher people to the boats on Miota's southern shores. Abner and I would use the Queen's Guard to direct people southward, away from Julia's grasp.

"What happens when someone gets in our way or tries to stop us from leaving?" Abner asked as I drank my afternoon tea in his office seven days before Corinn's arrival.

The countdown was waning. *Three weeks, two weeks . . . and now one.*

I sipped my tea from my seat and eyed the pacing king. "You think that'll happen?" I tracked the pacing king with my calculating gaze.

"I *know* it will." Abner tossed a hand in the air. "Things will escalate, and you'll need to be prepared. What are you willing to risk?"

I chewed on his question and drained my tea to the dregs. I would give anything for this cause—except my family, the remaining pair of souls on this island I cared for completely and wholly. Without them, none of this mattered as much. I also grouped Corinn with them, since she would be back on Miota the night of our stunt.

My thoughts untangled, and I settled back in my chair. "The guards can use sedatives—they tranquilized us almost weekly during Accolade, so there must be a supply somewhere. Then we can get Julia's sympathizers out of the way without hurting anyone."

Abner's brow raised. "That could cause quite the moral predicament." Something like amusement lined his statement.

My cheeks heated. "It's the best idea we have. I'm open to suggestions." I didn't bother hiding my scorn.

Abner's jaw twitched, causing a stiff ruffle of his beard, before he spun on his heel, pacing the opposite way. "Speaking of predicaments . . . does Addison know about this plan of ours?"

"Of course not."

Abner tossed me a quick, reproachful look from over his shoulder. "And why not?"

I gawked. "Because it's not *safe*. She's allied with your wife—"

"My wife," Abner interrupted, flicking his hand, "hasn't spoken privately with Addison in weeks. I'm not sure how strong their partnership is these days. And if you . . ." Abner's pace slowed. "If you disappear on her, will you be able to live with that?"

I'd mulled over that same question too many times to count, and I'd yet to produce an answer. I kept brushing it off, vowing to think of it later.

But my time would run out soon. I'd either have to tell Addison our plan and offer her a place in the mission at hand, or I'd have to hold off on telling her and chance her being left behind.

Addison would do anything to save her skin—but she'd also do anything to gain power. I couldn't predict how she'd react to news of the supercontinent and the plan to leave Miota.

I *would* tell Addison and give her the choice. Just not yet. Because once I did, she would hold the power to bring this entire ploy crumbling to the ground.

CHAPTER 32

CORINN

"You beat Emerald Barracks," Zephyr shouted from the front of Scarlet Barracks' gym, a drafty room carved into the ground below our building. "But it's in the past"—he accented every next syllable—"and I don't give a damn about it." He blew his whistle, and the twenty-five of us collectively rose from the floor into plank positions.

My core and shoulders seethed—we'd already planked for over fifteen minutes. I wouldn't last much longer, but I concentrated on my sweat spots on the concrete floor. If I fell now, I'd have to run extra miles later on.

Zephyr shouted over our shaking bodies. "You need to work harder than ever, and together, to win the next trial against Cobalt Barracks."

Nothing but Zephyr's shouting, sounds of breathing, and sweat slapping against the floor filled the room, echoing eerily off the concrete. We stayed here for minutes.

"The mind," Zephyr called, "will break! A *hundred times* before the body!"

I'd grown into the habit of reciting Bernard's sentiments each time Zephyr delivered his phrase.

Dig deep and find strength.

This was not a lost fight. This was not—

My arms collapsed, and my face hit the ground with rattling force. My skull vibrated, and blood, wet and warm, fell from my nose to the floor.

"FIRST TO FALL." Zephyr's voice pounced. "JANUSKI. Ranked seventy-fourth in the overall team—take that as you will, folks."

I gritted my teeth and resumed position, fighting off the acrid shame in my mouth, its own metallic taste slicing through my blood.

After morning conditioning, I didn't grab a shower in time, and I was left to scrub blood off my face in a sink.

Most recruits avoided me, now more than ever. *That* didn't help anything, considering the circumstances. If I was deemed one of the outcasts in the barracks, I'd never be able to sway people against Arlo.

I sulked on our walk down to the basement lecture hall as Anya and Dalton carried the conversation.

Anya shoved my shoulder with hers and waved her notebook in front of my face between flights of stairs. "You alive in there?"

"How did I get here?" I blurted monotonously. *Here.* Everything about this was wrong. The supercontinent, the barracks, the current events.

"You're dramatic." Anya inspected my nose. "It was a fall and a nosebleed. I think you'll survive."

I shared a skeptical look with Dalton from over Anya's shoulder. He knew where my mind truly lay. He offered a tentative smile, though we didn't speak until we made it to the lecture room.

We packed into the lecture hall, which wasn't unlike the classrooms on Miota: blank white walls, rows of desks, and a large monitor screen at the front. Brood and Broody—whose real names were something like July and Pattry—stood at the front, surveying us as we filled the room.

I slipped into a seat in the back row, to which Anya and Dalton begrudgingly followed suit. Back home, we'd take notes on our panel and interact with the monitor screen at the front; but here, we didn't have devices, so we used pens and pads of paper for notetaking.

Recruits shuffled around, shouting at each other about exercise drills, dipped in laughter. Others balled paper and threw it across the room. Everyone chattered until the lecture's start time.

Meanwhile, I stayed quiet, unsure of what to say. I rubbed at the rat bite on my wrist.

Dalton narrowed his eyes. "You've been rubbing that wrist like crazy."

"Poison ivy," I replied, giving my practiced response. To that, Anya whipped her head toward me and tapped her pencil rapidly against her desk. I glared at her for only a moment, praying to the moon she'd keep my secret. "It'll be better soon."

Anya gave a sharp laugh and picked at the ends of her braids.

Dalton eyed Anya, but before he could ask anything, Brood and Broody started our latest lecture on how to read terrain.

I silently thanked the timing, though my unease didn't dissipate for the entire first hour. Upon finishing the lecture, we received a short break, and I shot out of class to hide in a restroom stall.

During afternoon training, my assigned weightlifting partner was a brawny older woman, Leo, with cropped blonde hair laced in silver and biceps the size of my legs.

"What do you think of all this?" I asked between sets at the bench press. From my supine position on the bench, I looked up at the woman. "Working for Biourica, I mean."

Leo shrugged, scrutinizing my form as I began my next repetitions. The weighted bar suppressed my quivering arms.

"Biourica's a huge company," Leo droned. "So it'll be interesting to see where we go from here—Januski, your form is horrendous."

I scrunched my face and pushed through the sear of my muscles, feeling like the fibers were splitting apart. "Sorry," I grunted.

Leo only rolled her eyes. "Engage your core. Keep your back flat. And push with your chest, not your shoulders."

I modified the exercise as best I could, and once I finished, I sat up and wiped the salty sweat off my brow. "Thanks."

Leo added extra plates to the bar before completing her reps. I shook out my arms, which hung limply from the overexertion. Every muscle in me vied for attention.

"What if . . ." I clenched my jaw shut, though I ultimately continued. I *had* to start making progress toward my goal. "What if this unit gets called for combat? What would you do?"

"Combat?" Leo echoed. "Don't be—ridiculous," she gritted out between repetitions. "What makes you—ask—that?"

I shrugged. "Think of everything they're making us train for. What's . . . the point, really? Does Sector A have enemies?"

Leo stretched her arms. "Not that I know of."

I didn't get very far with Leo, but I didn't think she grew suspicious of me and my motives, so I took that as a win. We finished strength training, and Leo left me quickly, not appearing to think any differently than when I'd first spoken to her.

I tried the same tactic after dinner, during my clean-up tasks with Garrison, who said he thought we were learning combat techniques just in case someone else tried invading us—something he apparently thought could happen.

"I'd be on the lookout from Sector C," he offered in whisperings. "Since they hold the other half of the Old Lakes and all."

The Old Lakes? Since he seemed to imply Sector A held half of these, I didn't dare ask what those were. I wasn't even confident in what the word "lake" meant. I believed it was like a smaller ocean, but I wasn't certain.

"If Biourica mobilized us," I dared to ask, "would you fight blindly against whatever target we're given?"

Garrison dried off a stack of plates before answering. "I'd want to hear both sides . . . Whatever we feel toward the other sectors is how they feel about us. And I'd want to know why."

My eyes flared. "You'd do that?" *Question the only place you've ever known?*

He nodded. "There's two sides to stories. If you only surround yourself with one, and then make serious decisions based of it . . . who's to say how much of the truth you're missing?"

Garrison's words gave me blind hope. Growing up on Miota, it hadn't occurred to me to question the regime in charge. We believed the monarchy was correct and legitimate in everything—yet we were clearly wrong. There were so many truths shielded from us. Why wouldn't the same be true of Sector A?

That night, while recruits juggled finishing homework assignments in the common room and completing their daily chores, I sat with Dalton on his bunk.

"We compete against Cobalt in just a few days," I said, hugging my knees to my chest to calm my nerves. It didn't work. My back ached as I simultaneously hunched to keep from hitting my head on the top bunk's mattress immediately overhead. "I think there's a chance I can sway some of these people. Or at least make them question Biourica."

Dalton nodded from his lounged position against his pillow. "I've been talking to others, too. Talking about how my dad disowned me, how he's had dangerous thoughts in the past . . . It's helped turn some against him. Or at least put a sour taste in their mouth."

I parted my lips and sat up, effectively scraping my scalp and tangling my hair in the top bunk's metal support beam. "You *what*? You did all that without telling me?"

"That was the plan," he said, almost accusatory. "*We* talk to people. *We* sway them together. I've just been doing my part."

I opened my mouth, though I couldn't produce sound. Dalton was doing more for Miota than I was. It was empowering to know I wasn't alone . . . but it also stamped guilt on my heart for not trying harder. I was supposed to be the one leading this internal rebellion.

"Aren't you scared?" I whispered. Everything in my life seemed to have unspeakable consequences. When I acted against Julia Delldova, my best friend paid for it with his life. When I acted on my own accord, matters didn't end up in my favor. *That* was why I procrastinated—why I moved with sticky hesitancy and unyielding fear.

"Yes," Dalton admitted. He eyed me intently. "But you're brave, Corinn. I've seen your courage."

My heart wrenched. "It's gone now," I admitted, barely a whisper. "I lost it. I . . . don't know how to be brave when all I feel is this *fear*."

Fear of losing my friends, my family. My island. Fear of feeling the same pain I'd had after losing Salem. If anyone else got hurt because of me, I wasn't sure how I'd dig my way out of the darkness.

I was stuck under the weight of it all, and while I wanted—*needed*—to free myself for others' sakes . . . I didn't know what moving would mean. Who it would affect.

I needed every inch of this load on my heart; I needed to feel Miota's weight and hear the clock ticking against me.

Dalton bunched his lips. "Well, that's the funny thing about courage. You can't usually have it unless you're terrified of something first."

I blinked back tears, obscured from Dalton in the dim lighting. "What are you supposed to . . ." My voice wavered. "How do you replace the fear with courage?"

"You make the choice." His mouth twitched upward into a quick half-smile. "Bravery feels a lot like fear; it's just about the choice you make in its face. It's that easy, and that hard."

I softened to his sentiment, trying to mold my thinking toward it. "You're pretty damn wise for a kid younger than me, you know that?"

Dalton huffed a laugh through his nose. "Yeah, well, Colton . . ." Dalton trailed off and tipped his head back. "Colton did something for me a long time ago." He paused. "It's not my story to tell. But I didn't think I'd ever see him again, and . . . being brave was the only thing left for me to do."

I stayed silent and mindlessly rubbed at my wrist, almost healed but still wrapped in gauze.

"Is there any way for someone to survive red bite?" I blurted.

Dalton's face turned unrecognizable as his eyes glazed over, donned in shadows, and his mouth turned to stone.

"No one survives," he muttered after a long breath. "Trust me. My mom . . . it's complicated." Dalton fidgeted and curled his legs close. "She had cancer first, which was when Dad became all obsessed with Biourica turning to medical inventions. But after we found out Mom's case was terminal . . ." He swallowed hard. "She volunteered to undergo Dad's red bite experimental vaccines."

He didn't need to say more. "I'm so sorry," I offered. I knew the words wouldn't serve him any real purpose, or ease any pain, but it was the best I could do.

"It was a quicker way to go than cancer, so . . ." Dalton clenched his hands into fists and wiped beneath his eyes.

I was *going* to tell him of my bite, of the disease I'd evaded, but now I couldn't. Not as he shed tears over his mother.

"Anyway." He sat up in his bed. "Focus on classes and training. It's how we'll beat Cobalt Barracks next, and then we'll be free to pick our assignment and head to your home. Then this whole plan can finally kick off."

"Right." I straightened my legs, dangling my feet off the bed. "Thank you. For everything."

"Keep your courage, Corinn." Dalton reached for my hand. "You'll need all of it in the weeks to come."

CHAPTER 33

CORINN

My lungs seethed, seemingly ripping to shreds with each breath I took. This trial against Cobalt Barracks was a three-quarters marathon, a term I didn't know.

"It's approximate," Zephyr had told us on the bus while giving us the rundown. "Twenty miles."

Twenty, and my lungs already begged for air after three. Not to mention the searing ache in my shins with each step I took.

This competition, much like our last, lay on a mountain, meaning we ran uphill as a team. We had water and quick food supplies as needed this time around, but instead of walking at our own pace, it was a race to the top.

I'd been too nauseous to eat this morning, and Anya had tried helping me with a pep talk, though it did nothing but unravel me.

"Win or lose," she'd said, "we do it together."

Her promise rang through me now like a chant, taunting me and burning deeper into my skin with my every step.

Together. If we lost, we'd do it together.

This event wasn't complicated; it was an all-out race to the mountaintop, and the first team to have every recruit there would win.

One person could hold the power to destroy our team—one person could haunt us all.

I only hoped it wouldn't be *me*.

I sniffed, cursing the chilly morning. Though it was still September, autumn had started slinking its way into the world, slowly gripping at the earth. This was the type of early fall morning that foreshadowed winter, where cold laced the air in my nostrils and against my skin. Back home, in these brisker temperatures, Mom would have to work more hours out in Miota's fields, spending her days toiling away in and beyond the Grove, yielding as much food with her farming unit before winter came and destroyed plant fertility.

As sharp winds whipped around me, slicing through my clothes, sweat formed at the nape of my neck, underneath my long sleeves. The sensation slowed me down, and the mass of both barracks swallowed me as I fell toward the back of the pack.

I couldn't be the weakest link.

"Hey." Stella, my bunkmate, clapped my shoulder. "Focus on your breathing." She took a huff of her own. "It's tough, with the . . ." *Inhale, exhale.* "The thinning air, I know. Just . . . Focus."

I nodded and channeled my thoughts toward breathing as I'd learned back during Anya's initial training.

In through your nose, out through your mouth.

Time and bodies raced forward. I internalized Zephyr's sentiments of the mind breaking before the body. Heavy thoughts would do nothing but weigh me down even more. The lot of runners were still together, still collected within a hundred or so feet. Some were so far ahead they couldn't be seen—those like Dalton and Gordon, a lanky man who ran marathons for fun. But none had fallen hopelessly behind yet. Hope still remained.

Remember why you're doing this, a deep voice echoed through me when my legs wanted to stop churning forward. Griff's spirit was with me, even now.

At the seven-mile water checkpoint, I found Anya stretching out a cramp, nearly ready to start running again. I quickly whispered to her the plan I'd created a few miles back. She understood my breathless fragments of words, and she pushed on ahead of me with a smile.

I caught my breath and waited for every Scarlet to come through—only a few had fallen behind me.

Garee, an ex-convict, came first. His dark hair glistened with sweat, and his cheeks housed red circles from the frigid air.

"Why aren't you running, Januski?" he ground out. "If you aren't trying, I'm not gonna—"

"I'm waiting for our whole team," I replied and jutted a water cup out to him. "No one should have to do this alone."

Anya had been right. We'd either win or lose—*together*.

Garee rolled his eyes, but he must've found strength in my words, because he set off at a quicker pace.

Two others came, flanking our team: Leo, one of my previous weightlifting partners, and Stephan, a man who'd recently sprained a ligament in his knee. The three of us pushed onward as Scarlet Barracks' fringe, sweeping others forward as we ran on with increased speed and grit, feeding off each other's energy. We collected a few others, refusing to leave them behind. Though shaky and ragged, we were unbreakable in spirit. We willed our way forward.

The second half of the course turned onto a steep path of rock, and we soon had to crawl to traverse the inclines. I clamped my jaw shut and tried focusing only on moving forward. There were still two recruits from Cobalt Barracks behind us; we just had to keep them there.

I stopped in my tracks at the sight of the river. Dark water roared, which dipped my spine in shock, dousing my energy. Too much water . . . the ghost of Julia and her kettle licked at my legs.

The sole path across the river was an unsteady wooden beam, not even a foot wide, which dipped in the middle, hovering just above the tumultuous current.

"Keep your core tight as you go," Leo offered to the group. "And keep your arms out for balance. Or crawl if you have to."

"Just don't fall," Stephan said with a snarky chuckle, "or we're toast."

Fear grabbed my stomach as I stepped onto the wooden beam, ready to scuffle across to the river's opposite bank. The five of us that made up Scarlet's final group inched across the board. It dipped under our weight, leaving the middle section to kiss the river.

No matter. We *would* make it across.

Until a Cobalt man appeared at the end of the board, effectively blocking our exit.

"Move!" Leo snapped.

The Cobalt sneered.

Behind us, the last two Cobalts had caught up. A woman with buzzed hair cackled. "Nowhere to go now, huh, Scarlet?"

The lot of us realized what this meant. We were trapped on this narrow bridge; we wouldn't make it across.

I cursed. We couldn't fight these people while teetering above rushing waters.

But before my thoughts tangled into too many knots, Garee and Stephan, at the front of the pack, shared a look.

"You thinking what I'm thinking?" Garee asked.

Stephan grinned. "Together."

At the front of the line, Garee inched toward the Cobalt man. As Garee neared the end of the plank, Stephan ran up behind him, pushed Garee, and barreled him straight into the Cobalt.

Cobalt Man hadn't expected to be toppled, and in his brief heartbeat of staggering, Garee knocked him in the gut. Then Stephan grabbed the man's hands to pin them behind his body. Cobalt Man snarled, but before he could free himself from Stephan's grip, Stephan and Garee swarmed and pushed him into the roiling river.

His head became a small dot as he washed away.

Victory unfurled in my chest. We needed to hurry, before he banked and found his way back to the race course.

The other Cobalt on the opposite side of the bridge screamed and charged toward Vianka, the Scarlet closest to her. Vianka whipped her curly hair out of her face and solidified her stance before bringing her fists up in front of her, ready to throw punches as the Cobalt neared. The Cobalt woman lifted a leg to kick Vianka, but Vianka was quicker and swept the Cobalt woman's legs from beneath her. The river drowned out the Cobalt's scream as she, too, rushed down the current.

"Way to go, Vi!" Stephan shouted. Vianka blushed and rolled her eyes.

The five of us made it across the bridge because of teamwork. We couldn't have done it on our own, but together, we'd accomplished so much more.

The triumph gave us energy, and we passed multiple Cobalts. As we encountered Scarlets, we pushed them forward with us. At our next water station, we sipped and kept running. We were *so close.*

I didn't like having a small slew of Cobalts on our backs, but it was necessary if it meant we didn't finish last. As the terrain became rockier and more vertical still, something told me we'd see the Cobalts again.

My vision morphed into hues of red and blue and green. I likely hadn't drunk enough water, and I doubted I was alone.

"The air," Vianka wheezed to Garee and Stephan.

"Dizzy," Stephan chimed breathlessly.

No, no, no. We only had three miles to go. I could nearly taste the finish line, the victory for Miota. Since we'd already beaten Emerald Barracks, we only had to beat out Cobalt Barracks today to get our pick of Arlo's three assignment options.

We'd go to Miota, and together with Dalton, I believed we could still carry on as planned. These Scarlets could help free Miota against Julia's forces.

The purpose of saving Miota buzzed through my blood. It overtook me as our group passed Charlie, evidently a member of Cobalt Barracks. My friend from Anya's pre-logistics training group crawled up the rocky slope, breathless and dazed.

Guilt pressed on my chest as we overcame her.

The path leveled in the final two miles—still steep and winding, but less rock made for less climbing on all fours.

"This race is bigger than us!" I shouted. "We can *win!*"

The group of amassing Scarlets further honed their resilience, and we ran like hell.

Until Stephan collapsed with a sharp cry.

I smashed my jaws together. This could *not* happen now. The flock of trailing Cobalts would catch up at any minute.

"Keep going!" I shouted at the group. Though reluctant, they listened.

My hands shook as I approached Stephan; this felt too similar to when Salem had needed medical help in Miota's tunnels. I'd failed my friend then, as I was sure to do now, too. Besides, I hadn't done anything with my schooling in so long—who was I to help this man?

Just try, Corinn. I chided myself—this wouldn't end up like it had with Salem. I *couldn't* make that same mistake. Salem Redding was now the compass I lived by, and if I made the same choices now, he would've died for nothing.

"Knee," he said through a sucking breath. "Still sprained, and . . . can't put weight on it any longer."

I surveyed his knee, where the lateral ligament was surely frayed beyond repair right now. Stephan needed weeks of proper rest and healing.

Next, I scanned the terrain below for any signs of Cobalts progressing on us. Nothing yet, but I sensed movement in the woods. They would soon catch up.

"You go on," Stephan said as he tried standing. "I'll be fine."

"You know the rules. We *all* need to finish." I met Stephan's eyes, and the same helplessness I felt behind my ribs resided in his irises.

"Januski, I'm not finishing this one."

Footsteps battered closer—Cobalts had gained on us.

But the familiar gait stopped upon reaching us. I almost let out a fresh sob when I looked up and saw Dalton alongside three skilled runners, Gordon, Hayden, and Jerome.

They must've received the plan from Anya, the one I'd told her over ten miles ago. This group had already finished their race and were now back to help the rest of us. They'd push us forward and help our barracks win.

"Thank the moon," I whispered on a shaky exhale. I realized too late the mistake of letting out a Miotan phrase, and Stephan eyed me with a knit brow.

Hayden, Jerome, and Gordon helped Stephan to his feet, and the trio helped carry him forward. I scanned the path behind us; still no Cobalts. Stephan and the three carrying him would need all the head start they could get.

With what little spare air I had, I ensured Dalton knew the second half of this plan to slow the Cobalts. He nodded, understanding the task I wouldn't trust anyone else with.

We all staggered forward, and with less than a mile to go, the thundering footsteps of the remaining Cobalts came behind us in tandem with their cackles and taunts.

This was the battle to the finish line.

I helped thrust Stephan's group onward, shoving them forward. The end was *in sight*, sprawled ahead in the distance, our beacon of hope. We *had* to get there first. The Cobalts closed the distance between us as they hollered and yelped, shouting vile things to try shocking us into submission. It wouldn't work.

Dalton, running next to me, tripped over a rock and stumbled down to his hands and knees. He lay on the ground, too motionless for a breath, and my stomach lurched as I craned my neck to look back at the boy.

"DALTON!" I shouted. My lungs tore in two at the effort. "HURRY!"

The Cobalts surpassed him, but I didn't turn back. I trusted the plan.

I was the group's next target. Pure adrenaline drove me forward as hoots and aggressive snarls came from the Cobalts. Surely, this was a tactic of theirs, trying to wear down their opponents' minds.

The mind will break a hundred times before the body.

I blinked and peeled my feet forward, step by step, propelled by nothing but raw grit and bruised courage, the kind Dalton told me I carried.

We will win. We will win. We will win.

Many paces ahead, the three carrying Stephan crossed the finish line; now, only Dalton and I remained on the wrong side of the mark.

The Cobalts snapped at my heels. They nearly caught me; I blended into the group. Feet beating, heart pounding, I *pushed* off the ground and forced my way to the finish line. I crossed before the last Cobalt, though *they* cheered.

I froze. Dalton wasn't here. His fall, according to plan, should've been fake. But if he hadn't crossed . . .

"Congratulations, Scarlet Barracks."

The gang of Cobalts froze, their jaws slack and eyes wide. But the slew of Scarlets gave way, revealing Dalton lying on the ground, winded as ever.

"I snuck . . . around . . ." he panted. "Wasn't that hard."

My eyes fluttered shut. We *won*. We'd beaten the other two barracks making up the whole logistics team—we deserved to pick our assignment. I'd harness my courage, as Dalton told me.

Because I was coming for Miota with everything I was.

CHAPTER 34

CORINN

My barracks certainly knew how to celebrate our victory.

When three recruits snuck out to bring back a keg of malt alcohol to the barracks, Zephyr turned a blind eye. "Get back before the other two see," he'd said to the trio.

The other two—*Brood and Broody.*

That night, after our win against Cobalt Barracks, we'd collected in the boys' quarters, using their bunks as sofas and the floor as a serving counter.

My head buzzed all night, and my muscles tingled through the morning, too. But I was in better shape than most. Dalton and I surveyed the cafeteria during breakfast with amused looks. He hadn't drunk—something about wanted to keep a clear head at all times. It seemed like a move Julia Delldova would make; then I remembered who Dalton's father was and how he'd likely been raised. Were he and Cass truly that different?

I wondered how Cass was doing. Was he still trying to live as a Miotan in a foreign world?

Anya, sitting across from us, aimlessly scooped her oats. After she'd stirred her breakfast no less than a dozen times, Dalton grabbed her spoon and ate her protein oats himself.

Anya's mouth gaped. "You ass, that's my food." The entertained glint in her eyes didn't help her case, though.

Dalton shrugged as a laugh rolled in his throat. "You weren't eating it." He handed her spoon back.

"I need food," Anya pouted, frowning and slumping in her seat.

Dalton eyed her bowl. "You've had food in front of you this whole time."

"I need *different* food."

"How drunk did you get last night, Anya?"

Her eyes flared. I couldn't blame her; her name slid off Dalton's tongue like a prayer. "Not any drunker than *you*."

"I was sober all night."

"Right . . ." Anya resumed stirring her oats.

Garee and Stephan hadn't even made it down to breakfast this morning—which earned them extra miles of running alongside double chore duty.

No one could deny the hungover state of our barracks, which was why we were so startled when Zephyr called us for an emergency meeting in the living room immediately following breakfast.

I stood in the back of the space next to Dalton. Anya sat cross-legged at his feet and played with her braids' ends. Stella, my bunkmate, stood to my other side.

"You've beat out the other two barracks," Zephyr told us. His dark eyes combed the crowd in an effort to command attention. "Now, you all have orders to report to Arlo James after lunch to select your position in the logistics team. He said to come ready to fight, which means we should probably warm up this morning. Hindsight twenty-twenty, the keg should've been a negative, considering the looks of you lot." To that, Brood and Broody blinked at Zephyr with shock. "And be ready for anything today—you never know what the guy's gonna do." Zephyr crossed his arms, which rippled the permanent ink on them.

We ran through morning training, some more groggy than others, and my apprehensions grew. Time ticked toward officially confronting Arlo James, the all-consuming leader I'd heard horror stories of but had never met.

Miota weighed on me like never before. The last time I held this sort of pressure on my shoulders, I'd acted so rashly, I'd gotten Salem killed. I couldn't do that again, with everything on the line.

Our barracks prepped for combat before lunch. I wrapped my legs in compression bandages before donning slick pants, and I taped my wrist, concealing the fading scar of my rat bite.

My survival should've encouraged me. But I sensed *I* was the defective one, not the rat. No one survived red bite.

No one until me.

Dalton scarfed his food down as usual, unable to eat at any speed besides as-fast-as-humanly-possible. He picked at my food too, as my appetite was nowhere to be found.

After lunch, we piled onto a bus reeking of exhaust fumes and drove not out to the base of a mountain, as we had the past two times we loaded this vehicle, but toward Red Fox's inner city. We then rode a maglev into the heart of Sector A's capital, straight to Biourica's base.

Being back in civilization, seeing so many people enthralled with their own lives, made me feel a little better—my problems weren't the center of the world, nor the end of it. Maybe I could handle this coup, succeeding to overtake Julia *and* this fraction of Arlo's logistics team in one blow.

It wouldn't solve every problem; part of the logistics team would still likely expand beyond Sector A, and the last thing we wanted was Arlo solidifying power in another sector. But maybe this victory would be enough for now.

A ball of bile sat in my throat, and I clenched my jaw to keep it from making an appearance. My ears rang; my shoulders slumped; my feet went numb.

"You good?" Anya asked, taking my hand as we unloaded from the maglev. Being back on Biourica's grassy lawn was like being slammed back in time. This was where Anya had first given me hope for helping Miota. "You look freakishly pale."

"Fine," I lied.

"Hey." Anya squeezed my hand. "Dig deep and find strength, right?" When I whipped my head toward her, shocked by her echo of my old tutor's words, she grinned sheepishly. "Charlie told me the phrase way back when. Said she heard it from you. I like it."

A tentative smile shimmered across my lips. For a small moment, peace surrounded me. Anya using Bernard's words seemed ritualistic, providing a blend of friends, old and new.

"Thanks, Anya."

"Kick ass today." Her mouth twitched.

"Kick ass," I echoed with a light laugh.

We entered Biourica through a back door and took an elevator down into the building's bowels. Unlike the gilded elevator in Lorella's apartment building and the metal one in Cass's and my hotel, *this* elevator housed rust and copper wiring.

I slithered my way toward Dalton. "You don't remember anything about this place?" I challenged him.

"I've already told you." Dalton blinked furiously and crumpled his brow. "*No.*"

I pushed, hoping he would remember by being *here*. "Tunnels, passageways, doors . . ."

He ground his teeth. "No, no, and, n-no."

I didn't believe it. This place *had* to house covert passages. I recalled the skills I'd learned to spy—not that they'd ever gotten me very far—and took it upon myself to pinpoint distractions and potential hideaways.

We landed in a cavity large enough to hold the castle's ballroom, the very location I'd first met Griff. Fluorescent lights beat down from the towering ceiling, and dusty metal shelves, each one seemingly the height of a full-grown tree, housed stacks upon stacks of boxes. The shelves cleared a spacious area at the front of the chamber, and in that gathering space stood a man who made Dalton stiffen and tremble all at once.

Arlo James.

The man responsible for hijacking Miotans—stealing their bodies and brains for his own malicious intents. I recalled seeing Hallan in this very building, up in the medical wing, and I bit back a snarl.

While Griff warred with the Queen of Miota in her domain, I was now at odds with the most powerful man in Sector A at his home base.

I wrapped my arms across my chest to keep from shaking too much. Thank the moon I hadn't eaten much lunch, or I'd be sick all over myself.

I tried humanizing the infamous Arlo James by prying his features apart. His smugly set mouth mirrored his oldest son's in an expression I'd seen too many times to count on Colton. His hair, though graying now, clearly used to be dark in color, matching Dalton's inky strands. Arlo was as lean as Dalton and muscled as Colton, with eyes as roving and stature as intimidating.

Arlo stood erect, radiating power, even with the downward slope of his shoulders. He knew we'd entered *his* dominion, and it made us vulnerable against him.

The twenty-five of us, plus our three leaders, closed in around him, awaiting his instruction. When Arlo's leaden eyes skirted over me, my heart stopped. I *swore* he saw through my disguise; he surely knew I was Miotan. But his gaze moved on without anything more than a small smile.

I let out a quick sigh and rubbed at my taped wrist.

"You are the cream of the crop," Arlo began without warning. Everyone stilled. "The elite of the elite. Congratulations. As promised, you'll receive your reward: your selection of assignment. This logistics team will help Biourica expand its benefits and resources past current markets, and that is no simple task. The choice is yours, Scarlet Barracks: expansion, enforcement, or allocation."

Our team searched each other with blank expressions. "Can we get job descriptions, Arlo Sir?" Leo asked. "It just seems hard to choose—"

"Unfortunately," Arlo interrupted, "you don't have the security clearance to get the full schematic. You'll only know the part you play a role in. Trust me, it helps drive efficiency upward."

"Spoken like a damn bureaucrat," Dalton muttered.

"What was that, Dalton?" Arlo perked, lifting his brows.

Dalton's cheeks reddened as he answered his father—his *father*, who stared at his son as if he were a stranger, a logistics recruit with no significance. "I, uh—er, allocation."

Allocation. Would that get us to Miota? Expansion was likely the team that would bleed into another sector, in the Sector B encampment Lorella had heard about. Enforcement could nod to regulating rules here or enforcing Julia's trade terms on Miota. Allocation, similarly, either meant gathering and distributing supplies here or people on Miota.

"Interesting decision," Arlo hummed. He grinned. "Anyone oppose?" A few grunts and shrugs met his question.

I hoped this was the path to Miota.

Arlo hmphed. "All right. Scarlet Barracks"—he mimed a checkmark with a finger—"allocation. Only thing is, I need to know your hand-to-hand combat skills and endurances are up to snuff. So in this case, I have one more test for you."

A few recruits groaned, and Dalton's frame shrank.

"My company, my rules!" Arlo harnessed our attention back to himself. "And here they are. You'll be completing hand-to-hand sparring, right here, so my organization and I can ensure you all have the necessary skills for the job."

If hand-to-hand combat was in the job description, that meant Dalton had chosen correctly; we were going to Miota to fight. And if I had it my way, I'd help ensure we fought *for* Miota instead of against it.

"You'll all be paired up. There'll be three one-minute rounds of sparring, with the intent of knocking out your partner. After the three rounds, everyone will run one mile—unless you're knocked out cold, I guess. The person in the partnership with the combined better fight and faster run will win. If over half the Scarlets win, you guys will carry on with your allocation assignment, and I'll give you my congratulations."

I narrowed my eyes. Dalton's hands flexed, spasming without control. This didn't add up at all. Something else was at play, and we were about to confront it.

Our barracks shimmered with anticipation and questioning as Arlo James called our names and assigned us our sparring partners.

"Corinn Januski and Shea Nowans: front left corner."

Shea Nowans. I didn't recognize the woman's name, meaning she wasn't a Scarlet. Was she part of another barracks? I didn't recall her belonging to Anya's training group.

Would Shea be lean and powerful like Anya? Or stocky and intimidating like Leo? Was she bent on seeing me fail, or could I somehow hold my own against her?

I focused on a spot in the distance and blurred out the world around me as I located a fierce headspace. I'd improved my punches and blocks, thanks to the training we'd done on our shoulders and arms and backs. The lean muscles honed power. Even my legs, once burned by the Queen of Miota, had healed well and provided me with a strong base of support.

I created my battle tactics with that knowledge. I'd have to get Shea stuck in one area, firmly plant my feet, and throw all my upper body strength into defeating her. One solid punch could have her eyes rolling back, deeming me winner of the round.

But doubt still managed to creep into my mind. I wasn't sure I'd *let* myself deliver such a harsh blow to a woman I didn't even know. If that were the case, I just had to focus on not letting her get *me*. If neither one of us beat the other, we'd still have to complete the run, and hopefully, I'd run faster to get a better overall score.

Once Arlo finished assigning us, we each took to our foretold spots on the floor. It was hardly enough room to clear the other partnerships; one fight would likely bleed into the next.

With glazed eyes and splintering nerves, I searched through the crowd—which had grown to comprise of more than just Scarlet

Barracks—for the woman I would fight. With each passing foreigner, my voice squeaked. "Shea?" I tried. "Shea?" No luck. One woman's face nearly knocked me to my feet—she looked exactly like a Top Tier from Pointe.

"Corinn?" a familiar voice called. "Januski?"

It was Dalton. But what did he want right now? I spun—

I was on the ground. *"By the moon,"* I muttered. My lip quivered. I choked on a laugh and let him help me to my feet. Anything to get closer to those irises of seawater. As he touched my skin, helping me stand, I knew this was real. It was *him.*

"Salem," I huffed quietly, relief and confusion washing over me violently, threatening to drown me. *Salem Redding* was here, alive. I wanted to vomit, to faint, to do *something* with all this shock. "Salem, it's you—"

"Shea," he interrupted. He tightened his eyes—his *naked* eyes, as if he wasn't blind without his thick, wired glasses. "It's Shea Nowans."

The chill in his tone, leeched of *any* sort of recognition toward me, rendered my body and mind frozen.

Shea. Shea Nowans.

When the pieces clicked, I broke.

CHAPTER 35

CORINN

I opened my mouth.

It hit me. *Shea Nowans* was no woman. It was him.

Salem.

He'd been erased. Just like Hallan, and just like Lorella's crew had alluded to.

Arlo James had erased Salem Redding.

A tear slid down my face. I trembled. "Do you . . . do you remember anything?"

"What the hell are you talking about?" He furrowed his brow instead of quirking one eyebrow, as he'd do *before*. He crossed his arms, now too bulky for me to register as his own, and he carried his features in a way I didn't know. This person . . . he was foreign to me. This wasn't Salem.

It might've been his shell, his physical appearance. But this wasn't *him*.

"Do I know you?" he challenged.

My heart cleaved. "You're supposed to."

He only rolled his eyes. "I'm not in the mood for mind games, Januski."

"Where are you from?" My voice shook. This was *not* real.

"Born in Hart, raised in Red Fox," he rattled off flatly. "Why's it matter to you? I'm just the guy who's about to beat you in a fight."

"Salem—"

"It's *Shea*," he growled, and took a fighting stance. "Our minute's about to start."

"I won't fight you." This wasn't happening. It *was not*.

Arlo blew a whistle, signaling the start of our first minute of sparring.

Salem cocked his head and strode toward me with collected fists. "Suit yourself, Scarlet."

He'd died. He was charging for me . . . but he'd *died*. I'd seen his lifeless body. I'd mourned him every second since then. But had I seen the moment he died? No, I wasn't sure I had. I saw a body, disconnected from a heart monitor, after I'd woken up from a medicated spell of unconsciousness.

He must've been on the shipment to Red Fox. To Biourica, to Arlo James and this damned company, hellbent on brainwashing Miotans. Making them forget their pasts, forcing them to take on new identities. It happened with Hallan, and now my worst nightmare was standing in front of me.

Salem Redding was too good for a place like this. His brain had been scrambled, fried, whatever . . .

A set of heavy eyes bared down on me, snapping me out of my trance. Arlo James watched, fixated on Salem and me.

I couldn't show any sign of recognizing Salem *now*. If Arlo realized I knew him in another life, he'd know where I came from. He'd see through my façade.

So I mustered what little strength I possessed into stopping my tears and clenching my jaw. It was useless. I screamed, channeling rage toward Arlo into the sound, as Salem—Shea, whoever—raced toward me.

Salem punched me. The ground slammed up into my jaw. Before I could recover, Salem delivered blow after blow to my ribs, my back.

I did this to you, I thought. *This is all my fault. I got you erased.*

He didn't know who I was. Who *he* was.

When he hit my head, pain sent my skull buzzing.

Salem Redding did not exist. Not in the slightest. Because if there was any inkling of Salem inside this body, he wouldn't beat me into a bloody pulp. It was all the proof, all the information, I needed to know that though Salem was here, walking and talking and breathing, *he did not exist.*

"Please," I gasped. "P-please." I kneeled, straightening my spine, before he punched me in the face, and red lights overtook my vision. I wailed.

I flailed and protected my head, thankful for the mercy of not having to look Salem in the eye as he pummeled me.

He hit again.

Again.

Again.

I deserve this—all of this, and more.

What had Arlo done to Salem to make him this way? My best friend, my sunshine and light, had been replaced by a twisted monster.

I coughed, spitting blood onto the ground. Salem's foot found my back, crushing my quadruped position, and I keeled onto the ground, flat on my stomach. His elbow connected with my back, over my lung, and it sent me hurtling toward oblivion as I sucked in for air I couldn't find.

This was a nightmare, surely. I'd wake up soon, and Salem would be dead instead of a stranger.

"Stand up, Corinn," he taunted. "Didn't realize how *easy* this would be."

I cried. This was real. I would know Salem's voice in any version of reality, even in this one, where his tone was devoid of all life and color. Where he lilted his words differently to possess a poisonous twinge I didn't recognize.

When the pain resonated through my whole body, I begged for

Salem to end me. Put an end to this. But my body seemed to know I *deserved* this because it held on, forcing me to witness this cruelty from Salem's husk. My heart fractured further as he went, and I didn't have the strength to rise.

I didn't have *anything*. Not when Salem Redding had been erased from time and space because of *me*. He'd been tortured, experimented on in a lab, and erased.

This was what happened when people relied on me.

"End me," I cried, barely audible even to my own ears. Guilt flooded me. Who was I to beg for mercy? My actions hadn't granted that gift to Salem months ago. "End me now."

Salem's elbow came down on the base of my skull.

When I opened my eyes through the pain lancing down my torso and around my head, I saw ghosts.

Salem Redding was dead. He was supposed to be. But the fact he was *here*, under a new name, with an entirely fabricated history, meant they'd done something to his brain. Something to change him entirely.

"Good." Salem huffed. I shut my eyes at the sound of his voice. "Thought you weren't coming back for a second."

Funny how I could've said the same about him.

"Can you stand?"

I opened my eyes at the approaching footfalls, and Salem outstretched a hand to help me to my feet. His face—his body—was technically his own. But his gait, his voice's intonation and rhythm, his muscle tone . . . not a *damn thing* was familiar. "Let me help—"

"Stop!" I screeched and curled into a ball. Pain exploded in my abdominal cavity. "Please, *stop*."

Salem was gone. *Dead.* And Shea was the replacement who stole his body.

"Really? You're a sore loser, Januski." His tone turned bitter and ugly, something I'd never once heard from my best friend. No matter his anger, whatever his mood, I'd *never* tasted hatred in his words. "I'm just trying to be nice."

"Well, I don't need your help," I choked before wiping the tears caking my face. "So just get away from me."

Salem's face morphed into an entirely new expression—resolution dipped in smugness. "It's a wonder you made it onto Arlo's logistics team at all."

"Just leave!" I begged. This wasn't Salem; it was Shea Nowans, and I *hated* him for it. Shea was too sharp, too angular, where Salem had been warm and light.

This person was *too damn dark*.

Had Salem suffered? When they changed him, what had he felt? Had he known what was coming, or was he simply gone at the drop of a hat?

However it came about, it was my fault. I never should've let him leave Castle Circle with me, all those moons ago. If he'd stayed there, he'd still be safe, on Miota where he belonged.

This Salem spat a curse at me and retreated. He gave a light taunt at how he'd certainly win the race between the two of us.

I didn't care.

A woman donning Biourica's green colors knelt over me and offered a watery smile. "I'm going to touch your ribs," she informed me. "They appear to be broken. I'll send a med-bot down here to help."

"Leave them," I croaked. *I deserve it—deserve this.*

"But your ribs—"

"*Leave them.* They'll heal." And my ribs would. But I wouldn't. My soul would never, so long as Salem walked this earth as someone else. That person who just beat me was not my best friend.

I'd already seen this cruelty done to Hallan, and I now added Salem to the list of victims. I couldn't imagine how many other Miotans were like that. How many of Miota's ghosts were still living whispers of their old lives, stuck to conform to new ones fit for Arlo James? It was the most barbaric thing I could imagine. Salem was dead, but his body was forced to beat on relentlessly in the name of someone else.

The woman quirked a brow. An action so *Salem* I nearly screamed at her. "Let me at least fix your hands. They took a beating." She reached for my wrists, and in my stunned state, I hadn't realized the tape had unwound around my wrist.

The world moved too slowly as the woman's eyes flared and she inhaled to yell.

"Stop!" I cried in the same instant she shouted, "*ARLO!*"

I tried standing, but pain vibrated through my entire body at a vicious rate. It was no use as I scrambled, failing to stand. Failing to do *anything* as my nervous system paralyzed me, accepting how detrimental this was.

Biourica's leader materialized at my side. He reached out for my wrist, doing more than examining the healing rat bite. I couldn't pinpoint what he'd done, but it had violated my entire bodily freedom. I felt . . . *him* beneath my skin. In that split second, Arlo had done something internally to my blood and bones and muscles, and I wanted to destroy him for it.

But I couldn't move.

I couldn't do anything.

Help! I shouted—except no sound came from me. As far as I could tell, my mouth didn't even open.

"Now, what have we got here?" Arlo beamed at me with a malicious grin. "Almost every other recruit is running right now. But you, my dear, were knocked out. You took the hardest beating, and you didn't even *try* fighting back!"

He gave a sharp laugh that spider-walked down my scalp, my spine. Arlo then crouched to my level on the ground—only inches from me, completely aware I could've reached out to hurt him, if only I could move. But whatever he'd done when he touched me had rendered my body useless, and he dangled that fact in my face now.

"You knew him, didn't you?" Arlo continued. His hot breath on my face did nothing but smolder my temper. "You knew who he used to be?"

When Arlo's hold on me dampened, I regained the ability to speak. "How could I?" At least he hadn't taken away my free will to speak in half-truths and lies. Not *yet*, anyway. Besides, I didn't need Arlo's incentive when every fiber of my being yelled at my betrayal to Salem. *You coward!* a small voice said. *Tell Arlo about your best friend!*

Arlo's face hardly rippled as he dug a gray button, no bigger than a fingertip, from his pocket. The instant he pressed it, I stood up through the pain, unable to control my own limbs. Arlo had straightened my spine and my legs. He had complete control of me.

Arlo was the poisonous puppeteer, more cynical than Julia Delldova. I hadn't thought it possible before coming here.

Yes, ending Julia's reign on Miota was essential. But without also finishing Arlo and Biourica, it wouldn't matter. Not really, when every Miotan would likely march straight into Arlo's hands.

I tried unleashing my rage, but it was no use. *Nothing* happened. I couldn't cry for help, and I couldn't fight back. Arlo ripped the tape off my wrist completely, where it had been secured to my skin by only a few hairs, and he beamed.

This was the end. Nausea rolled over me in deep, unceasing waves. I dry heaved with each breath, completely unmoving, unable to thrash against Arlo's heavy hold on my body.

"This is red bite." Arlo's eyes flicked to my wrist. He still swallowed any sense of personal space. "*Old, healing* red bite. And do you know what that means?"

HELP ME! I tried screaming. Arlo had once again rendered me speechless. *I hate this, I hate this, I hate this.*

Arlo retreated and turned his back to me. "It means you're Miotan in blood. They're the only ones who survive. I would *love* to learn how and why, but it's unclear. And that frustrates me." He threw a disgruntled look over his shoulder. "Think about it. I can regenerate limbs—I've done it to my own son—and I can cure certain cancers. I can stall the effects of diseases, and I can practically read minds by sifting out truths. I can even control a person's entire motor functioning, as I'm doing to you now. But I cannot for the *life* of me figure out why Miotans are immune to these vermin. Do you see why that pisses me off?"

Potent dizziness slammed into me. I needed to get out of here.

"You're coming with me," Arlo growled. As if my muscles were butter to his command, I followed him.

STOP! I willed myself. Every cell of my being went into turning around, leaving this place, escaping Arlo James. But my body was *not my own*.

Desperate panic slinked further into me. I gulped down air, but it wasn't enough to sate the weightless feeling in my head. This was the end. *The end.* After being minutes away from achieving our assignment with Scarlet Barracks; after almost being able to have a way to save my home.

None of it mattered anymore.

"Try and call for help all you'd like," Arlo offered nonchalantly. "You do what *I* say from now on. I can't wait to find out how a Miotan ended up roaming my city free as a bird!" The genuine excitement in his voice was a slap to the face.

I will never tell, I silently responded. I couldn't jeopardize Lorella's crew and Arlo's own children. But would I have much of a choice? Hopefully, the minute Dalton realized I'd been compromised, he'd alert the crew. Maybe they'd still make it to safety.

"I will break you and remake you so many times, you won't even remember who you are," Arlo snarled in a vicious promise. "Just as I did to your friend. At least you'll finally be back with your people, hm? Miotans, reunited."

I could have wrung his damn neck.

We stepped into the elevator, and every ounce of hope dwindled, submerged completely by fear. Dalton had said I needed fear to have subsequent courage, but in this moment, as we shot upward to a higher floor, *nothing* warred against my terror.

Dalton surely had the forethought to realize what happened. He'd help get Lorella's crew to safety—he *had* to. I would hold out on telling Lorella's plans and secrets as long as I could, but soon, not even my thoughts would be my own. For the crew's sake, and for Miota's, I would put up a fight.

But how was I supposed to win against an all-controlling monster?

The worst was now knowing Salem had been here this whole time. He'd been tortured and erased.

He wasn't himself, and I didn't know which was worse: that he was alive as someone else, or that I wished more than anything for him to be dead.

CHAPTER 36

CORINN

Arlo had me walk into a hallway of black metal, lined with numerous brightly lit cells, all to our left. They encased people of various states—some restless and honed, others subdued and vegetative.

My stomach clenched. *Miotans*, all of them. I was certain.

You're despicable, I tried grounding out to Arlo. *I hate you with everything I am.*

Arlo had the audacity to whistle as he stepped down to the end of the hall, to an empty cell, all-white from its harsh lights to the linens on the small bed. Biourica's leader grinned at me as I walked in.

When the glass sealed shut, cutting off all sound and leaving me with a vacuum of silence, my eyes widened. I whirled—*on my own accord*—and pounded on the glass.

"YOU BASTARD!" I screamed. "YOU'RE A DAMN COWARD! OPEN THIS DOOR AND FIGHT ME!"

If Arlo heard me, he didn't show it. With a placated smile that made me want to punch him, he spun on a heel and left.

I didn't know how long I paced and wondered what I could do to shake Arlo. Despite the injuries Salem just gave me, despite the desire to curl into a ball and weep, I strode on through the pain.

What could I do to free these people I was with, and how could I keep Lorella's crew and the rest of Miota safe?

How could I help Salem, if it was at all possible?

I paced and schemed, though came up short of anything worthwhile.

Too much and too little time had passed when Arlo reappeared outside the glass. I pinned my rage at him, charging at the window.

I didn't make it across the cell. A gas blew into the room from one of the ceiling's corners, and I jolted.

The white room went black.

I woke in Pointe's hospital. Finally, I'd made it *home*.

It worked out after all, then. Our plan for Scarlet Barracks to infiltrate Miota and help. Griff must've been here somewhere—

My view of the white-tiled ceiling became obscured by Arlo James leaning over, looking down at me from where I lay on the exam table.

"You're here?" I blurted. "But that means the plan won't work—"

"*Hear me* when I promise you this, Corinn Januski." Arlo arched his brow, which shot up clear to the bottom edge of his blue surgeon cap. "There is no plan of yours I don't already know."

"Why are we in Pointe?" I demanded. "How did we get here?"

He scoffed and retreated from my vision. "Silly *girl*. We haven't left my compound. But that certainly makes it easy. Pointe is the farm city, right? That's where you're from?"

Still in the compound. We were still in Biourica. I strained to recall how I got onto this table. But the last thing I remembered . . .

Salem. Salem was alive, as someone else entirely. And then I'd been taken over by Arlo, my actions overridden by his commands, and marched into a cell. The smoke . . .

I sat up, only . . . *nothing* happened. I remained flush against the cold, hard table. My worries quickened my pulse, and a pounding pain thrashed through my skull. I couldn't move—

"Welcome to my lab, Corinn." Arlo wheeled over a cart of metal objects clanging about, and I could tell each was as sharp as the next as blades sheared and sang against each other. "You've made it into my experimental rooms, where I aim to figure out what causes red bite. I've already drawn vials of your blood—quite a few, hence your probable lightheadedness. Sorry."

I couldn't hide my eye roll at the sound of Arlo James delivering a half-hearted apology over something so *trivial* against everything else he'd done. I strained again, still unable to conjure motion. Aching lanced through my head and trunk.

"While your blood is off being tested, I hope you'll answer my questions, Corinn. I trust you don't want to make an *enemy* of me, correct?"

"I don't answer to you." I kicked—or, I *tried* to. I couldn't tell if I was truly restrained by thick straps, or if I only imagined them and Arlo contained me with nothing but his brainwaves.

Biourica's leader chuckled as I sat up—rather, as *he* sat me up.

Salem sat tied to a chair across the room, staring blankly ahead, unseeing and unhearing.

"Don't hurt him!" I snarled.

"Silly, silly," Arlo hummed, and he *tsk*ed. "I already *have*. The boy you knew suffered unto his final breath, and then after frying his brain and giving it a good *slosh*"—he scrunched his nose and flicked a hand— "I remade him into something worthwhile. As I do with *all* of you Miotans, after the first phase of experimentation. Consider this the taste test of your own future."

I hiccupped. I was either going to choke, or vomit, or, *or . . .*

Arlo James did this to Salem Redding. My best friend had been tortured and erased completely.

"I was there when he snapped," Arlo continued as my blood seared. "He put up *quite* the fight." He grinned. "Don't look at me like that, Corinn. In the end, we get you all. No one can stand torture forever."

Arlo's grasp on my body lessened, granting me the air to dry heave at the implications. In Salem's last moments as himself, he'd suffered. He'd *fought back*. Even knowing the odds were stacked against him, he'd combatted Arlo James and the inevitable.

It decimated me for a few moments. But if Salem chose to hone such bravery, I could certainly do the same. Just as Dalton had said I could.

As I looked to the lost boy in front of me, the one defiled and remade into something new, I dug deep for my strength and courage.

Whatever Arlo unleashed, I would endure.

I coiled all emotions toward Salem into a tight ball. I couldn't afford to crack now—one moment of weakness would sever me. "You're a monster," I whispered. "And I will *never* answer—"

I gave a clipped wheeze as my lungs convulsed. I couldn't breathe. *I couldn't breathe.*

"This is the best part, Corinn" Arlo said as he sat, lounging in his seat. "I have full control of your body. The voluntary muscles are easy to command, as I'm sure you've realized by now, and luckily, there's a voluntary component to breathing to help speed up the process when I decide to . . . *dive deeper.*"

I couldn't tell if he continued speaking. My mind whirled; my ears rang. Fire licked at my lungs. I couldn't breathe.

I. Couldn't. Breathe.

Salem's ocean eyes stared at me, devoid of all thought and emotion. Until even he faded, and the cacophonous ringing grew. I was going to pass out. But as my eyelids fluttered shut, air slapped my lungs, and I gulped it down.

"So how'd you get to Red Fox anyway?" Arlo asked too casually, as if he hadn't just cut off my ability to breathe.

I burned behind my ribs as I gathered an answer. "I . . . by boat." That was vague enough. I was going to protect everyone I loved.

"No *shit.*" Arlo's eyes of hot coals drifted to Salem for a mere breath of time before Salem cried out. "Shea here is currently getting volts of electricity shot up his spine—feels like tiny bugs in the vertebrae, probably some vibrating of the teeth. I'm increasing the intensity each second you stay silent."

Salem brought a hand to his jaw, and his face twisted. After blinking profusely and grunting, he let out a roaring scream.

My mouth hung as my mind raced. In every form, in every life, I still managed to hurt Salem Redding.

If only I could think of him as Shea Nowans. Then I could spare my friends' secrets. But the agony in the sea-colored eyes . . . the disheveled blond hair . . . he was foreign, but this was still my best friend's body.

His limbs jerked, and he fell forward in his seat. Unconscious.

It was now my turn to scream. "WHAT DID YOU—"

Arlo robbed me of oxygen again.

"Stubborn girl," Arlo snapped. He hadn't even lifted a finger, and he'd rendered Salem unconscious and cut off my air supply. "I'll try my best to keep this grit in you when I remake you."

The white room blurred. Pain nearly drowned me, and I drifted away . . .

Air burned my lungs as Arlo let off my diaphragm.

The cycle continued. I didn't know how long.

Eventually, Arlo let me pass out before granting me air. I was a wilted body, with withering lungs and fractured courage.

Arlo's question clattered somewhere in my subconscious. *How did you get to Red Fox?*

But he never gave me another chance to answer. My mind broke.

My throat cracked, too dry. I needed water. I doubted it was something Arlo would give.

Time passed in days or seconds—with air, and without.

Arlo's next tactic was to contract every one of my muscles to full capacity—the most excruciating, agonizing pain of being splintered apart by hot nerves and zingy flesh.

I broke.

Each time I glanced at Salem, still keeled over in the corner, Arlo sent shock waves through his spine. His ribs no longer expanded.

I arched against the table as my muscles spasmed and locked into place, rendering me unable to breathe. My throat made a gagging, screaming sound, my only remaining outlet.

The mind would break a hundred times before the body. But if that were true, had I almost extinguished my mind's efforts? Because my body was going to collapse and give up.

I was . . . was . . . going to . . .

I blinked, and Salem was gone. Had I passed out? This was too much like his death on Miota—I needed to see him, to see proof he was alive.

Or dead.

I'd failed him yet again. Just as I was destined to fail Lorella's crew and all of Miota. I hoped they were all safe, all completing the plan on their own. That hope kept me holding on.

More time passed. Neither food nor water came. As my muscles buzzed and head trounced, I stopped trying.

Diaphragm malfunction.

I wasn't getting out of here.

Lockjaw.

I wasn't saving Miota. I'd tried playing a game bigger than myself, and this was where it got me. I should've known from the start, should've been more adamant to Lorella: I wasn't made for the games of kings and queens.

No air, no air . . .

I was going to die. During one of these spells, I eventually wouldn't recover. It was the least I could do to hold my secrets.

"I'll give you one more chance, Corinn," Arlo said during one of his sessions. He'd just recently switched tactics again—electrocution this time—to see what would ultimately break me. I would've hated him for it, if I had the ability to *think*. "Tell me how you got to Red Fox, and tell me how you of all people managed to join my logistics team."

I didn't know. I couldn't remember. I was a sack of flesh, and nothing more. I couldn't, couldn't . . .

One of the overhead lights shone in a perfect circle, a beacon. The sun or moon, I didn't know. Didn't care.

Or did I? This meant *something*, didn't it?

The light of the moon. The rays of the sun. *Griff and Salem.* Moon and sun.

"No," I said with a snarl. I gnashed my teeth and clenched my fists with what little movement Arlo currently allowed me to have. "*No!* I will *never* let you jeopardize the people I love!" I found the moonlight, the sunlight. "I have information you don't, and—and—until my dying breath," I fought to finish the sentence, "*I will keep it from you.*"

My vision tunneled.

Arlo paled. Then he snickered maniacally and tilted his head back. "Silly little girl." He wiped under his eye before locking up every muscle in my body. I strained to exhale. My ears rang, and the room went scarlet. "Tell me, then, how this sounds to you. You're Miotan, and you were brought here by my own two *chummy* sons. Lorella Anzalone of all people tried to turn you into a spy, but you weren't having it. So you joined Anya Steele's training group to get on *my* very own logistics team because you thought it would lead you back home—and right you were, I'll give you that. Oh, and best of all, Miota's only heir has been living here, too. Cass Delldova. Have I left anything important out?"

By. The. Moon.

He knew everything—*he knew everything.*

When Arlo released his grip on my muscles, I let out a sob and worked through the tears racking me. I hiccupped for air when I wasn't gagging.

"Why," I rasped out, "am I—am I—"

"Still here?" Arlo guessed. He strolled to his tray of blades and other medical devices and fished out a hypodermic needle. "Alive?" He filled the syringe with a red liquid, and my stomach clenched. "Remember what I told you? Your *blood*, Corinn. It's still proving useful.

Your immunoglobulin levels and ratios, coagulation pathway, platelet count, prothrombin and fibrinogen . . . I *do* need you alive. All of this other stuff—the prolonged torture—is just my way of seeing what Miotans are made of mentally before I remake them into someone of my own army. To see what type of person they are, how much fight they have, and where they'd fit best in my company. You, Corinn, are proving to be quite the tough nut. I only asked about your friends because I wondered if you'd *rat them out*—see what I did there? Like I said, you don't have plans I don't already know. But I guess I *did* underestimate you."

He brought the needle close and aimed for my thigh.

I screamed as the flames burned me alive, charring my flesh to ash.

CHAPTER 37

CORINN

Zephyr said the mind breaks a hundred times before the body. So I started counting.

One. Two. Three . . .

Arlo pumped me with needle after needle. *Eight.*

He burned me alive. *Thirteen.*

Turned my skin to acid. *Twenty-one.*

Broke every bone in all my fingers, one by one. *Forty-two.*

Slit me open in various spots on my arms and legs and chest. *Fifty-seven.*

Stretched my limbs apart until they dislocated from my trunk. *Sixty-six.*

Broke my ribs with blunt force. *Seventy-five.*

The methods changed often. It didn't matter. Whenever death lingered too close with sharp jaws, black as night, Arlo healed me with his revolutionary medicines—to force me to hold on. So he could then break me again. So he could test my mental limits now and let them serve as a reference for when he inevitably remade me into a stranger.

Let me go, I thought. *The ghosts call my name.*

The pain, the agony—I couldn't do this.

I had not been enough on my own. I couldn't win against this man, so it was best to let me meet my end.

Eighty-nine, ninety, ninety-one . . .

I was nothing as the world progressively washed away. In seconds or days, in minutes or hours. It didn't matter. I'd lost the fight. This was the end, and somehow, Arlo already knew all there was to my plan with Lorella's crew. Meaning there was no purpose left for me.

I'd known I wasn't strong enough, known it since—

Since the night I endangered Salem during Accolade. I'd been grasping for atonement since then, and I thought I'd find it in freeing Miota. In saving the people left I loved. But instead, *I* was the one in distress. And Salem had still been undone, defeated, by me.

The new moon had returned. I'd waxed, only to wane.

Arlo had confirmed my suspicions earlier: every Miotan who came into contact with him underwent this sick cycle of blood draws and torture until eventual transmutation of the brain. The thought of every Miotan suffering like this was *unbearable.*

I didn't know when I passed out, but when I woke, my room's occupant was no longer Arlo, but Salem. Was this real?

I would've cried if Arlo hadn't left me paralyzed, hadn't sank his invisible claws into my muscles. He'd undone my restraints only enough to let me breathe shallowly, a weight sitting on my chest. My breathing shallowed even more at the sight of Salem, and I dizzied, *needing* more air, needing relief from this trap—

"Hey." My best friend's voice snagged my attention. "It's you."

I stilled. Stopped breathing, stopped *everything.* "Salem," I whimpered through what little air I had. "Salem, I'm so sorry—"

"Shea," he corrected me, and my heart dropped, slamming back against my spine from where I lay. "It's *Shea.* Remember? We fought for control of B." His gravelly voice scraped against my skin.

Control of B?

Those words might have meant something to me in another life. But I couldn't form thoughts or mold logical conclusions. Not when

Salem Redding stared at me like I was a damned stranger. It drove a knife through me.

"Are you okay?" I uttered at the state of him. Bruises kissed his puffy jaw, and a necklace of fingerprints maimed his neck—some dark and new, others old and yellowing. Adorning the ring, like a crown jewel, was a perfect slit, still encrusted and healing. It would scar, leaving a fine white line forever on his neck.

He shrugged. "Been better. They've been torturing me for days now, for what reason, I don't know." His eyes grazed me. "Same as you, by the looks of it."

I swallowed. If only I could move my head to see the door . . . "Who let you in here?" I asked.

"One of the Biourica lab assistants. She told me to *rile you up*, but you already seem . . . well, riled."

I huffed, then coughed as my lungs slammed into Arlo's artificial restraints. "So does the name Corinn Januski mean anything to you?" I didn't care what punishment this would ensue. I was already on my ninety-sixth life. I'd lost all feeling, all sense of living, long ago. If I met my end at Salem's hand, it would be a fitting welcome home.

"Outside of fighting you?" Salem rubbed at the wounds on his neck. His eyes scanned the room. "No. All I know is you're part of the missing crew."

"Missing crew?" I got out. Curiosity, mixed with some foreign, fluttery emotion, shrouded me. "What's that?"

"I—" Salem paled, bringing out the plum-colored layer of his scars. "I shouldn't say anything. I wasn't supposed to hear. They thought I was unconscious—"

"Salem, *please.*"

"*Shea.*" He paused and narrowed his brow at me. The motion twisted in my chest; it was so *un*-Salem of him. "Why do you keep calling me Salem?"

"I'll tell you if you—" I wheezed. "Tell me what . . . what the missing crew is."

I was . . . bargaining. With my last four lives, knowing death's jaws lingered, I was still attempting to gain the upper hand against Arlo.

This fire was *new*. I'd been so hopeless, alone in this room, stuck with no reprieve. But now that Salem's face was here, even if he wasn't the boy I grew up with and knew like my own flesh, I felt . . . lighter. More *hopeful*, and it expanded life outside of this room. There were plans in motion outside of this place.

The missing crew. Lorella's crew, surely. I only needed Salem to confirm it.

And he did. "They're missing, apparently—the James boys. And the ultimate tribunal's vice judge." *Lorella*. "A few other names I didn't recognize. Yours was included, too."

"They're missing, but are they—are they *here*?"

Had Arlo taken them hostage too?

The door whipped open, and Salem's face fell at the visitor. A woman's husky voice shouted at Salem to leave, that he'd done his job, and Salem tossed me a glare so quick, I would've missed it if I hadn't tracked those eyes for the last seven years.

As Salem passed me, his voice was so low, I nearly mistook it for a hot exhale. "No," he muttered, the word bleeding out, unable to clot.

I recalled what I'd asked. Lorella's crew . . . No, they *weren't here*. They'd vanished, then—they'd likely either left the sector or were making their way to Miota. Either way, Arlo didn't hold them hostage.

The load on me lightened. Though I was alone again, I felt brighter for the first time since entering this building. Salem—no, *Shea Nowans*—had granted me a gift, had given me final words of assurance before sealing me off in this tomb.

It wasn't much. But it was enough.

CHAPTER 38

CORINN

While I succumbed to pain and rode out the waves of consciousness, I let my mind churn. I thought of every possible way to escape this room.

Because I had finally realized what was always churning beneath the surface, just out of grasp.

I couldn't beat Arlo on my own—but I was never *supposed* to. And if I'd accepted that fact from the beginning, I might never have ended up here, in his grasp, on the precipice of oblivion.

This plan was always a team effort, each person with their own forte. I'd rammed through all implications of teamwork, all notions of collaboration, hellbent on toppling Biourica *and* Miota myself.

But such a feat wasn't possible. Salem's presence helped me finally realize it. People were not made to do this life on their own. Just as Miota and Biourica had been built at the hands of many, they would have to be uprooted in the same way. Lorella's crew housed the pieces to pull off a plan groundbreaking enough to shake Biourica to its core, and I held my role close. I was Lorella's spy.

Together, we could do this. Together, we could change the world.

My friends were now missing, undetectable to Arlo, and that meant they were still carrying out their schemes.

"Where's Arlo?" I choked out to the lab assistant who'd taken to healing my broken bones with an osteoblast elixir, making them stronger so it would hurt just as badly the next time someone snapped my fingers and toes.

"Busy with his latest shipment," she told me. "And with his army."

Shipment and army. I latched onto the information, knowing it meant our plan was in action. If all went accordingly, Scarlet Barracks would be on their way to Miota—without Dalton and Anya, given what Salem said about my friends being missing. And Griff, Max, and Abner were leading a movement off Miota, away from Julia. Into Sector B, outside of Biourica's jurisdiction, where they'd more likely have a temporary haven.

I needed to help. I needed to escape. I'd before been so focused on how to take down Biourica from in here, but that wasn't my fight yet.

Yet.

One day, it would be. But I needed to first live to see that day, and I would gladly watch the light leave Arlo's eyes—as I ended him alongside my friends of Red Fox *and* Miota.

"We've put your body under enough physical stress," the lady continued. I wished I could see her, but with Arlo's restraints still embedded in my muscles, I couldn't crane my neck. "And you passed most of our tests, so you're a viable candidate for cerebral fragmentation and deletion. Arlo wants you back in your old room as you wait to make the transition."

"Transition?" I strained against the invisible shackles weighing me down. "What's that?"

"I thought Arlo told you about erasing memories and identities to create something more suitable for life here."

My pulse thrummed. It was what they'd done to Salem—meaning he'd undergone torture already and *passed* their tests, surviving it, though ultimately losing the real war.

"More suitable?" I spat. "For who? *Arlo?*"

"For *whom*," she corrected me. My vision darkened. "And yes."

I received no warning when the needle punctured the inner crook of my elbow, and I went numb. Darkness sank its teeth into me.

I woke with the ability to move within this sealed cell.

I didn't mind the lapse of sound created from the air-tight door; I hardly noticed the blindingly white color washing the chamber. I was finally free to *move*. Of course, it also meant I felt every stitch and ache and pain, and movement wasn't easy.

I studied the crinkly paper clothing I donned, caked with brown blood and some unidentifiable stains. Portions of the clothes stuck to my skin, and that was how I pinpointed which of my wounds still oozed now.

But my physical state didn't hold my attention for long. I needed to scheme up a way out of this cell.

I came up short. Panic didn't set in until my muscles once again tensed. I couldn't look around to see who had opened my door, couldn't even inhale to speak. Someone shuffled inside and set a plastic item on the floor.

Once the door closed, I regained movement.

I have full control of your body, Arlo had said. So someone still controlled my voluntary movements when I wasn't alone.

My sights and thoughts froze and snagged on the tray of food now on the ground. I hadn't eaten since my last breakfast at Scarlet Barracks. I crawled toward the oats and ate them, not minding how the food condensed into a thick paste that made swallowing difficult.

I would have eaten *anything* right now.

Arlo and his crew must've still found use for my blood if they were keeping me alive, granting me autonomous movements and food. If only I could find a way to break the frustrating hold Arlo and a select few of his colleagues had on me.

An idea formed. I chewed on my thoughts in time with the sticky oats. I'd learned the brain's functions and pathways, back home in Pointe, in my schooling with Salem. I'd also studied the side effects of medicinal drugs.

It helped me now.

I didn't believe I falsely recalled any information. Assuming I was on track with my thinking, I'd just discovered my way out of this prison.

I coughed gradually. It came out forced at first. But after what felt like a few hours since the oats had come, I threw every ounce of consciousness into this plan. I counted to twenty. *Cough.* Forty. *Cough.* Sixty. *Cough.* Repeat, and repeat.

When my next plate of food arrived, I tried not to get discouraged when two coughing pills didn't come with it. I summoned my patience, and I wielded my determination into a weapon. I would *make* them give me medicine, if it was the last thing I did. I didn't believe they'd give me medicines intravenously because they were still using my blood, so I coughed until my throat burned and waited for pills.

At my next meal, two blue pills arrived on the serving tray. I contained the victory unfurling within me. I rode the emotion like a fall breeze, full of freedom and possibility. I was stuck in Arlo's compound, yes, but he had not ruined me. He had not—*would* not—end me like this.

My friends and I still had too much to do to change the world.

I swallowed one pill and stuffed the other in the pocket of my paper clothing—the first to see if the pill made me drowsy, alluding to active ingredients, and the second to see if anyone would come fault me for stashing a pill.

My eyelids went heavy, and no one appeared to abduct my pill.

The moon waxed again, as it was always set to do. Maybe I'd make it out of here after all. *The light is there, waiting,* Griff had told me in another life. *You just have to learn to let it in.* There was still hope, even with an empty moon. The darkness wouldn't win.

Next, I internalized time as best I could. I did so while pretending to be asleep, hoping people mistook my idleness for hopelessness. In reality, I was like the sun my Salem had always carried. Maybe he'd shared some leftover rays with Shea, and I now bore the remnants of my best friend.

Time passed in odd waves, and before long, I couldn't trust myself to keep consistent count. The absence of sound in here, save my guttural, forced coughing, messed with my mind more than I thought possible. I never realized how powerful and loud silence could be, demanding all attention, unleashing its power of insanity onto victims.

Trays seemed to come every six hours. Of course, that didn't sound right, but it was my best guess. Two pills accompanied each meal, and when I covertly stashed them in my paper clothes, no one ever came to force them down my throat.

But then Arlo James paid me a visit. He seized me so I couldn't move, though he didn't clamp hard enough to stop my breathing or head movements. It was a small grace, one I gladly accepted.

"What the hell is wrong with you?" he said and marched up to me to slap me. The impact stung on my cheek, and the world rattled on its axis.

"What do you mean?" I kept my voice raspy.

"That cough, you *pathetic little girl.*" He seethed as he smoothed his clothes. "Where did it come from? You've been *here* for the last six days."

Six days. Six days . . . total? Or six days in this cell? No, I couldn't have been in this cell more than two.

"I . . . don't know," I admitted. *Cough.* "It just kind of came on. Maybe when I was being transported from that lab room to this cell?"

Arlo rolled his eyes and cut another slap across my face for good measure. "Well, it better resolve *quickly.* Your transition is in the morning."

His words stung more than his palm on my cheek. *Tomorrow morning.* I would have thirteen pills by then—if that wasn't enough, then this plan was cursed from the start. I only needed to be impaired, not killed off by my own stupidity.

"What's my transition?" I asked as dumbly as possible. I bumbled over the words, using the lessons Lorella taught me. *Become unassuming; play the innocent part.*

Arlo gave a low growl. "Use your *brain*, Corinn. You *know* what your transition is. If you're lucky, you'll end up in the same shape as your little friend, Shea Nowans. But if you're immunocompromised, there's a chance the serum won't hold, and it'll simply kill you. But I like your spirit, and I want you to *survive.* You should really be thanking me."

Too many emotions rattled within my chest. Fear, anxiety, scorn, hope . . .

Courage. That was what Dalton had said. In the face of fear, *choose* courage. It seemed easier said than done, but I gave it a try.

"Thank you," I said. "I'll try my best to recuperate. But, now that I'm remembering . . . that brain fog stuff made me loopy last time, didn't feel good . . ."

"Brain fog stuff?"

I blinked and averted my gaze. *I am innocent; I am clueless.* "When you transported me, you knocked me out, right? My cough started after that. Probably coincidence, but . . . thought I'd mention it. I don't know."

I saw in Arlo's eyes the moment he latched to the idea I'd just planted. I'd just used Lorella's spying tactics on Arlo James, and if all went off without a hitch, it will have *worked.*

"I'm feeling better now that it's rubbed off," I continued with a shrug. "And the medicine has been helping." A pry for the truth—if anyone watched my cell close enough, he'd know I wasn't taking the pills.

But he only kept his face long. "I'll see you tomorrow, Corinn." He left me alone to succumb to the void of silence.

Solitude wasn't good for my mind; I'd learned that already, when

I'd been in the Hold under Miota's royal grounds. Things might have been different now, but in many of the ways that mattered most, they were exactly the same. I was stuck in the jaws of a poisonous ruler, and my country needed help.

This was the same story, but it would not end identically; I wouldn't let it. I would make my mark, find my courage, and best Arlo James. I would help my friends save my country.

Time proved too difficult to track against my buzzing nerves, but I did my best, calculating when to take the pills before I was taken for my transition.

Please let this be right. Still lying underneath my cot's thin sheet, I unleashed my stash of pills and gulped them down. My success now relied on timing, dosage, and my transportation method out of here.

I wasn't sure if the pills worked until sound hit my ears—the glass door had unsealed, and a redheaded woman wearing Biourica's green color entered.

"Ready for your transition?" Her grin was too wide, showing too many teeth, and the sight sent a chill up my spine.

"Yes." I . . . got out of bed. *On my own accord.* The invisible clamp on me was gone! I was—

The world tipped, and I fell to the floor to match the room's spinning. I stumbled to my feet and didn't know which woman to look at; she'd duplicated, her two bodies blending and blurring.

The pills worked, I supposed.

The woman eyed me warily before turning on a sharp heel and leading me out of the room. I followed, figuring she had no idea the hold on me had disappeared.

I'd done it—the pills had scrambled my brain's motor pathways enough to sever the connection. I didn't feel any external control.

Then again, I couldn't feel much at all. I swayed with each step, and the walls blurred by. *Pay attention,* Lorella's voice chided me. *Watch your surroundings.*

"Shush," I whispered to Lorella as my eyes fell shut. They flew back open as my head dropped, its weight suddenly too heavy.

The redhead narrowed her eyes at me. "Who are you talking to?"

"You," I blurted. "Shush."

She rolled her eyes. "Hurry up. The sooner you get this done, the sooner we can stop worrying about you."

"Why would you worry about me?" The effort of talking and walking made me stumble, but I kept my core tight and continued onward. Even as the walls swayed. Even as the floor rolled. Even as my stomach became a hardened pit, nearly pitching itself.

I followed the beacon of red hair through swinging doors, down a fluorescent hallway. My steps mirrored the woman's until we reached a moving box . . . it was called . . .

Elanator. No. Yes? Maybe. Whatever.

The doors gaped open to swallow us, and once we were sealed shut, the box lurched downward. My knuckles went white from gripping the rail.

"You look sick," Red Girl observed. Her voice came out fuzzy, unclear.

"I have a cough," I replied and kept my gaze on a single spot on the ground, trying to ignore the roiling mass in my stomach.

She wrinkled her nose. "Don't get sick in this elevator. Please."

Elevator! That was the word.

Something deep and warm in my stomach told me to stay quiet, so I did as we escaped the metal contraption. I didn't think to look at what floor we'd landed on until we were long gone.

Pay. Attention.

Everything looked identical here; it was a living, breathing maze, and I started to wonder if I would ever escape Arlo's layer. I wasn't confident. Especially as bile rose in my throat at the whirling world.

My senses sharpened as we entered a room whose ceiling I knew too well. This was my torture chamber. This was where I'd been broken and remade over one-hundred times. Salem had been here, too, with his own ringlet of bruises and scars.

I struggled to breathe. I couldn't come back here—*couldn't* do this again. No, no, no. *Get out of here!* a voice snapped at me. My courage found me in this labyrinth. I'd too comfortably followed the woman in here, and it might've blown my one chance to escape.

Get. Out. Get out. Get out!

No, it was too late. I'd realized *too late*. I was about to be erased. The deadliest man in the League, on the entire supercontinent, had me in his grip.

I coughed on the thought, choked on the fear flooding my every nerve and cell. It triggered my gag reflex, and my churning stomach could take no more.

I vomited.

The girl shut her eyes. She stumbled and wrinkled her face, scoffing at me. "Stay seated." She mumbled the next bit under her breath. "Not that you have a choice." In a swift moment, she was gone from the room, leaving me alone.

"Sorry," I babbled, much too late.

The thought collided into me again, brighter and sharper than the last time. *She was gone.*

This was my one chance to escape! This was good. I needed to find a way out of this building. Right? That *was* my plan?

The girl thought I was under full control of Arlo's muscle contraction . . . *thing*. They wouldn't give me full reign in this room, unlike in my cell. I'd been able to walk around, breathe, eat, sleep . . . but in here . . .

Eighteen years of living on Miota cut through my impaired state. There was a way out of here, unlike in my cell. The Delldovas hid their secrets, and that wasn't a trait unique to dictators. *Everyone* had secrets, and people usually obscured them to keep from being discovered.

I stood, and I tried the door. With a quick rattle, panic set in. It was locked. My discouragement quickly morphed into courage, though. If I couldn't leave through the door . . . then there was likely another way out, hence my strict constraints in here.

The restraints that were now only *presumed* by Arlo and his team.

Either by blind courage or sheer ignorance, I tore at the cabinets, looking for an escape. Nothing. *Think, Corinn. Think.*

I poked and prodded at the wall, but nothing gave. The cabinets also housed nothing. The only remaining thing in the room was the sink and pane of reflective glass hanging on the wall. I pried my fingers behind the mirror and *ripped* with unchecked strength, thanks to the coughing pills unbridling my panicked state. Though, after getting sick, I felt a little better in the head. *A little.*

The mirror came off the wall. It unsheathed courage and action, and I leapt into motion at the dark chamber sitting like a prize within the wall. I *knew* there were passages here. Dalton either had never known about them or his memories had been altered upon his disownment. The way he'd stuttered when speaking about this possibility led me to believe the latter.

Get out of here.

I laughed and stepped into the cool passageway, setting the mirror back against the wall as best I could from within the threshold. I only had a limited amount of time before Red Girl returned to the room.

I couldn't lose this chance. I ran with all the momentum I could muster, only the longer I went on, the more my terror undid me. Where was I supposed to go? I was rushing through a maze within a maze—there was no chance of escaping. Arlo James would send a search crew, and they would find me. I wasn't even sure what floor I was on; what if I was hundreds of feet above Biourica's ground level, running only closer and closer to my death?

I followed the fragments of light, figuring I could find a tunnel outlet that way. Once I was outside of Biourica, I'd have to continue on foot, as fast and far as I could, to leave Red Fox entirely. Lorella's crew was missing, meaning they were either on Miota or in Sector B.

As I scurried onward, I decided I'd go to Sector B, knowing Miotans would eventually end up there.

I only stopped short when I came to a fork in the path. Which way to go? They looked identical. How would I choose? Would one lead to victory, the other to my demise?

I nearly started down the left path when a rustling motion came from it, echoing through the bleak metal hall. Someone else was here.

I froze as a shadowed figure ran at me.

PART FOUR

"My dear sister, listen . . . Firstly, keep Maintenance in check. Don't act against the crown unless you have direct support from my son-in-law or grandson. Secondly, keep a distant but watchful eye on Charles Howard of Salford when you overlap in Castle Circle. Julia may love him, but she would still kill him if he's found guilty of treason."

—Letter from Elizabeth Delldova to Jyn Hepper, dated 17 November, 20 JD

CHAPTER 39

GRIFF

I held every breath too long, knowing treason infiltrated the castle walls tonight. It reeked wherever I looked, wherever I went . . . it haunted me like a phantom presence, and it was all culminating now.

I paced my bedroom as I waited for Addison and Abner. I didn't know who would come first. Addison was set to arrive any minute—already late, which was unusual for her. And Abner . . . I glanced at the time on my panel. He should've been in Julia's bedroom right now, expertly poisoning her in the form of an unassuming laced wine.

He still had twenty minutes, according to schedule, before I was supposed to worry. But I couldn't help it, and my limbs bumbled about. I tripped over my feet as I paced.

Things had already gone so wrong. We'd planned for Corinn's team to help escort Miotans off the island, using their presence to our advantage. But Max had received word from Lorella Anzalone that Corinn's team was being shipped off to a different part of the supercontinent, and instead, a second team unrelated to Corinn and our plan now sailed toward Miota. The only way to save ourselves was to get everyone off the island before they landed.

We were now racing death, and it was too early to predict the winner. If death didn't come in the form of invasion, it could certainly strike as revolution here, among and against Miota's own people.

Calm down, I schooled myself. Yet my nerves ramped up with every ticking second. I marched to my balcony and threw the doors open, welcoming the chilly night air. Each passing day grew colder as autumn heightened, slowly summoning the descent into winter. It was jarring to know that at summer's height, Corinn and I had just discovered the supercontinent's existence. Now, just one season later, Corinn was on the supercontinent, and I was set to free Miota and join her there.

Assuming all went to plan.

Someone rapped on my door. My heart lurched. I didn't know if I hoped for it to be Addison or Abner—I needed them both. My gut twisted into too many knots as I reached for the door and cracked it open.

Addison. While temporary relief found me, I also hurtled quicker toward full-on panic. Was it safe to tell Addison what was happening? Abner was still in Julia's room, meaning we weren't in the clear yet. Abner's current role was essential to this entire plan working. If he couldn't subdue Julia, we wouldn't win.

"Ads." I forced a stiff smile, though I knew it hardly reached my eyes. "Come in." I could stall for time until Abner showed himself.

My fiancée's gaze choked me as she entered. I motioned toward the bed, gesturing for her to sit, while I continued pacing. I couldn't stay still right now. Not when so much—too much—was about to happen. Not when I was about to march to Miota's southernmost tip, razing our island home in the process, riling up anyone and everyone who'd listen.

It was risky, yes. It was more stress than I'd ever wanted to put on myself. But with a supercontinental army sailing for us, it was the only way to keep everyone on this island safe.

"What's going on?" Addison tried silently prying me open, as if she could read my mind. But I tucked my intentions inward, only letting my nerves show through my clenched hands and pacing.

"I just thought we should probably talk," I started. My voice went in and out. "About the future. *Our* future."

Her throat bobbed, and she nearly slid off the bed. Her words came out rushed. "Griff, you *have* to marry me. It's the law, and we're going to rule together. There's no way out of this!"

"It's not that." Except, wasn't it? The unbending steel in Addison's voice gave away her thoughts: she'd assumed I was breaking up with her. Not that we were ever really *together*.

I guessed I was, in a way. Once we left Miota, I would have no reason to stay bound to her. And Corinn would be there . . . I couldn't dwell on this now. Addison would be a problem for later. In this moment, I just needed to convince her to leave with me. Because if she stayed, if she succumbed to Julia's wrath and the oncoming army, I couldn't live with myself.

"I just wanted to ask," I restarted, hardly above a whisper. "What do you know about . . . the world outside Miota? Anything at all?" What a stupid question to ask. This wouldn't stall her long enough.

Addison's dark eyes pinned me to the floor. "Like, the ocean? What's this, Griff? You've been acting weird all night."

I swallowed. My hands shook, and she watched as I came undone. As the truth and all its implications ruined me.

"And . . . what if I told you there's more than jyst the ocean?"

"*Okay*," she reluctantly mused. "Like what? The sky? The stars?"

"Ouch." Addison knew Dad and I watched the stars back home in Salford, when he was alive. She'd always called me a fool for it. "And yes, but there's still more."

How long would she play this guessing game?

Addison slipped off my bed, and adrenaline kicked through me as she marched toward the door. She spun back around before reaching the threshold, and I realized she was pacing.

Just pacing. Not running to Julia.

"What do you mean?" Her voice rose with the question. "What's '*still more*' than all that?"

I held her gaze and braced my legs, ready to lunge at my door to keep her in here. She needed to know the truth, and quickly. I'd already risked her refusal by waiting this long. But with Abner still in Julia's room, I couldn't give the queen any reason to believe anything suspicious was happening. Would Addison yell if I held her here?

Maybe all I could do now was sate her with confusing riddles and let her arrive to her own conclusions.

"There's more," I started, "but it's . . . lower than in the sky. It's level with the ocean."

Addison grasped at the ends of her hair and picked at them. "But nothing's out there except the serpents and ghosts. And bodies."

"What if there were other *places*?" I challenged. "Other islands? Wouldn't that be . . . well, how would you feel about that?"

Addison froze before her shoulders slumped. And she *laughed*. "Thank the moon, Griff. You scared me for a minute there—I thought you were talking about something real!"

My defenses rose thickly on my tongue. "Maybe this *is* real."

"And maybe flying limos are real," she retorted. "What did you *actually* want to talk about?"

There was no easy way to do this; I'd have to jump and place my trust in her. I angled myself in front of my door, ensuring she couldn't leave, and I spoke. "Ads, listen. Miota isn't alone. There are other places out there, bigger than our island, with people and cities." *And some of them are sailing toward us now, poised to attack.* But I'd get there in a minute.

She pushed me square in the chest, and my ankles and knees swayed to maintain balance. "You're delusional!" she hissed. "I know you're going through a lot right now, but seriously? You don't have to try embarrassing me. I'm not going to fall for that." She tried swerving around me. "I wish I could *hate* you."

My emotions tightened as I blocked her path. "Please. *Addison.*"

She stilled. Then she tipped her head upward, and the question in her eyes shone brighter than her glittering jewelry.

"Yes," I answered levelly. *Keep her calm until Abner shows.* "I said it, and I'll say it again. Addison, I'm telling you the truth here."

Her lips parted as I spoke her name—her *full* name. "Don't." Her trembling lip pouted. "Don't say it if you don't mean it—"

"I mean it." I gathered her hands in mine, as though I held some physical power to convince her to cooperate. "I need you to hear me out, okay?"

She didn't answer behind her dazed glare. She sized me up, like she was deciding if I was a worthy predator. I took her temporary silence as an invitation to continue.

"Miota is a prison, run by the Delldovas. There are other islands with other people, and they're bigger than Miota could ever dream up. And . . . well, one of the cities has an army coming for us now, to invade and attack. So we have to leave Miota."

Addison retracted her hands. "You're lying."

"*Not* lying." I stepped closer; she skirted backward. "Addison, please come with me. If you don't, you'll have to deal with a pissed off Julia, and a revolution, and whatever chaos will come from the outsiders marching in. Please do this for me."

"My father," she uttered. When I furrowed my brow, she posed a question. "Are our families coming? My father's the mayor . . . He can't just leave . . ."

"Everyone on Miota is welcome to come with me," I replied. "If your family can be convinced, bring them. *Save them.*"

"Well, they won't agree." She spun away, and it snapped any tentative promise of cooperation.

"You can still try," I urged, trailing her. "Tell them what's out there. Tell them there's more."

"There is *nothing* outside the Fort!" Addison shouted. Her cheeks blushed.

I stilled. Could Julia hear if Addison yelled loud enough? The queen was only a few doors down. "Ads, you have to be quiet—"

"What happened to my name?" she charged as her face contorted with rage. "You're so selfish, Griff Howard! I forgot you only use me to get what you want. Use my own name as a damn weapon against me!"

"That's not true." Except, wasn't it?

Addison snarled and stalked toward my door. "I've had it." Before she grabbed my doorknob, I grabbed her wrists and easily pinned them behind her back. "*What are you doing?*" she shouted. Addison kicked at me with alternating legs, but her shifting weight only helped me steady against her.

"I'm sorry." I *was*. It wasn't supposed to happen like this. I repeated my sentiment, unable to think of anything else to say. "I'm sorry, Ads."

My unlocked door burst open, and Max Reno entered.

"*Officer!*" she shrieked. "*Help me!*"

Before I could ask what he was doing, before Addison could voice another command, Max approached Addison and revealed a needle. He stuck it in her arm and slammed on the plunger.

Addison fell silent and slumped in my hold. Before her eyes shut, she pinpointed me, her gaze flashing nothing but vile hatred and betrayal.

CHAPTER 40

GRIFF

Wide-eyed and trembling, I lowered Addison to the ground, out of my arms. "What was *that?*" I hissed at the guard.

"She was being too loud." He discarded the needle and wiped his hands on his pants. "We don't know if Abner's done, and Julia could've heard her screaming—*I* did from out in the hall."

"I know, but . . ." I sighed. "What did you *do?*"

Max knelt and pressed two fingers to Addison's neck. "She's alive. Just sedated."

I couldn't pry my eyes from her: my broken promise, the girl caught in the crossfires of a rogue heir and despicable queen. I saw it now, how involved *I* was in this royal game, and there was *no* innocent player.

"What do we do now?" I asked. "We have to take her with us."

"No." Max stood and rolled his shoulders. "She stays here."

I furrowed my brow as dread absorbed through my skin. "She's not the one who decided to be unconscious right now—"

"What're you suggesting? We lug her all over the island with us?"

I paused, swallowing hard, looking at the girl who would be

tortured if she stayed here to endure the chaotic aftermath we'd surely cause. "Maybe that's exactly what I'm suggesting."

"By the moon, Griff." Max clenched his jaw and paced, alluding to his inner turmoil. "I thought you couldn't stand her!"

"I can't," I replied, my voice a jagged edge. "Not that it's any business of yours. But who are you to keep Addison from freedom because *you* sedated her? Because *you* don't want to bring her with us? She should've had the choice."

"She doesn't, though."

"No thanks to you—"

My door unlatched again, snapping the boiling tension. Abner entered, blood coating him where a deep laceration carved his leg cleanly across the width of his thigh.

All apprehensions crashed at the sight, pointing themselves toward worry instead.

"What happened?" Max charged toward Abner and removed his shredded pants fabric from the wound. "She's gone?"

"She's out," Abner said on a rattling exhale. "Wasn't easy. Before she went under, she realized something was wrong . . ." He inhaled sharply and winced as Max pressed a handkerchief to his leg. "We have twenty-four hours maximum to get off this island, because if she wakes and we're still here, she'll make sure to kill us all."

"And you're fine?" I asked. Everything about this plan was falling apart—from Corinn's absence, to a foreign invasion, to Addison and now Abner—yet we were still going through with it. Was this smart? How could we guarantee success?

"It's just a cut," Abner replied, seething. He wrapped a spare sheet around the wound to act as a bandage. I didn't know if that was the right medical move, but Corinn wasn't here to check our work as was the plan, so it wasn't something to dwell on.

A muscle ticked in my jaw. "Fine. Let's get going, then." I squatted near Addison, unsure of how to transport her.

"She okay?" Abner nodded toward Addison's limp body.

"Max sedated her." I scowled at the guard. "She didn't get to choose if she wanted to come with us or not."

Abner hmphed. "Then it's up to you, Griff. Make a choice, and make it fast."

Julia was gone. We needed to act *now*, while the castle remained unaware of the fact their queen was unconscious.

This choice was Max's doing. I could either kidnap Addison and force her to go with us, which would hinder us all, or I could leave her behind. I knew—I *knew*—if Julia woke up and found Addison here, the girl would be tortured. Addison was too tied to me, especially since I'd told her of the supercontinent in some capacity. Julia would try wringing information from her, and Addison didn't know anything useful.

Bringing Addison was the only way to save her from the queen.

"She comes with us." I draped Addison across my arms. She wasn't heavy, but the weight would catch up to my limbs before this night was over. I would eventually need help.

Max rolled his eyes at my decision, and Abner's face remained unreadable as stone.

"Keep her here," Abner offered as he produced Julia's panel from his pocket. "I'll set up control of the Guard from Julia's panel, then I'll take Addison to a limo with me. The rest of the plan stays: Griff, you worry about the video message going out to the island. And Max, get the sedatives from the hospital wing."

While we'd already spoken about this plan, it felt insurmountable now that it was upon us. Now that there was an unconscious body to haul around, a physical representation of my guilt and shortcomings. And now Max and I had different agendas with Addison; we weren't perfectly aligned, and I was left to only hope it wasn't the first piece in a cascade of downfalls.

Max nodded. "Let's go bring Miota to its knees."

Once I recorded this message and scheduled the broadcast to each city, there would be no undoing the chaos it would create. Anyone who came with us would be risking their lives, taking a leap of faith on the moon and every star in the sky. There was no guarantee, after all, that we'd make it to the supercontinent unscathed. But the alternative was staying here, trapped with Julia Delldova and succumbing to whatever fate the supercontinental army brought. And once those events happened . . . I didn't want to be on this island.

"Let's hope people follow us," I chimed. "To the end of the world."

Abner nodded, agreeing. "To the end."

I sat on Julia's throne, set stoutly in front of the camera. I'd only been in this studio once before. I knew I didn't have much time to say what *needed* to be said before leaving and enacting the next phase of the plan: getting people out of the cities.

Though my hands quivered, I set my face in bravery upon recording. I knew what to say; I'd known for years what I would tell people, if given the freedom to speak Dad's truths. I had to sway Miota toward escape by ensuring they *knew* what doom they would encounter if they remained on this island.

An unshakable army was headed toward Miota, a tidal wave of destruction. No one needed to be here when that swell crashed.

I stared into the camera lens and the red dot signifying my recording status. "Citizens of Miota, I'm Griff Howard, appointed to be Miota's next king. I come to you now with *your* best interests in mind. I beg you to listen to me, for your own sake. Because after living in the castle, and after hearing stories from my father, who died at Julia's hand over three years ago, I know things about the monarchy and our country that I can't keep to myself."

I took a breath. *Please listen.* I hoped the sentiment showed in my face; I hoped it banded citizens together instead of tearing them apart. I hoped they accepted this as fact instead of dismissing it as conspiracy.

I laid the pieces out: the supercontinent, asympton, the malice of Julia and the crown as a whole, and the developing story of the forthcoming army. And as I did, I realized how big of an ask this was. I was urging people to leave their home, the only known structure in the world, without proof of anything else existing beyond the Fort. To commit blatant, crude treason. To leave the haven of the Fort. To live on the ocean and plow forward into an unknown world.

At least there was a plan. I told the camera about the location we'd be sailing to, in a place called Sector B. Corinn and her army would meet us there, and we'd have a safe hideout in a cave, hidden from the world until we grew and trained together.

After laying out all the pieces, I directed citizens to meet us at their city's door so we could get them onto the monorail, down to Cape's tunnels and beyond the Fort quickly and safely. I cut the broadcast, not realizing I'd talked for over five minutes, and launched into motion, ready to schedule the broadcasts to play in each city at staggered times.

But just before I secured the footage schedules, the studio door opened. I grinned, expecting to come face-to-face with Max Reno. But my stomach dropped. *By the moon.* I thought either Abner or Max would've dealt with Jameson Klemmins, Julia's closest ally, by now. Yet here the vile man stood.

"What on earth are you doing here?" the doctor said, fumbling in his pocket, revealing a scalpel pointed at me.

Why was he here? *How* was he here? I couldn't dwell on it as I ducked, avoiding the arc of Klemmins's arm toward me, blade in hand, ready to harm.

"Klemmins." My voice was tight, strained. "Get out."

He ran after me, and I evaded him, going in circles and jumping over furniture and camera equipment. Breathlessly, I ducked behind the throne as he once again swung his scalpel, bent on slashing whatever he could reach.

"I knew you were up to something," Klemmins said in a reedy

voice as he gasped for air between words. "You're *trying* to ruin the crown, aren't you?"

As I made another lap around the room, keeping one eye on the doctor, I searched for anything to use in self-defense. I could take his scalpel, but it would require letting him get close enough to potentially cut me. And though I assumed I was stronger than him, there was no guarantee I'd get it.

The room didn't have a worthy weapon, so I resorted to throwing whatever I could get my hands on. He stopped at nothing to get to me.

My breaths dwindled, becoming quicker and shallower. I only hoped that, as I tired, Klemmins did too. I'd trained for this, in a way. In Salford, some physical training was a Top-Tiered requirement, thanks to an almost successful Low-Tiered uprising two generations ago.

"You're insane," I gritted out. I cut directions, leaving Klemmins to run into the camera mount. "I'm not trying to ruin anything."

"You're a terrible liar, Griffith." He swung again, each jut of his blade sloppier than the last. Running him breathless seemed to be working, but it would soon catch up to *me* as well.

"Why would I want destruction?" Maybe getting him talking would help speed up his fatigue.

"Because of your father!" Klemmins heaved. "Julia was too in love with him to realize the truth."

What? What could he know about my father? The answer distracted me, and when Klemmins lunged, I didn't jump in time.

A deafening *crack* echoed through the room. Klemmins fell onto me limply, and his scalpel clattered to the floor.

I pushed his body and whipped toward the door, finding Max with a gun outstretched.

A *gun*. By the moon. I crouched toward Klemmins, who must've still been alive, judging by the gurgling in his throat. Or . . . was he . . . bleeding out?

"Is he alive?" I asked Max. Did he have *any* regard for people right now? Was he at all worried about collateral damage?

"Let's get out of here," Max replied. "Before we find out."

I bit my lip and finished scheduling the broadcasts, staggering each one in the order in which we'd visit the cities. Klemmins didn't move, and I shoved that from my brain's forefront. No thinking about Klemmins; no thinking about the murder Max might have committed; no thinking about what might've happened if he *hadn't* intervened.

Julia was too in love with him. In love with Dad. I knew my father had made it far into her Courtship, but . . . *love?* I couldn't imagine it.

Within half an hour, the four of us—Max, Abner, the unconscious Addison, and me—sliced through the midnight fields, our sights set on Pointe. Max drove our limo, and a fleet followed, driven by the other guards, all under Abner's control.

Pointe would have received my video message by now. They'd be assessing it, and I hoped they would take my word for what it was. I couldn't offer them guaranteed safety, but there wasn't such a thing. The Fort was no haven when a tyrant queen ran rampant within it.

I braced myself in the few moments before we opened Pointe's singular gate, the one weakness in their city wall. I didn't know what to expect, but I held my breath and tightened my grip on Addison, slumped against my shoulder in the backseat.

Nothing could have prepared me.

The dark loom in front of us was one of terror and hostility. Sentinels had their weapons, non-lethal, pointed at citizens who threatened to overrun Pointe's internal security force. Chaos was woven into every person, every particle of charged air. These people were going to destroy each other.

Without thought, I laid Addison's head on the seat and jumped out of the limo. "STOP!" I waved my hands, directing attention toward me. "Please stop! I'm telling you the truth. The supercontinent is real."

Some weapons wavered while other sentinels directed their barrels at my head, and the motionless air felt tense enough to slice.

"Lower your weapons!" I barked at the sentinels. "By order of the future king!"

Pointe slowly listened, and the voices dampened into silence, falling into stillness, every movement ceasing as the Queen's Guard members filed in behind me. I used the army to my advantage.

"You're all free to come with us," I said, "and hopefully gain a free, autonomous life. Or you can stay here and witness the aftermath of a broken throne, corrupt monarchy, and an oncoming foreign invasion. The choice is yours."

"Is it?" a stray voice met my ears. "Because it looks like we either go with you or you'll use the Queen's Guard."

"The Queen's Guard isn't here to shoot!" I insisted. "Their weapons aren't lethal. They're here to help escort anyone who wants to come with us."

The crowd didn't move, though. I hadn't imagined backlash from Pointe, of all places, since this was Corinn's home, and a longing for freedom stewed within her.

Corinn. "Corinn Januski is still alive," I said. "I wasn't making that up, in my video. She's waiting to see you again. Along with many others who you only *think* are dead. Like I also said, asympton isn't real. Come with me and get the chance to start again."

"Corinn's really alive?" A blond head of hair stepped in front of the crowd, approaching me too quickly. In a moment, I realized who the man was.

Corinn's brother.

"She's alive?" Theo rasped.

"Yes." I smiled. "Let's go see her."

Theo came to hug me, but before he reached me, a weapon fired. Corinn's brother crumpled as a bullet entered his stomach.

CHAPTER 41

GRIFF

Time stretched into nothingness as Theo's head bounced on the ground. As his hand clutched his abdomen.

I couldn't think. Couldn't see.

A piercing scream slammed into my ears, bringing me back to reality.

"*THEO!*" A child's cry.

The small brunette girl rushed forward, undazed while everyone else seemed to be frozen. She must have been Tellie—she looked around Jess's age. The sight of her screaming for her brother—no, *cousin*—ripped me into a thousand tiny pieces.

Theo's lip wavered. "I . . . *Go*, Tell. Don't let them get you, too."

My head felt too big for my shoulders as I looked around the crowd. For what? What did I want? "Who did that?" I finally asked. "*Who. Did. That?*"

A small Pointean sentinel stepped forward, his weapon raised at me in his shaking hands. My vision turned red, even with the Queen's Guard raising their own firearms. Tensions within Pointe rose as high as the moon. "I did, Your Highness. I . . . I thought . . ."

I kept his gaze. "Drop your weapon."

"You'll be okay," Tellie whispered frantically, her voice hardly reaching me. "You're okay, Theo. You're fine. You're *fine*."

I couldn't snap my gaze tethered to the sentinel ready to shoot me, scared my next movement would trigger his weapon, which would in turn activate the Queen's Guard and their sedation bullets Max managed to scrap together. The cascade could doom Pointe; they wouldn't make the boats if they were all sedated.

But I needed to know if Theo would survive this. Sentinels' weapons were only made to harm. Killing weapons weren't allowed in general cities—only Julia's mind-controlled guard could have them. But if that were the case, why had Theo collapsed so violently? Why did he gasp for air now?

"You don't believe what I say," I guessed, speaking to the bald sentinel as Tellie's hushed whimpers met my ears. "Is that what this is about?"

"No." He looked at Theo on the ground and flinched. "I'm terrified you're *right*. Because if you are, then we aren't safe anywhere in the world. Not even our own home."

We *weren't* safe here. And we couldn't even guarantee safety by leaving. The Fort gave an illusion of peace and security, but it was false. There were risks, there was loss of life, everywhere in this world. On and off Miota. We were *human*, after all. If the sentinel thought safety meant outwitting death . . . then our very existence, from the moment we were born, meant we were not safe.

But we could still gain a shot at *freedom*. This plan of ours had already caused too much pain—to Addison, to Klemmins, and to the Januski family.

"You can never promise assured safety," I said. I glanced upward at the waxing moon, drawing strength from it. Somewhere across the world, Corinn looked at that same moon, and her spirit smiled down on me now. I inhaled the night air. "You can't hide from death *anywhere* you go. But I can promise you this: a better life exists beyond our shores.

Corinn Januski is alive and fighting for our cause with a powerful group of people—I just spoke with her two weeks ago."

I glanced at Theo for a mere second, and his face encapsulated the moon, full of hope and light. He embodied his sister exactly.

"Stop fighting each other!" I begged the crowd, raising my voice. "The Queen's Guard is here, but they will not end your life, as the queen would have it. They will sedate you, though, and you won't wake up until after we've left the island. You'll be stuck with Julia Delldova, in her arena, and she *will not* have mercy. And you'll realize soon enough that I tell the truth about this army from another world: they're coming, and you won't know it until it's too late."

I captured more Pointean gazes, and I poured every ounce of persuasion into my tone.

"I'm here with Abner, a Pointean who wants nothing but the best for you. I'm here with Max Reno, a guard who spent his life looking after Prince Kierran. We're able to leave now and get to a safe spot on the supercontinent—I'm not sure how long we'll be there until we're free, but *we will be free.* By staying here, you'll only meet death sooner. Leaving Miota is the first step to creating a better world, and you can help create a new and freer future. The choice is yours."

My words sent a ripple through the crowd. Sentinels lowered their weapons, and citizens surged forward to leave Pointe. They only cowered before the Queen's Guard, still standing with weapons at the ready.

I continued speaking, aiming for the stubborn ones, prepared to leave my heart here if it meant bringing more people with us.

"Life on Miota is ending tonight, no matter what. You can either stay here and let Julia bestow her punishment on you. Watch as an army overtakes our lands. Or you can come with us and help rewrite the future—to make it something you want and believe in. To make it something worth fighting for."

More weapons rattled to the ground. More Pointeans left their city wall, heading to the monorail.

The sentinel with his weapon pointed at me threw it to the ground with a brash clutter, and he marched forward, nearly shoving past me on his way out of Pointe.

Thank the moon. I knelt beside Theo and Tellie, whose head was on his chest and thin arms clutched his shirt so tightly I wondered if he could breathe.

"Theo. It was a sentinel's weapon," I confirmed with him.

"Yes," he croaked. "I . . . should be fine. Damn, these things *hurt*, though."

I rattled out an uneven laugh. "Can you make it to the monorail?" He'd hit his head hard on the ground after falling; that would concuss him, surely. Corinn would've known for certain.

Theo's mouth worked as he glanced at Tellie. "My parents. Our grandma. They wouldn't come. I think Yvette—our grandmother—wanted to come, but . . . her hip is really bad. She's been falling lately, and usually Corinn is here to keep her from doing that . . ."

"Corinn *is* alive," I told her brother and cousin, putting weight behind my words. I volleyed my gaze between Corinn's family. "Look, I don't know if I can slow down this plan in action, but Pointe is the first city we've seen. Go get the rest of your family, *convince* them to come, and make a run for Cape. *Do your best.*"

Tellie nodded with a child's hope while Theo's lip quivered.

"It won't be easy," I agreed with Theo's thoughts. "But it's not impossible."

Theo and Tellie held a silent conversation, their mannerisms reminding me so much of Jess and myself, I couldn't stop tears from biting at my eyes.

"We'll do it," Theo stated, full of determined bravery, appearing so much like his sister. "I mean, I didn't get shot at not to at least *try*." His wry smile broke some of the tension.

I nodded. "Good. If the monorail is outside Pointe, board it. If it isn't, run for Cape like your life depends on it. You can make it in time."

"Can't you stay with us?" Tellie asked.

I swallowed, reaching a hand out to hers. "I wish I could. But I have to go give speeches to a few more cities first. I'll find you guys on the boats, okay?" I stood and grinned at the girl. "I have a sister your age, you know. Corinn and I decided you two would be great friends."

Tellie's eyes danced in the flickering lights of buildings and streetlamps. "What's her name?"

"Jessalyn."

She grinned. "I can't wait to meet her."

Once Theo was standing, I bid the two farewell and jogged toward the abandoned limo where Addison still lay unconscious. Max and Abner were escorting people onto the monorail. Bernard now joined them, the two brothers united under the same dark night. Their plan was finally happening, and I couldn't help but smile as they offered help to countless Pointeans, jumping and climbing onto the monorail cars.

These people were the brave ones. They would forge new paths for Miota and rewrite history. They were fearless enough to take their lives and make the most of the time they had, and I admired them endlessly for it.

So many Pointeans came. And while it was a success, I couldn't help but think of everyone staying behind. Was this what Jyn would have wanted? Did she want me to force everyone off the island?

That wasn't feasible. So I focused on the task at hand: getting to Salford. Doing this all over again with *my* home city.

After ensuring Addison was still in the limo's backseat, I took the wheel and ogled at the pedals and buttons. After a minute or so of testing the mechanisms, I drove at an uneven pace toward the road.

Right pedal is go, left pedal is stop.

I didn't want to take the road back to Castle Circle and *then* go around . . . I would have to cut straight through Pointe's fields and Salford's agricultural pens. That would be fine . . . I hoped.

Addison's body bobbled in the backseat as I took us over rolling fields, through bramble and weeds. Pointe's harvest had already started slowing as winter approached, which meant we luckily weren't driving through tall chutes of plants or stalks of corn.

Time didn't seem real—it was frozen until we came upon the city wall, looming starkly in the night, encasing Salford and those I loved.

Mom and Jess. Lorenzo. Countless friends from school and work.

"We're home," I told Addison, knowing full well she wouldn't hear me. "Let's do this again."

This would go better than it did in Pointe. It *had* to. We couldn't keep igniting fighting among citizens. These people were supposed to band together, not be shorn apart.

I held hope. Lorenzo and I knew a small handful of skeptics who despised the crown. But would it be enough to help my mission now?

I would soon find out.

I drove the limo through Salford's single gate, and my hope collapsed. When I parked and opened the limo's door, sounds of shouting and gunfire alike found me. Chaos ensued inside Salford.

CHAPTER 42

GRIFF

In hindsight, I should've kept the limo outside Salford's wall. But I was already here, within the havoc, and I didn't trust this vehicle to stay under my control if I left it. So I heaved Addison's body out of the limo—surely she was safest with me—and ran toward the fights.

My city had a reaction similar to Pointe's. Sentinels grabbed weapons from the armory and blockaded the exit, threatening to shoot at those wanting to flee.

In the face of fear, habit ran deep. In a world where we only ever served the Delldovas, spirits were surprisingly stubborn to the notion of change.

But I noticed the breakdown as I recognized faces and names. The upper-Tiered citizens held the weapons, while many protests came from the Low Tier. The laborers and backbone of our city. The most essential workers.

Had it been this way in Pointe, too?

Shouts came from every direction—in protests, in cries for help, in anger toward my family.

I was naïve to think Salford would listen to me because I hailed from the city. They still had to war with my claims, that life existed outside Miota and I could safely integrate us into that world. There were too many layers to this, and my identity wouldn't be enough to calm this crowd.

Lorenzo materialized in the horde, his eyes drifting to Addison in my arms. Hesitation claimed him.

"Hey, Enzo." I flicked a brow. "Long story. She's alive."

"You're damn gutsy for this," he muttered. "What's your plan?"

"Get everyone to the monorail," I ordered. "Direct them out. It's going to Cape. I'll deal with the sentinels here."

Lorenzo slapped me on the back, his version of a hug, and left. In the lamplight, I made out his parents trailing him, and I couldn't hide a grin. Lorenzo would have his family, as I would have mine.

They were somewhere in this mess.

While Pointeans had stopped their standoff when I'd arrived, Salford *didn't*. I might as well have been invisible without the king and guards behind me. This *was* my home; I couldn't stand out in a mob when I'd breathed this air my whole life. Though I'd been recently named royalty, Salfordian blood hummed through my veins.

When I spotted my family in the crowd, I took my first full breath of the night.

"Mom." My voice cracked as she ran over and crushed me into a hug. "Jess."

Jess wrinkled her forehead. "Did Addison fall asleep?"

"Something like that," I replied drily.

"Your father would've loved to see this," Mom said, bringing a soft palm to my cheek.

A knot rose in my throat. "I wish he was here."

"You and me both, love." She rested her chin atop my head for a brief second, a singular family moment in the pandemonium of tonight.

"Let's get to the monorail," I ordered, tucking Jess under my arm. Some protective spell overcame me, and there was no stopping it. "It's safe there. We'll take the train to Cape."

"You're coming with us?" Jess asked, her big eyes scanning the crowd.

"Of course," I answered at the same time Mom said, "No."

"I'm coming," I told her. "Just until I know you're on the monorail and safe."

A few times in my life, especially when I'd done stupid things with Lorenzo, I'd wished I were taller than Mom. Even for all my height, she was taller. And she used it against me now.

"And who's going to get this city in order?" Mom challenged. "Who's going to keep ushering citizens toward Cape?"

"The Queen's Guard is coming."

"They're the brawn, but *you* need to be the brain."

I opened my mouth and shut it, letting my teeth clamp my tongue. I thought of Max, how he'd let people be collateral tonight; Addison in my arms was proof enough of that.

"I can't let you go with Max," I uttered, grasping to change Mom's mind, but it felt like reaching for frayed ends of a rope that had already been undone, and I couldn't hold them together anymore. "*He* did this to Addison. *He*—" I cut myself off, noting Jess's widening eyes. "He might've killed Julia's doctor. I don't know for sure. But I don't trust him to take you two without me there."

Mom pushed Jess behind her, a protective move. It stoked fire in my stomach. Was she shielding my own sister from *me*? "You aren't just *our* future king, you know. Who's going to help get everyone else out?"

"I'm here for you two!" I hoisted Addison upward, getting ready to move her outside the city wall. Amid the screams and shouts of Salfordians, I had to yell for my mother to hear me. In the background, the monorail whistle bellowed, and for what reason, I couldn't say. "I'm *going* to help the rest of the cities. But right now, I just need to make sure you both stay safe, because I couldn't *live* with myself if anything happened to you."

My family was my moral compass tonight, and if either Jess or Mom got hurt—or worse—in my absence, the shortcoming would haunt me for all my days. Pictures of Theo, of Addison, and of Klemmins rose behind my eyelids.

Mom's face turned tomato-red. "You won *Accolade*. You didn't do all that for the good of only your family! You didn't risk everything that you are just to save the small handful of people you care about—"

"I did!" I screamed, raking a hand through my hair and using the base of my palm to rub my eyes madly. Saying it aloud, voicing the unbearably selfish fact, was an unlocked key that shredded me. I was like a great pine, the kind outside Salford, that grew to the skies just to crash in a glorious downfall for all to see.

Timber! they'd shout in the Low Tier if they saw me now. This was the destruction of Griff Howard.

Because this was all an illusion. It wasn't my salvation; it was my demise. Was I truly freeing these people? I was leading them into a world I didn't know. *No one* on this damn island knew a thing about it. Really, how could this be the right decision? The right thing to do?

Nothing was going to plan tonight, and I couldn't guarantee anything in the place we were going. The only thing I *could* dictate was staying with my family to protect them to my very last breath. If I couldn't even do that much now, this was all for nothing. I was a catastrophe. I wasn't avenging Dad; I was dooming our family. I was *failing*.

"Griff Howard." Mom pointed her chin down toward me, looking me squarely in the eyes. "You were made for *more*. Look around."

I'd lost myself completely. This trip to Salford was my breaking, and my people would be the ones to see my destruction. But I could still obey Mom's commandments, so I surveyed the scene.

Citizens fled, leaving Salford's wall. The only home we'd ever known. The one place that provided security—at the cost of freedom.

Except, Salfordian sentinels held weapons to others' heads. Our lives were now a lie, and our wall did not offer peace and safety. Now, it spurred war between citizens of the same upbringing. It waged insecurity to ever again see the light of tomorrow.

It didn't matter how I *felt*. It didn't matter who I thought deserved saving, or who I wanted to help most. I won Accolade alongside Addison. These were our citizens, in name and in blood. And it was my *duty* to help them, as Dad would have wanted.

I nearly choked on the dryness in my throat. "You're right." I glanced at Mom as bodies slammed into us, fleeing the sentinels and only harbor of civility we'd ever known. "You and Jess, go."

Mom smiled, her eyes glassy. "You're a good man, Griff."

A good man. Not because of who I innately was, but because of the people I'd surrounded myself with through the years. Because of my family, and because of Lorenzo, and because of Corinn.

I would hold them all in my heart until I could once again hold them in my arms. I bid my family farewell. "I'll see you later tonight, then," I whispered, unable to say more. Anything else would be too official.

I watched my mother and sister leave, holding onto them in my mind's eye, pressing their touch and voices and looks into memory. Because I would need their strength to get through tonight.

I turned around, ready to command the crowds, ready to give the same speech I did in Pointe. I strengthened my guts, remembering which arguments swayed Pointeans the most. Instead, I was met with the eyes of Addison's father, black in the night, swathed in shadows, looking as volatile as ever.

My stomach dropped, and I tightened my grip on Addison. "Mayor Maybee, I can explain—"

"Griffith Howard, *is she dead?*"

"No!" I cupped her head, protecting her from her father's snagging grip. "No. I swear it. Max Reno, a guard, injected her with a sedative against everyone's will. I'm the one *saving* her right now!"

Addison's father snarled, leaving his pearly teeth to glint beneath his dark mustache. "You're abducting her onto a damn suicide mission! How is that *saving* her?"

I hesitated. Addison didn't want to leave the island, but I was delivering her to ensure her safety. Because no matter how I felt about

Addison, I wouldn't be able to live with myself if she stayed here and suffered the consequences because of *me*.

I tore in two. Because I also knew the mayor loved Addison. He thought of her as an asset, yes, nothing more than a living commodity. But she was a valuable one—heir to the throne of Miota. He wouldn't let anyone, Julia or foreign army, harm his daughter so easily.

I faltered. "There's an army coming. Everyone needs to escape *that*, if nothing else."

"She's my daughter. I will protect her best, from a tyrant queen or make-believe army."

My temper rose, billowing up my lungs and into the hectic air around us. "It's not made up. They're coming. Please, Mayor Maybee, come with me. Bring your family and our city. It's your safest option, given what Miota will become. Once Julia wakes, and once the island is overrun by an army, no one will know peace."

The mayor cocked his head, and a lightweight smile held firm to his lips. "Are you sure about that?"

It sent an icy jolt through me. "What . . . what's your plan? What do you know?"

He shrugged, brushing off his suit. "Let's just say Addison will be fine with me. I'll keep her safe, and she'll get everything she ever dreamed of." He paused, running his shadowed eyes up and down the length of me. "Well, except for *you*, but no matter."

Addison would never forgive me for this. It wasn't my fault, since *Max* was the one to rob her of consciousness, but it still wasn't fair. Addison would hate me for the rest of time, no matter if I left her here or if I brought her to a strange new world.

Something about the steely determination in the mayor's eyes made me question everything. *Would* Addison somehow be safe if she stayed here with him?

"It wasn't . . ." I inhaled shakily. "It wasn't supposed to be like this."

"No." The mayor smirked, the rest of his foul grin finally playing out. Instead of reaching out to intercept Addison, he produced a knife glinting in the moonlight. "It wasn't."

He lunged at my side to slice me open.

CHAPTER 43

GRIFF

Some quick survival instinct had me dodging the blade, narrowly avoiding its arc. I dropped Addison in the process, noting in the back of my mind the harsh thud of her head as she crumbled.

The mayor might've killed me for that.

"Stop!" I shouted, caught in a deadly dance against Maybee's knife. "Your daughter—" I crouched to avoid his spinning move, and I lunged at his legs, aiming for the back of his kneecaps. He caved under my direct pressure and stumbled forward. "*Stop!*"

Maybee flashed an expression toward me, one as sharp as his weapon, as he bent backward to hack at whatever he could reach. "I— need—you—*here!*" He curled his knife and swung again. "I won't kill you, Griff. I need you alive. But I need you here in Salford. To be my bartering chip."

"Never," I spat. The longer this went on, the more I realized I moved in the same sequence to avoid getting hit—which meant the mayor was attacking in a pattern. I needed to anticipate and disrupt his next movement . . .

When he shifted his weight to lunge and swing left, I caught his wrist in the moment and squeezed, making the weapon clatter to the stone ground. As Maybee gawked, I stole the knife and pointed it at his throat. The mayor froze.

"I'm leaving tonight," I said through tight teeth. "And I'm taking Addison with me, where I can guarantee her safety."

"You can't guarantee *anything*," Maybee retorted. He bared his teeth as his knife now rested against his throat in my hand. "Not here, and certainly not there."

I knew that to be true; I'd already said as much in Pointe. Theo Januski had been hit tonight, harmed within his city's wall. Addison and Klemmins had been betrayed inside the castle. Meanwhile, Corinn lived unharmed beyond this island, in the heart of our supposed greatest danger.

I didn't know the reasons, and I couldn't pretend to sort through the riddles life gave us. But I *knew* I would never be able to guarantee safety. The best I could do was to try granting it to those around me.

I pressed the blade harder against Maybee's neck, nearly slicing the outer layer of skin. "Leaving Miota is safer than staying. Now order Salford to come with me, or I will slit your throat."

I couldn't; I *wouldn't*. Not when Max's actions from tonight still haunted me. This night was supposed to be about saving people, not harming them. I couldn't bring myself to hurt Addison's father.

But he didn't know that.

Still, the mayor laughed, growing eerily still. "No." He reached up for his knife, and I ground a knee into his stomach, pushing him backward, toward his daughter's unconscious body in the road.

Maybee and I, in different capacities, both held promises to protect Addison. And in this small stroke of time, Maybee honored that oath to his daughter.

I betrayed it.

I ran and called for everyone to follow me.

Much of Salford listened. Mayor Maybee only watched, though. He wouldn't leave the city, and with the oncoming crowds, he was forced to hold Addison's body to keep her safe. He'd decided having one royal was better than none.

I only hoped he was truthful to his word and he'd protect Addison from all forthcoming evils. There was no telling what would happen to our home after this night, between Julia and the supercontinent.

The mayor's black eyes traced me through Salford, until he was a pinprick in the distance, wearing Salford around him like a jacket.

As suspected, the limo I'd arrived in was now missing, so I helped usher citizens toward the monorail by foot. Beneath the moonlight, we raced toward freedom.

Still, as I helped the last of the willing citizens out of Salford, I looked back at our city, encased in its brick wall. And I wondered if this would be the last time I ever saw my home.

Go to Kendall. Give another speech. Direct everyone to Cape. Trust the monorail to deliver my family. Usher Miotans outside the Fort.

Find Mom and Jess. Track down Theo and Tellie. Ensure their safety.

Start and sail the boats. Ration the food and supplies.

Navigate the ocean, to the cave Lorella Anzalone picked out for us. Stay hidden until Corinn and her crew find us.

Raise an army to bring down the people enslaving Miota. Defeat Julia. Free the rest of our home.

"Howard." Abner's harsh summons snapped me back to the dark, quiet limo. Good thing, because breaking this plan down into smaller steps only made me dizzy.

"I'm ready," I assured the king, though I didn't know how true it was. In the shadows, in the silence, we all prepared our hearts for the second half of this battle, the part of holding our breath and crossing our fingers and toes before taking the plunge.

Tackling southern Miota had relied heavily on Corinn and her logistics team being here—our plan had more cracks now, built on an unsteady foundation, one peppered with doubts.

After Salfordians had piled onto the monorail, it bolted off to Yorkinson, where Max Reno and half of the Queen's Guard would land. He sat in front of me now in the driver's seat, dipped generously in shadows, though I made out the tense hunch of his shoulders. Maybe his decisions from tonight were taking their toll after all.

Bernard tied a new piece of fabric tightly above Abner's wound, still flayed open from Julia's ruby-hilted dagger. Blood seeped through the cloth Abner had placed within the castle; apparently, a makeshift tourniquet had been necessary. The Pointean doctor had already reprimanded his brother for not applying pressure on the wound sooner.

"You can't be losing blood and fainting on us," Bernard growled at the king. "Cape will only be a success if *you* pull through."

Cape. Jyn's city, where a secret rebellion lurked in alleyways and under roofs. The group Maintenance occupied Cape, and according to the old woman, they would answer to Abner and me in her absence.

Abner and his brother would collect and rouse them while Max and I funneled people from Cape's two surrounding cities—Kendall for me, Yorkinson for Max—to a tunnel entrance just outside Cape that led to Miota's southern beach, outside the Fort. We should've had the logistics team's help leading people to the beach and beyond, but we'd have to settle for the Queen's Guard.

I wasn't sure how these final three cities would fare compared to Pointe and Salford, but we had to try our best, to save them from an oncoming army and a poisonous queen's future wrath.

Max stopped the limo at Kendall's perimeter wall, where I let myself out to head into the heart of the city. Half of the Queen's Guard would soon follow, a few minutes behind us.

I couldn't think, could only go through the motions, as I stepped out of the limo and toward the city wall. I held no space to think of my family, of Corinn's family, of the fates of those who chose to stay behind tonight.

Before plummeting into the city, I glanced back at the limo and shared a look with Max in the driver's seat. In this transient moment, we were united—two allies with different tactics but the same targets.

Kendall was laid out exactly like Salford and Pointe. I guessed that was a perk of a man-made island—no reason to create anything outside manageable symmetry. Their video hadn't played yet, so the city still remained contained, each citizen in their home.

It would quickly change, and I'd witness it.

Now on my own, my legs swayed beneath me, and I nearly fell a few times, stumbling on the coarse streets here. These roads were made of the same material as Pointe's: stones, pieced together in a craggy manner. Much unlike the even surface of Salford's asphalt streets.

Focusing on little things like this helped keep my head on my shoulders. Otherwise, I'd realize how tantalous this all was, and I'd crumble like the street beneath me.

I first made my way to the arsenal, already locked—it was only a matter of *keeping* it locked, no matter who tried opening the door.

Someone would have to scan their panel to open the door, which meant I needed to break the scanner. Using Maybee's knife I'd tucked in my pants, I slashed through the metal as best I could, scraping and lacerating wires.

With that finished, I turned back to the streets and prepared for the citizens to flood the walkways. I rehearsed the words internally, ready to get as many Kendallians out of here as quickly as possible.

There would be no time for arguments or incivility. The longer we stayed here on Miota, the longer the other cities were given time to revolt. The deeper Miota would descend into madness. And now, with Abner and Maintenance about to access the boats, *everyone* needed to leave as quickly as possible.

On schedule, Kendallians emerged from their residences, taking to the streets in an unsure manner. I intercepted them, along with half the Queen's Guard trickling in, and spoke of freedom. Of rewriting the future. Of joining the brave Miotans already headed toward the boats.

That was the thing about Miota—we loved to do what the *group* wanted. We were praised for following a strict path, for doing what everyone else was doing. It was how the Delldovas maintained their order.

Citizens were hesitant to listen, slow but not reluctant. The arsenal had evidently stayed locked, so Kendall remained weaponless. Their helplessness made their population listen to me without much of a fight, and I tucked away my shame bubbling upward as Kendallians cowered beneath the Queen's Guard and their sedative powers.

I instead tried focusing on Kendall's success—citizens were escaping a raging queen and supercontinental army. But as citizens averted their gazes and spoke together in violent hisses, I wondered what these people truly thought of me, of this escape.

My panel buzzed, and Max's name glowed on the screen. He was likely in Yorkinson by now, ushering them toward Cape, mirroring my actions from the island's other coast.

I read the message, and my heart stuttered to nearly a stop.

POINTE TOOK CTRL OF MONORAIL. WHOLE THING LOST GET TO CAPE SAVE YRSLF

Time stopped. My blood turned to ice. The monorail was *taken?* What did that mean? My mom and sister were on it—*countless* Miotans were, ready to find freedom.

Tears blotted my vision as I thought of all the Miotans who wouldn't even make it to Cape now, if Pointe had control of Miota's transportation.

The whole thing is lost.

I didn't need specifics to deduce what Max was saying. He wanted me to save myself, to ditch this plan and get to the boats. I would escape along with a small, lucky fraction of citizens. Everyone on the monorail would be lost.

But I wouldn't be able to live with myself if I did that. I'd sat for too long already on the precipice of a throne, bumbling blindly through life, trying to gather myself and protect my family. And while my family's safety mattered more than anything, it wasn't my sole duty to keep them safe.

You aren't just our *future king,* Mom had said.

From the day I joined Accolade, and especially after becoming Miota's newest heir, I should've thought of everyone on this island. We *all* needed to be free. I was future king for all of Miota, and I was going to break our country's shackles.

I *had* to stop the monorail.

An idea sifted through me. As fast as my shaking fingers would let me, I messaged Max. Once he confirmed he could still see the monorail from his spot just outside Yorkinson, and he could still reach those people, I told him what to do.

I acted quickly. I was poised for this to work, from here in Kendall, the heart of Miota's power grid. I *knew* this city held supreme power, and I was going to use the privilege now.

I called my twenty-five guards for help: they would use their weapons to blow Kendall's grid sky-high. If Miota went without power, the monorail would stop. From across the island, Max could use his half of the Guard to usher those from the unworking monorail down to the southern boats. Everyone could escape Julia's loyalists while they were distracted by the power outage.

Kendallians still fled around me as I made for the city's center, and I shouted at them, urging them to continue onward toward Cape and beyond. When the power went out, they would need to run toward the southern beaches. Toward a new world.

Ripping myself from the rapidly unraveling scene, I hiked toward the thick-wired, locked fence housing Miota's power sources. The metallic maze contained too many tubes and wires to count. I didn't know where to set my sights, all of it flashing under the moon's gleam.

"Blow up anything you can!" I ordered the guards. They pointed their guns between the fence's ruts and shot.

Wires frizzed, and metal poles sparked. Smoke started, but as far as

I could tell, Miota still possessed power—meaning the *monorail* still held power, and everyone on it was in danger.

"He's cutting electricity!" Kendallians shouted, muted voices hardly hitting my ears. "The future king is dooming us all!"

Future king. I was no royal. But I would be damned if I couldn't be these people's *savior.*

"*Keep shooting!*" I growled at the guards, ignoring the raw bite in my throat from all my recent shouting.

Just hold on a little longer.

I didn't know who the thought targeted, but I hoped it for everyone involved. We were so close—and I didn't come this far, execute this much of the plan, just to fail *now.*

I snatched a weapon from one of my guards, and he hardly put up a fight. Maybe it wasn't a matter of hitting everything in there, but the *right* thing.

I gripped the fence desperately and studied the mechanics within it. What would do the most damage? It would be protected, surely, to prevent exactly what I was aiming to do . . .

Ah. I locked my gaze on a metal box, large and in the middle of the electric field. If enough guards shot at the box, it could cut through to whatever was inside it.

But as I breathed in to command the order, one of the guards must have hit something meaningful.

I didn't see the guard hit true as much as I *felt* it.

I let go of the fence, though only after it was too late. Electricity jolted through my body, zapping my bones and slicing my very essence, before the world turned black.

CHAPTER 44

GRIFF

I didn't know what was real.

I saw nothing, felt nothing. Was this death? Maybe it was. Maybe I'd been so worried about saving my family and everyone else, I'd forgotten to protect myself.

Glowing stars filtered into the dark sky above me, punching holes in the darkness. They flared with yellow and orange light, too bright and near to be the stars hung in the heavens . . . but what else were they?

Get up, urged a whispering voice, light as wind. Corinn. It was Corinn.

I bent forward and pushed off the stone ground with my hands to stand. But nothing happened. I didn't move.

I tried again. Nothing.

Panic set in, trapping me in a small, inescapable box, narrowing the world to the size of my body. *What is happening to me?* I threw all my weight and strength into rising to my feet. While my muscles felt on fire, like they were working, I didn't move.

Couldn't move.

"Help," I croaked. Who would hear that in the midst of the chaos around us, though? Maybe those who'd been there, at the electric fields, when I'd ordered the guards to shoot at it.

Had they left Kendall? Were they near? If any of them had the intention of hurting me, it would be easy. I couldn't defend myself because I could not *move*.

Each second of passing time slipped through my fingers, rolling beyond our island, disappearing for good. The ships were set to leave soon, and I was *lying here* in the middle of Kendall.

I needed to get off this bloody island. And I *couldn't*.

Get your panel, I commanded myself.

My arm moved, twitching and spasming, but I couldn't close my hand to grasp anything. I couldn't produce any meaningful movement.

If I couldn't even get to my panel, I couldn't tell Max where I was. No one would know I needed help.

The boats would sail without me.

What happened to the guards? They'd been with me before one of them blew Miota's power grid—and its surrounding fence. In retrospect, I cursed myself for holding onto that fence so tightly.

"Your Highness." A guard's face clouded my view of the glowing, fiery sky. His navy uniform cut up the stars.

I let out a cry. *Help me. Please, help me.* "To Cape," I rasped. "Take me."

The guard scooped me up, which he somehow managed despite my stockier frame. We traipsed through Kendall's streets, the guard carrying me, stumbling and tripping over obstacles.

I was thankful now for the numbness in my feet, the buzzing in my limbs. Because it almost felt like we were wading our way through *bodies.*

When we left Kendall's wall, smells of wild winds and pungent grasses filled my nose. *Thank the moon*—at least all my senses seemed to be intact. Then again, who cared if I could smell or see if I couldn't *walk?*

"To Cape," I repeated. The guard's keen sights led us through the fields. He dragged me when my feet stopped working.

When my legs twitched and muscles trembled.

We neared Cape's wall and searched for the underground tunnel entrance, hopefully still wide open, just outside the city and leading to the beach.

In the small trickling of running bodies, a familiar blond head winked in the night. I wailed at the sight of Max Reno.

"*Griff.*" Max intercepted me, and I collapsed against him as the guard handed me off. My body was damn near useless. "By the moon, what happened? Never mind. Bernard will look at you once we're sailing." He tried giving me my weight back, but my muscles wouldn't accept the load. "Can you not walk on your own?"

"The fence," I uttered. My voice worked; my arms were weak; my legs spasmed. What did it all mean? Corinn would know. Bernard would, too, I reminded myself. He would tell me if my legs would soon work . . .

The mere thought of them *not* holding me again sent a knife through me.

"What fence?" Max scoffed, then shook his head. "Not now. We need to get to the boats—Yorkinson and everyone from the monorail already came through. We're some of the last to board. Your idea to blow Miota's power worked, but it turned the island into an all-out war zone. I was able to get a lot of people out, but . . . Pointe's backlash was more than expected . . ."

We hurried through a sloping threshold that would funnel us underneath the Fort and onto the beach, and Max used this as an opportunity to stop talking and adjust my weight across his shoulders. Once we were fully in the dim tunnel, a shocking mixture of iron support beams and muddy soil, Max continued speaking.

"The important thing is most were able to make it. And Jyn was right about the boats; the instruction manual gave us everything to get them up and running. Abner, Bernard, and Maintenance have been loading people onto boats—Pointe, Salford, and Yorkinson onto one, and Cape and Kendall onto the other."

After too many shallow breaths passed, we made it to the tunnel's end, passing from oppression to liberation. To something much *more.*

The ground shifted, causing Max to stagger, as I tasted freedom.

No, not freedom—*salt.*

In the night, I couldn't make out the beach as much as I wanted; only the sporadic lantern and still-charged panel light provided relief from the darkness. The dirt here was slippery, catching my legs like a trap, encouraging me to stay ensnared on Miota.

This was my first time on Miota's beach, and I couldn't even appreciate it for what it was, what promises it held and what vows it kept. Would the supercontinent have similar beaches? Was the land different there, natural outcroppings and jutting shores? Was Miota smooth and refined, manmade in more ways than I realized?

How different would these two worlds look?

As we slipped along the shifting grounds, hardly stable, I couldn't help but gawk at the *stars.* They were so abnormally bright out here, so close, I could run to reach them

If I could've *run*, that was.

How was I going to help raise an army to defeat the supercontinent's evils if I couldn't use my legs?

"Those are the boats," Max said, pointing to the stars.

Oh . . . *oh.* Those were *windows*, letting buttery light bleed out into the dark night. These boats were enormous. The name *boat* didn't do it justice—these were entire *cities*, floating on the water, only claiming another name. These were the biggest things I'd ever seen in my life.

Before I had time to fully inhale the salted air, or hear the water roaring against the beach and boats, or let the sharp wind seep into my skin, we ascended a ramp onto a city-boat. We'd officially stepped foot off Miota.

This was the end goal. I'd achieved it, even without Dad. Without knowing my family's whereabouts. Without functioning legs.

"Where's Mom?" I asked Max. "And Jess?"

"They made it. They're around here somewhere." He navigated the steel hallways, dark and resounding with distant voices, a blurred cacophony that didn't help the ringing in my ears.

"Take me to them," I demanded.

Max didn't say anything as he clomped through the boat's tunnels. *My family—take me to my family.*

We stopped at a door leading into a room full of people, bloody and broken. Bruised, damaged, spoiled. My stomach roiled.

"My family's in here?"

"No." Max forced me onto a rigid cot. "This is the infirmary. *You're* staying here. Bernard will visit once we're on open water. Just sleep for now. Everything will be fine." He paused, straightening his posture, poised to *leave me here.* "Hold on tight, okay? You'll see your family and Corinn soon."

Yes. My family. And Corinn. I shivered. I needed to see them as much as I needed my legs to work again.

"Where are you going?" I asked.

But Max ignored me and left.

I tried getting up. My arms could barely push me off the cot, and my legs still twitched. I tumbled off the cot and thudded to the ground, now staring at someone's bloody hand in my line of sight.

I was among the injured. And I couldn't leave. I couldn't walk. I couldn't do anything.

I can't walk. I can't walk . . .

The thought echoed until sleep pounced.

"Howard."

Abner slipped into sight, fuzzy initially.

No, Bernard. *Bernard* narrowed his lead eyes.

"Where are we?" My throat seared. I let my eyes close, welcoming the familiar darkness.

"You tell *me.*"

I sighed, and the movement singed me. My insides were fiery, splintered. But my skin . . . was damp. I lifted a hand to my forehead and met a towel, wet with cool water.

Soggy towels littered me, sprinkled over my limbs and core.

Where are we? Last I recalled . . .

My heart pinched. "Infirmary. Boats." My throat still screamed at me for using it. I'd run it ragged during our rounds to each Miotan city, and I assumed my electrocution hadn't helped that.

"Yes." Bernard's shoulders drooped a little.

I blinked, straining to remember all that had happened. "Max said . . . *war.*"

"A bit," Bernard admitted. He was the king's twin right now, full of sharp angles and gray hair and gruff words. "Once the power went out—thanks for that, by the way—everyone raced for the Fort." A pause. "Most made it."

I grimaced. "How many didn't?"

"Hard to say, but based on estimates . . ."

He looked to the ceiling, as if the answer were written there. Or a trap door he could escape this conversation through. "A couple hundred?"

I broke at the number. A couple *hundred.*

Max had told me *most* made it out. How could he belittle such a number? It choked me now, and my vision blackened.

"My family," I demanded. "Max said they made it. What about Corinn's?"

Bernard's face twitched, nearly imperceptible. Maybe I'd only imagined it in the soft light. "Yours did. And Tellie made it, Corinn's cousin. One of the Pointeans carried her. But Theo and the rest . . . didn't."

A knot bunched at the top of my throat. Corinn's brother, her parents and grandmother . . . they were still on Miota.

You can't save everyone, Abner once said.

I knew this, but now I was living it, and it brought on a new level of agony. I'd failed with Addison, and now I'd failed with Corinn's family. If I hadn't been electrocuted, if I hadn't hung onto that *damn fence*, they could've been here. I could've looked out for them, as I promised I would.

I tried wiggling my toes. I swore they moved under my brain's command. Only *then* did I realize someone must have nursed me after I'd fallen off the cot earlier. I now lay on my back, staring at the metal ceiling, dark and ominous and low-hanging, as if death were here, ready to pounce on the injured.

I wasn't sure if my heart palpitations were caused by emotional or physical agony. Either way, I gasped for air, not able to suck enough down for a moment. My lungs and heart then returned to normal, as if nothing had happened.

Bernard froze as my world frayed at the edges. "Howard. You need to *hold on*, okay? When we get to the supercontinent, I'll find a way to examine your organs and the internal damage. I think . . ." He blinked rapidly. "Actually, aside from the electrocution, I'm not sure *what* I think, and that's scaring me."

Bernard had me sit on the edge of the cot, which I was able to do with some struggle. He gave instructions, testing my muscles' abilities, and I followed. Relief crashed into me with each successful motion.

Lift your knees. Straighten your legs. Point your toes upward. Now the big toe. Tilt your foot outward—

The muscles below my knee quivered, but I couldn't fully complete the motion. I whipped my head to Bernard, who only nodded with a neutral expression. Damn doctor knew exactly how to mask his feelings.

"Tell me what's wrong," I demanded, using the voice I'd practiced in the castle, even if I was no longer Miota's future king.

Bernard only flicked his brow. "Point your toes. Then curl them."

I came up short on both commands.

The doctor grunted. "Could be a lot worse. The lesion is relatively low, first off, and it's paresis, not paralysis. That's all good news."

"How is any of this *good?*" I spat, stoking the flames in my belly. "My legs don't work—not really, anyway—and you won't let me see my family, and *so many people* didn't make it! Too many are still stuck on Miota!"

The king's brother shushed me with a wary glance around the room. Everyone else seemed too involved with their own injuries to notice my upheaval.

"Everything is under control." The comment seemed to be directed at more than just me. "We're passing out food and bedding now. We have competent captains on both boats, able to read the manuals and navigate us to Anzalone's coordinates—these ships were definitely a secret from the supercontinent, and they're our saving grace now. We've been lucky so far."

"And it'll run out eventually," I barked back. I would wish on the star-studded sky, if only I could see it above this metal infirmary. "Bring me to my family."

"*No.*" Bernard met my cold tone with equal fervor. "They'll come to you in a bit, but you're staying here. That little dance your heart just did? Don't think I didn't notice. It's not supposed to *do* that, Howard. I'm keeping an eye on your vitals."

His certainty dropped a hammer on my ribs, crushing everything I'd worked for. We'd made it off Miota, and we were sailing for freedom . . . but why did this victory feel so *wrong*, so hollow?

"I can't just stay here," I argued. "Let me help. I need to do *something*."

"You've helped enough. You got over six-thousand Miotans off the island." Bernard delivered the statistic like an achievement, except that number meant about four-thousand citizens had stayed behind . . . it gutted me. "The best thing you can do now is get some sleep. Once we dock, you'll travel into the supercontinent with us, and we'll need you at full strength. So do us a favor and rest."

"Fine." I raked my tongue across my teeth, forcing subsequent silence. This wasn't the time to say something stupid.

I kept quiet until Bernard left.

And then the tears fell. My shoulders shook, and each sob carved at my heart, robbing me of life. This was only half a victory. Addison,

Theo, Corinn's parents, countless other Miotans . . . they were trapped in Julia's fortress with an oncoming army.

How could I celebrate the free people surrounding me now when all I could think of were the ones left behind? What could I have done differently to ensure their safety? When had I turned down the wrong path?

I tore myself apart at the possibilities.

There was too much to be done, too much to solve and remedy. And Bernard expected me to *lie here*, as though it was the most effective thing to do.

No, I'd learned to see past his and Abner's lies spun into gilded distractions. The brothers had tucked me away—they were taking full charge of this mission.

And I would never trust them to do what was right for others; they only did what was beneficial for themselves.

How had I not seen it before? We'd *run* from Julia, as was Abner's original plan. Though Max and I had set the foundation to get off Miota, tonight's plan was ultimately one of Abner's design.

And the king's deliverance was not enough for me. I needed to see the queen's demolition. I needed to see her *burn* and *crumble* and *fall*.

I would. Once I reunited with Corinn and her forces, we would bring chaos to Julia's home.

I silently vowed to never get caught up in the king's selfish antics again.

Abner had run. But I was born to *fight*.

CHAPTER 45

CORINN

I sucked in a cold breath. Every muscle in my body tensed. I couldn't have made it this far through the tunnels, this far from Arlo's grasp, just to be found *now*.

Get out of the way, idiot! an internal voice chided me. But where could I go? I didn't know this maze of Biourica's tunnel network. Not even Arlo's own sons did.

If only I'd thought to grab some sort of weapon—I'd used syringes and scalpels before, collected for me by Griff Howard before I'd faced Julia in her courtroom.

That seemed like something of another lifetime now.

I had only my body, which I could fight with, if I could somehow school my movements to be quick against the fog of the coughing pills.

The shadowed figure approached, and I sucked my stomach inward, as if I could meld into the tunnel wall behind me.

My defensive spirits softened as I noted the lean frame and mop of hair, dark aside from the murky lighting. At the sound of his rattling breaths, I paused.

"Dalton?"

He spun, aiming a small firing weapon at me, before letting out a choked sound. "Holy hell, Corinn—" He gave a quick, skittering laugh. "You're alive."

"And you found the tunnels."

"Your prying questions helped," he admitted and crushed me into a hug. "I only remembered this place because of you. You were right about my dad. He veiled my memories."

I wasn't sure why I was surprised at Arlo's ability to manipulate memories when I'd lived through torture of another kind at his hands— and when I'd seen him strip Miotans of their entire identities.

"Do you know the way out?" I asked.

"Yeah." Dalton spun and began back the way he came at a pace I couldn't keep. I had so many questions, yet I couldn't get any of them out—not when I struggled to keep my breath, my wits, and my bearings, at this speed.

I thought I'd been walking quickly before, but Dalton's pacing was so frantic now, I must've been moving like molasses, barely inching along this pathway.

"Keep up," he called. "No time to waste. We'd pinpointed the section of cells you must've been in, and I was ready to put up a fight against Arlo—how'd you get out, anyway?"

Why didn't Dalton sound breathless at all? Had I lost so much endurance in my time here, or was it more because of the pills I'd swallowed?

"I . . . I'm going to throw up, Dalton." I panted. "*Too fast.*" We were moving *too fast*.

"Woah." Dalton assessed me as best he could in the dimness and pressed the back of his hand to my forehead. "What? What'd Arlo do to you?"

"What *I* did to me," I corrected him. It made Dalton's dark brow knit together. "I took too many coughing pills. To break the connection. He can't control motor pathways if they're scrambled."

The whites of Dalton's eyes widened as realization hit him. "You overdosed on *coughing pills?*"

"It was my way out," I whispered. A tear tracked down my cheek. "Sorry."

"Don't apologize for *anything* you've done," he insisted and took me under an arm. "You *saved* yourself, Corinn Januski. Like I knew you could. I only worry about overdose. Do you feel okay, other than the . . . what is it, do you feel drunk?"

"I don't know. I guess." The only time I'd had a large amount of alcohol had been at our Scarlet Barracks celebration, the day before we went to Biourica and everything had gone wrong.

Dalton stayed silent, but he offered his hand. I took it, and he led me through the maze.

My eyes darted around the obscured hall, trying to make sense of my surroundings. But I couldn't make out anything important until Dalton heaved open a door and we landed in a cleaning closet, stocked with chemical bottles and washrags.

The place reminded me of the Queen's Guard and Griff's lips.

"We need to make a run for it," Dalton said. He grabbed plastic gloves off a shelf, along with hard hats, which needed dusting off. "Wear this and keep your eyes on the ground. We'll head to the OneTube, but once I scan in, the system will know who I am. Lorella and Cass are waiting on a spare maglev, which we'll take to the edge of town. Aunt Sea—Saoirse—and Anya are waiting for us at the edge of town on a trans-sector train."

My tongue hardened at the number of questions raised from Dalton's explanation. The OneTube . . . that was the chute that connected Red Fox's ground-level streets to the Platform, the elevated and safe streets for the rich and affluent.

Lorella and Cass were waiting on a maglev, and Saoirse and Anya . . .

Anya.

"Anya knows?" I piped.

Dalton's cheeks grew red. "Yes." The one syllable fronted a long story—one I'd have him tell later. After all, I'd noticed how Dalton's eyes recently started tracking Anya's every move, and how his chest expanded toward her when she was near.

I fixed the hard hat to my head, wondering how this bright orange color would keep us hidden. "What about Colton?" I asked. "And Neave?" The remaining two in our group.

Dalton glanced at me as he wrenched his gloves on. "Colton's already in Sector B—he's meeting with the Miotan leaders once they dock their ships and make sure everyone's set with rations."

Miota was *here*, on the supercontinent. Griff had done it. He'd saved our country. And I would soon see him again. I couldn't mask my grin.

"And Neave insisted on staying behind for the next day or so, to help us get out of the city. She's holding a maglev for us out on the Platform, and she helped Saoirse gain control of the trans-sector train farther south. Then she'll join us in a few days, I think, when she can make a break for it."

The information washed over me, an unceasing wave I couldn't fully comprehend, but I knew enough. Neave was staying behind. The rest of us and Anya would travel to Sector B, where Colton was already waiting with Miota.

Griff and Abner and Max. My family. My city, my home.

The excitement only made bile rise in my throat, though, and I swallowed hard as Dalton opened the door, spitting us out into one of Biourica's white-washed hallways.

He led me down the hall, through the front lobby, and out the door, to the field where I first met Anya and began training for Arlo's logistics team.

I targeted the OneTube's entrance. I'd never been in the rising glass chute before, given my contrived status in Sector A, and nerves flitted in my core.

"Once we get to the top," Dalton muttered as we swerved through crowds of people, "we run like *hell* for the maglev. It'll be the first one you see. Can you do that?"

I nodded. I *had* to, despite my altered state. Our escape from Arlo counted on this.

Dalton squeezed my hand as he swiped his grid, and the glass doors yawned open. Time was ticking. We stepped into the glass pipe and shot upward. How I kept my stomach contained, I didn't know. We now hovered above the shining city from our spots in the sky.

The doors peeled open at the top. I swayed for only a breath before splitting from the tube toward the first maglev. Its front door opened as Dalton and I frantically approached. Dalton dragged me across the Platform's central road as bystanders gawked.

"Dalton James?" onlookers echoed.

Dalton cursed and ran faster. I kept up as best I could as the shouts grew around us. Would Neave help us keep control of the maglev? Would we escape Red Fox? Though I'd fled from Biourica, I still remained in Arlo's domain. He ran this sector, his eyes rampant and ears omnipresent.

We hopped into the maglev, crashing to the floor. In the same instant, the door sealed behind us, and the transportation shot forward. I went rolling on the ground at the jolting speed.

Dalton helped me up, and as I reoriented myself, I realized who else occupied this maglev's front compartment.

Lorella grinned at me, teary-eyed.

Cass studied me, noting every scar and wound on my body, before wrapping both arms around me. "By the moon, Corinn. I thought I'd lost you."

"Not so easily," I said in a breath, smiling against the contours of his chest. Miota's prince was lost, but not for much longer. He and I were on our path toward home, toward safety and unification. All of this *had* to end in Miota's survival and security.

"You're incredible," Cass said against my hair.

When I peeled away from the prince, Dalton clapped a hand on my shoulder. "Have a seat, Corinn. There's a lot to catch you up on."

CHAPTER 46

CORINN

The maglev fell from the sky, sloping on its downward track to ground level upon exiting Red Fox. When we reached the end of the line, as according to plan, we transferred onto the vacated train waiting for us on a separate track. Its stakes bled southward, winding through the country and disappearing into the distance, laying out our road ahead.

Anya ran from the second train to tackle me in an embrace. She trembled and whispered my name. "I knew you'd survive Biourica," she cried.

I sniffed. "I was strong enough because of *you*." Everything she'd taught me about friendship, about being stronger together, had been true. Without her light, I'd never have outlasted that place.

Dalton wrapped an arm around each of us. "As much as I hate to break this up, we need to leave the sector. Now."

Yes. We were fleeing Sector A into a bigger, better, bolder world. Into a place I would *not* hide away in silence, or blend in to covertly spy, but to cause a spectacle for all to see. I would shine brighter than the moon, and I would do whatever I could to save those I loved. Those on Miota, and those like Salem, stuck in Biourica, who knew no peace.

Salem. I had to tell Cass . . . and at the right time, I would. Salem had been his friend too, and I didn't know how the prince would take the news.

Saoirse waved us into the train's front compartment and half-heartedly scolded Anya for leaving the train upon our arrival. Once we all sat, Saoirse and Lorella started up the train and led us down the supercontinent's coast, away from Sector A's capital city and toward our neighbor to the south.

I slumped into a seat and crossed my hands over my stomach in a weak attempt to sate its unease. And I listened to the story, told primarily by Dalton with Anya chiming in every few sentences to embellish his words.

After I'd been taken by Arlo, Dalton took Anya and ran to Lorella's apartment, explaining Miota to her on their way. The three of them—plus Cass and Colton, who'd been staying at Lorella's—then went into hiding on Red Fox's streets, never staying in one place for long.

Scarlet Barracks had been sent down to one of Sector B's major cities, Charston; evidently, our assignment of *allocation* had been the directing of resources to Biourica's newest outpost in Sector B, to be completed by winter's end.

Once the group learned that, Lorella sent warning to Miota. Colton had left for Sector B, where he now resided to create space for Miota's oncoming boats. And for us, who'd join them all by tonight.

Lorella eyed me carefully at the mention of Griff, but she didn't reveal my secrets to Cass, thankfully. I scratched invisible dirt off my clothes to keep from locking eyes with the woman—and with Cass.

The prince, though, stared at the ground, mind spinning behind his royal eyes. This was quickly becoming too much for him, and I knew it. But he was Miota's only heir; he was designed for a fate like this.

"Neave heard talk," Dalton said, thinning his lips and adjusting his pants, "of where the other barracks ended up. Cobalt Barracks was assigned enforcement, and they're patrolling the streets of Red Fox and a few neighboring suburbs. Emerald Barracks was given expansion, and they're sailing off to Miota. To . . . I don't know, *expand*, I guess."

A lump formed in my throat, settling nervously in the back of my mouth. At least Griff and the Miotans had made it off the island; there would be no one left for Emerald Barracks to overtake. What had happened, I wondered, to Julia? The Queen's Guard? Had anyone stayed behind on Miota, or was our home completely vacated?

I instead asked a question I'd been holding too close to my heart. "And . . . what of the people we'd fought after picking our assignment? Do you know who they were? My best friend from Miota was there."

"Biourica employees?" Dalton guessed with a shrug. "I'm sorry, Corinn. Clearly trained in combat and who knows what else. I . . . suppose that's Arlo's Miotan fruitions coming to life."

I only nodded, silently accepting the answer. Arlo had said it himself: those people were erased entirely, scrambled down to the neuron, and built wholly into someone else.

My Salem was gone forever.

Cass excused himself and fled our compartment. *By the moon.* He'd put the pieces together; he knew I spoke of Salem, and he must have deduced the rest. Guilt overtook me, fractured only when the train rattled over a bump that sent us jolting in our seats.

Dalton stood to peer out the window, where his gaze stayed glued for too long.

"Dalton?" Anya prompted. She patted the seat next to her. "Is someone out there?"

"No," he said, and he flicked his gaze toward Anya. His expression melted slightly as he neared her to take a seat. "*No,* and that's the problem. Arlo has to have caught on by now. Rogue transportation, Corinn escaped, his son and crew on the run . . ."

"He already knew everything," I added. Every pair of eyes turned my way, and the weight pressed into me. "When I was . . . when he . . ." I couldn't speak of the details. "When I was in Biourica, Arlo knew who was in Lorella's crew. He knew I was supposed to be a spy, and he even knew Cass was hiding among us all."

"*What?*" Dalton's hands clenched, and his face went ghastly white. "Then . . . does he know where we're going right now? Does he . . . is he waiting for us in Charston?" Dalton paced the compartment, treading footsteps into the dark carpet.

"He's not," I assured Dalton. Even though Arlo's assurance rattled through my skin. *There is no plan of yours I don't already know.* "He can't know everything. Or else we never would've made it out of Red Fox, let alone *Biourica.* He might've known the past, but he doesn't know what we plan for the future."

"He'll figure it out," Dalton grumbled and slouched next to Anya. She bit back a smile as he leaned his shoulder against hers. "And we'll need to be ready when that happens."

"Do we carry on with the original plan until then?" Anya voiced. She angled her face toward Dalton, her lips now inches from his ear.

He nodded. "We'll cover our tracks by staying far away from Scarlet Barracks, and we'll meet with Miota's leaders to help turn their population into an army."

Butterflies swarmed me. Either that, or the coughing pills were still affecting me in waves. The plan was to make an army out of the Miotans willing to fight . . . civilians, family, and friends, bred into soldiers.

They would need time, months that weren't on our side. If Arlo expanded fully into Sector B before this theoretical army was ready, our current plan would be useless.

My head swam. I chewed on each implication, trying not to ruminate on any one thought by switching mental subjects every few breaths.

"I'll go find Cass," I volunteered. "Bring him back in here, in case anything happens."

The group let me leave without a fight. I swayed on my feet, courtesy of the whirling train and the pills. After gaining my balance, I staggered through the metallic door leading into the next chamber, some sort of plush sitting room. This trans-sector train held plenty of luxuries, usually used to sweep people across the League on long trips.

Cass lay on a red-cushioned sofa, plated and finished with brass.

One arm was sprawled across his eyes, and the other rested on his slow-rising abdomen.

It didn't surprise me, the prince obstructing his view. As much as he was fated to shake the heavens, he didn't want to. But he would need to accept his position, acting as a bridge between Miota and the League. He held untapped power back home, and it would prove crucial in the upcoming weeks.

"Hey." I sat across from him, in a black leather chair that felt cool on my exposed skin. I sank into the furniture, and I was so tired, I could fall asleep in this thing. "About Salem . . . I'm sorry."

I fell silent. Nothing—*nothing*—I could say would help ease the pain. Salem had been a true friend to both of us, and now we had to share his memory on our own. We had to carry his spirit . . . his *true* spirit.

Cass uncovered his red-rimmed eyes and blotchy cheeks. "How'd you find out?" he croaked. "You saw him?"

"I had to fight him," I answered plainly as my throat caught. I swallowed the painful lump.

Cass shook his head and let his eyes fall closed again. "You were never supposed to know." His throat quivered. "I'm sorry."

I reached out for Cass—

And *stopped.*

Froze.

Something *cold* whittled its way through my every organ, every cell, every thought. Time crawled toward a halt as my thoughts descended on what he'd just said.

"What do you mean?" My voice was not my own. The chamber yawned until there was *so much space* between us. "I *was never supposed* to know? What. Does. That. Mean?"

Cass didn't need to answer. His red eyes slammed into me, and the guilt burrowed in every line of his face was a punch to the gut.

My upper lip twitched. "You *knew.*"

"Neave's shown me the name of every Miotan brought here—she

hacks into Arlo's systems to scrap together the list of names every month." His words drifted upward, like smoke, aimless and wafting up, up, *away*. I didn't want to hear them. I wouldn't listen. "Look, I knew you wouldn't take it well, since there's no fixing him, so it was better for you to think he was gone."

"Better for who?" My legs pushed me upward, and I drew near to Cass. My hand punched the sofa just above his head, and I let out a frustrated scream. "*YOU KNEW!*"

Cass cowered, using his arms to shield himself from me. *As if* he could stay safe from me. *As if* I hadn't trained every day of my life for the past few months, unknowingly toward this moment.

I was going to beat the stupid Prince of Miota into a pulp.

He. Knew. He knew my best friend was *still alive*, and he hadn't told me. Hadn't bothered.

"Corinn—"

"*Stop!*" I kicked the coffee table, wishing I could shatter one of the metal-enforced legs. If I brought a kick down on the glass tabletop, would it break? I needed *something* to crumble in this room besides me. "I don't *care* if he's someone else now! You should've told me! You told me *no more lies* between us!" I unleashed another round of punches onto the couch cushions, the table, the pillows. They were all weak substitutions for Kierran Cassius Delldova. "*You promised!*"

He'd *promised* not to lie. Granted, I'd promised the same, though I still held Griff close to me.

I would *never* show Cass my true heart now.

"I was scared, Corinn. I didn't know how you'd take it! Or what you'd do—"

"Stop trying to *put me* inside your cages," I spat. Fury hummed through my blood, my bones.

Cass was so much of his mother right now, trying to keep information from me. Trying to control me, to tell me how I was supposed to react to things.

It was in this moment I realized the difference between us. While Cass and I had both been stubborn to change according to this new world we landed in against our will, he refused to accept it as his new reality. He still wanted to go back to Miota, back to the castle he called home. He chased his life formed at society's pinnacle; he grasped for his parents' ways, the only constant he remembered.

Meanwhile, I'd been forced for flight. I guessed that was one of the perks of being lowly my whole life and *wanting* more. My organs were imbued with determination.

Coming from the bottom meant I'd been born to rise. To *soar.*

The lights cut out without even a flicker, and the sound of the hovertrain screeching to a stop found my ears, reminding me there was a world outside this chamber, this bubble of rage.

"Arlo probably just found us." No emotion reached my voice; how could I waste *feelings* on this person in front of me? He *was* a Delldova, raised by a queen of poisons and a king of cowards. He didn't know a life outside of deceit and self-preservation. "We need to go."

Cass looked like he might curl his knees to his chest and stay plastered to the sofa. Anger seized my limbs, giving me the strength to lug him to his feet and force him in front of me. Cass was avoiding his problems, just as his father would have done. And I refused to let him stay here and become a curdled version of his parents.

Cass trudged back into the front compartment. I followed him, and shock hit me in the face as I surveyed the scene outside the train's front window.

The tracks were on *fire.* And with the train's power severed, the best we could do was use the emergency brake and hope the train stopped in time.

It was unlikely.

Staring at the flames sent hot fear up my spine. My legs throbbed at the thought of burning. *Not again, not burns again . . .*

On either side of the track, a vehicle hovered with a word stamped onto it: *BIOURICA.*

These people, sent by Arlo, would watch us burn.

CHAPTER 47

CORINN

My eyes stayed hitched to the scene on the tracks in front of us. Our train's brakes screeched before fizzing out completely, dooming us to hurtle toward the wall of fire.

I braced myself, spitting out a curse on a shaky exhale.

Heat, Julia Delldova, boiling water . . .

Dalton fumbled and pulled at different levers. Lorella clutched the main navigation panel and strained to change our current course. And Anya, with clenched teeth, found my eyes amid it all.

I remembered what she'd been trying to tell me from the start. We were better together. That was why, after all, we were a *team*.

These were *my* friends, bound to me not by blood, but by loyalty and love. Whether we rose or fell, we would do it together. Just as Anya had said—the promise that was now strength and grit.

Together.

Banded alongside each other, we stood a fighting chance. It was better than the alternative; the fire held no future for us.

"We have to jump!" I shouted. "Then we storm one of the limo things. Hijack it and drive to Charston."

The others nodded, their faces glistening in the firelight we flew toward.

We had to jump *now*.

The door was jammed shut, only powered by the absent electricity, so Dalton took the butt of his gun and broke the glass. It shattered and rained glittering, deadly pieces, giving off an ephemeral ring.

The trance was short-lived.

The train's speed and motion tried sucking us out through the open door, and we let it. Without thought, we jumped from the metallic structure.

For a fleeting moment, I sailed on winds. As I launched from the rattling hovertrain, as I sliced through the merciless air, I *soared*.

So this was what it felt like to *rise*.

But I was thwarted not even a full breath later. As green grass rose to meet me, my heart kicked, and I tried keeping myself limp. Going stiff wouldn't help anything; it would only increase my risk of breaking a bone or dislocating something.

Every joint in my body vibrated upon impact. Pain lanced through my legs and abdomen, through my shoulders and ankles.

There was no time to regroup. Shots rattled. Dirt and chunks of grass flung from the ground around me as bullets pelted nearby.

I hardly had time to scan for my teammates before running in the zig-zag pattern we'd learned in the barracks. My legs weren't as steeled as they'd been before Arlo had locked me up for a week, but I'd make do. My survival depended on it now.

As I half ran, half limped, toward a lone vehicle housing a half dozen snipers, I fortified myself. My friends had already saved me from Biourica once, and now, I would help them in return. They were my supercontinental family—one I didn't ask for, but one I'd needed all my days.

I reached the vehicle and kicked two of the grounded men in the spot I knew would hurt most. A sharp buzz rolled through my lower limbs. One man dropped his weapon and cried out. The other cringed, though barely moved.

Anya came up behind me, and she punched the latter man square in the face. His brow split open.

We grabbed the two grounded weapons as Dalton and Lorella took out two more on the opposite side of the limo.

It was now four against two.

The empty-handed men didn't cease, though. They popped upright and rained fists and feet on us. Amid dodging stray punches and kicks, I eyed one of the snipers, focused on a far-off spot across the field. I pointed my firearm with clammy hands. The gun nearly slid out of my grip.

I had to act *now*, had to shoot while the gunman was distracted.

But before I gathered my wits, the sniper fired his own weapon, and I heard the distant wail. I glanced at the target and found Cass—I'd forgotten about him. In the frenzy…

He'd jumped, which beat death by fire. But now he'd been shot.

My limbs froze as blond hair and blood and friendly faces morphed, past and present, until I didn't know who I was looking at.

Cass. *Salem.* Salem was friends with Cass. Cass knew about Salem being here. Salem was now Shea. *Kierran Cassius Delldova. Salem Redding.*

Salem. Redding.

Cass.

This gave me the clarity to cock my gun, ready to impair Cass's perpetrator. But before I had the chance, he crumpled.

Lifeless.

Dalton nodded at me from across the vehicle. "Get to Cass! We have this under control."

As I ran, the others fought, each person unable to rip their gaze from their partner lest they'd get shot in the eye or kicked between the legs.

This wasn't the plan, I wanted to tell Dalton. Even though it had been my idea to do this, to jump off the hovertrain and storm the vehicle, I didn't want it to come to *this*.

I didn't know what I'd had in mind, but it certainly hadn't been to *kill* our opponents. Even though they were shooting at us. Even though we would die, and it was nothing more than self-defense.

I'd been ready to shoot.

I had been ready *to* shoot.

If Dalton hadn't done it, I would have. And I would've come to this realization with the blood on my own hands.

Cass lay in the grass with blood smeared across his face, dripping from his ear and down his neck, meeting the collar of his shirt.

"Cass," I said, grounding him.

His eyes found me. They were blue, from Abner, and they were brown, from another branch of the family tree. Julia's green, her malice, was not present here.

"Corinn." Tears slid down his cheek. He made no effort to move. "I'm sorry."

I blinked tears away. Surely he wasn't… No.

No. I couldn't lose *both* my Miotan friends to gunshot wounds. Different times of day, different continents, different circumstances, different people.

Same outcome.

"You're fine," I said, breaking every rule I'd learned in my medical classes. "Cass, you're *fine*."

He tried a light grin. "Help me up, then."

I swallowed the knot in my throat. Maybe he *was* fine. But I'd done the same with Salem, thinking he was fine, except he wasn't.

Maybe he would've been, though. It was hard to say how much of his condition had been real; his death had been staged.

I wouldn't let Cass meet death. No matter what he'd done to hurt me. I would protect him, always. He was part of this family, too. The one who shared a room with me while I trained; one of the first to meet me in this strange new world. He was the boy I once thought I'd never see again in this lifetime, except now he was in front of me, still alive and breathing.

For now.

I helped him up, and as he stood, I watched his breathing. I felt his heartbeat in his neck, still strong, and I checked his wound.

The bullet hadn't entered him, thank the moon.

"You should be fine," I said. *Insisted.* "Looks like it grazed the skin. Head wounds bleed a lot, but if we get that under control, you'll be okay."

"Hurry!" Lorella called, sprinting over to help me escort Cass to the currently vacant limo. "The other Biourica car is almost through the wall of fire. We need to *go.*"

Dalton took to the driver seat, and the rest of us piled in the crammed back row, save Lorella who volunteered herself for the spacious front seat next to Dalton.

"Next stop," Dalton muttered, igniting the vehicle's engine, "Charston." He slammed his foot downward, and we took off with a *screech.*

Charston. Yes, if we could keep Biourica off our heels, we might actually make it there.

To see Miota. My family. *Griff.* If this small crew of Lorella's could do so much, I couldn't wait to see what we could accomplish with an army on our side.

As Dalton drove, we took turns looking behind us, but we never found more Biourica minions following us. Still, we couldn't rest, even upon making it to the sand-dusted city of Charston after hours of driving through Sector B's hill country and briny coastlines.

We couldn't rest because we knew what was coming: the merging of two worlds, and they would collide spectacularly, for all the League to see.

CHAPTER 48

CORINN

My legs cramped by the time we reached the city. When we made it into Charston, trading sand-lined streets and towering trees for neutral-colored buildings and heavier foot population, Dalton parked in an alley.

"We'll have to walk the rest," he said, glancing back at Cass to quickly assess his condition. "No cars allowed here—they have one main maglev within the city. No limos either, Corinn."

I stuck my tongue out at him—after I'd called this vehicle a limo for the second or third time, Dalton told me this was called a truck. Between the two Miotans and three Sector A citizens, we'd come to the conclusion that every vehicle on Miota was a limo. Meanwhile, limos were rare in the League, and most personal vehicles were cars or trucks.

Anya bent, looking upward, gawking as Dalton parked in the alleyway. "No Platform," she murmured.

Dalton grinned. "Just blank sky. Makes for a great view, right?"

We exited the car, and I helped Cass keep pressure on his head. I knew walking could only worsen his wound, but he didn't have another option. I wrapped Cass's head in gauze and offered him a hat once belonging to one of the lost Biourica employees.

Dalton and Lorella led us through the city, talking wildly now to align their tactics on what to do upon reaching the hotel. Anya and I matched Cass's slower pace behind the chattering pair.

This city was much smaller than Red Fox, with few buildings reaching toward the clouds. People swarmed, hot bodies baking together under the sun, and salt pricked the wind as the ocean's scent infiltrated the city, percolating through manmade layers, reminding us of its presence.

I couldn't believe I was locked in a room within Biourica just this morning. I was a prisoner of Arlo James, and now I was about to reunite with my loved ones.

How quickly things could change. I embraced it.

After walking for what felt like *much* too long, as the sun dipped behind us and turned the ocean a dark blue, we reached a high-rising hotel. While the buildings around us were made of clay and sand, with peeling shutters and colored front doors, this place was composed of glittering metal, all modern angles and majesty. Life seemed to happen *around* it, as if everything welcomed the beach except for this place.

I read the sign atop the golden sliding door: *Gull & Hand.* This was our meeting spot.

I wanted to rip from these people and run inside. They would be waiting—Griff, Abner, Max, and maybe a couple others.

And my family was on a boat nearby. Thousands upon thousands of Miotans were.

I shook, wiggling my fingers, letting out all anticipatory energy. I wasn't sure I'd be able to hold it in upon seeing Griff. My beacon, my hope.

Dalton and Lorella entered the hotel first. The lobby, though apparently dipped in gold, was a dimly lit space. The windows were tinted, keeping away the evening light, and my eyes couldn't adjust quickly enough. I strained, blinking furiously.

Show me Griff. Show me, show me…

They weren't here. That was probably for the better, since I likely would've caused a scene here in the lobby. Too slow, Dalton pecked his fingers on one of the hotel's central screens, reserving our rooms, coordinating with where Colton and the Miotans were staying.

"Can I help you carry anything to your rooms?" a beaming woman asked, approaching us swiftly.

"No, thank you," Dalton said a little too dismissively. "We don't have much luggage with us."

The woman tried helping again, but we denied her. Still, she persisted, up until the elevator doors closed in her face.

"Didn't like that," Dalton muttered, breaking our ride's silence.

I tried not to rush past everyone as we landed on our floor.

Griff. He was behind one of these doors. The stars had led us home, strung us together. And we were on the precipice of their culmination, now about to crash into each other, two shooting stars burning one in the same.

Dalton told me which doors belonged to the other half of our team. Our Miotan half.

Led by something not of this world—something intangible but very *real*—I knocked on their door. Shuffling came from the room, and in a moment, Abner's gray face met me, with Bernard on his heels.

The king wrapped me in a suffocating hug before passing me off to Bernard.

They were *here.* They'd made it. Even with everything the brothers had put me through during Accolade, they'd helped bring this about. And I was thankful for it.

"Thank the moon you're okay," my old tutor whispered into my hair.

"*Cass?*" Abner's gruff voice caught. "*Kierran Cassius.*"

I sidestepped from Bernard and studied the reunited father and son. Abner's arms shook as he clung to his only child, still alive.

I searched the room for Griff and Max, but they weren't here. No one else occupied the room.

The question showed in my face, and Bernard must've caught it. He nudged my side. "They're in the other room. Max had just gone to check on him. Here, I'll show you."

Him. Griff. Griff and Max were *here.*

"Check on him?" I echoed absentmindedly.

Bernard hummed in confirmation, shuffling toward the threshold between the two adjoining rooms. The door was cracked, and voices bled through, even where light did not—the other room's curtains were shut and lights were turned off.

"It'll take time," Max's higher-pitched tenor came through. "You'll heal, though."

"Not quick enough," a deep, rattling voice responded.

The sound of his husky voice undid me. I barged into the room, and time ceased to exist.

"Griff," I choked, pinpointing where he stood, hunched and supporting himself on the back of a chair, at the closed window. He wore a thin blanket around his shoulders, even though it wasn't cold in here, and his hair splayed in a thick, dark crown around his head.

He wobbled when his eyes landed on me, and he shuffled toward me. I ran for him, drawn by gravity, and we collided.

"*Corinn.*" His chest shook, and it took me a few moments to realize he was *crying.*

We melted into each other, resting in one another once and for all. Finally, *finally,* together.

I would *never* let him go.

He didn't need to say anything else; I *knew* he thought the same. Our tears, our skin on skin, his lips on my hair and the outer shell of my ear, was proof of this vow. We weren't separating again.

"No more distance, lovely," he finally whispered, his voice heartbreakingly raw.

"No more," I echoed. "By the moon, Griff. I missed you."

"I missed *you.*" He ran his lips across my cheek, my jaw, placing a light kiss with each word. "*So. Damn. Much.*"

I exhaled and turned my head to meet his lips with my own, unable to take this *almost*. We were together again, and I wouldn't waste another second.

This was a reckless kiss, messy and hurried. As if we could make up for lost time with desperation. This was teeth catching; tongues sliding; lips whispering hasty things, promises for the future.

For as much as he was still Griff, *my* Griff, he'd changed in our time apart, just as I knew I had, too. His hair had grown out—I realized as I twined my hands through it—waving at the ends where they kissed the shells of his ears. His hands were smoother, more refined, as I was sure happened to all Miotan royalty. His voice was rougher and air more somber, and I could only imagine what he'd been through in Julia's court.

Still, despite his changes, he was the *same*. He still held me with delicacy; his lip still tugged upward in the same omnipresent, devious grin; and he still held the weight of the world in his eyes.

When we pulled apart for air, he rubbed a thumb along my jaw, the other digits still grazing my neck. "You are so *lovely*. You know that, right?"

I smiled. "So you keep telling me."

"Today and every day. You may never hear the end of it, I'm afraid."

"Oh no," I laughed. I closed my eyes and inhaled. Even with time and distance keeping us separated for some time, they'd ultimately failed. I knew the charted stars led us back together because even *they* knew that Griff and I were not made to be apart. "I can't wait to hear about how you got everyone off Miota."

At that, his smile dropped. And his eyes left mine.

"Griff?"

He gingerly lowered himself onto his bed, staring at a spot on the wall. "I . . . *by the moon*, Corinn. I know this was the plan, but there's so much I'd change if I had the chance to go back and do it all again."

"What do you mean?" I followed him and wrapped my arms around his shoulders.

"Is this some sort of joke?" a voice ambushed the room. I looked at the doorway and found Cass glowering at us. "What the hell, Howard?"

I stiffened. "Cass, stop."

Griff blinked. "You're as alive as Corinn said, Your Highness," he got out, the words possessing a bitter edge.

Cass's gaze pinned Griff and me to our spots, and when the pieces fell into place, the prince's features became like a stone statue. "No secrets," Cass said to me, "right? I thought that was the deal."

My heart cleaved as I thought of Salem. "I thought so, too." I swallowed. "I guess we aren't very good at promises."

At that, Griff glanced at me. I'd have to tell him of mine and Cass's deal, and of Salem, later.

Cass only gawked at us. "Not that a promise means much if you're lying through your teeth from the start." He snarled out the last word. His jealousy contorted him into someone I didn't know, didn't *want* to know.

"Cass, trust me," Abner chimed, appearing behind his son, glancing fleetingly at Cass's head wounds. "You never stood a chance against Griff. And *you*," Abner said, narrowing his gaze at Griff, "should be in bed. *Resting.*"

The same icy sensation as before seeped through me, a slow-reacting poison. "Why?" I asked Griff, tethering my sanity to his reply. "What happened? Are you okay?"

"I'm fine." Griff pointed a sour look toward Miota's king.

Abner cleared his throat and crossed his arms, surveying Griff and me. "Okay, meeting in here"—he signaled to the adjoining room behind him—"in ten minutes. Everyone needs to be there, so say what you need to say to each other now, then get over there."

Abner spun on his heel and left. Max slipped out in the same instant, whom I'd forgotten had been in the room that entire time, and Cass's jaw remained slackened until his father shut the door between us.

I whirled on Griff. "What happened? Are you hurt?"

"Electrocution." Griff passed the word off to me as if I would somehow know what to do with it. "On our way off Miota, I had to cut the island's power. I was in Kendall, so I had the Queen's Guard blow out the grid. I was holding onto the fence, and . . ." He looked at his toes. "My feet don't work, Corinn. Not like they *should*, anyway."

The room's shadows clawed at me, attempting to sink into my skin. "Oh, Griff . . ."

"And Bernard thinks there's more internal damage. In my organs. I'm not . . . my heart and lungs, every so often . . . I don't know what's wrong, and it terrifies me." The knot in his throat quivered, and I set a tender hand on his cheek.

"They have good technology here," I said, trying to channel light into my voice. "You can get help. The things Biourica is capable of . . ."

My voice died. Because we were aiming to destroy Biourica and their cruel ways. Arlo needed to be gone, and if the company was only gaining medical knowledge by experimenting on Miotans, they didn't deserve any of it.

"We'll get through it," I finally decided. It delivered with a flat ring.

And though Griff seemingly noticed, he still pressed a light kiss to my temple. "It's *we* now, lovely?"

I held the weight of his stare, the one that so often nearly unmade me, seeing past all my defenses. "Yes, *we*. From now on, it's me and you."

Griff's smile reappeared, shining like moonlight in the dark. "You and me."

I chewed on my bottom lip. "What did you mean just a second ago? You wish you could do things differently?"

This snapped Griff into the dark place I imagined he'd burrowed into before my arrival, when I'd first spied him in this room with Max. He'd been made of taut muscles and tired eyes.

Now, in this space, he told me everything. I listened, refusing to react or even digest the words until he'd finished.

There had been a plan to get *everyone* off Miota. Or, at least, as many as able. Max sedated Addison, and Griff left her in Salford with her father—Griff and Addison were no longer engaged, would never be a forced couple again. Pointe formed an uprising, which targeted the monorail, and that event had kicked Griff into cutting the island's power.

My family had been on the monorail. Only Tellie had made it off Miota.

My brother, parents, and grandmother were still on that island. As Emerald Barracks charged for Miota. As Julia would wake with a bloody need for revenge.

I was numb. I waited for tears, would have *welcomed* them, but they never came. I just . . . lay there. Helpless. Stupid. Useless. Not *enough*. Nothing would ever be enough, until I laid claim to Julia and her island *myself*. No matter what Biourica forced Julia into, *she* was a monster herself.

She needed to be destroyed.

"Abner *ran*," Griff said, breaking my thoughts. "I thought his plan to free the island was a good one, but it only would've been worth it if there weren't people left behind. *Julia* is still ruling. *Julia* is still free to do what she wants. I'm going to make her suffer for all she's done."

"I'm with you," I promised. "Whatever you need, whatever I can do to help . . ." My eyes fluttered closed as images of my family flooded my brain. They were still subject to the vile queen. I cursed.

"Months have gone by," Griff said, "and you're still the same. My moonlight. My faith. We'll stop Julia."

I let Griff stoke my own vengeful flame. "Julia and Arlo both— you know about Arlo James, right? Colton's told you, I assume?"

"Yeah, Arlo, the ass who's at the top of this whole scheme?" Griff sat up with a shudder. "Colton's said Arlo is his *father*. I don't envy the guy, that's for sure."

I confirmed with a shake of my head and wry grin. "Yeah. Arlo . . . well, he tried turning my brain to soup just this morning, actually."

Griff whipped his face toward me, his features stone-cold. In a moment, with my words, he'd turned into something deadly, ready to set havoc to the very ends of the world.

"*What.*" It was a growling command, dripping with violence.

I pecked a kiss on Griff's jaw. His shoulders hardly melted. "But I survived, brain and all. Besides, his sons are nice. Colton's brother, Dalton, has become one of my closest friends here."

Griff slowly blinked away his trance. "Yes, you'll have to tell me more about that. Something tells me you have *quite* the stories."

"I do." I stood. "But first, we have a meeting to get through."

CHAPTER 49

CORINN

The Bartholomus brothers were going to kill Griff.

Not quickly, like I'd seen happen to others today, but slowly and *surely*. He was already clearly running on nothing but fumes and sheer willpower, and he didn't need more stress.

"I said no," Bernard snapped from his seat. Though he was seated at the wooden table, leaned back and hands clasped, it was clear to everyone in the room that he led this.

Even though Abner, King of Miota, stood. Even though Miota's prince paced along the room's perimeter. Even though the sons of Arlo James were perched on the edge of their seats, ready to act.

Bernard led this.

Griff sat as straight-backed as I'd ever seen, with a spine of metal and eyes of cold shadows. His dark features consumed him now, and his tousled hair gave him an even more roguish look as he challenged Bernard's gaze.

"I'm going back to Miota," Griff said again, as he had minutes ago, proposing his plan to the group. "Because *I* need to save the people *you* let go! They were on the train, coming, and *your plan* didn't work. You ran." He looked up, pinning Abner to his spot. "*You ran.* Like a coward."

In my periphery, Cass threw his hands in the air. Tensions rose yet again, thick enough to cut through.

"You seemed to like my plan *just fine* back on Miota," Abner chimed in, his own voice unsteady. "This is what we wanted from the very beginning. It was the plan even with Corinn, with *Cass!* Why are you trying to argue it now that it's happened?"

Griff raked his hands through his hair, bottling a deep breath before speaking. "Because I didn't think we'd be leaving so many behind. Now that we're gone . . . all I see are the people still there. The ones who wanted to be here but got stuck. The ones who couldn't decide in time—" His voice wavered, and his next whispered words broke me. "The ones I could've gone back to help. If I hadn't . . ." Griff stared into his lap, toward his legs.

When Julia had burned me, she'd melded the action with my failure to Salem, so the physical scars would always carry my shortcomings, too. I knew when Griff felt his quivering muscles, his stuttering heart, he also endured the weight of every Miotan left behind.

It wasn't his fault. But there would be no convincing him otherwise.

"You see the thousands who aren't here," Bernard finally said, shattering the deafening silence. "*I* see the thousands who *are*. We did a good thing."

Griff glared at the man. "We did *nothing* to stop Julia or the army headed to Miota. All we did was save ourselves."

His words sobered the room, smothering every movement into stillness. Griff held all attention, and his posture adjusted to the load. *This* was a refined Griff I hadn't come to know yet, since he'd emerged only in the past few months, during his time living in the castle. In Julia's domain.

"Besides." Griff's voice cracked. "Mayor Maybee has a plan, having to do with Addison and Julia." Griff had already briefly mentioned his failed attempt to bring an unconscious Addison here with him. I didn't, *couldn't*, dwell on that. "Maybee didn't seem to believe

Miota was in any danger outside of Julia's grasp, and that scares me. A lot. Oncoming army or not, the thousands of people left on Miota are still at the mercy of Julia."

"It's certainly something to keep in mind." Bernard's practiced voice, made to placate Griff, only boiled my blood.

Without another breath, Bernard changed topics entirely.

I offered my hand to Griff below the table, and he gripped me as if hanging his sanity on my touch.

At least Griff and I matched sentiments. Emerald Barracks sailed for Miota, and only the stars knew what Julia planned to do with her remaining country once she realized what happened.

Miota was going to sink, and if nobody went back to defend our home—my *family*—it would be a defeat unlike any other. Ever since I'd competed in Accolade and learned Julia's secrets, I tried living by the standard of saving and protecting Miota. But I was quickly beginning to feel like I was in waters too deep, pulled by ocean currents too strong.

We listened to Bernard's rendition of the plan, collaborating where he let us and fighting him otherwise. My old tutor was stubborn, a brute force equal to the Fort.

Bernard crossed a line, though, when he told Colton how Arlo would act from within Biourica.

"I'm his son!" Colton spat, red-faced. He ripped his jacket off, and—his *arm*.

His entire *left arm*.

Dalton had hinted at something unspeakable happening between Arlo and Colton, and Arlo had even mentioned something of limb regeneration experiments done on his own son, but nothing could have prepared me for this. "He did this"—Colton waved his prosthetic—"to me on purpose! He used me for experiments! On prosthetics and afferent signaling, because that's all I'm worth to him, right? *His own son.* So don't you dare tell me what I know and don't know about that man."

Dalton watched his brother with embers burning in his eyes. I knew Dalton sided with him. That made it Griff and me, Dalton and Colton, against the rest. But the brothers would bring in support, surely, from Anya and Lorella, and therefore Saoirse, too. Of the two sets of brothers, Dalton and Colton could prove to be the stronger force.

As Colton fumed and stalked toward the exit, I tucked away my scheming for now. "I'm with Griff Howard," Colton called behind him. "You could save damn near everyone on that island, but you're just happy you finally checked the box of leaving that hell hole, right?" He opened the door, letting out into the hallway, and slammed it shut behind him.

I shared a look with Griff, transient enough to be indiscernible to the rest. Warmth surged through me at how intimate the communication was.

Colton James was publicly on our side. We could work with this.

Bernard and Abner's plan was clear: slowly move the Miotans from their ships to the plots of land where Scarlet Barracks now resided. There was unused land where Miotans could learn to fight, and Dalton assured the room that Scarlet Barracks would turn a blind eye to it, if not even join our cause entirely. I verbally agreed as I thought of the soldiers like Stella, Leo, Garee, and Stephan.

Once Miotans made landfall, we'd build an army with those willing to fight against Biourica. And once we were strong enough, we'd strike and sink Arlo.

"I was thinking . . ." Anya spoke up, slowly outstretching her arms on the tabletop. Hesitant to contribute, until Dalton gave her a soft smile. "Arlo is brainwashing Miotans with a serum that rots their brain. Turning them into someone they're not." Her eyes briefly met mine. "What if we used the serum on Arlo? What if *we* controlled him, and therefore, the company? If Arlo falls, it'll be messy. But if we use his own serum to control him, we could peacefully break up the company. Help bring down the people who've already been given too much power for something so inhumane."

Her proposal burrowed into the room as everyone grunted,

thinking. Dalton smiled. Bernard laughed.

"What's your name again?" Abner asked.

"Anya," she answered, looking into the eyes of a king and not balking in the slightest. "Anya Steele."

Abner's mouth tugged upward. "I like your idea, Steele."

Even Bernard folded, amending the final step from "sink Arlo James" to "brainwash Arlo James."

Catching up and scheming made everyone hungry. A few hours before midnight, we left the meeting where it was, feeling solidified in our plans. We'd configure final details in the clarity of morning, then start acting immediately.

Currently, Miota wouldn't be tended to until Biourica was sorted out. But if Griff and I had anything to say about it, and maybe Colton and Dalton too, we would change that. We wouldn't give up on Miota so easily.

It was a problem, I told myself, to solve tomorrow.

I liked Charston, but not its food.

Too salty; too sour. *Briny*, Anya commented. Fish—a creature from the ocean. The other foods were better: creamed corn, fried green beans, and sugared dates.

We'd eaten in separate rooms, which was when I'd reluctantly left Griff for fifteen minutes to eat in the room across the hall with Lorella's crew. Of the original team from Red Fox, only Cass was missing now, spending the time with his father, uncle, and courtier instead.

Even though this was the crew's continent, their homeland, *they* seemed the ones out of place. Maybe that was because we Miotans were reconnected, and I now knew that home was comprised of people with heartbeats, not the soil beneath one's feet.

Lorella's crew spoke tactically of our plans and itineraries for upcoming days and nights, and I knew this was their way of trying to maintain control. Lorella and Colton strategized, while Dalton tried poking holes in their schemes. Anya brought in even more absurd potentials, which helped ease tensions. Saoirse only grunted as she ate. I sat in a high-backed chair and watched, slowly chewing my food as I processed the people in front of me.

I couldn't bring myself to urge them to relax tonight; they were each far out of their element, and this was their way of maintaining sanity. Bernard seemed more of a madman than ever these days, and to these people who didn't know my tutor, their fear was justified.

When we started on the dessert that had been delivered to our rooms—*cherry pie*, a golden and flaky crust filled with a tart red filling—I ate one bite before excusing myself, gravitating back toward Griff.

It almost felt like if I let him leave my sight now, he'd disappear again. I entered through Bernard's room, where all the Miotan men sat, save Griff, whose room I trekked into through the adjoining door.

Griff sat in bed, fork midair, and his face lit up when I entered, glowing like a waxing moon. "*Lovely*. How are you? How are your friends?"

"Eat this." I jutted my slice of pie toward him. "And . . . I'm good, for now. So are they—stressed, but who isn't? They're quizzing each other over deadly scenarios. It's exhausting."

Griff let out a shaky laugh. "Well, speaking of deadly scenarios . . . Not that this is deadly, but . . . Just don't let Abner catch me, okay? *He might kill me*."

I tilted my head, and Griff gave me a cheeky grin, my favorite kind.

He stood, and before I could open my mouth to protest his leave, he threw open the curtains, letting milky moonlight flood his room. "Max and I found this little gem last night," said Griff.

He opened the window using a crank lever at the windowsill and yanked the mesh screen out of its place, bringing it inside. Then he straddled the window and *slid off*—

He landed squarely. His entire torso was visible; he hadn't dropped in height. "This path leads to a stairwell that takes you to the roof."

I widened my eyes and wandered to the window. "The *roof?*"

"Yeah, at the top of this building."

"This is allowed?" I asked.

"Doubt it." Griff shrugged, tugging one side of his lip upward. "But I want to watch the stars with you. Just like you said you do at home."

Home. He pressed the word to his lips so matter-of-factly, so casually, as if I had no other home than Pointe. It made me long for Miota, for my family. I'd see Tellie soon, where she stayed with Griff's family in the concealed caves, but the rest of them held unstable fates. I couldn't dwell on it, or I'd collapse, and that wouldn't help anything.

"I told you about that?" I asked. *And you remembered?*

"Yes." My anxious spirits fell to rest as Griff reached out a beckoning hand. "Once, in passing. The time I asked if you were *a rain person* and then bombarded you with personal questions? Not my best move."

I laughed. "By the moon, Griff. I still feel awful for running that night."

"You shouldn't, when I was the one who drove you away."

I threw Griff an incredulous look before following him out the window. I carried our plates of pie as he led me up the too many stairs bleeding upward. Griff's pace gradually slowed, and as we reached the top of the sixty-something steps—I'd lost exact count—Griff used his arms more than his legs to pull himself upward.

"Are you okay?" I asked quietly when he needed a third break.

"Fine." Griff's breathless tone said otherwise, though. "Look."

As we made it onto the roof entirely, my jaw fell at the view.

Night made the sky bleed a deep blue, and stars gleamed, crackling pinpricks of light. They seemed closer from this side of the ocean.

In the distance, the open sea roared. We were a few streets away from Charston's beach, but without any taller buildings between us and the water, the shore stretched in my view. Silvery moonlight swathed the white-tipped waves crashing onto the beach, leaving bubbling seafoam behind on the damp sand. Beyond, blue-black waves churned and bled into the dark horizon.

"It's beautiful," I whispered.

Griff planted a kiss on my forehead before sitting cross-legged on the roof to finish his pie. "*You're* beautiful. This view is just a bonus."

I scoffed. "Griff Howard, ever the flirt." I'd said it before, and I still meant it just as much now.

He smirked, giving his identical response, too. "Only for you, lovely."

I sat next to him on the cement, and in silence, we ate our pie and watched the waves. Watched the stars twinkle in their places. Watched the moon command the waves.

Though *so much* had changed, and there were things Griff and I would have to tackle in the coming weeks—together and personally—we'd transcended time and distance. And I was thankful for everything that brought us here, back together, because we were stronger for it.

"Seriously, though," I returned to my worries. "How're you feeling?" I combed him over and took a bite of my pie.

Griff shifted, still focused on the distant waves. "Seriously, I'm fine. Good enough, anyway."

But I'd just witnessed him crawl up here when the Griff Howard I knew on Miota could run up and down stairs all day. So I raised my brow and forced him to look at me. "Don't lie to me. Please. Does it hurt?"

I recalled when we'd been in reversed roles, just after Cass's mother had scalded my legs. That was something of another lifetime now, when I'd been in the castle's hospital wing.

All of that—Accolade, the burns, life on Miota—seemed so trivial now. Life and death and all their subsequent problems were so much bigger, so much more.

"I couldn't tell you what's wrong," Griff admitted. He hugged his knees and clasped his hands together. "Things just don't feel . . . quite right. Quick movements hurt. My heart will—jolt sometimes. I stumble around on my feet. I get tired easily, and I'm never that hungry."

"Except for this cherry pie?" I motioned toward his half-eaten slice of pie.

He shot me an amused look. "*Except* for this cherry pie." He chewed on his cheek, something I knew *I* did. "I don't want you worrying, though. There's enough to worry about without *me* adding to the mix."

I knew the feeling well. "You know, Anya taught me something during my time in Scarlet Barracks. The people who care about you don't do it because they feel like they *need* to. It's because they *want* to. I . . . Griff, it's not a burden to worry about you. We're together now, me and you. Which means we're a team. It's only natural for me to want you to be okay."

Griff smirked, his eyes deepening as he took a bite of pie. "Okay, when did *you* become the one who's good with words? What has this place done to you?"

I laughed lightly. "It's done *a lot* to me. All for the better, I hope."

"Just what I said all along," Griff replied. "You're a waxing moon, Corinn. And I—" He cut himself off as his eyes flared. Griff's slender fingers curled around mine, a blanket of warmth in the cool air. He selected each word carefully, strung together like a delicate constellation. "Lovely, there isn't a star in the damn sky that doesn't know your name. I've wished for you on all of them. And now you're really here, and I get to see your light again . . ." Griff moved his pie from between us and scooted closer, closing our small gap. His arm came around mine, and I fit his hollows. "I realize that what I'm looking for out there, in charted stars and moons, is really just *your* spirit."

Trembling, I brought a hand to his chest. *I know,* I told him in our silence. Our souls of stardust wanted both a great love and great adventure, and in each other, we could find that. It was possible.

We'd always been the same in that way.

When Griff's lips found mine, languid and warm and lingering, I welcomed them, delighting in his touch. His taste. This kiss was something new, something freshly burning for the first time, and we explored its feel. Its implication.

It was soft, starting small, a flame to stoke. Sliding of hands down arms and backs. Brushing of lips, featherlight and sweet. We fanned the flames, letting this kiss grow and deepen in *no* hurry. As if this hotel was our place of solace, safe from all outside worries. The kiss became a caress of tongues, and Griff let out a low rumble in his throat. I delighted in this feeling, this moment, savoring every bit of it.

"You and me, lovely," Griff groaned against my lips.

I smiled. Outside this place, we would wage war. We would *fight*. But right here and now, we would find our strength in each other. "Me and you," I whispered. "No matter what."

Yes—no matter what came with the rising sun, we could handle it. The lot of us here in the hotel were hiking to the caves tomorrow, to set foot back on the pair of what Griff called "city-boats" brimming with Miotans. We would assess the rationing of food and supplies, and Lorella's crew would begin rallying for troops.

I would see Tellie. And Griff's family. And countless more from home.

But not my brother, my parents. My grandmother. Hundreds more who'd aimed to escape Julia, but hadn't made it in time, thanks to my *own city* sabotaging Griff's plan.

I pulled away as a chill slinked into my bones. "How's Tellie holding up?"

Griff's gaze softened as it settled onto my face. "It's been hard on her . . . but Jess and Tellie are becoming friends. And the Rivera family is helping her, too—Jubilee Rivera said you two were friends in Accolade, and I think Tellie likes that."

I couldn't help but break for my cousin. Theo, according to Griff, had been *with* Tellie. She'd watched him get shot by a sentinel, and I was sure she'd witnessed his downfall, too. How had she gotten to the boat without him?

Jubilee Rivera *had* been a solace in Accolade, one of the only other Low-Tiered Pointeans in the competition. Jubilee had a younger brother around Tellie's age, and they were likely friends, especially given her current intensive year at school before choosing a career path for life.

Not that any of that mattered anymore. No matter what came of

Julia and Emerald Barracks' attack, our past ways of life on Miota were over.

"I'm ready to see her tomorrow," I told Griff.

His lips brushed against my skin, swathing me against the breeze's salty bite. "She's ready to see *you*. I think it's the only thing getting her through."

We sat on the cusp of something greater, made of both Miota and the Sector A crew, and I knew we'd need every bit of help we could get. I only hoped the Miotans who came here, who followed their future and current kings, were also willing to take a stand against Arlo James.

While Arlo hid behind the reasoning of finding a cure to red bite, he'd clearly taken full advantage of this trafficking agreement between countries. He had countless extra hands to help, bodies to use, without any of them raising suspicions or dissenting against him. Arlo had manufactured his *own* Miotan army.

Would our side have the heart to fight Arlo and his army contrived of our own people? He'd deliberately fortified himself against us, I realized, by doing this. He'd pitted Miota against itself—we couldn't win either way.

I sighed and buried my face into Griff's shoulder, letting his hands weave into my hair, tangled by the whipping winds. "I think we could convince Colton to take us back to Miota and save everyone left behind. Even if we just claimed another leader, stripped Julia of power . . ."

"We'd need to do more than that," Griff replied. "She has loyalists too willing to bleed for her. They think Miota is the safe haven and *we're* the insurgents trying to kill them." His chest rumbled against me as he spoke in his low voice. "But yes, I think we could figure something out, the two of us. We've seemed to manage so far."

I huffed a laugh. "Even though we were separated for months."

"And look at how we found our way back to each other," Griff said in a breath. He lifted my chin with his thumb and index finger and dipped his mouth until it hovered just above mine. The small gesture sent sparks tingling across my cheeks.

"Right," I said. "Maybe the stars *were* smiling when they placed us together?" It was a sentiment he'd delivered after we'd discovered the supercontinent's existence.

"I think they led me here, to you," he replied in the shape of a vow, an invisible stamp on my heart. His swirling dark eyes fastened on my mouth, and a shimmering grin crossed his face. "But even if all the stars went out, I'd always find my way back to you."

The moon shone brighter. Griff closed the aching inch of distance between us. We collided once again, and I became clay in Griff's delicate touch, letting him mold me however he wished. One of his hands cradled the back of my head while the other pressed my torso flush against his. Griff's skin burned, evident beneath layers of clothes, reminding me of his ill state.

I groaned against his wandering tongue as it recommitted my mouth to memory. "Are you sure you feel okay?"

His lips only cut me off sharply as he swallowed my words, drank my breath.

We lay on the roof long after the moon arced on its journey across the sky. Griff and I were two points of a constellation, always connected. I'd been on my way toward him my whole life, unknowingly.

And now that we were together again, we would unleash ourselves on the world trying to throttle us.

We stayed there for our own infinity of time. The rising sun, we knew, would come with a start into motion toward justice for all Miotans across continents. But for now, each brush of our bodies was a future promise to destroy Arlo and Julia. Each caress was a vow to save Salem, my family, the Miotans left behind, those within Biourica . . .

Retribution would come. So I lay my worries down, knowing in this moment alone, I was home.

EPILOGUE

JULIA

The knocking returned, resounding through the attic corridor. Yet again, I ignored it and schooled my breathing to stay even and shallow.

You've been betrayed. Father's incessant voice taunted me on repeat. He stated facts I already knew. Facts that already tortured me and made me want to scream. *They're coming for you now. Your people are going to kill you.*

"My Queen?" Klemmins's voice filtered through the door's crack. "Your Majesty, I know you *must* be in there. We need . . . we should probably talk about our next move. What will you do?"

The question resounded and splintered me to the core.

What can you expect me to do? I wordlessly replied. I came close to voicing the thought merely to break the tension surrounding the topic. I was queen, and I was supposed to lead a counterattack. But I did not know who in the country stood with me, and it was too late to wreak destruction on the rebels who had escaped.

I sank into the hopeless depths of my mind—the void seemed to only grow darker with each passing day. If Josiah had lived, would his reign have ended so spectacularly? Would my brother have controlled his people? Surely, they would have loved him too much from the start to ever rebel.

Again, Father's voice rang until it melded with my conscious thoughts. I was not certain which voice was mine and which was his anymore.

You've been betrayed. They're coming for you. Your people are going to kill you.

I tried to make sense of the events, but I could not deduce what had happened that made things go so poorly.

Abner had been with me last, and once I realized the wine he had given me was laced with something, I had sliced him with my dagger as the world's edges blurred. But he had opened the sealed wine bottle *in front of me*, and I had watched him pour our glasses with merciless eyes. How had he slighted me?

I had failed with my husband when it mattered most, and it cost me my island. Abner clearly had aid from Griff, which should not have surprised me. When I had chopped down Charles Howard, I should have tended to his roots more, extinguishing his wife and children, too.

After slipping out of my room upon waking, I had gone immediately to my media room, where I saw Griff Howard's video, filmed in my very home, blasting on my projector. I had gone to see if it played everywhere on the island, which had brought a new surge of conflicting emotions. It was not playing in the cities—which I soon after realized was because Miota did not have electricity.

Only the castle still had energy. My Guard and panel were gone, so I did not have a military to control. Would these facts lead my citizens into the castle, bloodthirsty and ready for vengeance?

Surely *some* Miotans had stayed. The thought of me and Klemmins stranded on this island did not settle well within me; we would die slow deaths, set to succumb to starvation or lack of fresh water without functioning desalination.

"They left Miota, so I hear," Klemmins started up again. I was hoping he had left.

They left Miota: my husband, my chosen heir, and my childhood best friend. There were no words, no emotions, to appropriately wrap around this. If given the chance, I would cut them all into miniscule pieces. I would make them *writhe* and *bleed* and *suffer*, as they had aimed to do to me.

Klemmins had told me of Max's betrayal the last time he had wandered to this door, my only remaining shield. Max's implant had not worked as it should have; he had shot Klemmins with intent to kill. From what I could tell from behind my warden door, Klemmins was quite injured.

You've been betrayed. They're coming for you. My mind seemed to only know circles, always ending at this same point. *Your people are going to kill you.*

I had not heard word of Addison in all this. She could still be lurking around the castle somewhere . . . or she could be with Griff. It was difficult to know what now happened outside my castle, without my eyes and ears of guards. Without my cameras and surveillance technology.

Klemmins continued. "They took thousands with them to the supercontinent. But those who stayed behind are still here because of *you*. We can still regain control if we act now. Please, think about what we can do."

With that, Klemmins's footfalls retreated.

If his news was true, it was justice at last. If they set foot on the supercontinent, I had no doubt Sillian Reeves, leader of Red Fox, would kill them all—

Sillian. That was it.

Maybe it was too late for me, but I would not be the only one brought to my downfall. Father's delight crawled up my face and neck.

My very own citizens had followed Abner into what they thought was safety. But if it was the *last thing* I did, I would ensure that what they thought was the king's deliverance was nothing more than their ultimate demise.

When I opened the attic door, feeling more exposed than I ever had in my life, I found a tray of food on the floor. I snatched a piece of stale bread and bit into it. It only soured in my stomach. I had not eaten since waking, whenever that was, yet I could not find the strength to be hungry.

I dared to leave the small attic. It had been my safe space for as long as I could remember. Father used to hide up here, and I would follow him, to this place he called his *lucky abode*. I tried drawing any last bit of luck from the room before shutting the door behind me.

Carefully, knife and poison in hand, I navigated the empty hallway, making my way to my office. Where had the castle staff fled to?

I made it down the stairs, down the ruby hallway, to my office, and I successfully shut myself in before drawing the key out to unlock access to the radio room.

Time inched forward, seemingly frozen, but I eventually got the monitor up and running. I called Sillian myself, hoping he answered.

He did. Sillian's gray face, eternally scrunched in a condescending smirk, appeared on my projector.

"Julia, darling," he began, "what a surprise!" He remained cool and calculated. It reminded me I must do the same.

"Reeves, I must tell you something of great importance." My throat burned; this was the first I had spoken in . . . well, since waking. "My husband, the king, has betrayed us. He and a few others have taken Miotans, and they are rumored to be sailing toward your own home. *Thousands* of Miotans, no less. I cannot say where they are going exactly, but I will help you—"

Sillian cut me off with a squawking laugh. The sound skittered down my shoulders, and I clenched my jaw to keep from wincing. "Julia, Julia," he said. "As if we wouldn't already know this."

My heart thudded into a spontaneous beat. "What?"

Sillian's aging face smirked, which gave him sinister lines at his forehead, beside his eyes, and down his cheeks. "Yes, darling, we've been betrayed, too. But not to worry; we know everything. Abner Delldova, Griff Howard, and Max Reno . . . yes, I've heard those names *plenty* lately. They're working with a pathetic band of rebels from Red

Fox, who spilled their whole plan on a rogue maglev. Clearly, they didn't realize how extensive my surveillance runs."

Rogue maglev? By the moon, what did that mean? And Sillian *knew* Griff and Max's names . . . While his extensive knowledge should have brought comfort, it only chilled my bones.

"So you know where my husband is taking the Miotans?" I prodded.

"Of course!" Sillian laughed. "Of course, I know that—oh, thank you, Neave." For a moment, Sillian ignored me and grinned at a blonde girl who handed him a full teacup and folded paper.

"From Arlo," she said.

"Yes, thank you, dear. You've been an angel. I'll transfer the bits into your bank account after I finish up this call, okay?"

"No rush," she sang, then flitted out of the camera's lens.

"Sorry about that." Sillian sipped at his tea, making an irritating gulping sound that made me want to disconnect our call. "Yes, darling, I *know* where over half your country is. My armies have them pinpointed. They're inside sea caves outside Charston—that's a city—and all your leaders rounded up with my rebels at the *Gull & Hand* hotel."

Charston. Sea caves. Hotel. I masked my confusion; Sillian was handling it all. "Your armies have them pinpointed," I echoed. "What, exactly, does that mean?"

Sillian's lip twisted into a smile. He leaned back and played with the note that the girl, Neave, had delivered with the tea. "It means my partner and I have troops marching toward them as we speak. The armies will arrive before the sun rises tomorrow, and they'll kill them all."

I sucked in a cold breath. "You are bluffing."

"I don't bluff, Julia. Those in the caves will be easy to deal with. We'll crumble the caves and drown them all. And as for your leaders on land? There's ten of them against an army of hundreds, and they have no idea troops are moving through the night toward them. It'll be impossible to survive."

Before morning, they would all die. Miotans and Red Fox rebels alike.

It's better this way, Father sneered. *They deserve it.*

Yes, that was right. This was their own doing, for leaving the Fort's security.

I blinked my way out of silence. "I have heard rumors of an army of yours sailing toward Miota?" I investigated. "Do you know anything of this?" If Griff's video was correct, and Sillian was sending an army toward us, we were *all* doomed, no matter what.

"Yes, I'm sending them," Sillian replied simply. "To help you rebuild your island. You can regain control of your country; you *need* to, for everything it's worth. Miota will not be brought to ruin so easily. Do what you can to rebuild bigger and better. Show your people you care for them, and that *Abner* was in the wrong. *You* were betrayed, not the other way around. Show your people how powerful you are."

"They will not believe me—"

"People will believe whatever lies make them feel *safe*," Sillian interrupted. "Tell them you'll protect them. Tell them that everyone who left Miota has been killed swiftly, and there is no future outside your island. Use my army to help you, please, in whatever way you deem fit. They're coming to *aid* you, Julia." He paused. "But *do* try to keep them out of sight of the public, if you can help it."

I nodded, too stunned to speak. Rebuild, act as if this was something I could recover from.

Was it?

Sillian's words *had* managed to summon a soft, flickering hope. Maybe I could continue ruling my country after all. Maybe it would not fall into ruin as I had suspected. Besides, I had Sillian's support, clearly.

"Why are you helping me?" I wondered. "Why do you send troops for me to command?"

Sillian sipped his tea. "We both benefit from the survival of your country. I'm only trying to make this easier for you."

Sillian needed my people—Miotan people—but for what exact purpose, I could not say.

It did not matter, I supposed, so long as he helped restore my island to its ordered state. Maybe I could build something worth saving. Something worth regaining control of.

"You promise to end the Miotans?" I asked. "To kill everyone who betrayed me?" I fantasized Abner, Griff, and Max burning alongside every citizen who chose to flee. They thought they were safe, but chaos would rain down on them.

"They'll all be dead in just a few hours," Sillian responded. "Abner, Griff, Max . . . and every single other Miotan here. I promise."

I nodded. My silence was not long-lived. "Then I will rebuild. I will do that. For us."

"Yes," Sillian growled. Victory emerged on his face, and I wondered what I had just unleashed. So long as I kept my crown and country, I did not care. "Yes, you'll be a shining, thriving country in *no time*. You can do this, Julia." He flicked his brow. "I have to go, but we'll be in touch. Daily, please. You know my hours."

He shut his screen off and disconnected our call.

I cleaned up the radio room and hardened myself in front of this insurmountable task of rebuilding Miota. I would fight tooth and nail for my island. My family's dynasty. We could come out better and stronger.

This is why it had to be you, Jules, Father said. *And not Josiah. I am so proud of you.*

The citizens who had stayed on Miota were still *mine*. And I would make sure they never left. I would ensure they never threatened to ruin my empire again.

I left my office and began my search for Klemmins, the only person I could place half-hearted trust in. From within these castle walls, we would rebuild Miota. Sillian would demolish the traitors on his side of the ocean—all I had to do was worry about my country.

For the first time since waking from Abner's poison, I smiled. There was work to be done.

END OF BOOK TWO

WHAT'S NEXT?

This crew's story continues in the last installment of The Royal Codex trilogy, where lines will be crossed and sacrifices will be made…

Don't miss this epic conclusion, with a Kickstarter coming in 2026.

THANK YOU FOR READING!

To you, my wonderful reader, who is reading this message here and no only because you reached the end of the book. Thank you for investing precious time into reading not just one but two of my books. I hope you found pieces of yourself in these characters, and I hope you experienced some magic along the way.

As a self-published author, each and every review helps this book reach new readers. Please consider leaving a written review on Amazon, Goodreads, or social media.

And if you'd like to be the first to receive news on the Kickstarter for this trilogy's final installment, please subscribe to my newsletter.

Thank you!

ACKNOWLEDGMENTS

Wow! Fourteen-year-old Brittany never thought she would go on to publish one book, and now this makes TWO. So I have to thank her for starting this story, and thank twenty-two-year-old Brittany for recommitting to this trilogy.

Thank you to my dear husband, my #1 supporter, who's the only reason I was ever able to publish anything at all. He took the chance on my author career while I attended medical school, and I'm forever thankful for that. I couldn't have done this without his endless love and support.

Thank you to my beta readers, who once again turned this story into something unrecognizable from its early drafts (and thank goodness for that!). This book wouldn't be half of what it is now without them. To Kiara, R.J., Michelle, Kimberly, Autumn, Taylor, and Teresa—you truly deserve so much credit for your insights, very necessary tough love, and support.

Thank you to my editor, Angela Knotts Morse, and my proofreader, TJ Shiree. You two were amazing hype women, and your expertise did not go unnoticed. Thank you for helping me shape this story into its final version.

Thank you to Maria Spada, my cover designer, for creating a mesmerizing cover yet again. And thank you to Rachael Ward, my cartographer, who has now brought my entire fictional world alive in a very artful and beautiful way.

Thank you to my Instagram family. You know who you are — the ones who take up much-loved space in my DMs, who always show up no matter what, and who are always cheering me on even when I have nothing left to give myself. I will always cherish your support and our connections. Thank you for being a true friend.

Lastly, I want to than **you**. Us readers have a million and one books we want to read, and time is so precious; life only seems to get busier by the day. So that fact you've now read two of my books is no small thing. I see you, and I appreciate you more than you know! I've thoroughly enjoyed going on this journey with these characters as their author, and I hope you've enjoyed yourself as the reader, too. From the bottom of my heart, thank you.

ABOUT THE AUTHOR

Brittany is a physical therapist by day, author/bookworm by night. She loves nothing more than curling up with a cup of coffee and a good book. Brittany loves going on walks, trying out new restaurants, and visiting all her local bookstores. She lives in the Midwest U.S. with her husband and two cats.

Brittany is active on Instagram @writerbrittanymack daily, where she talks about her books, self-publishing, and the books she's reading.